THE PRODIGY SLAVE

Book One:
Journey to Winter Garden

Londyn Skye

The Prodigy Slave

Book One:

Journey to Winter Garden

(Revised Edition)

ISBN: 978-0-578-24039-8

Londyn Skye Novels

Copyright © 2020

Library of Congress Control Number: 2020920199

Reference information for Slave Codes: District of Columbia Slave Code Manual of 1866

WARNING!!! Please be advised that this entire series features the following material that some readers may find disturbing, inappropriate, or triggering: Extreme profanity, racial slurs, extremely graphic violence, sexual misconduct, master/slave intimate relationships, explicit sexual content, violent mistreatment of slaves.

Reader discretion is advised!!!

Prologue

Slave:

A human being who is by law deprived of his or her liberty for life and is the property of another.

Slave Code
Article II Section IV

A slave cannot become partially free. The law recognizes only freedom on the one side and slavery on the other. There is no intermediate status. The status of any Negro child's mother is the status of the child. Therefore, a Negro child born of one parent who is a slave and one parent who is free is considered free only if the free parent is the child's mother. All Negro children born of slave mothers shall be slaves during their natural lives, regardless of their father's status.

Virginia
Slavery Era
January 14, 1845

The shrills of an innocent little girl paralyzed an entire field of slaves as they watched her mother fighting with the strength of a wild beast to hold on to her during a vicious battle that had kicked up a massive cloud of dust. Somewhere in the middle of the haze, Maya, a slave, held on tightly to her daughter's arms, while her master, Levi Collins, stood at the opposite end yanking at her little legs. They were locked in a tug-of-war, with the little girl nearly being torn apart in the middle. Levi was hell-bent on selling the little girl. Maya was prepared to die before such a thing transpired. The mere thought of life without her daughter inhibited her fear of the punishment she would receive for disobediently fighting and pleading with her owner, in heartbreaking cries of desperation. Her cries were like the sounds of a woman who was being tortured to death. They were sounds born from the immediate pain of the inevitable loss of her child ... the *only* child God had ever blessed her with.

Just minutes before their struggle ensued, Maya and her daughter were taking laundry down from the clothesline. When Maya removed a sheet, Levi was directly in her line of view, stalking toward them. The way he walked and the look on his face was a sight she had seen before. It was a walk that said he was on a mission, a mission to steal another innocent child away from its parents, no different than grabbing a bag of cotton to take into town for profit.

Maya was usually just a bystander during Levi's despicable missions. She was typically unable to do anything but watch from a distance in horror and then help comfort the distraught parents after they had seen their child for the last time. But this day was different. Levi stalked toward her and her child now with that familiar menacing look in his eyes. Maya looked to the right and to the left and saw that she and her daughter were the only ones in his view. When she realized that her little girl would be the lone casualty of his mission, tears instantly erupted from her eyes. For the entire nine years of her daughter's life, Maya was convinced that Levi would never sell her, the way he had with other children, because he was not only her child's master ... he was also her father.

Levi had come into Maya's cottage the day their baby was born. He walked over to where she lay in her mother's arms and reached down to pick her up. Remembering that Levi had sold other children, Maya pulled her baby from his reach and held her tighter. Despite Levi being her daughter's father, she suddenly feared that it would be the last time she would ever see her. That fear, however, quickly subsided when

Maya finally let Levi hold her, and she saw a heartfelt smile emerge on his face as soon as he looked at the beautiful newborn girl he had created. "Lily," he called her, because she had initially come out of the womb of a brown-skinned woman so pale and lily-white, before settling into an almond-brown complexion months later.

Levi's wife, Emily, had given birth to six of his children. But of the seven Levi was responsible for producing, the child he had created with Maya was the only little girl. Emily always assumed that her husband had secretly indulged with his slaves from time to time, like so many other slave owners in the South. But, oddly, it was *not* her husband's infidelity that made her rife with unrelenting envy and anger. She simply could not handle the fact that he had given some other woman the little girl she was desperate to have, and to a lowly slave at that.

It further sickened Emily to watch Lily grow and morph into her father. Lily resembled Levi far more than the sons Emily had birthed for him. Lily's skin tone and the texture of her hair were a blend of her parents, but her father's traits dominated every other one of her features. Lily was in nearly every way a honey-brown female version of her father. And it was impossible for Emily to gaze at her and not see her husband's seed staring right back at her with *his* sparkling green eyes.

Levi did his best to keep his distance from Lily after his wife learned the truth about her paternity. Despite Levi's distance, Maya was confident that he would never hurt or sell her beloved child. Her belief in that had been so strong because of the sentimental reasons behind the brilliant smile she had seen on Levi's face the day of Lily's birth, as he cradled her in his arms and whispered her name while gazing at her for the longest time. It was not until Maya stood in the middle of a dirt field, fighting Levi with the strength of ten men, that she realized how wrong she was. She was forced to accept that her confident belief was an illusion she had created to give herself a sense of peace. As Levi tried to wrestle Lily away, he was proving to Maya that money was worth far more to him than his own child. But those painful realizations did not

3

stop her from fighting mercilessly with Levi to free her little girl from his death grip.

"Masa' Lee, don't do this! Nooo!" Maya repeatedly cried as she attempted to snatch Lily from Levi's hands. "Pleeease! Dear God, don't let 'em take my baby!" she prayed aloud, as tears flowed down her cheeks. "Pleeease, don't take our baby! She's yo' daughta' too! Why you doin' this to yo' baby?" she pleaded, in a desperate, last-ditch attempt to make Levi feel some sense of connection to his child. Then, with the searing burn of a lash across her back, Maya was instantly brought to her knees and lost her grip on her beloved child.

Unexpectedly, Levi's eldest son, Wyatt, had whipped Maya from behind. When she dropped Lily, Levi immediately picked her up and placed her into the back of his wagon. As the wagon pulled away, Lily watched through tear-filled eyes as Wyatt brutally beat her mother into unconsciousness. Levi's wife, in turn, took twisted pleasure in watching the entire scene play out from the porch with a joyous smirk etched on her haggard face.

Chapter One

Slave Code
Article II Section I

Sundays and holidays are to be strictly observed. No slave shall be permitted to work more than 15 hours per day in summer, and 14 hours in winter, or on any holiday or Sunday, except as a punishment or unless they are paid. All Negroes otherwise found at work on these days shall be confiscated.

Fourteen years later
Fayetteville, Virginia
January 14, 1859

Lily sat quietly at the piano, on this, the fourteenth anniversary of the day she had been stolen from her mother. Although she did not know how to read a calendar, she was certain that this was indeed that fateful day. No different than one's circadian sleep rhythm, Lily's internal body clock set off an alarm to reawaken her misery and anguish on *every* January fourteenth. Today, much like every January fourteenth before it, she had woken up in a cold sweat, gasping for air, after the grisly lingering memories of that life-altering day began haunting her dreams. From then on, those revitalized memories continued to relentlessly invade her mind, making it nearly impossible for her to focus on anything else. Having gone through this torture in the past, though, Lily now knew that playing the piano was the *only* thing that had the power to halt the persistent painful imagery from that nightmarish day.

5

Preparing to play a song she had composed in memory of her mother, Lily lifted the key cover to the piano. She then sat there a moment, blankly staring at the keys, as visions continued to roll through her head of the momentous day that had landed her in the place she now considered as her own personal prison. With the curse and blessing of Lily's photographic memory, those horrific images were now locked in her mind. With crystal clarity, every miniscule detail from that day began replaying in her head, drumming up every excruciating emotion, as if she was experiencing it all over again. She recalled the cloud of dirt that surrounded her during her mother's struggle to save her, the desperation in her mother's voice, the pain in her extremities as her parents nearly tore her apart, the sound of the whip as it snapped across her mother's back, and the sight of her mother lying motionless on the ground after her severe beating.

In vivid detail, Lily still remembered being dragged from her father's wagon and being put up on the auction block at Virginia State Negro Auctioneers. She still recalled standing there barefoot in her tattered dress, riddled with terror as tears poured from her sparkling green eyes, making tracks through all the dirt still left on her honey-brown cheeks. Lily remembered being deaf to the pale faces in the crowd, who yelled out bids in hopes of becoming her new owner; she was far too focused on the man who had put her up for sale. Up until that day, she had only known him as *Master Lee*. But after hearing her mother's desperate pleas, Lily had inadvertently learned that the man who had placed her on that auction block was her very own father. As Lily shivered there alone, she could not pull her eyes away from Levi, noting the lack of expression on his face as he stared unblinking back at her, waiting for the final bid to come in. When it did, he took his daughter by the hand and ushered her down the steps to take her to the man who had just won the rights to her life.

"A-are you r-really my fatha'?" Lily cried, looking up at the profile of Levi's face as he dragged her along.

6

Levi did not reply.

"A-are y-you?" Lily sniffled, asking him again after he had lifted her into the back of her new owner's wagon. After securing shackles around her legs, Levi looked up and met a set of eyes that were undoubtedly his, penetrating him with their innocence, as tears careened in steady streams from within them. *"Daddy?"* Lily whispered. She had spoken the solitary word in a sorrowful tone that pleaded to know why her own father would do this to her.

After looking deep into his only daughter's eyes, Levi turned and walked away, without a word or even a second glance at the beautiful child he had created.

"Daaaddyyy! Pleeease! Take me back to my maaama! Daaaddyyy! Pleeease!" Lily erupted as her new owner began to roll away with her in tow. Still, though, Levi never broke stride.

As Lily continued to yell, the wagon came to an abrupt halt. With tears blurring her vision, she never saw the swift hand of her new owner as it made its way across her face. "Shut y'ur goddamn mouth, you hear me girl?!" he yelled, a devilish glare in his eyes as he loomed over her. Lily had yet to even learn her new master's name, but his brutal introduction instantly painted a clear picture of the sort of heartless man her father had just callously sold her to.

Jesse Adams had purchased Lily to work alongside his ailing house slave, whom everyone called Auntie. Auntie had worked on the plantation with two generations of Adams family. The decades of field and housework had finally taken their toll on her body. Her multitude of health problems were making it a struggle for her to keep up with the needs of a large family. Jesse and his wife knew that it would not be long before Auntie would need a replacement. Lily was to be that girl.

The Adamses had three sons, who all lived at home when Lily first arrived at the farm as a child. Their eldest, Jesse Roscoe Junior, whom they all called J.R.; Jacob, the middle child; and their youngest, James. A few years after teaching Lily how to run the Adams household, with its three rambunctious boys, Auntie passed away, leaving Lily to handle the needs of the family alone. It was an overwhelming burden for a thirteen-year-old, but she handled the grueling responsibilities with the grace of someone three times her age.

As the years rolled by, the household duties began to lighten for Lily. In that time, J.R. and Jacob had both started their own families and moved into plantations nearby. James had gone away to medical school. And their mother, Elizabeth, passed away suddenly just a few months after Auntie.

Before her death, Elizabeth Adams was a schoolteacher, who also taught piano to children in her home on the weekends. During every piano lesson, Lily would disregard her duties and secretly stand at the top of the stairs, watching as each child attempted to play their music pieces. Those simple melodies would replay joyously in Lily's extraordinary mind, long after the sessions had ended. The uplifting music soothed her and helped her through her daunting weekly tasks.

Before moving to the Adams farm, Lily had never even seen a piano. Once seeing and hearing one, she became fascinated at how the simple movement of fingers across the keys could create such beautiful music. Day after day, that notion obsessively drew her to the piano. Knowing that touching it was off-limits, she would only move her fingers in the air near it, pretending to play.

One day, though, Lily's obsession took control. Despite knowing the punishment she would receive for touching the piano, she could not fight off the urge to tinker on it. After seeing the Adams brood off to school and work, she hesitantly sat down on the piano bench. She was reluctant to touch the keys at first. She got up to look out of all the windows to reassure herself that Elizabeth and the boys were truly at school and that Jesse had already left to make his daily trip into town. Once Lily was confident that she was alone, she sat back down and proceeded to play a classical song that was taught to all of Elizabeth's students. Lily played the entire song purely from her memory of the mechanics of Mrs. Adams' fingers across the keys. She stumbled her way through the first attempt, then used her precise memory of every note's sound to guide her fingers toward the accurate keys. With great determination, she found every appropriate combination until she could play the song in its entirety without a single note missed along the way. When Lily completed the song, her joy was instant; and so, too, was her addiction to playing.

Using that visual copy-cat method, Lily continued to sneak onto the piano and play every new song she learned from her secret hiding spot. After only a few weeks of familiarizing herself with the piano, though, she no longer needed to hide and watch any more lessons. As she went about her chores, her mind began imprinting melodies into her memory by sound alone. When she replayed them, her fingers instinctively found every key combination with ease. Not long after that, she began creating music on her own. Within only a few months of teaching herself, ten-year-old Lily was playing as flawlessly as a professional who had had years of training.

Lily did not even realize the incredible gift she had. All she knew was that playing the piano brought her joy, numbed the pain of missing her mother, and gave her an escape from the misery of her new environment. The temporary reprieve became a vital part of Lily's daily routine. She cooked breakfast for the family, saw them off to school and work, and escaped on the piano.

And so, on this fourteenth anniversary, it was that obsessive daily *need* to mentally escape that led Lily to sit down at her beloved piano. Most days, she played with the need to drift away from the world around her. But today, she needed to escape the visions in her own mind. As with *every* January fourteenth, she needed music to override the memories of her mother's beating and of her father callously exchanging her for money. Attempting to wrestle those torturous thoughts into submission, Lily began to play the very first song she had ever composed. Blended within the song was the melody from an old music box that her mother had. The song reminded Lily of the way that she and her mother used to dance together, just like the tiny couple spinning around inside the music box. Lily's new extended version of the old tune allowed time for dozens of other wonderful memories with her mother to resurface. The array of cherished moments never failed to trump the yearly nightmarish visions that invaded the serenity of her mind.

On this morning, however, unbeknownst to Lily, she had an audience, who had walked in just seconds after she began playing. Her uninvited guest stood there quietly, listening intently as she flawlessly played her music piece. As she swayed gracefully to the rhythm with her eyes closed, Lily never once felt a presence in the room. She was far too lost inside the recesses of her mind, reliving the highlights of the nine years she had spent with her mother.

After the song had helped restore peace to Lily's mind, she wiped away the tears on her face. Still none the wiser to the fact that she was not alone, she carefully replaced the lid to the piano keys and got up to continue her household duties.

"My fatha' know you playin' my motha's piano?"

The deep, southern accent startled Lily as she rose from the piano bench. She was instantly paralyzed with fear, unable to turn and look at the man whose voice she instantly recognized, even though she had not seen him in years.

"Answa' me, girl!" he snapped.

"Naw sa' Masa' James," Lily finally responded, her heart pounding.

After six years away, James had returned home from medical school, entering through the back door, hoping to surprise his father with his arrival. Instead, he had become Lily's uninvited audience member, catching her in a role she knew full well she was not purchased for. "Then who gave you permission to play it?" James asked, coldly glaring at her.

Lily began trembling. "No-nobody. But I beg you not to tell yo' fatha'," she added, tears forming in her eyes. She had seen Jesse Adams' wrath before when other slaves had stepped out of line, and she was not eager to become one of his latest victims.

"Who taught you to play that way?" James asked, ignoring her plea.

Lily still had her eyes locked on the piano. "No-nobody."

"You 'spect me to believe that? You think I'm some kind 'a fool?!"

"Naw sa'!" Lily answered with urgency.

"Then I'm gonna ask you one more time. Who taught you to play that way?"

Lily finally turned around and gazed at James with unshed tears glistening in her eyes. "Masa', I'm tellin' you the truth, ain't nobody taught me to play."

The sincerity in her eyes and her voice forced James's better judgment to believe her.

"But I beg you not to tell yo' fatha' ... *please*," Lily added again, as a tear finally made its way down her cheek.

James motioned his head toward the piano. "Play," he demanded.

Lily looked confused.

"I said play," he demanded again.

Unsure of what his goal was, Lily sat back down at the piano bench. She lifted the key cover and looked at James, asking permission with her eyes before touching the keys again.

"Go on," James insisted.

Without another moment wasted, Lily began playing the song she was most familiar with. James instantly recognized it as one that his

11

mother had forced him and his brothers to play as children. Unlike their mother, however, they were not musically inclined enough to master the classical piece. Ironically, though, the way Lily played the song made James wonder if his mother had ever truly mastered it. She now seemed like a beginner in comparison to Lily. He recalled his mother always playing so slowly and cautiously. But Lily's hands were gracefully dancing, her fingers effortlessly floating from key to key, like that of an accomplished performer. She was playing the song so smoothly it was as if the piano was playing itself. Lily never opened her eyes throughout the entire piece and never saw James walk closer to her, his eyes unblinking. He was scrutinizing her every keystroke as the wheels spun in his head. He simply could not comprehend how such skill was possible without any formal lessons.

When Lily finished, she nervously glanced at James as he loomed over her; his face remained unreadable. She was unsure what to say, as was he. Judging by the tense scene in the parlor at that moment, one never would have guessed that such coldness between them had not always existed. There was once incredible warmth between the pair. As children, they formed a unique bond that was very profound and instantaneous…

On this exact day, fourteen years prior, James had watched from his upstairs bedroom window, as his father took a very young new slave out of the back of his wagon. Something about seeing a child his size, shackled in chains, tore at James as he stared at the little girl. He continued to watch this new little girl curiously for a few days after that, secretly peeking his head around corners or peering at her from the top of the stairs. Whenever or however he had the chance to spy on her, he would.

Soon, what drew young James to watch this new little girl began to go beyond the sorrow he felt about seeing a child his age bound in chains. There was something about her that made him look at her in a way he had never looked at any other girl before. Without even realizing he was doing it, his eyes would often linger on the almond-brown glaze of her skin, the curvature of her little bee-stung lips, and the array of colors swirling in her eyes. He even became curious about what her hair was like underneath the scarf she always wore. He did not understand at that time why he was so captivated by all the nuances of her unique features, nor why he was so compelled to follow her everywhere in secret.

One afternoon, James quietly followed behind the new little girl as she neglected her duties and snuck off into a thickly wooded area near a creek. After seeing her pick up a turtle she had found, James's fascination with her grew even more. The day before, he had watched her effortlessly climb into the tree he was currently hiding behind. He was surprised to see a girl scale a tree but saddened by the way she then perched herself there and quietly cried, as she mindlessly picked leaves and dropped them to the ground. And now, the fact that she fearlessly held onto a turtle further proved to James that she was nothing like the dainty girls he was used to.

James continued hiding and watching her as she sat down with the turtle on a log. Her sadness was still obvious to him by the tone of her voice when she then began to speak to the turtle. "Don't worry, little fella'," she sniffled, "I won't take you away from your mama. I just wanted to play with you for a while. Maybe we can be friends." She suddenly turned her head quickly to the right when she heard leaves rustling nearby. James had stumbled over a tree root as he moved to get a better view, tripping just enough to fall into her line of sight. She immediately jumped to her feet in a panic, thinking for sure she would be in trouble for leaving the farm without permission.

Embarrassed that he had been caught, James just stood there staring at this new little girl in silence. Although he felt a little foolish, he was glad he had finally been discovered. After noticing the way that she always cried when she was alone, he had a question he had been wanting to ask her for days. "A-are you okay?" he stammered.

"I-I'm fine," Lily stuttered back, still feeling afraid that she was in trouble.

"Sho' don't look like it."

"I-I'm fine," Lily insisted, quickly wiping her tears away with her free hand. "Just thinkin' 'bout my mama is all."

"I know," James said, cautiously approaching her. "I-I been prayin' real hard every night that you'll get to see 'er again," he admitted. It was something he began doing after overhearing her crying to Auntie about how badly she missed her mother.

Considering what her own father had just done to her, Lily was deeply impacted by this stranger's touching confession. She did not even know what to say in return. She just stared at him in silence, stunned that he would do and say something so incredibly kind. Her ability to speak became even more lost on her when she was suddenly captivated by the innocence of this young boy's piercing blue eyes, as they peeked out at her from underneath his loose, curly brown hair. Lily had never looked at a white person in the eyes for long, because she knew better. But for reasons she could not understand at that moment, she found it hard to turn away from the beauty of his. She had seen James amongst the family members before, but this was the first time she absorbed every detail of his features: how skinny he was, how he stood eye level with her, and how his blood-red lips stood out against his pale skin ... but mostly his *eyes*. They were innocent eyes that somehow made her instantly feel at peace.

"I-I'm James," he suddenly announced, switching the subject swiftly, not even realizing how his words had profoundly touched Lily.

"I'm Lily," she replied, still staring at James as he stepped closer to her.

"What's your turtle's name?" he asked.

14

Lily finally managed to pull her eyes away from James and look down. She had been in such a deep trance that she had forgotten she was even holding a turtle. "Don't know. Hadn't even thought to give 'em a name."

"I've seen 'em around here before. Maybe we should name 'em," James suggested.

"Okay, let's think 'a somethin'.'"

Lily sat down on a log next to her newfound friend. They sat shoulder to shoulder, looking just as comfortable as two people who had known each other from birth. James then reached over, took the turtle from Lily's hands, and gave him a once over. "Maybe Jimmy?"

Lily leaned over and looked at him again. "Nah, he looks more like a Willie to me."

"Hmm, yeah, kinda. Or maybe a Wilbur."

"Yeah! I like it!"

"Wilbur it is then!" James said, lifting the turtle high in the air. That simple moment instantly ignited an incredible bond between the pair.

After that day, it became a ritual for James to return home from school and secretly help Lily with her housework while talking with her about his day. But *Sunday* was the day James looked forward to the most. It was the only full day the slaves were given off. While his family was distracted by their post-church gatherings, James would sneak away and spend the entire afternoon with his new best friend.

Every Sunday, James and Lily went on extravagant childhood adventures in their wooded playground paradise. They had foot races, pretend sword fights with sticks, fishing contests, and competitions to see who could collect the most crickets for Wilbur. James taught Lily how to skip rocks across the creek and how to swim. Their favorite pastime was climbing the tree where they had first met. Perched high up on its branches, James would read stories of fantasy adventures that they would later reenact. They were wise enough to keep their time together a secret. Their efforts worked well, allowing their friendship to blossom while they went about creating unforgettable memories that strengthened their bond over six long years.

As James and Lily grew older, rock skipping, cricket collecting, and tree climbing turned into long walks and laid-back fishing in the shade while having long conversations about all aspects of their lives. Despite all the things they had conversations about, though, Lily never revealed to James her ability to play the piano. Fearing punishment, she refused to utter a word about it. James, however, hid nothing from her up to that point. Lily had become his greatest confidant and the closest person in his life. She was the sole reason James was excited to get out of bed in the morning, the reason he disliked going to school, and why he ran like mad to get home at the end of the day. James drowned in thoughts of Lily along the way to school, during class, and he often dreamed of her at night. James's mind always seemed to be inundated with ideas of what new things he could share and experience with Lily. In fact, it was on the very last Sunday that they ever spent together that he revealed one of the new experiences he wished to have with her. Lily was sitting shoulder to shoulder with James underneath their childhood tree, listening to him read a story. When James finished, he turned to Lily and promised her that he would teach her to read and write. His willingness to do such a thing brought appreciative tears to Lily's eyes. But just days before her lessons were set to begin, an unforeseen circumstance caused their innocent six-year-long friendship to crumble.

James had come home from school eager to help Lily get done with her chores as usual. The two of them were on their hands and knees scrubbing the kitchen floor, laughing hysterically about an embarrassing incident that happened to James at school. They were laughing so loudly that they never heard James's father walk into the kitchen. Jesse had left to go into town but had briefly returned to the house after forgetting some important paperwork. Instead of finding the papers, he found his son crouched on the floor like a servant. The very second James and Lily saw Jesse's boots, their laughter immediately ceased. They both sprang to their feet, but Lily fell back onto the floor before she was completely upright. She lay there in tears, holding an eye that was quickly swelling. Jesse swung so quickly that Lily never saw his backslap coming. His heavy knuckles had connected right alongside her eye socket.

James was instantly irate. "Why'd you hit her?!" he screamed, stomping closer to his father, his face fire red.

"Who the hell you think you talkin' to, boy?!" Jesse snarled. "She knows goddamn well she ain't to be askin' y'all for no help!"

"She didn't ask! I *wanted* to help!" James fired back, fearlessly staring his father down.

"Have you lost y'ur goddamn mind?! What the hell you helpin' 'er for?!"

"She's my friend!" James erupted.

James suddenly stumbled backward and fell over the kitchen table, blood gushing from his mouth. The ferocity of his father's punch sliced his lip wide open and loosened two of his bottom teeth.

Jesse realized at that moment that his sixteen-year-old son had become too spoiled over the years. He had always believed that James's intelligence would take him to great places in life, so he had not worked him hard on the plantation. He had not taught James about the sort of man he expected him to be like he had with his two older sons. But that all changed. From that day forward, Jesse became strict with James, hardly ever letting him out of his sight. He forced his son to work side by side with him in the fields after school, overseeing the slaves. Jesse indoctrinated James with how God expected master/slave relationships to be conducted. He constantly preached that Negroes were born to be property, and that they were far too inferior to be worthy of being friends or family to anyone in the white race.

When Jesse's racist lessons began, Sunday strolls and fishing adventures between James and Lily immediately ceased, right along with Lily's chance to learn to read. Deep conversations about life turned into demeaning demands from her best friend, with the expectation that respectful replies of "yessa'" or "no sa'" were to be her only responses. For the two years remaining before James went away to medical school, he never spoke another kind word to Lily nor made another memory with her worth cherishing.

... Now, after six years apart, Lily was once again reunited with her *former* best friend in his father's parlor, a place they once dusted together as they talked and laughed. But instead of Lily feeling a need to laugh, James's dark presence began unburying the memories from the last months of their dying friendship. The way James used to look at her with such disdain and talk to her like she was nothing immediately came to her mind. No matter how Lily tried to empty those ugly memories into her music over the years, they had remained locked in her mind in perfect detail. Reliving those moments now had reawakened the loneliness, the hurt, the sorrow, and every other emotion that accompanied how horribly James began to treat her before he left for school. But being caught at the piano made the feelings somehow seem much more intense this time around.

After completing the song, Lily sat there stiffly, feeling a chill race down her spine under the icy glare of a man whose face she once smiled at seeing. James's presence now only caused her to feel inferior and keep her eyes on the piano keys. His coldness was proving that Lily's prayers had gone unanswered; he had not reverted into the kind boy who had befriended her in the woods. He seemed to *still* be the unkind man his father had taught him to be, one who was about to speak to her in a tone that she had grown to hate in the months before his departure.

"My fatha' would whip you good if he knew you were touchin' this piano for anything otha' than dustin', don't ya'?" James finally said.

"Yessa'."

"So, you *chose* to defy his rules?"

"Masa' James, it won't eva' happen again." Lily sprang from her seat, suddenly wanting to get as far away from the piano as possible. "But please, I beg you not to tell yo' fatha'," she pleaded.

"How long've you been usin' this piano like it was yo' own property?"

Lily lowered her head, fearing the consequences of a truthful answer.

"Answa' me!" James demanded, taking a step toward her.

Lily's body stiffened, and she closed her eyes tightly, fearing that James would hit her. When he didn't, she finally spoke. "S-since a few weeks afta' your fatha' bought me," she confessed softly, her head still hanging low.

Her confession felt like a punch in James's stomach. He thought that he and Lily had spoken about *everything* as children. He now wondered why she had not shared something of this magnitude with him all those years ago. Her major omission suddenly fueled his anger. "You've been playin' for *fourteen years?!*" he shouted.

"Y-yessa'," Lily stammered, her body trembling again.

"Did Auntie know?"

"Yessa'."

"Well, it's a good thing she's dead then, isn't it? 'Cause I'd have my fatha' whip *both* 'a y'all good for this!"

James intentionally tried to hurt Lily by mentioning Auntie. He knew she was the closest thing Lily had to a mother since being sold away from hers. Lily was devastated over her death, especially considering the way Jesse had not bothered giving her a proper funeral. After loyally taking care of two generations of the Adams family, Jesse showed his appreciation by tossing her remains in the woods for animals to feast on. Lily had leaned on James during those days when she never seemed to be able to stop crying over Auntie's loss, in much the same way that James had leaned on her after his mother's death. With compassion, they had supported each other through every moment of unrelenting pain. But now, James spoke of Auntie to intentionally reopen old wounds. His venomous words instantly ignited a rage inside Lily. But she had learned, by watching other slaves over the years, that emotional outbursts were only rewarded with countless lashes of thick leather. She, therefore, exhaled and calmed herself before she replied. "Please, Masa' James. I know I've broken the rules, but I promise you it won't eva' happen again."

"Lily, you say that like this is your first time on that piano, and you're a child who knows no betta'! Your deceit has dragged on for ova' a decade! This simply *cannot* be ignored!"

Lily erupted in tears, fearing that her back would finally bear the brand of his father's brutal punishments. "Masa' James, please..."

"I don't wanna hear your tearful pleas and apologies, Lily!" James interrupted. "*Fourteen years* of your deception will *not* go unpunished!" He crouched down to look her in the eyes. "You're lucky my fatha' didn't catch you sittin' there. You'd be strung up to the whippin' tree by now for disrespectin' my motha's belongin's!" After a moment, James finally stood up and marched around the room, his hands gripped around his suspenders as he strutted. "Way I see it, though, I caught you, so I decide what to do about it. You're my property just as well as my fatha's." He began to walk up the stairs but suddenly stopped before reaching the top and turned toward Lily again. "If you wanna avoid yo'self a whippin' then … well, let's just say your duties are about to exceed far past fixin' a cup 'a coffee and scrubbin' floors," he smirked. "You do what I tell ya' if you wanna keep that pretty little back 'a yours unscathed, ya' hear?"

"Yessa'."

James then turned and walked up the stairs without another word, leaving Lily trembling and crying in the middle of the parlor alone. She turned and looked at the piano through the blur of tears in her eyes. Instead of feeling joy, the sight of it made her feel sick to her stomach.

Chapter Two

Slave quarters:
An oftentimes rundown or dilapidated village of makeshift lodging or homes for slaves to reside in, located on their owner's plantation.

Slave Code
Article II Section XI
Be it enacted that every master shall provide all slaves, including the sick and the elderly, with a competent diet, yearly health examinations, clothing, and lodging. All such lodging and/or slave quarters are to be searched every two weeks for weapons or stolen goods. Acceptable punishments for these violations include: loss of ears, branding, nose-slitting, and death.

For nearly two weeks, Lily's fingers had not danced across her beloved piano keys. James's vague threat left her hesitant to even dust it. Without the comfort of her piano, Lily's mind never seemed to rest. Notes and melodies drifted endlessly through her head with no way to escape and infuse temporary joy into the suffocating atmosphere of her personal prison. Letting music flow through her fingertips made Lily feel free, but now the music lay trapped in her mind. It was a constant reminder that she, too, was trapped—like an animal. There was now not a single minute of the day she could escape from that reality.

Since her confrontation with James, the music that floated through Lily's head was always angry or heavy with sorrow. The dramatic music was always intertwined with the last words James had spoken to her: *Your duties are about to exceed far past fixin' a cup 'a coffee and scrubbin' floors.* That sentence looped in Lily's mind along with a new brooding melody as she stood at the kitchen sink washing dishes. She was in a trance, mindlessly wiping the plate in her hand. The plate had long since been cleaned, but she continued incessantly wiping it, wondering what James was planning as a punishment. The thought of the possibilities always stirred Lily's tears. She fought to hold them back, though; she refused to give James the satisfaction of seeing or even hearing her cry again. She was humiliated by the way she had emotionally cracked in front of him after he had caught her on the piano. She was now determined to prove to him that he did not have the power to affect her anymore.

Despite trying to summon the strength to ignore the pain that James had caused, Lily suddenly felt a wave of anger sweep through her. Amid the musical madness in her mind, her dishwashing became frantic. She started tossing dishes aside after barely wiping them until she accidentally cut her finger on a knife. Despite how deep the gash was, she hardly flinched at the pain. She lifted her hand and stared at the blood gushing from her finger. And then, as if ending a symphony with a dramatic crescendo, the music in her head suddenly stopped. "Lord, I wanna be with Auntie. I beg you," she whispered, her eyes suddenly fixed on the knife in her uninjured hand. It was the first time Lily had ever wished death for herself. There was not one thing she could think of that made her life meaningful enough to go on anymore; James had just made sure of that.

Even all these years later, Lily could not comprehend how a caring young man like James had so abruptly changed into someone capable of such mean-spirited acts. Oddly, the blood on Lily's hand reminded her of the sort of person James used to be. Her mind suddenly flashed back to a fond memory of when the warmth of James's heart was still evident, and the two of them were still as close as children could be. They were twelve at the time…

"I bet I'll beat ya' to the creek today!" James had said to Lily while looking up at her in her usual hiding spot. She had perched herself in their favorite tree, waiting for him to join her after church. He would usually climb up there with her, but after being beaten by her in foot races every Sunday, he decided to get an unfair head start this time. He sat his satchel down and took off running toward the creek before Lily could even make a move to get down.

"No fair, James! I'll catch you anyway! You run like a turtle with a broken foot!" Lily teased as she began quickly making her way down the tree.

James laughed at her comment as he hopped and trotted over the rough terrain toward the creek. With Lily's blazing speed, he was sure that she would be on his coattails within seconds. But when he reached the creek and turned around, he was only greeted by the sound of the flowing water and the panting of his own breath. He did not even hear the familiar sound of leaves crinkling underneath Lily's bare feet or her laughter. He quickly looked to the left and to the right. Not spotting Lily anywhere, James instantly had an unexplainable intuition that something was wrong. He then yelled Lily's name twice. When he got no response, he took off running toward the tree. In the distance, he could see why Lily had not answered. Tears began to flow down James's cheeks before he reached his destination. He slid on his knees, coming to rest near Lily's motionless body. She was lying face down near the base of the tree. She had sliced her knee open on a branch in her rush to get down. Her reaction to the pain had caused her to lose her footing and fall. She had hit her head hard when she landed and knocked herself unconscious. In James's twelve-year-old mind, though, her motionless body made him fear that she was dead.

He frantically turned her over. "Lily, wake up! Please get up!" he yelled, shaking her. "Lilyyy, can you hear me?! C'mon get up!" he begged, tears gushing from his eyes.

"D-d-did I win?" Lily responded softly, clearly confused.

Relief flooded James's entire body and returned his heart to a normal rhythm. "A-are you okay? I-I'm sorry. I-I should've helped you outta the tree," he stammered, wiping his tears away.

"Why you cryin' James?" Lily asked, still confused by what had just happened.

"Neva' mind that. Are you hurt?"

"My knee. I think I cut my knee," Lily replied, grimacing from the pain as she tried to get up and look.

"No, don't move! Lemme look." James hiked her dress up and saw blood covering her entire knee. The deep gash instantly reminded him of the way his mother would douse his and his brother's wounds with a stinging tincture. She always scared them into submission by telling them they would die from infections if they didn't sit still and let her clean their wounds properly. Infection and death suddenly had James's heart erratic again as he stared at Lily's bloody knee. "Your knee is bleedin' bad. The cut's real deep," he calmly told Lily. Inside, though, the thought of her dying had him ready to erupt in tears again.

"It'll be okay. Just help me up. I can go down to the creek and wash it," Lily replied.

"No! That wata's filthy! You need some medicated tincture, so it don't get infected!"

"Sorry James. You don't have to yell at me."

"Well, it's just that … that. Well, you need to clean it propa', okay? I don't want ya' to … to…"

"To what?"

"Nothin'. Neva' mind," he said, unbuttoning his white church shirt.

"What're you doin'?"

"Can you lift your leg at all?"

"Ow! Yeah, but it really hurts."

James helped her lift her leg and then tied his shirt around her knee like a bandage.

"You must've gone and lost yo' mind James! Yo' mama's gonna whup you good for ruinin' that shirt!"

"Neva' mind that. I gotta stop the bleedin' and keep it from gettin' dirty. Can you walk at all?"

"I think so." Lily tried to stand up, but the pain in her knee became even more evident upon trying to bend it.

James then helped her to sit up against the tree instead. "Will you be okay here by yourself?" he asked.

"I s'ppose so, but I don't really wanna be left alone. Not like this."

"I'll be back as fast as I can. I'll take care of ya'. I won't be long. I promise."

"Okay."

James then ran as fast as he could out of the heavily wooded area. It was nearly a half-mile journey before his feet hit the plantation grass of his home. But still, he kept his pace, running across the fields at blazing speed with his suspenders flapping near his sides. When he made it to the house, he stopped at the kitchen door and peered through the window. Seeing the kitchen empty, he quietly entered. He heard laughter and chatter in the living room between his mother and her guests. While everyone was distracted, he quietly tiptoed up the stairs to find a new shirt. Just before making it to his room, though, he was startled by his oldest brother, J.R.

J.R. certainly deserved to be named Jesse Roscoe after his father. Not only did he look exactly like him, but he was mean just like his father too, especially toward James. "Where's y'ur shirt, boy?" J.R. asked, towering over his little brother while smacking on an apple.

"Neva' mind that. Just let me by." James tried to step past his brother, but he blocked his path.

"You been tastin' that lil' nigga' girl, ain't ya'?"

"What?!" James snapped.

"I saw you," J.R. said, still rudely smacking on his apple. "Last Sunday, you were playin' with that pick-a-ninny." J.R. smirked when a look of guilt overtook James's face. "I's walkin' in the woods and I saw y'all wadin' in the creek. She the reason you ain't got no shirt on, boy?"

"I don't know what you're talkin' about!"

"I don't blame ya' little brotha'." J.R. leaned down close to James's face. "If she was old enough, I'd be tastin' that lil' nigga' too," he admitted, a devilish grin on his face.

With all his twelve-year-old might, James pushed and slammed his brother against the wall, breathing so hard that spit seeped through the cracks of his clenched teeth. He was not even sure what J.R. meant by "tastin'," but he knew it was something vulgar. He was further enraged by hearing him call Lily by such disrespectful names. His rage gave him the strength to keep J.R. pinned to the wall, while glaring at him through lowered eyelids.

J.R was shocked to see this angry side of his normally gentle little brother. But he refused to show it. He simply stared at James and bit calmly into his apple, as if a fly had landed on his chest. "I bet Pa would be real eaga' to hear you been tastin' that lil' nigga'."

"You wouldn't!" James spat.

J.R.'s face became hard and serious. He grabbed James by the hair with his free hand. "I suggest you mind me wheneva' I need you to handle my chores, or else the only thing you'll be *tastin'* is Pa's leatha' belt against y'ur skinny little ass, instead 'a that sweet little nigga' friend 'a y'urs. Then you can watch Pa tie 'er up to the whippin' tree and beat 'er good too. She'll be up for sale on the next auction block 'fore y'ur little ass stops stingin'." J.R. bit calmly into his apple again. They both heard somebody coming up the stairs and turned in the direction of the noise. James then broke free of his brother's clutches and dashed into his room before he could be seen.

J.R. had always been jealous of James. He hated the fact that their father had always gone easy on James with farm work because of his extreme intelligence. J.R. would be seething inside whenever he heard his father bragging about how his youngest boy was going to be a doctor and a fine upstanding man that people would one day look up to. J.R. craved to hear his father boast so proudly about him, but his father's words only ever made him feel worthless.

Jesse was hard on his two oldest sons. He raised them to never complain about hard work and to take criticism like grown men. J.R. was, therefore, infuriated by the fact that James lived the comfortable life and was exempt from such harsh treatment. But now, knowing about James's secret, J.R. felt he finally had the leverage to take the easy life away from his baby brother. And with J.R. having the upper hand, James felt he had no choice but to obey if he wanted to ensure that Lily—a little girl who had come to mean everything to him—was never abused and remained a part of his life.

Right now, ensuring that Lily remained a part of his life meant finding the stinging tincture that James was convinced she desperately needed. *Infection, death, infection, death,* were the only thoughts that were on his mind as he searched for the medication, more so than his brother's blackmail. Lily's superficial wound was mountainous in James's eyes.

28

After finding the solution, a clean rag, bandages, and another shirt, James made his way out of the house unnoticed and then dashed the half-mile back to where he had left Lily. "You alright?" he asked her, breathing hard.

"I'll be fine, but my leg is still hurtin' somethin' awful."

"This solution's gonna sting, but it's gonna stop it from gettin' infected. Be tough now," James told Lily as he began to pour it onto the rag. "It'll be alright, I promise. Just squeeze my hand to keep from screamin'." Lily gripped his hand hard as he worked on her leg with the diligence of a doctor. He took great care in cleaning the wound, patching it up neatly, and ensuring her comfort.

When James was finished, he dug in his satchel and pulled out something for Lily to eat. He then went to find Wilbur, brought him back to their picnic blanket, and read Lily's favorite story to her. Lily had been fine to walk for a while, but James would not let her until it was time for them to part ways. He helped her up and carefully walked with his arm around her all the way back to the slave quarters.

Later that night, James woke up in a panic, struggling to catch his breath. A nightmare about Lily lying face down in the leaves had torn him from his sleep. It took him a moment to realize he was only dreaming. Despite it, worry quickly settled in. He crept downstairs, avoiding every creaky spot on the floorboards on the way down. Too impatient to grab a coat or shoes, he slipped out of his house barefoot, in just his thin pajamas. The temperature had dropped considerably, but he did not let the crisp air stop him from his mission.

James made his way to the slave quarters, which could have easily been mistaken for a rickety barn. Much like horses, each slave slept in stalls with hay for padding. Auntie and Lily shared a room in the back, which was the only area that had a door and a decent amount of privacy. It was James's first time in the quarters so late at night. He realized that the chill inside was not much different from the cold air on the outside. He walked past each slave in their stalls. Their thin blankets caught his attention; he figured there was no way they were keeping everyone warm. It was not even winter yet, so he could only imagine the discomfort they endured at night during that season. It made him instantly think of Lily. He hoped that maybe she had been supplied with something more suitable for a child. But upon entering her room, he saw the harsh reality that his best friend was also vulnerable to the cold Virginia nights. James quietly made his way over to her haystack where she lay breathing lightly, none the wiser to his presence. He looked at her for a long time, studying the rise and fall of her chest, trying to convince himself that his nightmare had caused him to worry for nothing.

James then looked over at Auntie, who was snoring lightly. He stared at her for the longest time too, thinking about the fact that she was an ailing, sweet, elderly woman whose back had never known the comforts of a mattress. Suddenly, James felt unbearable sympathy for the inhumane life she had been forced to live. With tears welling in his eyes, James then walked back to the main area and looked around again at all the bodies resting on haystacks that were covered in thin blankets. He then stared up at the holes in the roof that easily let buckets of rain flow through. He could even feel the crisp night air whipping its way through the cracks in the walls. *The animals have better accommodations than they do*, James thought to himself, as emotion continued to constrict his chest. Thoughts of the slaves his father had whipped, and Lily being sold away from her mother began to weigh heavily on James at that moment. He again looked around at all the slaves surrounding him, and he began to quietly sob. The simple scene suddenly made him question the morals of humanity.

James felt an overwhelming sense of guilt about going back to lay in the comfort and warmth of his bed after that. He begrudgingly left the slave quarters, stood outside for a moment, and looked up at the stars. With tears rolling down the sides of his face, he silently asked God why He would allow such a thing to happen. Young James had been told all his life that this was the way things were supposed to be

30

for the Negro race, but his heart rejected those lies that night. He felt like there was no possible way that any such preaching could be true. He was convinced that nobody deserved a life like the slaves in those quarters ... *nobody*.

The next morning, Lily woke up with a strange feeling on her feet. She sat up to look and realized that her covers were heavier than usual. She didn't recognize what was resting on top of her until her eyes fully adjusted in the early morning light. She had made his bed enough times to know that it was undoubtedly James's comforter that covered her frail body, and so, too, were the socks that now warmed her feet. Lily sat up out of the haystack and nearly smashed the other gift left for her in the middle of the night: a piece of homemade apple pie. She looked over at Auntie, who was staring at her with a half-hearted smile. "You betta' eat up girl, 'fo Masa' Jesse catch you wit' that," she warned Lily.

Auntie had already eaten the piece of pie left for her and had long since hidden the pair of socks and the comforter that James had laid upon her too. She had caught him on his way out that night and grabbed his cold little hand as he was adjusting her blanket.

"You's a fine boy, James. Don't you eva' let the worl' change that, ya' hear?" Auntie told him in a weak voice, coughing slightly afterward.

James stared at Auntie for a moment as he absorbed her words. He then gave her the warmest hug he could muster before he quietly disappeared out of the quarters.

One year after that night, Auntie was taken away by the Lord, under the comfort of the blanket that James had stolen from his family's guest bed. That remained the single kindest act that anybody in the Adams family had ever bothered to do for her during the two generations she had worked for them.

Fortunately for Lily, it became the first of many wonderful acts by young James, many of which were unknown to her. James never mentioned to her the threat that J.R. had made. Nor did Lily ever find out about the hell that J.R. had put him through for nearly a year, so that their Sunday playdates remained a secret. Barns were cleaned, hay bales stacked, animals were fed, and wood was chopped in Lily's honor. James took on his brother's duties with pride to ensure that Lily was never sold and that her back was never scarred by his father.

... Lily reached down and briefly touched the twelve-year-old scar on her knee that James had tenderly taken care of after she fell from the tree. She had grown to hate the man that James had become, but the tears trickling down her face were an admission that she truly missed her childhood friend. She missed her mother, she missed Auntie, and she even missed Mrs. Adams too. Mrs. Adams always treated her wonderfully when Jesse was not around. She figured maybe it was because Mrs. Adams never had any daughters. When Lily began to ache for any of them, she was always able to release her sorrows onto the keys of the piano, but without that, the pain became too overwhelming.

Overcome with grief, Lily raised the kitchen knife and ran her bloody finger down its smooth side. Blood from her wound trickled down the sharp edges. As she stared at it, she realized that the small mass of metal could be a means of escape from a world she no longer wished to be a part of. One swift clean motion and she could be embraced by the arms of Auntie and Mrs. Adams again. And if the Lord had already taken her mother, then she could be in her arms again too. With shaky movements, Lily lifted the blade higher. It felt cold against the fragile skin of her neck. Her tears stopped and peace overcame her as she began to pray. When her silent prayer was over, the knife fell from her limp hand into the kitchen sink.

Using her apron, Lily began putting pressure on the still bleeding open wound of her finger. She had been startled by the opening of the front door and dropped the knife in a panic. She kept her back turned to the familiar voices that then entered the kitchen.

"Ain't you got lunch togetha' yet, girl?" Jesse barked at Lily.

"I'm workin' on it now, sa'," she answered, doing her best to sound calm.

Jesse wiped the sweat from his brow as he sat down with his youngest son at the kitchen table. "What is it you wanted to speak to me about?" James asked him.

"You decided where you gonna open you up a medical practice in town yet?" Jesse asked.

"No sa', I haven't."

"What's the hold up?" his father asked, sounding irritated. "Don't ya' think y'ur time would be betta' served startin' up a practice, or at least workin' with our ol' town doctor, 'stead 'a runnin' off for days at a time?" he asked, referring to the fact that James had left town for several days. His absence was somewhat of a relief for Lily. Feeling his presence now behind her sent a chill down her spine.

"Well, I been meanin' to talk to you about that," James replied, clearing his throat. "You see, I decided I'm not gonna be workin' in this town all the time."

"The hell you mean by that?"

"I decided I'm gonna be a travelin' doctor. I'm plannin' to go from state to state helpin' out as many sick families as I can, 'specially those with small children."

There was suddenly a long silence. Even Lily knew not to make a noise.

"Lily fix me some gin," Jesse ordered, staring coldly at his son.

33

"Yessa'." She knew from experience that such a request meant that Jesse was not happy about what he had just heard.

"Son, I been tellin' the good folks 'a this town since you was just a young'un that you'd eventually be this town's doctor. People 'round here 'spect me to stand by my word."

"I unda'stand that, pa. But afta' doin' some travelin', I realize that so many towns are in need of a good doctor. And I think I could be of good use with all the skills I've learned."

"Your gin sa'," Lily said, placing the drink on the table near Jesse. James caught sight of the blood on her apron and locked eyes with her briefly. She dropped her eyes to avoid a prolonged gaze, then turned around quickly to get back to her duties.

Jesse never noticed a thing. He picked up his drink just as quickly as Lily had set it down. He guzzled half the glass quickly, as if he was in a rush to prepare his nerves for a verbal assault. "Son, that's mighty noble of ya' to wanna help everybody, but the people in this town are like y'ur family. You can't turn y'ur back on all of 'em."

"I'm not turnin' my back on any of 'em. Just 'cause I'd be travelin' doesn't mean that I wouldn't treat those in need 'round here … when I was in town anyway. But I feel like travelin' is my callin'."

"Son, I've done everything in my powa' to be sure you got y'ur schoolin' paid for, unda' the premise that you were gonna be workin' right here in this town. Way I saw it, you could take ova' and run this farm when I'm dead and gone and tend to people's needs occasionally when they needed ya'."

"*Tend to this farm?!* I neva' had any intention on runnin' this place … *Eva'!*" James emphasized. "I neva' made any such agreement with you for payin' my schoolin'."

Lily jumped when she heard Jesse slam his glass down onto the table. "This plantation's been in our family for three generations! Y'ur brotha's done moved on and got married. They got kids and farms 'a

34

their own to take care of, so it ain't nobody left to run this place but *you!*" Lily heard Jesse's chair creak under the pressure of his large body when he leaned toward James. "Now, this ain't somethin' I'm *askin'* you to do ... I'm *tellin'* ya'!" He pointed at James. "Y'ur *gonna* run this goddamn farm! I ain't losin' this place to somebody who ain't none 'a my blood, ya' hear?!"

Lily continued to listen to their exchange in disgust, as she stood with her back to them. Her hatred for the man who had paid to have her imprisoned there grew every time she heard a conversation of that sort. The exchange was a reminder of Jesse's hunger to control *everything*. She hated it, and she hated him. There was not one thing Lily did not hate about Jesse Adams. She hated his condescending tone and the way he called her "girl." She hated the way he looked *through* her and never *at* her. She hated his walk, his dark yellow teeth, his stench, his wrinkly face, the look of his sunburned dried-up skin, and the sound of his voice. She hated the way his swollen belly protruded over his pants. She hated the disgusting grunting noises he made when he chewed his food, while moving his mouth like he had fashioned himself after a cow. She even cooked his food with hate. Her recipes were good, but she knew they could be great, a fact that she would never allow his tongue the honor of knowing. But most of all, she hated that Jesse was the sole reason she had lost her best friend.

Jesse had sculpted his youngest son into what he considered to be a masterpiece of a man. Lily hated that he felt so proud of his accomplishment, like some world-renowned artist. He ingrained in James all the traits that were his own, qualities that made her hate James too. However, she wished she felt differently because she knew that underneath the layers of ugly traits that Jesse had painted onto James, there was a boy who had once risked the belt to leave desserts by her bed late at night, and who escaped Sunday family life to climb trees with her. Underneath, there was a boy who once gave her his own blanket to keep her warm, and who looked at her with kind eyes of concern if ever she was hurt or sick. Somewhere inside of the man that James had become, lay a beautiful soul with a heart that was wrapped in pure love and innocence. But Lily knew that so long as Jesse was alive, he would continue to paint and mold his so-called masterpiece, and she would continue to hate him, and his disastrous so-called work of art.

Lily's mind had drifted off so deep into her hatred for Jesse that she had become deaf to a portion of the argument he was having with James. By the time her mind reconnected with reality, Jesse had succeeded in convincing his son to do as he wanted. Lily was not surprised at this outcome. However, she *was* surprised by what she heard next.

"This ain't the dream I envisioned for my life, pa. But in this family's honor, I'll bear the burden of inheritin' and runnin' this farm."

"My boy…"

"Only if…" James continued, interrupting the celebration it seemed his father was about to have.

"Only if what?" Jesse replied, annoyance returning to his tone.

"Since I'll soon be in charge of all the decisions around here, there's somethin' that I need to do, *immediately*. It's somethin' that'll help ensure the stability of this farm."

Jesse's face was cold once again. "And just what the hell is that?"

"This farm is always in need of a way for us to make more money. Not only that, but we also need to ensure that this plantation continues to have its fair share 'a slaves. I noticed that there ain't any young'un's runnin' around the farm these days."

"Get to it, son!" Jesse barked impatiently.

James paused a moment and looked over at Lily, evil dancing in his eyes. She still worked on their lunch with her back to them. "Well, Lily's young and strong." Lily stopped when she heard her name but kept her back turned. "I think she'd produce plenty 'a strong farm hands to sell and a few for this plantation to keep." James turned back to look his father in the eyes. "So, I want you to let me take 'er to a slave breeder."

Mortified by what she had just heard, the color left Lily's face and her body grew cold. She had been fortunate up until then. She was a beautiful slave whose body had not been mutilated by fists, chains, or whips. Her chastity had remained inviolate for her entire twenty-three years, which was a miracle considering that abuse was an inescapable horror for most female slaves before they even reached puberty. But now, Lily's once best friend wanted to take all of that away and use her body as if she were some meaningless workhorse. The notion made her nauseous. James's suggestion was beyond a punishment in Lily's estimation. She suddenly preferred the physical scars from heavy leather lashing her back over the agony of being ravaged, repeatedly, by some strange human being. She felt she could more easily live with disfigured skin on her back than to live with the mental and emotional anguish of having all her babies torn from her arms, just as she had been torn from her mother.

Lily remembered Auntie telling her that all seven of her children had been taken away from her. Auntie never got to look into their eyes or touch the soft skin of six of them. She never even knew the gender of any of them up until the last one was born. They had let her hold that baby girl for some unknown reason. She got to smell her, kiss her, touch her, and look into her beautiful brown eyes before they snatched her away too. It was a curse and a blessing for Auntie for the rest of her days.

Auntie began to lose her memory and her connection with the present world in her last few months alive, so much so that she began calling Lily, Sarah. Lily eventually stopped correcting her mistake but decided to ask another slave why she kept calling her by the wrong name. It was then that she heard the story of how Auntie had called her last baby Sarah before they took her away. Lily now feared that she was about to become mentally tortured by the loss of her child in the same way as Auntie, just like so many other slave women, in the name of money and business deals.

"You see fatha', that's what my trip was for: business," James explained. "I met with a gentleman who was willin' to strike a great deal with me for usin' Lily. If you tell me that I can't use her, you can forget about me takin' ova' this farm. If I'm gonna run this place, I wanna get things in orda' startin' *now*," he said, staring just as coldly at his father as he was at him.

"What the hell was you doin' makin' deals with folks 'fore I even told you 'bout inheritin' this place? Was you plannin' on takin' my property without my knowledge, boy?!"

"No, of course not. I was gonna come to you about it, but I wasn't sure what you'd say. I know otha' men have offered you breedin' contracts for Lily before, but you've declined because you said you didn't want a pregnant house slave workin' in here, and you weren't willin' to let 'er stay at anotha' farm durin' the duration of 'er pregnancy. But the man I just spoke to is willin' to pay damn good money for her offspring. And afta' lookin' at your finances, we need the money bad. And it ain't no otha' slave here of baby bearin' age otha' than Lily. Hell, we could even keep a few for ourselves to help populate this damn place. So, I figured since we're at this crossroad, this will ensure that I get what I want … and so do you."

Jesse sat there quietly, staring harshly at his son. He took the last swig of his gin and set it back down without removing his eyes from James. "I don't like you sneakin' 'round, doin' shit behind my back." He hesitated as if the next few words pained him to say. "But you go on and take Lily and let that travelin' doctor nonsense go to hell."

"Fine!" James replied. "But I ain't takin' on all the responsibilities of runnin' this place right away. Afta' I drop Lily off at the breeda's, I'll be headed back up to Ohio University for several months to make some extra money doin' medical research with an old professor 'a mine. More than likely, I'll stay there until Lily gives birth. I'll be back with 'er afta' that."

"I don't give a shit what you do in the meantime! You just keep y'ur word about runnin' this goddamn farm when I'm dead and gone like I'm tellin' ya'!" Jesse leaned in toward his son and gritted his teeth. "Or by God, I'll haunt you from my grave 'til the end 'a y'ur days." He stood up quickly, stomped out of the kitchen, and slammed the front door.

James briefly glanced over at Lily. She never bothered to turn around and look at her nemesis. James then got up and walked out without a word. Even after hearing his plans for her, Lily remained true to her promise never to let James see that his words or actions affected her. Inside, though, her soul was screaming as if it had just been thrown into the fiery depths of hell. As soon as she heard James exit the front door, tears rained from her eyes down into the filthy dishwater.

Chapter Three

Slave Code
Article XI Section I

Slaves have no right to own any kind of property. All that they acquire, either by their own industry or by the liberality of others, or by any other means or title, including their natural-born children, shall be the full property of their masters to do so as they please.

James rode slowly on his horse with his Stetson hat low and a piece of straw in his mouth. His blue eyes were fixated on nothing in particular. His thoughts were deep, removing him from the consciousness of his surroundings throughout his entire journey into Fayetteville's town square. He was headed there to pick up some much-needed supplies for his upcoming trip with Lily. Suddenly, though, his train of thought was interrupted by the memory of the fresh blood he had seen on Lily's apron while talking to his father the day before in the kitchen. James's heart began to beat rapidly, just as it had when he first saw the blood there. He recalled how Lily had quickly turned away when she saw him glance at the stains. Her reaction made him feel as though something deeper was going on with her, more so than any minor cuts. At that moment, James had to fight his old childhood instinctive urge to ask Lily if she was okay.

As a boy, James believed that he had a natural propensity to read Lily's emotions without her ever having to whisper a word. But he had since convinced himself that that was just childish nonsense. His reaction to Lily in the kitchen, however, proved that his intuitive reflex had not faded, even after six years apart. But James was a man now, indoctrinated with his father's teachings. He knew better than to tend to the emotional needs of an inferior slave, *especially* in front of his father. *Slaves are property, no different than mules,* his father had once told him. Remembering those words kept James from comforting his former friend, despite how confident he was that she had been emotionally broken before he entered the kitchen.

Despite still feeling the strength of his unique connection to Lily, it was not enough to stop James from traumatizing her with the threat of being bred. *She deserves this,* James thought to himself as he rode along on his horse. For the fourteen years that Lily had spent on his mother's piano, he was determined to see to it that her life remained forever changed. His plan drifted through his mind again, calculated, and unwavering. A sinister grin then emerged on his face after picturing the moment they would arrive at his chosen destination. He could not wait to drown in a wave of contentment when Lily finally faced the consequences of her actions.

"She deserves this," James reminded himself aloud this time, his sinister grin still in place. He then dug his heels into his horse's side, prompting him to pick up the pace. The quicker he could retrieve the supplies on his list, the quicker he could experience the elation of his plan finally coming to fruition.

Before going to Albert's General Store, though, James had another important stop to make. He dismounted his horse and tied it to a post outside of Dr. Gideon Whitfield's medical practice. He removed his Stetson hat before entering the good doctor's establishment. "Dr. Whitfield," he called out, after seeing him in the corner of the front office.

Gideon turned toward him after taking a vial from a glass cabinet. "Well, well, well, James Adams. Oh, pardon me," he said, clearing his throat. "I mean, *Doctor* Adams," he emphasized, smiling as he approached to shake James's hand. "Good to see you again."

James shook his hand. "No need to be so formal," he smiled. "James is just fine."

"I concur. I think we can certainly dispense with the formalities at this point. Call me Gideon."

"Well then, Gideon, I take it from the smile on your face that your son is doin' much betta'?"

"Well, why don't you see for yourself. He just so happens to be right back here with my wife. She brought 'em in for a follow-up exam." Gideon guided him to an exam room in the back where his one-year-old son, Brandon, sat in his mother's lap. He was wide-eyed, babbling, and shaking a rattle, a stark contrast from his condition nearly three weeks prior.

The first day James had arrived back in Fayetteville, he wanted to talk to Dr. Whitfield about the prospect of working with him occasionally to make some money and to continue gaining medical experience. When James stopped by his clinic that afternoon, though, he found that it was closed for the day, which was odd for the dedicated small-town doctor. James then decided to stop by Gideon's house. He indeed found him there. James barely recognized him, though; Gideon had not aged well in the last six years. His wrinkles were much more prominent, he was thinner, and so was his hair, which had lost all its color. Gideon looked nothing like the strapping man who used to give James and his brothers yearly examinations. But the aging doctor looked hale in comparison to his one-year-old son, Brandon.

James had come to talk business, but quickly set that aside when Gideon explained that his son's serious illness was the reason he was not at his clinic. Naturally, James took an interest in the boy's plight, hoping his new training could help. Gideon rattled off his child's symptoms with the most forlorn look on his face, as he slowly began to accept that his only child might die. He was further devastated by the irony that he was a doctor who was powerless to cure his son's unusual illness.

After explaining Brandon's ailments, Gideon took James upstairs where his son lay barely moving and unable to open his eyes. His mother sat nearby crying and holding his hand. From the list of symptoms, James already knew that Brandon's condition was grave. The disheartening sight of the frail little boy further proved that he was knocking on death's door.

All Brandon's symptoms reminded James of a little girl he had once come across while working with another doctor. James explained to Gideon that he had treated her with an experimental new drug concoction that had saved her life. He then offered to buy, mix, and administer the same medication for Brandon. Under the dire circumstances, Gideon was willing to try anything to give his son a fighting chance. He, therefore, allowed James to move forward with treating him.

Before leaving town for his business trip, James had stopped by and saw that the medication was helping Brandon to slowly improve. Now, with the way the toddler was smiling in the back of Gideon's medical practice, it was obvious that the treatment had been a success.

"Hey, little fella'," James smiled, happy to see a lively little boy this time around. Brandon smiled at him and reached his arms out, almost as if he knew that he owed James a hug for helping to save his life. James lifted him high into the air, settled him onto his hip, and tickled his neck, getting a laugh out of him. "No more scarin' your ma and pa like that, ya' hear?" he teased.

"Carolyn, darlin'," Gideon said, approaching his young wife. "Unda' the circumstances the otha' day, I don't think I eva' did get to formally introduce you to this young man." Gideon offered a hand to help his wife stand. "Meet the young man whose fatha's been boastin' 'bout bein' my successor for years now. He and his brotha's used to keep me so busy as young'uns, tendin' to their ailments, that I can make my way to his farm blindfolded," he laughed. "This here is Dr. James Adams. The man I'm now foreva' indebted to for savin' our boy's life." He then turned toward James. "James, this is my wife, Carolyn."

"Pleased to officially make your acquaintance, ma'am," James replied. Without all the chaos of dealing with Brandon, it was the first time James had taken a good look at Carolyn. She looked to be at least thirty years Gideon's junior.

James had not been home long, but he had already heard the whispers about the unusual couple. Their age difference had caused the conservative small town to shun them when they wed three years prior. Gideon had only lost his first wife a year before that, and so naturally gossip swirled, especially since Carolyn was such a young bride. Gideon and Carolyn did not let it damage their relationship, though, and went on to conceive a son together. The little boy was the first for the good doctor, since his previous wife was unable to bear children.

After the way the town had treated Carolyn and Gideon, the couple had been even more thankful, and rather surprised, at the lengths that James had gone through to help their son. It was with that in mind that Carolyn took James's free hand into both of hers. "I can't tell you how grateful I am to you for helpin' my little boy," she said, running her hand through Brandon's hair.

"And neitha' can I," Gideon added. "I tell you what, son." He placed a hand on James's shoulder. "If eva' you need anything, anything at all, you come and see me, ya' hear? I feel like I owe you the world for what ya' done for my boy, and I'll do anything I can to give it to ya'." He was nearly in tears as he conveyed his gratitude.

"You have no debts with me, Gideon. Your boy's alive, that's all I could eva' ask for."

"Carolyn, do you mind if I speak to James alone for a moment?"

"Of course not." She took her son from James. "I wanna get home and get Brandon down for a nap and get dinna' started anyway."

"Okay, I'll see ya' lata' then … Oh, and take this with ya'," Gideon said, handing Carolyn the vial of medication he had just retrieved from his cabinet. "Give 'em two drops 'a this before you lay 'em down."

"Will do." Carolyn turned to James. "Bye, Dr. Adams, and thank you again."

"You're very welcome. Take care."

Gideon walked his wife and son out to the carriage, kissed them both, loaded Brandon inside and then helped Carolyn up. "We'll see ya' back home, Giddy," Carolyn said, smiling down at him before she snapped the reins.

Gideon went back into his clinic afterward and quietly watched his beautiful wife from the window until she was out of sight. "I truly love that woman," he then said to James. "Just wish the rest 'a this town did," he sighed.

James stood there quietly, surprised by Gideon's sudden candidness.

"People around here can't seem to accept that I married Carolyn. I'm sure you can guess why," Gideon added with a lighthearted laugh, certain that James had noticed their age difference. "I get that we don't fit this town's mold of the ideal married couple, but I don't feel we deserve to be shunned because of it. If everyone just ignored us, I could live with that. But it kills me that people have treated Carolyn so poorly. She's so kind, such a truly gentle soul. She doesn't deserve to be mistreated," he sighed, still staring out the window.

"Everyone's treated *both* of us poorly, really," Gideon continued. "I haven't let it botha' me on a personal level, but it does hurt that my business has suffered for it. Hell, if it wasn't for the fact that folks truly needed my services from time to time, I doubt they'd come to

45

me at all anymore. They only seem to call on me now when it's an extreme emergency. Can't hardly get folks to come in for routine examinations anymore."

"Sorry to hear that, Doc. But I reckon you can't expect much else from small town, small-minded folks. They don't know any betta'."

"I agree," Gideon replied. He finally turned from the window and looked at James oddly. He had often used that same phrase in his head to help himself cope with the town's behavior. "Look, I'm sorry to dump all 'a my troubles on you. I'm just explainin' 'cause it's part 'a the reason I wanted to talk to you. You see, despite how harsh everyone in this town has been on me, I'd neva' walk away from helpin' anybody here in Fayetteville. Not unless I's certain I'd be passin' 'em along to the right set 'a hands to take good care of 'em." He looked down at both of James's hands. "And I just saw a pair 'a hands that worked a miracle on my boy. I could use those hands around here James," he said, wagging his finger at him. "And so could this town. That's why I's kind 'a hopin' there's some truth to what your fatha's been sayin' all these years. I sure could use the help takin' care of folks around here, 'specially from a man who's a masta' at savin' lives. And hell, maybe a fresh face is what it'll take to get folks rollin' back through these doors."

"That's actually what I'd originally come to discuss with you the otha' day when your boy was sick," James replied. "I wanted the opportunity to work with ya' from time to time, to get some more experience."

"Actually, I's hopin' for more than just your occasional help. I ain't gettin' any younga', as I'm sure is plain to see," Gideon laughed. "I'd really love to turn this place ova' to you in due time. I'm sure folks 'round here wouldn't object … 'specially the ladies," he teased. He had heard all the whispers around town from all the giddy young girls that were gossiping about James's return.

"Well, thank you, but I didn't originally plan on settlin' here in Fayetteville."

"I don't blame you," Gideon snickered.

"My hope was to be a travelin' doctor, and I's just wantin' to work with you before I set out on the road."

"I see," Gideon replied, looking rather disappointed. "That's certainly a noble unda'takin'."

"Thanks. But if my fatha' has it his way, that may not happen. So, right now I'm still tryna weigh my options. But I'm honored that you'd trust me to take ova' your clinic."

"Well, you let me know if you eva' change your mind. Eitha' way it goes, I'd be glad to have ya' here. Hell, far as I'm concerned, you can start now if you'd like."

"Well, unfortunately, right now I've got some much-needed business to take care of outta town that's come up unexpectedly. So, I'll have to postpone all 'a this for a while. But I'll certainly keep your offa' in mind for the future."

"You do that. Anytime you're ready, son. I'm here to help ya' in any way I can. You can count on that."

"Thank you, Gideon. I'll rememba' that. I certainly do appreciate it."

"No, son … Thank *you*. I won't eva' forget what ya' done for my family."

James nodded, shook Gideon's hand, and headed out the door toward Albert's General Store.

Dr. Gideon Whitfield's words about the women in Fayetteville could not have been more accurate. James Adams' return was undoubtedly the most popular gossip topic amongst many of them, especially after some had heard about him helping Brandon. Within days, James had become the talk of the town and, by far, Fayetteville's most desirable man.

There had always been something unexplainable about James Adams that gave women a sudden case of moral amnesia. As James crossed the road, it seemed that several young ladies had suddenly been afflicted by the rare disorder. Their lustful gazes were clearly conveying the fact that naughty thoughts were easily trumping their morality. Their reaction to James was an odd phenomenon considering that the presence of all the other Adams men triggered the flight response in most women. The fact that J.R. and Jacob had managed a bride was a miracle. James was certainly fortunate to be an identical copy of his maternal grandfather. Much like his grandfather, he never failed to catch the wandering eyes of his female peers in his youth. With the way all estrogen-driven eyes were currently fixated on James, it was evident that his ability to attract women had not changed … but his body certainly had. During his six-year hiatus, James had gone from an adorable teenager to a strapping, well-built, virile man. Even through his coat, it was easy to see that his once slender teenage body was now wrapped in a layer of chiseled muscles. His shoulders were broader, he had grown to an unusually tall six-foot-two, and the fresh shadow of a dark beard now covered his once smooth baby face. He had cut his hair short as a teen, but it had since grown back into a long mane of dark, loose curls. His dark hair contrasted with his crystal blue eyes, causing them to stand out even more than they already did. James ran his hand through his thick mane of hair as he walked mindlessly across the dirt road to Albert's General Store. He was lost in thought about the journey he was about to take with Lily, completely oblivious to the eyes that were glued on him … especially the eyes of one Mary Jo Parker.

Mary Jo was the only young lady that James's father had approved of out of the many girls who had an interest in him during his teen years. Jesse wanted only the classiest woman as a wife for the son he was certain would go on to greater things in life. But Jesse's approval of the beautiful, strawberry-blonde gem was mainly because he knew that a union between the two would be a great benefit to his bank account.

Mary Jo's father, Joseph Parker, was by far the wealthiest man in Fayetteville. He had cotton and tobacco contracts with the Adams family long before James and Mary Jo were even born. So, in Jesse's greedy mind, the merging of the two families would mean a definite increase in social status and his ticket to riches for generations to come. For that reason alone, Jesse was all but shoving James into Mary Jo's face every chance he got. Even when James was an infant, Jesse had sat him next to Mary Jo in the crib during her visits to the farm. He had hoped to build a natural connection between them long before they could even walk. However, Jesse's plan failed miserably. The more time James was forced to play with Mary Jo through the years, the more he disliked her.

As he got older, James recognized that the average man would probably consider Mary Jo pretty by traditional standards, but she was simply not his cup of tea. She was way too frilly for his taste, and she talked about things that rarely interested him. It did not help that she spoke in a high-pitched southern belle voice that was as pleasant to his ears as screeching nails on a chalkboard. He also could not stand her attention-seeking contrived ways. Even without those attributes, James simply was not physically attracted to Mary Jo's beady green eyes, red hair, fake smile, skinny shapeless frame, or her ghostly complexion. To him, she was far paler than the average white person, so much so that he often jokingly wondered if she naturally repelled sunlight, or if her daddy had dipped her in porcelain to preserve his pasty little "pumpkin," as he would call her. That term of endearment further annoyed James; he felt that that title should be reserved for little girls who were sweet, not ones who were snobbish with snotty attitudes.

Even Mary Jo's name bothered James; he hated that her father had arrogantly named a little girl after himself. It got under his skin enough that he began calling her, MJ. He hoped that it would irritate her just as much as she irritated him. But unbeknownst to James, Mary Jo thought it was sweet, and that he had given her that nickname because she was special in his eyes. Mary Jo was clueless as to the truth behind the name change and to James's true feelings about her as a whole.

Mary Jo's misconceptions had everything to do with the fact that James was always kind to her. He never once revealed the slightest hint of his distaste for her. In fact, it was quite the opposite. He went above and beyond to be sweet to her just to please his father, understanding that it was important for business. Deep down, though, Mary Jo meant nothing to James. He secretly loathed every minute of catering to her needs while she was at the farm. After he had befriended Lily, however, she helped turn Mary Jo's visits into a source of humor.

Whenever Mary Jo visited, Lily was notorious for peeking her head around corners and making "silly" or "kissy" faces at James that only he could see over MJ's shoulder. James would fight hard to keep a straight face, but Lily would not stop until he burst into laughter. It never failed to be poorly timed laughter that seemed bizarre to Mary Jo. Lily found it amusing to listen to James struggle to come up with ridiculous excuses for his unexplained outbursts. James and Lily's fun did not end there. Long after Mary Jo would leave for the evening, she continued to be a source of comedy for the duo. The mischievous pair would sometimes roleplay incidents that had happened that evening. Lily always did a spot-on impersonation of Mary Jo that had James laughing hysterically.

For Mary Jo, though, her visits with James were no laughing matter. While the secret best friends were laughing at her expense, Mary Jo was lying in her bed daydreaming about what her wedding day with James would one day be like. While Lily had James in stitches imitating her frilly little walk, Mary Jo was picturing the children she would one day have with him. While James was mocking Mary Jo's high-pitched voice, she was thinking about how sweet he had been to her while she was there.

James was simply making the best of the miserable position his father had put him in. He did not realize that the kindness he was forcing himself to show Mary Jo was creating a monster, one who had developed *serious* feelings for him. Mary Jo wanted James Adams in every way possible, and she was willing to do and say anything to acquire him. For Mary Jo—a spoiled, self-entitled, daddy's girl who rarely heard the word "no"—it was not a question of *if* she would have James, it was only a question of *when*. And as Mary Jo stood outside of Albert's General Store watching James walk across the road, she was about to attempt to have that question answered.

When Mary Jo heard that James was back in Fayetteville, she had been on the prowl like a lioness ever since. She was always coming up with some excuse to go into town, dressed up, made-up, and hair perfectly done, hoping to "accidentally" bump into him. Unbelievably, all her efforts were about to pay off. While she blended in amongst a group of her friends, her eyes coasted up and down the man she had been dying to sink her claws into for years. Mary Jo had lain in wait for long enough, and now she was finally about to seize the moment to pounce on her prey.

"James? *James Adams?* Is that you?" Mary Jo asked from behind him, as he collected a few things off the store shelf and put them into a wicker basket.

James was still lost deep in thought and did not hear a thing. He did not come out of his trance until Mary Jo tapped on his shoulder. Startled, he turned around and was greeted by the last face he had hoped to see in town.

"James Adams! What a surprise to see you! I had no idea you were back in town," Mary Jo lied.

"*MJ?*" he replied, sounding surprised after noticing how overdressed she seemed for a leisurely trip to the store.

"Why yes, it's me." Her bright tomato-red, lipstick-stained lips stretched into a wide smile. "You haven't forgotten me, I see."

"Of course not." *But I've certainly tried,* James thought to himself.

"One would think so. I sent you several letta's while you were away at university."

"You did?" James replied, trying to sound surprised. "I neva' received any letta's," he lied.

"You mean you neva' got a single one?" Mary Jo whined.

"No, not a one. I certainly would've written you back had that been the case," James fibbed once again. He had read the first few lines of two of her letters and tossed them into the trash. He never bothered to open the ones that followed before tossing them too.

"All that effort for nothin'. I put all my heart into those letta's."

"I'm so sorry, MJ. I have no idea what could've happened to 'em. Maybe you just used the wrong address."

"But I got the address directly from your fatha'."

"Well, all I can say is that I neva' received 'em."

"I s'ppose there ain't nothin' we can do 'bout it now, can we?" she asked rhetorically, forcing the fake grin that James hated so much.

"I guess not." There was an awkward silence before James resumed picking up items off the shelf. All the while, he was hoping Mary Jo would disappear, like the ghost she reminded him of. Much to his dismay, though, she found something else to talk about.

"Speakin' of your daddy, he's invited my fatha' and me to anotha' business dinna' at your home soon."

"Is that so?"

"That's right! This comin' Saturday, I believe," she announced excitedly.

"Well, I'll be travelin' for a while, so it looks like it just might be the three of ya'. Or maybe my brotha's might show up and keep ya' company."

"It's been six long years, James!" Mary Jo exclaimed, momentarily exposing her snotty attitude before calming back down and trying to sound sensual. "I's certainly lookin' forward to seein' you there and hearin' all about your time away at school. I thought perhaps we could even reminisce about all the good times we used to have togetha' when we's young," she smiled, touching him delicately on the shoulder.

What good times? "I wish I could, MJ, but this is a trip that I absolutely have to take. I'm sorry, but there's no gettin' out of it. It was good seein' ya' again though," he said, infusing a lie into the last part of his statement. James turned around and resumed his shopping, hoping Mary Jo would get the point and leave him be. But the porcelain-colored princess was nowhere near finished trying to seduce the man she had missed for years.

"Well, how about you and I celebrate your return before you depart? Just the two of us? I could make you a great home-cooked meal. I'm sure you could use that afta' bein' gone so long. And my cookin' is far betta' than that house slave 'a yours, Leela…"

"Lily!" James quickly corrected her.

"Whateva'." Mary Jo dismissed his correction with a wave of her hand. "It's much betta' than hers. So, what do ya' say? I can make your favorite … fried chicken and mashed potatoes."

That was not James's favorite. He suddenly felt a headache coming on, the kind with the strength to bring even the toughest man to his knees. "Listen, maybe some otha' time MJ. I have a lot I need to take care of before my trip."

"Maybe when you get back then," she insisted.

"That'd be nice. I look forward to it," James lied, saying anything he could to cease listening to the sound of a voice that was inducing a migraine.

Another broad smile stretched across Mary Jo's pale face. As giddy as she suddenly felt at the prospect of spending an evening alone with James, one would have assumed he had just proposed to her. "I can't wait to see you when you return then. It'll be an amazin' evenin'." She looked at James with hunger in her eyes. "I promise you won't regret it," she said in a seductive tone, as she glided her finger down his arm.

It took every bit of James's strength not to groan aloud. He let out a frustrated breath instead. "Bye, MJ," he uttered coldly. He then quickly turned around, ignoring the hungry look in her colorless face and the lust in her headache-inducing voice, knowing that he had zero intentions of spending one minute alone with her.

James stopped at two other shops before loading up the satchels on his horse and eagerly riding out of the town square. He had only been back a short time, but already some of the people in town were making him wish that he had never returned. He had tired quickly of all the long-winded conversations, of being questioned, and passively propositioned by multiple women that he had no interest in. He wanted to be polite as they welcomed him back to Fayetteville and asked him questions about his time away at school. But he was feeling oddly angry about the way people had treated Gideon and his wife, despite all the years he had spent selflessly serving the community. It didn't help that Mary Jo had his temples throbbing in unforgiving pain.

James remembered that he had always felt as if he did not fit in, in Fayetteville. His brief interactions since his return reminded him why. As he rode hard and fast out of the town square, he found himself already looking forward to escaping the place that had brought him so much misery as a boy. More than anything, he was eager to avoid dealing with Mary Jo and the vomit-inducing migraine she was sure to bring him again at his father's business meeting.

James galloped back onto the farm and headed for the stalls to feed and water his horse, and to begin preparing his wagon for his journey. However, his attention was drawn to another matter that suddenly became urgent to him. In the distance, Henry, a strong older slave on the plantation, was away from his duties in the field. James looked at his pocket watch and realized it was time for one of the two meals the slaves received daily. But Henry was not eating. He was having a leisurely conversation with another slave who James felt had no business being over there with him. They were tucked away behind the barn looking for a little privacy while they talked, but James could see them easily from where he stood.

"You've been lookin' so down the last few days, Lily. You ain't been smilin' that pretty smile like usual. That ain't like you," Henry said, in his baritone voice.

"Ain't got much to smile 'bout no mo'," Lily confessed, looking down at the empty clothes basket perched on her hip.

"What's wrong?"

"I'm gonna be leavin' here soon, Henry. That's why I wanted to come and say goodbye to you," she told him, placing her free hand warmly on his arm. "You've always been so kind to me."

"Jesse ain't sellin' ya', is he?" Henry asked, sounding genuinely concerned.

"Truth be told, I wish that was the case."

"I don't unda'stand. Don't tell me you's runnin' away."

"No, masa' James decided he's gonna take me to a breeda'."

"My God Lily, I'm so sorry," Henry replied, placing a comforting hand on her shoulder.

"It's okay, I…"

55

"LILY!" James interjected. He had heard and certainly seen enough. She and Henry jumped back with fear dancing in their eyes. "Looks to me like you done finished hangin' them clothes on the line, so you wanna explain to me why you're still out here, 'steada tendin' to your duties in the house?" he barked, all the while staring Henry down.

"Sorry Masa' James," Lily replied flatly.

"Don't be sorry. Just get back to mindin' your work. And you too Henry, if ya' know what's good for ya'," James threatened, still staring intensely at him.

"Yessa'," Henry nodded.

Lily walked away hastily with anger in each step. She could feel the heat of James's eyes on her back as she made her way up the plantation house steps. She busied herself in the kitchen, hoping that he would go on about his business and have nothing further to say about her conduct. Much to her chagrin, James leaned up against the frame of the kitchen door with his arms folded, letting his silence speak first.

"My fatha' informed me that you were pure, which is what I told the man who plans to breed you. From the looks 'a you and Henry, I'd say you done went and made a liar outta me."

Lily was appalled by his statement. She felt such a thing was none of his business. As much as she wanted to tell him to go to hell, she kept her wits about her. "May I ask why that makes a difference … masa'?" she asked, her irritation seeping into the last word.

"I can't present them with a slave that's already with child, Lily!"

Lily kept her eyes on the vegetables she was chopping and did not immediately react to the sudden anger in James's voice. She was calm and purposely delayed her response, which allowed more time for the visions of Henry having his way with her to graphically replay in James's mind. "No need to worry, *masa'*," she finally answered, never looking up from the vegetables in front of her. "I ain't made a liar outta you."

Her response finally returned James's heartbeat to a normal pace. But the brief visions of Henry lying on top of Lily had surprisingly destroyed his appetite for the rest of the day. "We're leavin' tomorrow mornin'," he mustered up the strength to say, while trying to force the images in his mind to subside. He retrieved a satchel from the parlor and tossed it onto the kitchen table. "Fill this with food and whateva' belongin's you have. Be sure it's enough for about two days 'a travel."

"Yessa'."

James then turned and headed to his room to gather his belongings. Before getting far, though, he turned back around and watched Lily from a distance for a moment. He knew she had to have overheard what was to come in only a few short days, yet he never once saw fear or tears in her eyes. He was amazed at her strength but wondered if those attributes would fade in the face of reality. He then turned and finally trotted up the stairs.

After James had left, Lily did as she was told and gathered canned goods, fruits, vegetables, and bread for their journey. She then went into the slave quarters to gather what little she had. There were no fancy shoes, nor shoes at all for that matter. There were no beautiful dresses or even ugly ones to change into; no pretty hats, expensive jewelry, or any other frilly things fit for a lovely lady. One scarf and an extra apron were all that lay next to her makeshift bed. She stuffed the extra scarf into the satchel, and her packing was complete.

Lily then walked over to the secret storage spot in her run-down room that still housed the socks and blankets that James had so kindly brought to her and Auntie on that cold night over a decade ago. She pulled out Auntie's blanket and hugged it tight. It still had her scent on it. As Lily inhaled, she began to think about all seven of Auntie's little babies and how they had been stolen from her, including baby Sarah. It made her wonder if she would ever get to see the faces of any of her own children, or know their genders, or be the one to name them. She wondered if maybe it was best to have them snatched away so that there was no chance to form a connection with them at all, no chance to be tortured by the memories of their names, their scent, the softness of their skin, and their petite faces as they lay snuggled in her arms. Either way, Lily realized she was about to leave the Adams farm with a filthy scarf and return with nothing but the same. Soon Auntie's blanket was covered in the moisture of her tears. The torture had already begun.

Chapter Four

Slave Code
Article III Section II

Slaves are forbidden from leaving their owner's property, unless accompanied by a white person, or carrying a license or letter showing he has authority from his master. If any be without either, they shall be considered as a runaway, and to suffer such penalties provided against runaways.

Lily sat in the back of James's covered wagon with her knees drawn up to her chest, watching her "prison" get further and further out of sight in the morning sunlight. It was the farthest she had been off the Adams plantation since her life sentence there began. While confined there, all Lily had known was the same miserable daily routine of serving her warden, a man she wished would return to his rightful throne next to Satan. Escaping her prison warden for a while was bittersweet. She was happy to be relieved of the irritating sound of Jesse barking orders at her all day but sickened by what that would shortly be replaced with.

Despite where she was headed, Lily was trying to enjoy the two days of freedom she had before her ex-best friend delivered her to hell. She prayed that James would not utter a word to her during their travels. She wanted to get lost in her own thoughts and pretend that she was on a journey to see her mother again for the first time since being tortuously dragged away from her. Thoughts of her mother only sustained Lily for a little while before the tears began to fall, collecting on her blood-stained dress. Every clip-clap of the horses' hooves reminded her that she was closer to being violated by some strange man and then experiencing the loss of her child, the way her mother and Auntie had. It was for those reasons that Lily lay with her head on her knees, crying silently, and begging God for infertility.

An hour into their journey, Lily turned and peeked through the wagon cover. She quietly stared at James in disgust as he tipped his hat to a passerby in another wagon. The lack of expression on his face reminded her of Jesse. It had been years since she had seen James smile. She missed that smile and the tender man it once belonged to. She once believed that James was the sort of caring man who would have fought tooth and nail to save her from the sickening things that were about to occur. She was now finding it difficult to come to terms with the fact that he was now callous enough to drag her to the wolves himself.

As Lily stared at James, she began to reminisce about her old friendship with him, just as she had many times since his return. She found that every time a negative thought of him crossed her mind, it was preceded by a fond memory of them together. Every lovely memory made his current transgression against her hurt even more. Lily became angry with herself for not being able to let go of the past. She constantly had to remind herself that the James she knew as a girl was dead. Despite feeling that way, though, the fond memories were far too strong and full of happiness to let dissolve. They played on in her mind along with her piano music, soothing her just as her beautiful melodies had the power to do. This time, she recalled an occasion one summer when they were sixteen ...

James had been sent away to work on his aunt and uncle's plantation in a neighboring town. He and his brothers were only gone for about two weeks during their summer breaks, but every time James left, Lily remembered feeling like each day dragged on for months. She was never sure when James was due to return, which made his absence even more intolerable. This particular summer, her heartache was far worse than usual; that fact was evident by her music. By the third day, Lily's loneliness presented itself in the form of a beautifully composed piano piece. She played no other song during James's two-week absence; it comforted her the entire time he was away.

After days of misery, Lily woke up one Sunday morning and found a gift that had been placed at her bedside in the late-night hours. Her face lit up the moment she saw it. Based on what it was, she knew instantly to go to the old oak tree in her playground paradise near the creek. Lily sat impatiently on a blanket at the base of the tree, gazing appreciatively at her gift. She suddenly turned her head to the right when she heard leaves crinkling in the distance. A brilliant smile illuminated on her face as she watched James dash quickly from tree to tree. Lily stood as he approached. James slowed his pace as he got closer, taking time to absorb the sight of a young woman who had dominated his thoughts while he was away, a young woman that he had missed beyond his capacity to express with words. James and Lily's smiles faded when they were within feet of one another. There were no words exchanged, just an intense gaze that they held for a moment ... and then a hug. It was a hug that dissolved any need for James to verbally express how much he desperately missed her. The length and strength of his embrace conveyed those words for him. He hugged Lily in a way that said, *please forgive me for leaving you here so long alone.* His arms easily proved to Lily that his misery and loneliness had been equal to hers. The warmth that radiated through her made her wish that James would hold her like that for a lifetime.

When James finally released her, Lily thanked him for the gift that he had placed at her bedside: a book that she was eager to hear. The pair sat shoulder to shoulder under their childhood tree as James read it aloud. The story instantly became Lily's favorite. The magnificent ending brought joyous tears to her eyes. It was those very tears that eventually brought forth James's desire to teach Lily to read. He wanted his gift to be the first book Lily was ever able to read to herself.

... After losing herself in that memory in the back of the wagon, Lily's emotions from that day were fresh again. During all the years that James was away, she had been able to repress all the feelings and memories associated with him. Now that he was back, though, it was all resurfacing again. It was crushing her to accept that those beautiful memories, and that wonderful man, were all in her past. She angrily wiped her tears away knowing that their relationship would likely remain severed, no matter how hard she prayed for things to be different.

Despite the onslaught of joyous childhood memories resurfacing, Lily refused to reminisce with James about any of it during their journey. In fact, she was happy with their limited interaction. They had simple conversations about food, water, and breaks to relieve themselves, but both seemed reluctant to say anything beyond that. Lily even chose to eat inside the covered wagon instead of taking the opportunity to sit in the warmth of the sunlight near her nemesis. She wanted to avoid looking at James for any unnecessary amount of time; the sight of him tended to destroy her appetite. It did not seem to make much difference to James either. They both seemed content with the distance and silence, two things that would have been inconceivable between them eight years prior.

After sleeping through a rather mild winter night, the pair proceeded on in the second day of their journey, much like the first ... in silence. Aside from a brief break for snacks, they rode steadily for a few hours until the sun was high in the clear blue sky. The beautiful conditions brought an unseasonable warmth to the winter day. It made a body of running creek water look inviting to James. Lily suddenly overheard him calling the horses to a halt. "Lily, we're breakin' here," he then said.

"Yessa'," she replied, even though she wanted to ask why they were stopping so soon. They had just eaten and relieved themselves not long before. She did not dare to step out of line by questioning him, though. Instead, she got out and found a place to relieve herself again. It was more of a way to distance herself from James than a necessity to go. When she came back, James was dropping bags onto the ground from the back of the wagon. She walked around the back to help him, but then quickly turned away when she saw that he was shirtless.

"Lily," James called out to her before she walked away.

"Yessa'," she replied, stopping with her back to him.

"Take this satchel."

Lily turned back around but felt uneasy with where to place her eyes as James handed it to her. "Is there some food in here needs cookin'?" she asked, being sure to keep her eyes glued to the satchel.

"Naw, there's soap, towels, and some otha' things for you in there. You can use that creek ova' yonda' to clean up. Quicka' you get cleaned up, quicka' we can carry on."

"Yessa'."

Lily walked a long way down the stream and set the satchel on a large rock once she felt she was in a place that gave her plenty of privacy from prying eyes. She opened the bag in search of the soap and towels but sitting in plain view were new undergarments, a neatly folded dress, and a scarf that matched it. Thinking that her eyes were deceiving her, she pulled the dress out, laid it on top of a rock, and stared at it in confusion. It was not an evening gown or even a dinner dress. She was not even certain if it was brand new, but that did not matter to her. She was just happy that it was free of holes, stains, and tattered ends, like the one she had on. She then held the dress up to her body and saw that it even looked to be a perfect fit, unlike her old one. It was basic but beautiful in her eyes, so beautiful that she almost refused to believe that it was for her.

James was in the distance tending to his own bathing needs. He wanted to respect Lily's privacy and kept his back to her for as long as he could, but his desire to glance in her direction was much stronger than he had anticipated. Discreetly, he turned toward Lily just in time to see her holding her new dress up to her body. The dress was among the many things he had picked up on his trip into town when he had run into Mary Jo. He wanted Lily to represent his father's farm well and figured that a new dress, free from bloodstains, filth, and holes, would be beneficial to their representation … at least that's what he told himself. After leaving Albert's General Store, James had gone into a clothing shop and found a woman that looked to be Lily's height and shape. He then asked what size she wore. He hoped that he had made an accurate assessment. He now stood in the creek, secretly peering at Lily, waiting impatiently to see.

Lily, however, had reluctantly put the new dress down. She was unsure why James would get her a new one but figured there was definitely some personal motive behind it. Although she appreciated it, she knew not to assume that James *wanted* to do something special for her. Nevertheless, she was excited to have a beautiful new piece of clothing, especially after having worn the same tattered garment for so long.

Before bathing, Lily leaned over and touched the creek water with her hand. She decided to take advantage of the rare warm day and go for a brief swim. Not wanting to put her private areas on display, she entered the water in her old dress. The chill touched her bones, but it did not deter her at all. Floating in the water reminded her of when James had taught her to swim. She suddenly found herself not wanting to rush the opportunity to enjoy the cool water while reliving that happier time in her life. She reverted to her childlike ways for a spell and began to swim around in the creek like she was ten again, not caring if her lack of urgency made James angry. She was already more than halfway to her punishment anyway and figured there was nothing worse he could ever do to her.

From the moment James had turned toward Lily, he had yet to take his eyes off her. He had mindlessly washed himself as he observed her backstroking in the water. Anger over her leisurely swim and lack of haste was not his reaction at all. He, too, was instantly reminded of their youth. As a boy, he admired how Lily was able to go from a disciplined, hard-working young woman, to a young woman with childlike playful ways and youthful silliness. Gazing at her now, he realized that she had not changed, nor did the fact that he still appreciated those beautiful qualities.

After swimming for a short while, Lily finally decided to get to the business of cleaning herself. She moved toward the shallow end of the creek to get her footing, and then unbuttoned her old dress. She slid it off her body, unknowingly revealing her bare back to James's waiting eyes. Feeling a false sense of security, she walked toward the shore to lay her garments down and to retrieve the soap and towels. Little by little, her body emerged from the water, revealing the length of her long legs and the roundness of her buttocks. The sight of her nude body immediately cast a spell on James. He watched her in an unblinking trance. Not much detail could be seen from where he stood, but still his eyes followed Lily's every movement back down into the water as she began to lather herself.

James's own bathing and dressing needs instantly became irrelevant as he watched Lily. He knew where he stood with her as her master, but he was still a man. His status was not enough to stop a sudden raging desire, nor the envy he felt toward Lily's hands as she ran them slowly over her body. Countless nights as a teenager, James had woken up with the front of his pajama pants saturated by the end result of his dreams about Lily. His body began to react to the vision of her now, just as it always did then. No matter how cold their relationship currently was, it simply could not stop those fires from raging within him again, while watching a woman whose exquisite features he had always considered as a work of art.

"Hey there!" a voice called out from behind James that seemed to rain down from the heavens. His mind was so distracted by Lily that he had not heard a horse approaching behind him. He turned to find a sheriff glaring down at him. Luckily, James had just put on a pair of trousers that hid the truth about what was on his mind. "This here is private property. It ain't no goddamn bathtub!" the sheriff explained.

"Sorry Sheriff, it didn't look like it belonged to anybody."

"Well, I'm here to tell ya' that it belongs to the Blacksmith family, so I suggest you load up y'ur wagon and be on y'ur way, if you don't want no trouble." Lily was so far down the creek that she did not hear any of what was going on. She was still diligently bathing herself when the sheriff caught sight of her movement in the distance. "She with you?" he asked James.

"Yessa', she is."

"She a nigga'? I can't hardly tell from here."

James felt the heat in his blood start to rise upon hearing the way he referred to Lily. He could not stand that word. Despite it being typical slang, he felt it was degrading. "She's a *Negro,* yes," he said, through gritted teeth.

"She y'ur slave?"

"Yessa'."

"You carryin' her papers?"

"Yessa'."

"Finish gettin' dressed and let me see 'em."

James put on a shirt, retrieved the paperwork, and then handed it over.

The sheriff took a moment to read the documents. "Well, you and y'ur lil' monkey need to move it along, 'fore I arrest the both of ya'," he said, handing the forms back to James.

"LILYYY!" James called out. She turned around abruptly to find not one, but two pairs of eyes centered on her. "COME NOW! WE HAVE TO MOVE ALONG!"

"YESSA'!" she yelled back, feeling the heat of embarrassment crawling all over her. She frantically retrieved her belongings while trying to keep her body as covered as possible.

James tried to distract the unwelcomed visitor with unnecessary conversation to stop him from looking at Lily. Slave or not, Negro, Caucasian, or otherwise, he knew men would be men, and he did not like the idea of the sheriff using Lily in his fantasies, the way he looked to be doing.

After Lily had dressed and walked back to the wagon, the sheriff continued to watch as they loaded up, pretending as if he did not trust that they would move along as he had demanded. But Lily knew better. For the first time in her life, she felt the disgust of an older man conveying his desires for her with his eyes. She had not experienced such things on the Adams farm. Although Jesse was in every way an evil man, he would have never allowed such violations to take place with his most valuable slave. Slithering eyes from a repulsive man was, therefore, not something Lily was used to; it made the hair stand up on the back of her neck.

Lily was not the only one seething inside as the visual assault took place. James had tried hard to turn it off over the years, but the urge to protect Lily began to swell within him again. He had to dig deep to find the strength to keep his anger from spilling over into a physical assault that would certainly have landed him in jail. Just as Lily fought with herself to let the memories of their past subside, James, too, found himself constantly fighting to be the man his father had taught him to be. James naturally wanted to protect Lily in more ways than a typical master should. He was usually able to gain control over himself. But as the sheriff sat on his prancing horse, raping Lily with his eyes, Jesse's teachings had become nearly impossible for James to obey. He was so irritated that his eyelids had squinted into hateful slits, and his face turned a deep shade of red. But the anger he exuded did not deter the sheriff in the least.

"What you got worth showin' me unda' that dress, nigga'?" the sheriff suddenly asked Lily, continuing to stare at her with his mouth open.

"Nothin' that ain't gonna cost you your fuckin' eyesight!" James barked, jumping in front of Lily to block the sheriff from glaring at her any longer. Lily remained hidden behind him, feeling appreciative of his maneuver, but stunned by the fact that he would bother to come to her defense.

"Don't you threaten me, you uppity white boy!" the sheriff bit back.

"That ain't a threat!" James snarled.

The sheriff purposely spit near James's foot. "Y'all move it along 'fore I arrest the both of ya'!"

When the sheriff finally left, James and Lily continued with their journey, in the silence that they had become accustomed to. As they rode away, Lily realized that the dirty old man was only the first of many who would soon look at her as an object to be used in a sexual way, be it for pleasure or financial gain. The tears began again, christening her new perfectly fitted dress, as she tried unsuccessfully to swallow that painful reality. James, too, had a difficult time accepting what had just happened, as well as his uncontrollable reaction to it. It took him hours to settle himself and put his focus back on the benefits of their journey. When he reminded himself of things to come, he instantly calmed down. A faint smile even emerged on his face. He then prompted his horses to pick up the pace to his desired destination.

* * * *

ATHENS, OHIO

James tried to reach his destination before nightfall, but darkness had long since settled in by the time he finally pulled through the decorative steel gates of Werthington Estate. In the distance, William Werthington, an older white British man with a goatee and a full head of graying hair, emerged from the front door of his massive white mansion. He stood on the porch wearing a plain gray suit, smoking a pipe, waiting for James to walk over and greet him. William had anticipated their arrival, but he had expected them much earlier in the day. James pulled up in front of the porch, climbed down, and walked up to William. "Good to see you again, Mr. Werthington," he said, extending his hand.

"Good to see you again too. Glad you finally made it. I was starting to think maybe you'd changed your mind, or decided to take her elsewhere," William replied, in his proper British accent as he shook James's hand.

"No. I'm a man of my word. I wouldn't dream of backin' out on such a thing," James replied. "I'm so sorry we're late. I had to make a few more stops along the way than anticipated."

"No need for an apology. Just glad you made it here safely."

"Listen, Mr. Werthington…"

"William. Please call me William."

"William, if ya' don't mind, I know you wanted to get things started when we got here, but it's been a ratha' exhaustin' day, and…"

"Say no more. I wouldn't dare let her jump right into things at this ungodly hour."

"Thank you kindly, sa'. I think we could both use a little rest."

"After two days on the road, I can certainly understand that. By the way, where is this … umm, *Lily*, I believe you said her name is?"

"She's in the back 'a the wagon, more than likely asleep."

Lily had overheard every word of their conversation. Her body did not crave sleep, it craved death. Despite hearing that this William character had no intention of turning her into a breeding animal that night, she still sat with her knees drawn up to her chest, quivering, rocking side to side, and praying for God to make her heart stop beating right where she sat.

Lily thought that by the time she arrived, she would have gathered the strength to face the physical, emotional, and sexual abuse that was about to take place. But as soon as the wagon halted on the plantation, all she could think about was Auntie's baby, Sarah. That one name lingering in Auntie's demented mind was proof to Lily that this entire experience would be like infecting her brain with an incurable disease that would eat away at her sanity until the day she drew her last breath. That thought trampled Lily like wild horses, paralyzing her where she sat. She did not have the power to speak, to scream, or even to run. She just sat there like a weakened flower waiting to be destroyed by an oncoming thunderstorm.

"Lily!" James called out to her.

Crickets and croaking frogs were the only sounds in the air.

"Lily!" he called to her again.

Still, she did not budge.

James sheepishly turned toward William again. "Just like I thought, she's probably asleep," he said, feeling a little embarrassed.

"It's quite alright. Take your time waking her and gathering your things. I'll go check and see if Anna Mae's got your room ready. She's already made dinner and put it away, but I'll have her warm it up and set it out again for the both of you."

"That's mighty kind of ya'. We'll be in shortly."

James knew that Lily was awake, but he did not want to reveal that to William. He was glad that he had gone back into the house before retrieving her. Something told him that he may not be prepared for what he was about to come face to face with. He was right. Lily still had not gathered the strength to move from her upright fetal position. Her body was shaking uncontrollably, and her eyes were glistening with moisture. When she heard footsteps approaching the back of the wagon, she prayed quietly, "Dear God, give me strength."

"Lily," James said, as he looked inside the wagon.

She did not answer. She had her back to him, gathering their bags, maneuvering them toward the tail end of the wagon for James to collect. Her ploy gave her extra time to let her emotions and nervousness subside.

James stood there staring in astonishment at Lily as the bags piled up. It looked to him like she was still not fazed by his plans for her. He suddenly recalled how Lily's rock-solid inner strength had inspired him as a boy. He stood there now feeling like a fool for expecting anything less out of her.

"Lily, I've been callin' your name."

"Yessa', I's asleep 'til just a moment ago," she lied.

"Well, I can handle all the bags lata'. Mr. Werthington is eaga' to meet you," James told her, offering her his hand to help her down.

"Yessa'," Lily replied flatly. As she had gathered the bags, she was quietly inhaling and exhaling deeply to gain control over the quivering in her voice and in her body. She quickly cleared her eyes before turning toward James. She was thankful that the darkness was helping to hide any remnants of her tears. She was still determined not to give

71

James the satisfaction of admiring the ways in which he had broken her.

James led Lily up the mansion steps and held the door open for her, as any southern gentleman would do. After Lily walked in, her eyes panned around the foyer. She was mesmerized by the grand dual staircase and the long hallway in front of her that seemed to go on forever. She had never seen a home so massive. It could have easily fit four of Jesse's houses within it with plenty of room to spare. It made Lily instantly feel sorry for the house slave who had the unbelievable task of maintaining such a place. Just as that thought crossed her mind, an older dark-skinned man approached her and James, carrying himself much like a butler. "Good evenin'," he said, nodding to them.

"Evenin'," they replied in unison.

"I'm Ben. Mr. Werthington is right this way," he informed them. He then guided them toward the dining room.

James and Lily followed behind Ben in silence. Despite her predicament, Lily could not help but be fascinated by the beautiful art, sculptures, flowers, and furniture spread throughout the house. From the elaborate décor alone, she knew William was not a man who dabbled strictly in the sale of tobacco or cotton. She assumed he must have many other entrepreneurial endeavors as well. The grandness of the dining room further convinced Lily that William was no average man. Sitting on top of his massive dining table was silver cutlery, china for sixteen, and a spread of food fit for a Thanksgiving feast. Lily felt it was fitting to walk in and see William sitting like a king at the head of the table, smoking a rather expensive looking pipe.

As Lily meekly approached, William laid his pipe down and stood to greet her. "You must be the Lily that I've heard so much about," he smiled, gently taking one of her hands into both of his.

"Yessa'."

"I'm William Werthington. So very pleased to meet you. I hope the journey wasn't too rough for you."

"No sa'. I feel mighty fine, thank you," she said shyly, noticing he spoke with an accent that she did not recognize. It made him seem extremely intelligent to her and so, too, did the spectacles he wore perched halfway down his nose.

"I know you must be hungry, so please feel free to eat whatever you like. I wasn't sure what the both of you preferred, so I asked Anna Mae to prepare a variety of different items. I hope you find something to your liking."

"Thank you kindly, sa'." Lily had grown to feel over the years that kindness of any sort by rich white people was usually selfishly motivated. She thought maybe it was important to William that his breeding slaves had access to as much food as they wanted. Seeing that he was obviously a man who loved the finer things in life, she had no doubt that money and greed dominated his every decision, even something as minor as offering a slave an endless amount of food. So, despite his kindness, she felt uneasy with not playing the role of a servant. "Should I fix y'all a plate first before I eat," she asked, motioning to pick up William's plate.

"Nonsense," he quickly replied, gently grabbing her hand to stop her from taking his dinnerware. "You're a guest here. Besides, I'm plenty capable of fixing my own plate, if you can't tell," he laughed, patting his barely protruding belly. "Believe it or not, this body of mine used to be made of stone," he joked. "Seems that old age has chiseled away at that."

James gave a faint smile and a nod of appreciation in William's direction for his genuine effort to make Lily feel comfortable. He knew she probably felt out of place and nervous despite what her demeanor showed.

Lily, on the other hand, still believed that the jokes and the kindness were all an act. She only pretended to be amused and gave a weak smile in return for William's efforts. "My apologies, sa'. I'll leave you to make your own plate then."

"No apologies required, m'lady. It's quite alright," William smiled.

Lily forced another fake smile in return, picked up her plate, and began to scan the array of food on the table. After she walked away, James and William both sat down.

"So, James, are you willing to divulge the secret of how you were able to talk your father into this whole transaction?" William asked. "From all that you've explained to me about him, I'm surprised that he was okay with this little *arrangement* we've got."

"Well, truth be told, I don't think he was okay with it at all. But he's expectin' me to take ova' his farm soon, so I told 'em that I wanted to start makin' some of the decisions around there right away, especially matta's relatin' to the slaves."

Lily cringed after hearing James boast about his new duties.

"Ahh, very clever!" William exclaimed. "It's certainly true that there comes a time when a father has to start trusting his son to take over his legacy."

"That's exactly the point I's tryna make to him. But I guess it's a little hard for a man to let go of the reins sometimes, no matta' how much he might trust his own son."

"A statement I'm sure you'll fully understand when you become a father yourself one day."

"Yessa', I'm sure that's true. I'll just have to take your word for it for now, I guess."

"Well, in any case, I guess it's really not important how you got Lily here, is it? She's here, that's all that matters."

"I reckon it is."

Lily was thoroughly annoyed by their manly small talk. She did her best to ignore them as she decided what to eat out of the massive spread of food.

"I must admit, I've been looking forward to this since the day you came and talked to me about Lily," William continued. "One doesn't get many opportunities like this with a young lady such as her," he said, glancing over at her and smiling.

Lily had her back to William and did not see the way he smiled at her. But his words alone were enough to make her immediately stop placing food on her plate. She suddenly no longer had an appetite. She thought that it would be another one of his slaves that would impregnate her, but now she wondered if William was going to do the honors himself. It turned her stomach to know that he would truly be sick enough to pleasure himself and then callously reap the financial benefits of one of his own children, just as her father had done. Just the thought of it made her instantly deem him as lower than scum.

Lily suddenly turned to look at James. She could not believe that he had the audacity to make her sit and eat across from a man who looked forward to being her rapist. She had confided in James long ago about what her father had done, yet here he was now turning her over to a man with equally perverted morals. She waited for James to turn toward her. When he did, she lowered her eyelids and pursed her lips, hoping that her expression conveyed her vehement disgust for him.

"Mr. Werthington, is it anotha' table where us servants s'pposed to eat they food?" Lily asked, still glaring at James, not remotely fearful of what his reaction to her may be.

"Now, you just sit right down and eat your meal with us. You aren't on the Adams farm anymore. I know that may be a strange adjustment, but I won't have you thinking with that servant nonsense while you're here," William reassured her, with kindness in his tone.

Lily was hoping that he would have sent her away to avoid being in a room with two men who disgusted her. She instead sat amongst them as the pair chattered on for at least half an hour about topics that did not interest her. They were both completely unaware of how she was seething inside while she picked at her food, ingesting just enough to sustain her life. She did not remember tasting any of it. It was yet another symptom of her melancholy state of mind. Nothing gave her pleasure anymore; even breathing seemed like an insurmountable chore. She found herself wishing to find a means of escape from the dining room, from William's plantation … from her own life.

After sensing James's lack of remorse for bringing her there, Lily felt her heart further crumbling into pieces. He seemed so content for William to steal her innocence, to emotionally and physically wound her. She detested herself for believing that this very same man had once loved her. Even though there had never been any verbal admission by James about such a thing, she thought she had *felt* his love at one point in her life. But the fact that he had concocted this heinous life-altering punishment, made Lily realize that the love she once perceived was all an illusion.

"Well, it's awfully late," William said, putting his pipe down after his long-winded conversation with James. "And as you know, we've got business to take care of come early morning," he smiled, looking in Lily's direction.

Lily briefly glanced at William. The way he was joyously smiling over something that was about to devastate her life made her want to vomit.

"William," James said, standing and reaching his hand out for him to shake. "You've been more than kind to allow us to rest this evenin'. And I thank ya' for this fine dinna'. Again, my apologies for the late arrival."

"Not a problem at all. Life doesn't always go as planned, now does it? Better late than never," he smiled. "Come, come, let me show you to your rooms."

Lily followed behind William and James with her head hanging low. Absorbing the beauty of the massive mansion no longer interested her. She knew there was no point in it anyway. After James was guided to his luxury suite, she was certain that she would then be escorted to the dilapidated slave quarters.

"You'll be here tonight, James," William told him, after opening a set of double doors on the first floor. The room looked more like a miniature home than a guest bedroom. "Anything you need, you can call after Benjamin, the gentleman you met earlier at the door. He'll be glad to get you anything you need."

"Mighty kind of you, sa'," James replied, looking around at the beautiful room in awe, just as Lily would have if the heaviness of her sorrows had not been weighing her head down.

"Benjamin will also be waking you for breakfast, bright and early," William explained.

James nodded. "I'd appreciate that."

"Rest well until then."

"I certainly will. Thank you and goodnight."

"Goodnight," William replied. He then closed the doors and turned toward Lily.

Lily stood there with her hands clasped together in the middle of the hallway, now completely alone with the man she was convinced she would have her first *unwelcomed* intimate experience with. She did everything she could to remain calm as he walked toward her. She continued looking down at the floor as if she would somehow find a route down there to make her escape. She searched her mind for what to do: cry, scream, claw, scratch, run, vomit. Suddenly, though, the only thing Lily found was the strength to accept her fate.

William gently touched Lily on the arm. She jumped slightly and let out a startled gasp. "I'm so sorry. I didn't mean to frighten you," he said, speaking close enough for the sweet scent of his tobacco breath to overwhelm Lily's sense of smell.

Unable to conjure up a coherent reply in her racing mind, Lily simply stared at William and nodded.

William motioned his hand out in front of him. "Right this way, m'lady," he said.

Lily fell in step behind William as he led the way. For once in her life, she could not wait until she reached the slave quarters. She was eager to get as far away from William as possible. He guided her down the hallway back toward the front door and turned to go up the stairs. He began marching his way up but then heard the front door open behind him. He turned around looking perplexed. "Lily? Where in the devil are you going?"

"Out to the quarta's, sa'."

"The quarters?" William asked, looking confused.

"Yessa', the slave quarta's."

William laughed, making Lily feel embarrassed about her assumption. "Well, m'lady," he began, as he marched back down the stairs toward her. "As I told you at dinner, you are *not* on the Adams farm anymore," he reiterated, as he reached around her to shut the front door. "There will be no fixing food, nor serving it. There will be no cleaning and no washing dishes, and I most certainly will *not* have you sleeping outdoors." He motioned his arm in the direction of the stairs. "Your room is right this way. Now, please follow me," he said, placing his hand on the small of her back.

Lily did not like the feel of William's hand on her. Even through her dress, his touch repulsed her. The way his eyes lingered on her face disgusted her. The tobacco odor that oozed from his pores made her nauseous. The fact that she had to sleep anywhere in the vicinity of a man she believed to be a twisted pervert made her long for her haystack inside the rickety walls of the Adams' slave quarters. She would have slept in a horse's stall near piles of manure, if she was currently given the choice.

As William guided Lily up the stairs, she saw Benjamin out of the corner of her eye, staring empathetically at her. Her humiliation deepened, knowing that even the house slaves were privy to what was shortly to become of her. Thoughts of William's "business" plans caused Lily's legs to fight with her every step of the way as they ascended the stairs. But against her mind and body's will, she was soon standing at the top of the grand foyer, mere yards away from the room where she was sure her life was about to change.

Lily walked meekly behind William to the end of another long hallway that led to a set of double doors in the east wing. William pushed the doors open and revealed what Lily reasoned could not possibly be a guest bedroom. The room was so luxurious, she assumed it was William's personal master suite. There was a canopy bed decorated in lavish décor that sat on top of a stage-like platform. To the left of it was a fireplace with a reading sofa in front of it. To the right were bookcases with leather-bound classics and a writing table nearby. The curtains on the windows touched the ceiling and trailed all the way down to the floor, sprawling out like the train of a wedding dress. It was a room designed for a king, or in Lily's mind, the owner of the home.

Being offered an actual bed of any kind would normally have caused Lily to be overcome with joy. But under the current circumstances, she only fought to keep her food down. She thought that she at least had one more evening to herself before having to succumb to the evils of the twisted pervert standing beside her.

"This will be where you'll stay for the evening," William expressed with joy on his face, walking to the center of the room. "Come, come," he said excitedly, waving Lily over. "This room possesses some of my most treasured family heirlooms. My father and I built this desk together when I was just a boy. It was one of my fondest memories with him. And these books," he explained, grabbing one off the shelf. "They were all the books that my father would read to us after dinner every night." He paused as he thumbed through the one he was holding. "Oh, and over here," William continued, guiding Lily up the two small steps of the platform to the bed. "My mother hand stitched this quilt herself," he said, gliding his hand over the folded treasure at the end of the bed. "She was a master seamstress," he boasted proudly, pausing and staring into nothing as he remembered his mother for a moment.

With all that Lily was surrounded by, it confirmed to her that the room most certainly had to be William's. She offered no response or reaction to the excitement of his nostalgia. She was too busy numbing herself in preparation for what she believed was coming next. Standing so close to the bed with William just inches away, her heart began to beat wildly against her chest.

William suddenly reached over and gently touched Lily on the shoulder. Feeling her skin crawl underneath his hand, she flinched slightly. She closed her eyes, and her mind reflexively began to drift away into a parallel world to protect her fragile emotions. Suddenly, she felt William no more. His scent was gone, and she was all alone in the room, at least that's what her mind had convinced her of.

"Well, Benjamin has set your belongings in the chair over there," William said with a smile, removing his hand from Lily's shoulder. "If you need anything further, just let him know. He'll be glad to assist you. Get plenty of rest this evening my dear, you'll certainly need it for tomorrow."

Lily lifted her head and opened her eyes only to see William walking away. He turned, bid her goodnight, and shut the double doors behind him. To Lily's welcome relief, it seemed as though he was keeping his word about allowing her to rest for the evening. Shortly after his departure, Lily heard another door shut down the hallway, startling her. Although she was alone, she was reluctant to move from the spot she was standing in. She let only her eyes parade around the enormous candlelit room, looking at every corner as if someone might creep out of the shadows and attack her. But all she noticed was the silence. She did not hear crickets chirping or frogs croaking. She did not hear the rustling of hay, as the other slaves tossed and turned to find comfort. If any owls were hooting, she did not hear them either, nor did she hear the growling of her empty stomach.

Lily finally let go of enough fear to step out of the spot she was standing in. She walked slowly to the window and held her hand up to it, then ran her hand along the wall. She did not feel any cracks or breezes. There was no way for the cold night wind to access her tender skin. She looked up at every inch of the ceiling and saw that even the rain had no way of seeking out her face as she slept. She stopped in front of the crackling fireplace and saw that she even had an alternative means of warmth, a luxury she had not had since living with her mother. She then walked back up the two steps on the platform and ran her hand over the king-sized bed, adorned with William's mother's bed linens. Lily had never in her life known the comforts of a mattress on her back, nor the softness of a pillow underneath her head ... and she did not want to know. She wanted none of it, not at the price she had to pay. She would just as soon take back the croaking of the frogs, the chirping of the crickets, the hooting of the owls, the cold night air, the rain on her face, and laying on a pile of prickly cow's food while listening to the growling of her empty

81

stomach, if it meant never having to give away her body and her beloved baby to a rapist.

Lily lay down next to the massive bed on the floor, balled herself up like a lonely infant, and cried herself to sleep.

Chapter Five

Slave Code
Article X Section III

If it shall so happen at any time that any Negro shall strike a white person, even in self-defense, it shall be lawful upon proof made thereof before any justice of the peace for such justice to cause for one of the offending Negro's ears to be cropped for the first offense; the second offense shall result in capital punishment.

A single ray of sunlight had yet to peek along the ridge of the eastern sky. The nocturnal creatures of the night had yet to crawl back into hiding. Even the morning melody of the birds had yet to be heard. But there Lily lay asleep, still curled up next to the bed on the hardwood floor, with a cold hand slithering its way up her thigh. The chill jarred her from her sleep. She instinctively recoiled to get away and bumped her head hard on the edge of the nightstand. "Don't touch meee!" she screamed, slapping fiercely at the hand that had found its way underneath her dress.

"Shhh, this doesn't have to be a struggle," her invader whispered in a tone that was heavy with lust. He pulled her close. "Just let it happen," he moaned in her ear. The scent of his tobacco and his familiar British accent gave his identity away.

Despite his warning, Lily screamed again.

William tightened his grip. "I said be quiet! This is what you came here for. You might as well enjoy it," he said. Despite Lily's struggle to free herself, he buried his nose in the crevice of her neck and inhaled her scent.

"Why you doin' this to me?! Let me beee!" Lily began thrashing in the darkness, grabbing for anything she could. She gripped and tugged William's hair with one hand and knocked his spectacles off his face with the other. In her fit of defensive fury, Lily unintentionally dug her finger deep into his eye, instantly sending him into a rage.

"Damn you, nigga!" William yelled, slapping Lily hard in the face, instantly bringing her into submission. "I let you stay here in my home, and you dare to disrespect me!" He scooped her body up and threw it onto the bed. Lily continued to kick and claw, scooting back until her movement was impeded by the headboard. With no place to go, William was finally able to grab and steady her legs, planting his knees firmly on top of her thighs, catching her new dress underneath. He ripped it clean down the middle to gain access to what he wanted, then grabbed both of her wrists in one hand to cease all her movements. All Lily had left was her voice and the tears that now rolled in streams down the sides of her face.

"Jaaames! Dear God! Help meee! Jaaames! Pleeease! Anybody, Pleeease! Help meee!"

"Shut your goddamn mouth!" William yelled, slapping her hard again, drawing blood from her lip.

"Lily!" she heard as she thrashed, still fighting to save herself from the invasion. "Lily!" she heard again.

"Get away from meee!"

"Lily! Wake up!" Benjamin pleaded, as he watched her thrashing on the floor, acting out her dream. "Wake up, Lily!"

"Get away from meee!" she screamed in her sleep again before finally waking up. When she opened her eyes, she was instantly confused by where she was and as to who was speaking to her. When her eyes finally focused, she saw Benjamin looming over her. Startled, she retreated backward until she bumped into the nightstand. She looked around the room with her mind racing, her chest heaving, and sweat pouring from her face. It took her a moment to collect herself and realize she was trying to escape from nothing more than a nightmare. She shamefully looked up to meet Benjamin's eyes. He looked just as terrified and confused as she was.

"You alright? Sh-should I get Mr. Adams?" Ben asked.

"No! No, please don't … Please, I…" Embarrassment caused her to struggle with finding words.

Ben was not entirely sure how to react himself. He just stared at her, hesitant to touch her, fearful that he would only make things worse. "I-I just come to tell you that breakfast is on da' table."

"Th-thank you," Lily replied, still scrunched up against the nightstand like a scared little mouse.

Ben began to walk away but then turned around before grabbing the doorknob. "You sho' you alright?" he asked with compassion in his voice.

Lily lied and nodded her head only to get him to leave. She wanted to feel alright. She wanted to feel something good for once. She wanted to feel hunger, thirst, or any other normal human function to sustain her life, anything but the chronic emotional pain that pierced her body through and through and destroyed her desire to be alive.

After Ben shut the door, Lily continued sitting against the nightstand with her legs drawn up to her chest. She closed her eyes, buried her face on her knees, and drowned out all other thoughts and sounds, and listened solely to the music she heard in her head. The mood changes in the melody took her from laughter, to love, to a feeling of floating through the heavens and back, to start the myriad of welcomed emotions all over again. She opened her eyes suddenly, though, and slowly raised her head when she realized that the music she was hearing was not her own mental composition. What she was listening to was a beautiful melody that was penetrating her bedroom walls and had pleasantly invaded her ears.

Lily had not heard another pianist since Mrs. Adams' death, but her music paled in comparison to what Lily was hearing beyond the bedroom doors. What she was absorbing instantly ceased all her pain, dried her tears, and temporarily erased the memory of her nightmare. To her, it was the kind of music that healed, the way hers tended to do for her. The music gave her the motivation to stand and walk toward the double doors. She opened them quietly and let the sound rise and take over her room. Without any conscious effort, she had moved from the bedroom to the top of the stairs, standing there briefly to listen. Then, like a moth to a flame, she descended the staircase, drawn toward the sound.

With the music still guiding her, Lily soon found herself standing near the entrance of an enormous library. Every wall was made of shelves, on which there was not one inch of space that did not house a book or decoration of some sort. A sparkling crystal chandelier hung from the ceiling directly over the centerpiece of the room: a magnificent mahogany grand piano. It sat with its lid raised, allowing the deep tones to erupt into the room in a way that Lily's ears were unaccustomed to hearing with the old upright piano back on the farm. When the song ended with a few soft strokes of the lower register keys, Lily was torn between wanting to applaud and wanting to cry.

"It's considered rude to lurk in doorways where I come from," a voice called out from behind the piano.

From where Lily stood, peering around the corner of the doorframe, the raised lid was blocking the view between her and the pianist. She was surprised that he even knew she was standing there. "I'm sorry, sa'," she replied, sheepishly taking a step inside the library.

"Beautiful piece, don't you think?" he asked, sounding proud.

"Yessa'. Incredibly beautiful."

"Come, come. I'll play you another."

With hesitancy in her steps, Lily walked slowly toward the voice, her head hanging low like an animal chastised for its misdeeds. She had done nothing wrong, but naturally exuded a sense of inferiority in the presence of white men. She made her way around the open lid of the grand piano, and William's face came into view. He looked up at her through green eyes that were wrapped in wrinkly skin. His spectacles were riding low on his long pointy nose as usual. Lily stopped and stood next to the piano in silence, with her hands clasped in front of her. At that moment, William began to play again. Right away, he took Lily to another frame of mind. His music, and the way he played it, had a way of embracing her, like she was a child in the warmth and comfort of her mother's arms once again. She listened with her eyes closed, trying not to cry, absorbing every note, locking it all away in her memory, with the hope that one day she would have the honor of soothing herself all over again with the precious melody.

"Did you enjoy that one as well?" William asked, with a smile on his face when he completed the song.

"Very much, sa'. It was beautiful. Very soothin'."

"Please, m'lady. No more of this *sir* nonsense. Please call me William. It would make me feel like much less of an old man," he said, wrinkling his nose playfully at her.

"Yessa'. Sorry, I mean, Mr. William ... W-William," she stumbled, feeling the heat rise in her body from embarrassment.

"Much better," William smiled. "Well now, I've graced you with a song. It's your turn, wouldn't you agree?" he cheerfully insisted. He got up from the bench and offered it to Lily with a hand gesture.

The thought of James's vehement anger, after catching her on the piano, instantly came to Lily's mind. Playing the piano was the sole reason she was about to face a punishment more damaging than being whipped, in her opinion. It made the mere thought of touching the keys a terrifying prospect. "I-I don't know nothin' 'bout playin' no piano, sa'," Lily lied, quickly stepping backward, staring intensely at the keys, as if they were wild wolves ready to pounce on her.

"He knows," a voice suddenly said.

Startled, Lily turned around to find James leaning against the doorframe, his hands gripped on his suspenders. "Knows what, sa'?" she asked.

"That you can play piano. I told 'em. No need to lie. Go on and play if he wants you to."

Lily just stared at James, still reluctant to move.

As James often did, he easily read Lily's mind. "You won't be punished for it."

Lily briefly held his gaze. She, too, read him well and trusted that he was telling the truth. She then hesitantly turned to face William again.

William smiled and motioned for Lily to sit on the bench, allowing her access to yet another of his prized possessions. "Play anything you'd like, my dear."

Lily walked hesitantly toward him, looking at every inch of the piano in disbelief. She had not known they could be built like works of art. She sat down gracefully and looked at every key, familiarizing herself before lifting her hands. She knew exactly what she wanted to play, but she looked at William again, seeking approval from him with her eyes before she began.

"Go on, m'lady. It's quite alright," William reassured her.

Lily turned toward James one more time. They briefly held each other's gaze before he finally nodded his head in reassurance. Lily then turned her attention back to the piano, inhaled deeply, and closed her eyes. With lightness and agility in her fingers, she began tickling her way across the keys. For Lily, everything in the room faded away. The books, the shelves, and the chandelier all disappeared. William and James were no longer present. Her fears and worries melted away with just the lightest touch of the ivory. Like any addict who had fueled herself with her chemical of choice, Lily was on a high. Her mind had instantly taken her to a place where pain could not touch her, where heartache did not exist, where sorrow could not penetrate her, where tears were only from happiness. Mentally, she was in a place where nothing existed except the piano and the memory of the notes that guided her fingers gracefully along the keys.

The particular song Lily chose immediately motivated James to leave his stance against the doorframe. He began walking toward her, intently watching the beautiful expression on her face as she got lost in the melody. After he approached, he and William began scrutinizing her every keystroke. William's eyes were transfixed on the way her hands glided effortlessly across the keys without ever missing a note, even though her eyes were closed. It seemed to him as though she was reading the notes as they appeared in her subconscious. He was equally impressed with her bodily theatrics and the way her hands crossed one over the other, mimicking someone who had performed in front of an audience for years.

When Lily completed the song, William slowly removed his spectacles, as if he blamed them for deceiving his eyes. He stared at her in stone-cold silence. For once he was speechless. He then turned to look at James, who reluctantly pulled his eyes away from Lily to return William's glare. He looked equally as perplexed as William. "That sounded a lot like the song I heard you playin' just before I walked in here," James said to William, referring to the song that had coaxed Lily from her room earlier.

"That's because it *was* the exact same song," William replied, shock evident in his tone. He turned to look at Lily again. "Every note played flawlessly." Although it was indeed the song he had played, William was astounded by the lightning speed of Lily's fingers and the fluidity with which she had just played it back, especially considering that it was her first attempt. He felt as though her choice to add speed had enhanced the beauty of the song.

"It was so pretty and so soothin'. I just had to hear it again," Lily shyly explained.

"B-but how on earth are you able to accomplish such a thing?" William asked, truly baffled. "Is this some sort of game the two of you are playing?!" He turned to look at James again. "Y-you must have found the musical pieces I had laying around here and given them to her before your journey!" he accused, searching his puzzled mind for the answers to what he felt was an impossibility. "How else could she have just done that?!"

James felt slightly offended by the accusation but understood his skepticism. He, too, was shocked by the fact that Lily could retain music of that complexity so quickly and replay it with such accuracy. "William, I completely unda'stand your doubts, but I assure you I've done nothin' of the sort. I honestly had no idea she was capable of doin' that eitha'," he admitted, turning, and staring at Lily, as a wave of questions swept through his mind. It was another revelation about her that bothered him deep inside.

"With all due respect, William," Lily interjected. "I couldn't read my own name if my life depended on it, let alone read any music."

The room was silent, but James swore he could hear Lily's words echoing over and over again. He turned his eyes away from her, suddenly feeling overwhelmed with guilt and shame because of the truth in her statement. He would rather have taken a knife to the stomach than to hear her say it again.

After seeing the sincerity in Lily's face, William felt foolish for doubting her. "Lily, I'm so sorry. I shouldn't have made such an accusation. It's just that I've never witnessed such a thing in all of my life," he explained, the sincerity of his words confirmed by the expression on his face.

"It's alright. I unda'stand."

"Please, I must know how you've learned to play so magnificently. Somebody must have instructed you."

"No sa'. Bein' a slave, ain't nobody eva' been willin' to teach me anything."

Her words penetrated James once again. Such a simple conversation was affecting him in a way he had not anticipated. He propped his hand against the piano to steady himself, feeling like he had been punched in the stomach again.

"Not even the basics?" William questioned.

"No sa'," she answered. "I tell you no lie."

"Beyond your level of skill, your ability to retain music is simply remarkable. I must know how you've come to accomplish this."

Reluctantly, Lily began speaking, feeling unsure of how much of her story she should tell. "Well, when I's just a little girl, James's motha'…" she paused, and looked over at James, uncertain if she should continue.

Reading Lily's mind again, James nodded.

"James's motha' used to teach children to play piano. I used to hide at the top of the stairs and watch her. I'd memorize the way her fingers moved across the keys wheneva' she played, and…" she froze, feeling her fears surfacing again.

"Go on," William urged her.

"Well, wheneva' I's alone, I'd play back the songs I remembered her teachin', by mimickin' the movement of her fingers. But afta' a while I didn't have to hide and see the way she played. It got to the point where I could memorize just by listenin', and then play back the notes I heard runnin' through my head."

"So, Mrs. Adams never actually gave you any personal lessons?"

"No sa'. I just push the keys that match the sound in my head," Lily clarified, touching her temple lightly.

"May I?" William asked, motioning his hand toward the piano bench.

Lily scooted over and allowed him to sit next to her.

"Close your eyes," William told her. He immediately felt her apprehension. "Only for a moment," he reassured her. When she finally relaxed and closed her eyes, he played three random notes simultaneously. "Can you play the notes I've just played?"

Without opening her eyes, Lily quickly repeated the three notes. William proceeded again to play four notes, then five, and then used both hands to play six, and more at one time. Without ever looking, Lily played back every chord flawlessly.

James watched Lily in awe, just as he had many times throughout his life. He remembered thinking as a boy that she was always so great at everything she had ever done, but he knew that what he was currently witnessing her do was beyond great. The look on William's face further confirmed that he was justified in believing that Lily was born with an extraordinarily unique gift.

When William was finished running through dozens of various musical chords with Lily, he turned to look at her like he had found the most priceless treasure. "It is quite rare that anyone has the ability to hear a series of notes and play them back perfectly as you just did, m'lady. In the world of music, it is known as having *perfect pitch*. After all my years of training, I am unable to accomplish this feat. I've come to realize that you're either born with this ability, or you're not. It simply *cannot* be taught, and it most certainly *cannot* be learned." There was a sudden softness in William's voice as he continued. "I don't think you realize just how unique and precious a gift this is that God has blessed you with, or how special you truly are." He took Lily's hand in his. "Please believe me when I tell you that you are truly one-of-a-kind."

Lily raised her head slowly to meet William's bright green eyes and saw nothing but sincerity in them as they gazed upon her. She had forgotten what it felt like to receive genuine words of kindness, and almost did not remember how to respond. "Th-Thank you kindly, Mr. William," she said shyly.

"I would certainly love to hear you play some more, if you don't mind."

"No, sa', I don't mind at all."

Like two children who shared a favorite toy, Lily and William continued playing on through the morning, one song after another. Each of them showed the other their favorite compositions and, at times, easily played songs together in harmony. William was instantly captivated by Lily. Of all the people he had known with years of fine piano instruction, he had never seen one who had achieved the level of professionalism he was witnessing in her. He felt honored to be sitting beside a young woman whose hands and prodigal mind he was convinced had been touched by God Himself.

James had sat down and was watching the pair quietly from the corner, wondering how Lily was able to hide the musical side of her from him through the years. He wondered what he had done to make her feel as if she could not trust him with such an unbelievable secret. It stung him deeply as he watched her play and kept him from fully enjoying the symphonic sounds erupting in the room. He even began feeling a twinge of irrational jealousy after noticing that William and Lily seemed to have a profound connection with one another rather quickly.

"Excuse me for interruptin', but lunch is ready," Benjamin announced from the doorway.

"My goodness, is it lunchtime already? Why, we've been here all morning," William said, pulling out his pocket watch and glancing at the time. "You must be starving by now," he said, patting Lily's hand gently. "You go and have your fill. James and I need to head into town to handle some much-needed business, but you are more than welcome to continue playing whenever you'd like."

After being touched by William's music and his kind words, Lily felt a slight return of her appetite for the first time in days. She was initially floating on the clouds after being temporarily allowed to play her beloved instrument again. However, as she walked toward the door, she caught a glimpse of James in the corner, and she suddenly wondered the nature of the "business" that he needed to handle in town with William. It quickly reminded her that she would soon be forced to face her inevitable punishment. With that thought, Lily instantly fell from her high back into the hell of reality. Suddenly, the little desire she had for food vanished, along with her desire to continue playing.

Chapter Six

Manumission:
The act of a slave owner freeing his slaves.

Slave Code
Article IV Section III
Masters, when twenty-five years old, shall have the power to manumit their slaves, either by testamentary dispositions, deed of manumission, or by their last will and testament.

For three whole days, Lily still had no interest in playing William's piano. She was sickened by the way that he and James would traipse off together after breakfast every morning, claiming that they needed to handle some "business" in town. Lily assumed that "business" had everything to do with what James had originally dragged her there for. In her mind, there seemed to be no other explanation for the two of them to be conspiring together. Their daily excursions left Lily with no musical desires. Instead, she had a paralyzing fear that William and James would eventually take her along with them after their negotiations, and drop her off in some foreign place, leaving her there to do the "business" they were expecting from her.

Even though William and James were always gone until late evening, Lily refused to leave her room. She remained hidden there, politely declining every meal that was offered to her by claiming she was not feeling well. Having quickly plunged into an immobilizing melancholy state, that claim was not far from the truth. The emotional pain of her despair was indeed taking a toll on her health. Even her free rein to play the piano was not enough to alleviate her internal aching. There was not a song worth playing, or one she felt she could ever compose, that would soothe the thought of losing her child. Death, she felt, was her only solution.

The constant desire to end her life trumped most of Lily's thoughts as she lay on the cold hardwood floor next to her bed. Her obsessive thoughts of suicide even kept her from relaxing enough to fall asleep. On the few occasions she was able to doze off, she would have sickening nightmares, similar to the one she had had about William. The terrifying dreams would jolt her awake, robbing her of the sleep that would have given her a temporary reprieve from the rampant torturous thoughts that were bombarding her mind.

Knowing nothing about slave breeding, Lily's mind was filling in the details with the horrors she had cultivated in her imagination. Along with the awful images rolling around in her head, Lily had a curious question that was constantly gnawing at her. Ironically, though, it had nothing to do with breeding; there was something about William that did not make any sense to her. During their brief interaction playing the piano together, Lily had noticed a vibrant enthusiasm in William that was unlike any other man she had ever met. He exuded a love for people, life, and music that was extraordinarily infectious. His persona seemed a complete contradiction to the cold callous nature of every other slave owner Lily had ever met. But what impacted her most about William were the words that he had graced her with after discovering her gift of perfect pitch. It was not only his beautiful words, but the manner with which he had spoken them. Lily still recalled the warmth she felt as he held her hand and looked into her eyes while speaking with such tenderness and sincerity. The memory of that moment with him kept penetrating the darkness Lily had hopelessly sunk into, filling it with a brief spark of light.

Despite William's kind nature and extreme generosity, Lily still loathed him. Simply for the fact that he owned slaves, she considered him an enemy. James's injustices against her had taught her a painful lesson about gullibly trusting white men. Lily, therefore, remained guarded, convinced that William's kind acts were to make it easier to manipulate her into doing anything he wanted. But *still*, a nagging question about him dangled loosely in her mind because of that unforgettable moment between them at the piano. The nagging intensified when Lily finally found the strength to get up off the hardwood floor. After three days of lying there immobilized, she walked over to the window, drew back the curtains, and looked out at the endless acres of plantation land that surrounded William's enormous mansion. It was Lily's curiosity about what she saw that finally persuaded her to leave her room in search of an answer to her question.

Long after William and James had left for the morning, Lily quietly tiptoed downstairs and ventured outside. She stepped out from under the shadow of the porch and squinted her eyes when the sunlight hit her face for the first time in days. She appreciated the warmth on her skin as she then walked from one end of William's land to the other. What she was observing during her stroll left her even more perplexed about who this William Werthington really was. She walked back toward the mansion determined to obtain the answers to all the things she was puzzled by. However, she feared the consequences of questioning James. She had an intuition, though, that she could trust two people in particular to give her insight.

Anna Mae and Benjamin, the older Negro couple who took care of William's home, were in the kitchen together. They were working on their long to-do list to prepare for William's upcoming fundraising gala. It was an event that William's wife, Emma, had begun years prior.

It started small but then grew into a massive annual event that welcomed some of the town's most prominent citizens. Emma had put her heart and soul into perfecting the esteemed yearly gathering. Despite Emma's death, William continued the gala in her honor.

Anna Mae and Benjamin were working on party decorations when they suddenly heard the kitchen door open. They turned to find Lily meekly standing there. Being that it was the first time Lily had willingly left her room, the couple was happily surprised to see her. They had both become concerned about Lily's well-being after the nightmare Benjamin had witnessed her having. Since then, Anna Mae had knocked on Lily's door every day to ask her if she wanted to eat. Anna Mae always noted the sadness in Lily's eyes as she politely declined. Despite her opposition to eating, Anna Mae would set the meal on the nightstand anyway. Exuding a motherlike love, she would pat Lily gently on the arm and tell her to at least try to eat a little. Lily always appreciated Ben and Anna Mae's compassion and their efforts to make her feel comfortable. It was their warmth that gave Lily the confidence to approach them, hoping they would give her the clarity she was seeking.

The question Lily asked them brought the gala preparations to a standstill. Anna Mae and Ben soon found themselves seated with Lily at the dining room table as they told her a story that brought back a blend of painful and happy memories from a day that changed their lives forever. Even Ben could not hold back a few stray tears while recalling what had happened to them so long ago.

After hearing William and James approach in their carriage, Lily glanced out the window. "I knew a man as kind as that once," Lily told the couple while staring directly at James, comparing him to a certain man from their story. Lily was sure to wipe away her tears before James entered the house. He stormed through the kitchen door, looking extremely frustrated. He breezed by Lily without so much as a hello or even a glance in her direction. His actions did not faze Lily, though; her skin had become impenetrable to the coldness that her former friend now always emitted.

Later in the evening, Anna Mae was making her way up to Lily's room to see if she was hungry. However, she was surprised to see that Lily was already heading downstairs. Motivated by the story she had been told, Lily decided to join William and James for dinner on the porch, instead of hiding in her room as usual. Both men ceased their conversation after she quietly stepped outside and stood there looking nervous.

"Good evening, m'lady!" William said, smiling at her. "Please make an old man happy and tell me that you'll be gracing us with your presence at dinner this evening."

"I's very much hopin' to, Mr. William."

"Delightful!" William stood and pulled out a chair for her.

Anna Mae smiled from the doorway and went to retrieve a plate of food for her. Lily then walked meekly toward the seat William had pulled out. She sat down and placed a cloth napkin in her lap, feeling hesitant to lift her head after doing so.

"Please forgive my absence throughout the past few days. I'm afraid I haven't been much of a host since you've come here, but I hope that Anna Mae and Ben have been gracious substitutes."

"No need to ask forgiveness. I know y'all are busy. And, yes, Ms. Anna Mae and Mr. Ben done been more than kind to me," Lily replied.

"That's wonderful to hear," William replied. "So, tell me, have you taken the opportunity to play piano again since…"

"William, I'm sorry to interrupt, but Ben and I need your help for a moment, if ya' don't mind?" Anna Mae said after setting a plate of fried chicken and mashed potatoes in front of Lily. She had a tone in her voice that made the matter seem urgent.

"Not at all," William replied. He then excused himself from the table to go and help.

Lily already felt uneasy sitting there with James and William. But now, being there alone face to face with James caused her discomfort to increase tenfold. As uncomfortable and anxious as Lily was, though, she decided to seize the opportunity to speak to James alone. She nervously twirled her spoon around in her mashed potatoes, before clearing her throat and finding the courage to speak. "I-I, umm, been meanin' to tell you, thank you."

"For what?" James asked flatly, still shoveling food into his mouth.

"For the unda'garments and the new dress. They's real nice."

"I figured it was due time for new ones, that's all," he responded matter-of-factly.

"Whateva' the reason, I thank you."

James suddenly stopped eating. "You're welcome," he replied, sounding as if it was difficult to say.

It had been years since the two of them had had a civil conversation. The tension between them was so thick in the air it was almost visible. James returned to his meal when a few awkward moments had passed without a word, but Lily refused to hold on to the rest of what she wanted to say. "I had a real long talk with Anna Mae and Ben this afta'noon while you and William was out," she began, as she watched James continue to eat. He still did not bother to look up from his plate. She continued to speak, even though he seemed not to be paying attention. "They say they used to live down in Georgia a long time ago. They was workin' togetha' on the same plantation with their two children. Of course, they didn't like the idea of bein' slaves, but they was just glad they was all togetha' as a family. But, afta' a few years, their masta' decided he was gonna sell some 'a his slaves. Anna Mae, Ben, and they two children was among the ones he planned to do away with. Ben say his masta' needed the money any way he could get it, even if it meant splittin' up families." Lily's voice suddenly began to quiver. "So, h-he took 'em all down to the Negro auction and…" She stopped for a moment and looked at her wrists as they lay in her lap. She suddenly recalled the red marks that her mother had left there from holding on to her so tightly the day her father dragged her away to be sold.

James stopped eating, laid his fork down slowly, and stared at Lily in a way that let her know she finally had his undivided attention. When she felt a sudden shift in his demeanor, she looked up from her wrists and met a pair of eyes that were still stunningly beautiful to her. It reminded her of the first time they had come face to face in the woods as children. She had forgotten how easily she could get lost while looking into James's eyes. His gaze temporarily halted her ability to speak while simultaneously bringing her a sense of comfort, just as it had all those years ago in their playground paradise near the creek.

Lily had to force herself to look away. She cleared her throat and nervously continued. "B-Ben say his masta' dragged 'em all down to the Negro auction. When they got there, Anna Mae said she was cryin' like she ain't neva' cried before in all her life. She was holdin' on to Ben and her children so tight, she had to be whipped one good time just to let 'em all go."

Upon hearing of Anna Mae's whipping, the expression on James's face changed. Lily immediately noticed the way his eyes suddenly wandered away from her face down to the table. She always read James's subtle gestures well; she was surprised to see that he was pained to hear such a thing. But Lily did not let it stop her from continuing the story. She wanted to free her mind no matter how uncomfortable James might feel hearing what she had to say.

"Anna Mae say Ben was the first one their owna' marched up onto the auction block. Back then they called 'em Big Ben. He was strong and worth quite a bit 'a money. There was hands flyin' up in the air everywhere tryna get bids in to buy 'em, long before he could even get all the way up the auction block steps. Once they was well into the biddin', Anna Mae say she noticed it was one man in the crowd who was quickly raisin' the bids by a hundred dolla's every time someone tried to outbid 'em. One-by-one, folks was quickly droppin' outta the auction. Everyone's eyes drifted toward the extravagant bidda' when they realized that he just wasn't gonna quit 'til he got what he wanted … And they were right. When there was only one man left to challenge 'em, he raised the bid by five hundred dolla's and it was ova'. He had purchased Big Ben for twice the amount most slaves his size was goin' for. But despite all the money he'd just spent, he still wasn't finished. He stood out in that hot Georgia sun that day and didn't stop biddin' 'til he got himself three more slaves. And when he did, he loaded 'em all up in his carriage, and brought 'em all back to his home … *right here* on this very plantation."

James still just sat there quietly gazing at Lily, intently listening, entranced by the compassion in her voice as she spoke.

"*William Werthington*," Lily finally revealed. "He was ridin' through that town in his carriage right before that auction started and saw Anna Mae holdin' on to her family, cryin' like the devil was rippin' 'er soul apart. William pulled ova' and bid every dolla' he could to buy her, Ben, and they two children. And just as soon as they set foot on this here plantation, he signed they papers and set 'em all free. Every one of 'em," she whispered. "They's free as birds," she said, looking out into the trees, wondering what that kind of freedom felt like.

"William told 'em all they could stay here in his home for as long as they liked until they got on their feet. In return for his hospitality, Ben and Anna Mae decided to take on the responsibility of cleanin' and cookin' all the meals and helpin' with William's children. Eventually, they all became so close that William didn't want any of 'em to leave. William's wife especially begged 'em all to stay because her two boys had become so close to their children, and she sho' appreciated them keepin' 'er company in this big ol' house wheneva'

William was travelin'. And in all these years, Benjamin say William and his wife ain't neva' treated 'em like anythang less than they own kin folk. Both of 'em swear William got a heart bigga' than the moon itself." Lily paused for a moment and looked out onto the plantation fields.

"Masa' James, I's walkin' out on those fields today, and I realized that the very man you claim to bring me here to breed for don't have one row 'a cotton or tobacco in his fields, no slave quarta's, and not one slave eitha'. So afta' seein' how empty these fields were, I just couldn't help but ask Ben and Anna Mae who this William fella was and where all his slaves were. They both laughed and said I'd neva' see a single solitary slave roamin' around within these gates. Anna Mae said William neva' believed enslavin' folks was right. In fact, she said he worked for years with some anti-slavery society ova' in London, and even raised money to help fund their fight to abolish slavery. He was standin' there proudly side by side with memba's of parliament when they signed the Slavery Abolition Act into law in 1833. Ben said a big part 'a the reason William came to the United States in the first place was to help in the fight against slavery here. He was even heavily active in the anti-slavery movement with some group here called the Republican Party until his wife passed away.

"So afta' hearin' all those incredible stories, it just didn't make much sense to me why you'd bring me to a man like William to be bred ... not until Ben and Anna Mae told me one otha' thing about 'em." Lily turned from the fields and finally looked at James. "They said William ain't just some rich farmer that happens to know how to play a piano. They claim he's a man that done been all ova' the world playin' music in symphonies since he was just six years old, and that he became one 'a the most well-known composa's and musical instructa's in all 'a the United States, and even ova' in Europe. Ben and Anna Mae say he was a teacha' for years at the university you attended, and that he was even willin' to teach both 'a they children ... two *Negro* children," she emphasized, "how to read and write. But most importantly ... how to play *piano*."

James continued to stare at Lily for a moment before slightly nodding his head. "I know," he faintly replied, sounding as if he was ashamed to admit that he had withheld the knowledge of William's inspirational story.

After his admission, there was suddenly an immense amount of hope written into Lily's facial expressions. "Ben also told me that we's here in Ohio. This a *free* state, ain't it?"

James sheepishly nodded.

Lily's eyes drifted down to her hands for a moment as she searched for the courage to ask her next question. "You ain't eva' really had any intention on breedin' me at all…" She finally looked back up at James with tears sparkling in her eyes. "Did you?" she whispered.

"James!" William interrupted from the mansion door.

"Yessa'," he said, without turning his attention away from the beautiful woman in front of him.

"Could we borrow you for a moment?"

"Yessa'," he replied again while watching the tears that he knew Lily was fighting hard to keep from escaping. He kept his eyes on her for a moment longer before rising and leaving the table without ever saying another word. But he didn't have to. The expression on his face had answered all of Lily's questions. She had seen that expression often, once upon a time, during years that included some of the happiest Sundays of her life. Based on that expression alone, Lily now knew for a fact that her friend was still in there somewhere, and that he had undoubtedly revealed himself to her in a major way for the first time in many years.

While everyone was inside, Lily tiptoed past the kitchen where they had all congregated trying to fix something. She stopped in William's library to stare at his *grand* piano. She never knew such a beautiful style of piano existed. In her eyes, everything about it far exceeded the definition of *grand*. She walked around it and ran her hand along the artistically carved lines that were engraved on the side of it, then stepped back to absorb the entire view of the masterfully crafted piece. At that moment, the desire to play again began raging inside of her. She held off for the time being, though, and went upstairs, wanting to be alone with her thoughts for a while. She entered the room that William had so generously allowed her to stay in. But this time, everything looked different to her. Everywhere she turned, the colors seemed so much brighter. She noticed the patterns in the curtains, and every detail of the décor. The scent in the air was inviting, and there even seemed to be a warmth there she had never sensed before.

Lily walked over to the window, drew back the curtains, and watched the last piece of the sun hanging in the sky. It was one of the most beautiful sunsets she had seen in years. While the sun warmed her, she closed her eyes and let the images of James's gaze at dinner appear in her mind. Standing at that window with James in her thoughts, Lily began to breathe again without feeling as if she had to force herself to take every breath.

After every inch of the sun had faded away into the horizon, Lily lit an oil lamp. She then walked over to a bookshelf and glanced over the array of William's treasured books. She selected a rather large novel and opened it to a random page, only to be overwhelmed by a sea of meaningless letters staring back at her. She suddenly wished there was an oak tree with a blanket spread out at its base, and a familiar face seated next to her, who could dictate the words to her as passionately as he once did.

Lily then glanced up from the book, and the bed she had refused to lie in was in her line of view. Like the open arms of a mother, it suddenly seemed welcoming to her. As she walked over to it, she looked down at the uncomfortable area of the hardwood floor where she had laid for three days. It immediately brought back the memory of the disturbing nightmare she had had about William. She suddenly felt guilty for dreaming such a horrible thing about a man whose heart she now believed should be replicated and placed in the chest of every human being.

William's mother, Lily finally noticed, was certainly the master seamstress he had boasted about. The patterns of the quilt she had made were unlike any other she had ever seen. She now understood why William cherished it so much. Lily placed the book on the nightstand and reached down to feel the bedding. She suddenly could no longer resist the need to let her body experience the softness and comfort of linens that felt like they were made by a woman who wanted her children to feel wrapped in love as they slept. She lay down slowly onto the mattress and let the plush covers melt around her body. The feeling was so foreign to her, but it only took a moment for her body to admit that it never wanted to go back to hardwood floors or haystacks ever again. Nestled in the comfort of a real bed for the first time in her life, Lily drifted off quickly into a deep sleep. She fell into her slumber without her face surrounded by a puddle of tears, because she was now confident that James's heart still beat with compassion, despite all the evil that Jesse had tried to infuse into it.

Lily rested peacefully that night, but the same could not be said for James. He lay in his bed tossing and turning after being jolted awake by a recurring nightmare that he had become all too familiar with over the last eight years of his life. The nightmare was triggered by a gruesome event that had been seared into his subconscious several hours after his father discovered his friendship with Lily. The torturous memory was created after James was forced to witness an incident that took less than ten minutes to imprint itself on his impressionable sixteen-year-old mind. The grisly details left visuals in his head that would make him sick to the point of regurgitation every night for weeks following the horrific event. The horrors from that night drastically changed who James was as a young man and ultimately affected every decision he would ever make in his life moving forward, *especially* those concerning Lily. Even after going away to school, the nightmares, night sweats, and sleeplessness continued occasionally. But upon returning home, the night terrors had become more frequent, wreaking havoc on his ability to get adequate rest.

Since arriving at William's home, James was drawn to a certain place whenever the gruesome nightmare awakened him. Twice, he had stood outside of Lily's bedroom door fighting the intense desire to turn the knob and enter. On those occasions his rationale had won the battle, stopping him from doing something he might regret. But after sitting alone with Lily on the porch, absorbing the sound of her voice and the beauty of her soft features, his intense desire to see her finally obliterated his willpower to stay on the opposite side of the border in between them.

James unlatched Lily's bedroom door. He walked in as quietly as a church mouse, unprepared with an excuse if Lily happened to be awake. He simply did not care. There was so much he had wanted to say to her at dinner anyway. But he believed silence was his only sane option for the time being. If he said what he truly wanted to say, he had no doubt that the sprinkle of tears glistening in Lily's eyes would have turned into a downpour. With the way he was feeling now, he feared he would likely continue to abandon all rationale and tell Lily the perils that were at war in his mind … things that he had kept to himself for years. For that reason, he hoped that she was asleep.

James's eyes adjusted to the darkness and he walked over to Lily, happy to find her sleeping peacefully on top of the covers. He reached down to the end of the bed, pulled the folded quilt up and placed it gently over her body. He refrained from what he instinctively wanted to do next. But just the visual of himself pressing his lips against Lily's soft skin was enough to awaken another part of his body. He took a deep breath, regained control of himself, and reluctantly sat down in a chair near the bed and watched her sleep. It was a ritual he had started as a teenager when the night terrors began to strike. Much like this night, Lily was completely unaware that James was comforted by her presence while watching her chest rise and fall, as she lay there in those vulnerable moments. Such a simple tradition reassured him that she was still alive, a fact that contradicted his horrific recurring nightmare.

With the curtains still drawn back, the moonlight hit Lily's face in such a way that James was able to cherish all her angelic features for the few minutes that he sat watching over her. He then quietly tiptoed out and returned to his own bed. As soon as James lay back down, it was evident that his secret ritual still remained the one and only remedy that gave him the peace of mind he needed to quickly fall back into a deep sleep of his own.

Chapter Seven

Slave Code
Article III Section VIII

It is a felony for any person who shall transport, secretly carry, or send away out of any state, any slave belonging to an inhabitant within it, such offenses are punishable by jail time and costs to be adjudged by the justices of the provincial court.

L ily's assumptions and intuitions were accurate. Questioning Anna Mae and Ben about William helped confirm her suspicions about James's true intentions. Just hearing Lily play two songs on his mother's piano was all it had taken to convince James that she was far greater than the average pianist. Those two songs had James wide awake nearly all night in the hours after discovering Lily's gift. He lay there staring at the ceiling for the longest time, mystified about how beautifully she had played. Eventually, he began to pray. He prayed until he fell asleep. Hours later, James was jarred from his sleep. He quickly sat up, feeling convinced that God had just sent the answer to his prayers in the form of a dream. That dream drove him to immediately get out of bed and set out before dawn, headed to Ohio in search of William Werthington.

James made the two-day trek to Ohio despite having no idea where, or even if, he would be able to find the highly regarded composer. He had not heard anything about William since learning that he had retired from Ohio University years earlier. James hoped that his close friend and fraternity brother, Harrison Mitchell, might be able to help with his search.

Harrison and James had become friends after being assigned as roommates in the dormitories at Ohio University. Harrison was a strikingly handsome blonde, hazel-eyed rowing champion at the school. His tall muscular frame, chiseled jaw, infectious smile, and brilliant mind easily made him the pick of the male litter in the town of Athens. But when James arrived, Harrison was subsequently demoted to the runt. Despite being dethroned, Harrison took it in stride and quickly became great friends with James. The extraordinarily handsome pair were rarely seen without one another on campus, fraternity events, and around town. At Athens social gatherings, Harrison and James easily commanded the attention of the ladies. Religious convictions and social etiquette had no power to tame the duo's behavior when it came to women. They both took *full* advantage of the sinful benefits of their magnetic aesthetics, as often as any virile man could get away with in secret. Harrison's smooth-talking ways won him plenty of women, while James's quiet mystique easily tilted the female scale in his direction. James's natural introversion unwittingly caused dozens of women to attempt to prevail as the first to unlock his mysterious mind and capture his heart. But James dealt with women in a very selfish, cold-hearted manner and left a long list of broken hearts in his wake. Despite it, the gossip about his intoxicating prowess kept his female counterparts eager to win his affections. Harrison gladly capitalized on James's cold-hearted ways; he was more than happy to "comfort" the leftover heartbroken women that James swatted off like flies, after they had all failed at penetrating the rock-solid walls of his heart.

After graduating, Harrison put his smooth-talking ways and his fast-thinking mind to work as an attorney in his hometown of Athens. Knowing that Harrison had resided in Athens his whole life, James figured that he would likely know of William Werthington's whereabouts. His assumptions were correct. When Harrison was just

110

a boy, his family had been to several Fourth of July celebrations and Spring Extravaganzas that William held annually at his home. He was, therefore, easily able to give James directions to William's estate.

It seemed an odd request for James to be searching for William, but Harrison never once questioned James's motive for seeking the retired musician. The fact that Harrison never wanted to pry personal information out of James was a rare trait amongst small town people. It was something that James always appreciated about him. Harrison never wasted time trying to unravel who James was as a person, nor did he ever divulge stories about their scandalous weekend adventures and create unnecessary gossip. Harrison was always much more concerned with enjoying life with his longtime friend. He was trustworthy and loyal, and treated James like more of a brother than J.R. and Jacob. It was for those many reasons that James had come to his fraternity brother first when he returned to the city of his alma mater in search of William. With Harrison's proven level of loyalty, James never once doubted that his search would remain a secret, without ever needing to tell Harrison it needed to be.

After catching up with Harrison over a brief lunch at Buck's Tavern, James began making his way to William Werthington's estate. Despite venturing there unannounced, he was fearlessly prepared to ask the world-renowned musical genius for an astronomical favor. James prayed all the way there that his words alone would be enough to move William to help, the way that Lily's music had moved him to ride two days in search of a man he had never met. Following Harrison's directions, James's two-horse team eventually pulled him down a long tree-lined, decorated dirt trail. It led him to two large steel gates with the words "Werthington Estate" sculpted into them. Inside the gate, William's expansive, white plantation-style mansion sat perched in the middle of perfectly manicured grass, surrounded by shrubbery, trees, flowers, fountains, and sculptures. The entire visual looked to James like the grounds of a king's palace.

On his two-day journey there, James had gone over what he wanted to say to William a million times in his head, but as he climbed down from his wagon, a sudden bout of nervousness threatened to destroy his ability to even speak. He stood there a moment and looked up at William's beautiful home in utter amazement. It was a sobering reminder that he was about to speak to a man of great wealth and power, and that he needed to present himself as a confident man on an equivalent level. After reminding himself of the special reason he was there, pulling himself together suddenly became easy.

James dusted himself off, adjusted his attire, removed his Stetson hat, and fixed his hair before proceeding up the steps to knock on the artfully carved double doors.

"May I help you?" Benjamin asked when he finally answered.

"Yes. My name is James Adams. I's hopin' I might speak with William Werthington. Is this his residence?"

"Yes, it is. Is he expectin' you?"

"No, but the matta' is very urgent. I've traveled two days in hopes that I could speak with him about somethin' very important."

"Ah, I see. Come on in," Benjamin replied, inviting him into the foyer. "Can you wait here a moment?"

"Certainly." After Benjamin walked away, James blew out a breath and began pacing to calm the nerves he felt brewing again.

Benjamin walked into William's study, where he sat reading his mail and smoking a pipe. "Pardon me, William. There's a young man at the door here to see ya'."

"Who is he?" William asked, looking over the top of his spectacles.

"I believe he said his name is James Adams."

"Adams, Adams, Adams," William whispered to himself, trying to recall anyone he knew by that last name. "Doesn't ring a bell. Can't say I know anyone by that name."

"Me neitha', but he says the matta' is urgent."

"Oh, how so?"

"I don't know, but he claims to have traveled two days to get here in hopes 'a speakin' to ya'."

"Two days?"

"That's what he claims."

"Interesting. That definitely piques my curiosity. No matter what he has to say, though, I certainly don't have the heart to turn someone down who's that eager to speak to me. Send him in," William replied, as he snuffed out his pipe and laid it down.

Benjamin returned to the foyer and startled James, who was still incessantly pacing. "Right this way Mr. Adams."

"Thank you." James followed Benjamin, but only half focusing on where he was being led; the elegance of the home's interior had easily won his attention. It looked to him more like a museum full of fine arts and decorative antiques than a place where someone actually lived. His eyes roamed everywhere in wonderment until Benjamin suddenly opened the set of double doors to William's study. Nerves then instantly hit James again once he entered.

"Mr. Adams, this is Mr. Werthington," Benjamin announced. He then exited the den and closed the door behind himself.

James walked toward William who stood to shake his hand. "Hello, Mr. Werthington. Forgive me for showin' up here unannounced. I thank you for seein' me despite it."

"Not a problem at all."

"I'm truly pleased to meet you."

"Pleased to meet you as well, Mr. Adams. Can I offer you something to eat or drink? I believe Anna Mae's made chicken and dumplings. The *best* in the world!" he boasted with a smile.

113

William's smile and generosity calmed James at once. "Thank you kindly, but I've already eaten."

"Truly a shame! Your taste buds will never forgive you," he joked while motioning his hand to offer James the chair in front of his desk.

James laughed lightly and sat down at the same time as William. "It truly is an honor to finally meet you," he began.

William smiled in appreciation. "Well, thank you."

"I've heard a great deal about you and your music ova' the years."

"Ahh, so I assume your visit today is music related?"

"Well, that's part 'a the reason, but only if somethin' I once heard before about you is actually true."

"And exactly which *something* might you be referring to?" William replied with questioning eyes, wondering if he might suddenly need to be on the defensive.

"Well, to be quite honest, rumors."

"Ahh, *rumors!* Of course. I shouldn't have expected anything less with the way this town loves to jabber on about other people's lives," he said, waving his hand dismissively. "But now, if I might be quite honest with *you*, Mr. Adams." He leaned back, placed his elbows on the chair, and touched the tips of his fingers together, suddenly looking at James very seriously over the top of his spectacles. "If you have truly traveled two days to speak to me, as Benjamin has just informed me, then I have to believe that this conversation will eventually lead to something much more important than any silly rumors."

"Yessa', *far* more important, I assure you of that," James responded quickly. "But I can also assure you that there really won't be a need to carry on with this conversation if there's no truth in the whispa's I've heard about you around this town."

"And just which *whispers* might you be talking about, Mr. Adams?"

"Well, I've gotten different details dependin' on who was tellin' the story. But at the core of it was always the fact that you once helped a slave family out of an awful situation."

William immediately focused on the term that James used to describe their circumstances. "An *awful* situation?"

"Yessa'."

"And you say there's no need to carry on with the conversation if the story is *not* true?"

"Yessa'."

"So, you're saying that you'd actually prefer that it *is* true?" William asked, looking perplexed. He was intrigued by what this young man might want but wanted to be absolutely clear about his stance on the matter.

"Yessa', more than you know."

Because of his word choice, and the sentiment in his voice, William felt in his gut that James did not want to believe the story was true so that he could inflict harm on him, like many others had threatened to do in the past. Still though, James was a stranger, so he proceeded with caution. "Young man, why don't you explain to me the nature of your visit, then maybe I'll decide if you're worthy of hearing about my personal life."

"Fair enough." James leaned forward and put his elbows on his knees, clasped his hands tightly in front of him, and exhaled before he began. "Six years ago, I left home and went to school at Ohio University, where you once worked. I went there to begin my trainin' to be a medical doctor. I'd dreamt 'a bein' a doctor since I's just a boy. It was somethin' I wanted more than anything in my life. So, when I arrived there, I's determined to get through with my studies as quickly as I could. I doubled up on courses and even took courses ova' the summa' and durin' winta' breaks. Afta' graduation, I started workin' alongside a brilliant doctor. I worked with 'em because I didn't wanna be just an average doctor. I wanted to be *great*. And I's confident that this particula' man could guide me there. And I's right. He was one hell of a mentor. Any and everything he was willin' to show me, I clung to it. I locked it all away while I had the chance to work alongside a man who was a true masta'mind. In fact, he was so impressed with my eaga'ness to learn that he took me on a mission trip with 'em. We traveled togetha' from city to city helpin' folks. We treated all kinda people, no matta' who they were, or what their status was. I saw and learned things that a classroom could neva' have taught me. It was truly one 'a the greatest experiences 'a my life. From then on, I knew that's what I wanted to do. I wanted to travel and take care 'a folks all ova' the country, the way we did for all those months.

"That doctor was undoubtedly the inspiration behind me wantin' to take my skill on the road. And afta' everything I experienced with 'em, you'd probably think he was also the one who inspired me to work so hard to be *great*. But oddly, I can't give 'em the credit for that." James paused a moment and looked directly into William's eyes. "Because that honor belongs to *you*, Mr. Werthington."

William was taken aback by James's unexpected words. He was inwardly affected but kept a straight face as he continued to listen to the story.

"Because 'a you, I aspired not only to be a great *doctor* ... but to be a great *man*," James confessed. "I wanted to be the sort 'a man who was as compassionate as I had heard you were through all 'a those rumors. I know most folks were outraged by the fact that you'd supposedly helped a family 'a slaves. But for *me*..." James tapped his fingers on his chest. "It touched me deep." He shook his head, thinking back to the first time he had heard about William as a freshman. "It changed my life to finally know that there was a man like you that existed. It did wonda's for me just to *hear* that there was a person fearless enough to help otha's in need, no matta' who they were. And fearless enough to be his own man regardless of the rules 'a society. What that did for me, Mr. Werthington, I honestly don't have the words to adequately express. But I *can* say that in the six years since I heard your story, it's neva' once left my soul, not for one minute … And I swear it neva' will."

William still sat there quietly, completely gripped by the candidness of this unfamiliar man's confession, noting the sincerity in his voice and eyes as he spoke.

"Mr. Werthington, that story was truly an inspiration to me. And if it's true, the way I've always believed it was, then I know I've come to the right person."

"Come to the right person for what?"

"Ya' see, afta' six years of avoidin' goin' back home, I just recently…"

"*Avoiding?*" William interrupted, suddenly very curious. "A man only says that when he's running from something."

James noticed how William analyzed his every word and realized that perhaps he needed to be more cautious about what he chose to say. "Yes, well, it's just that at home…" He froze and closed his eyes for a moment. "The person I had to be there…" He stopped again as a rush of unwelcomed memories suddenly flooded his mind. "I, umm," he sighed. "Let's just say, I couldn't bring myself to be in that house unda' the circumstances."

William nodded and prodded no further, after seeing in James's face that he was deeply troubled by whatever had stopped him from returning home.

"But afta' six years 'a bein' away, I had to force myself to return," James continued. "I knew I needed to go back before I went off to live my life on the road. Of course, I had to see my fatha' and brotha's again. But more importantly, I knew I's gonna need some help while I's on the road and, umm … well, I had someone in mind there that I wanted to take along with me."

117

William faintly smiled when he realized that James's slight hesitation likely meant that this "someone" had to have been a woman.

"But when I finally got home last week, everything changed," James further explained. "All the plans I had for my career and for headin' out on the road ... *everything*. It *all* changed. Afta' what I witnessed that day, the dream I had for travelin' the country suddenly didn't seem so important to me anymore." He stared emptily at a bare area of William's desk as the memory resurfaced. "Not nearly as important as what I saw when I walked through the door that afta'noon."

"After you'd been dreaming for so long to be a traveling doctor, what could possibly make you have such a drastic change of heart so quickly?" William asked.

"The woman that I's hopin' to take along with me, she ... she has a *gift*, Mr. Werthington. A gift that could take 'er fartha' in life than I could eva' take 'er in the back 'a my dusty wagon, draggin' 'er from place to place while I take care 'a folks. She has a gift to play the piano unlike anyone I've eva' seen," he said with an intense look in his eyes. "Her abilities are so incredible that I feel she's worthy 'a me puttin' my dreams on hold for a while. What she can do is so astonishin' that it's guided me to travel for two days to find a man I ain't eva' met before, a man whose rumored story I pray to God is actually true. Because I'm hopin', with all my heart, that you'd be willin' to help this woman too, the way you allegedly did with that family all them years ago."

William leaned back slowly in his chair after being bowled over by James's words. Something so extraordinary was the last thing he had expected to hear on such an ordinary day. "I am certainly moved by your passion, Mr. Adams. But I still don't understand why the rumors have anything to do with this."

James instantly felt his heart start to race. He swallowed hard, nervously looked down and blew out a breath, knowing that his next few words could potentially be a turning point in William's decision. "Th-the young lady who was playin' that piano…" He paused and exhaled again. "She's … she's a *slave* on my fatha's farm, Mr. Werthington," he finally confessed, feeling ashamed that he had to label a human as such a thing. With hesitancy, James then nervously looked up and met William's solemn green eyes. Unsure what to expect next, James just quietly stared at him as his heart crashed mercilessly against his ribcage.

William silently stared back at James while contemplating his surprising admission. Before saying a word, he suddenly stood and went to look out the window. "And what exactly would you be hoping I could do for her?" he finally asked.

James was surprised not to hear any hostility in William's voice. Instead, it was a calmly stated question that showed interest. His compassionate tone seemed to confirm that the inspiring rumor was true, a fact that instantly settled the speed of James's racing heart. "Well, I'm aware of your level of musical talent, and the kind 'a powa' and respect you've earned in the field 'a music. So first, I's hopin' you'd be willin' to hear her play, and if you felt she needed any fine tunin' then perhaps you could help 'er with that. And if you think she's worthy of it, I's hopin' you'd use your influence to help me get 'er some work somewhere around here. Ohio's a free state, and I'm sure she could earn a good wage here. I don't know, maybe she could teach children to play, or perform in small venues somewhere, or perhaps even work with an orchestra. Anything along those lines that'll give 'er the financial means to take care of 'erself."

"I haven't touched a piano or any other instrument in over two years," William admitted, still staring out the window at his wife's heavily flowered grave site in the distance. "Haven't taught anyone in just as long either."

"I know this is askin' a lot, Mr. Werthington, but you're my only hope at this point. I really believe if you just give 'er a chance, just listen and watch the way she plays…" James closed his eyes for a moment, recalling how Lily's music had affected him. "Then maybe you'll think she's worth the trouble the way I do."

William turned from the window to face James. "Is coming here something she's asked you to do for her?"

"No sa', she has no idea I'm here."

"Hmph. Certainly lends credibility to how strongly you feel about this."

"Truthfully, Mr. Werthington, I don't think my words can do any justice to how strongly I feel about this."

"Trust me, if you were listening with my ears, I don't think you'd be saying that," William replied, staring down at James, still fascinated by the whole ordeal, and by the man who sat before him. "Have you any idea how long she's been playing?"

"Fourteen years." James shook his head in disbelief. "Said she taught 'erself to play."

"Really?" William smiled, recalling how he had done the same as a boy.

"Yessa'."

"And you'd truly be willing to put your medical career on hold for a while just to help her?"

James finally got up and stood with William near the window. "Afta' hearin' her play, Mr. Werthington, my medical career can go straight to hell for the time bein'. The sorta healin' I can do as a doctor pales in comparison to what she's capable of. She may not have eva' had one minute 'a trainin', but I swear 'fore God she could heal a man's soul the way she plays the piano. I ain't neva' seen or heard anything like it before in all my life. And so, *yes*. If puttin' my career on hold for a while is what it takes to help 'er pursue this, then you're damn right I would," he said with conviction.

"Young man, I don't think I've witnessed a grander act of altruism since my wife was alive," William said, staring at James as if to convince himself that he was not a figment of his imagination. "What is this young lady's name?"

"Lily."

The name instantly reminded William of something else about his wife. "Well, you bring your Lily to me, and I promise to do everything in my power to help her."

"You're certain?"

"You have my word."

"I can't thank you enough, Mr. Werthington! I can't tell you what this means to me!" James exclaimed, a great amount of relief in his voice as he vigorously shook William's hand.

"I think the fact that you're even here says more than enough about what this means to you."

"If only I could make my fatha' see that." James's excitement waned a bit while thinking about how Jesse would now be the toughest obstacle on his path to helping Lily. "Which reminds me, I'll have to send you word by letta' to let you know of our arrival. Knowin' my fatha', it might take me some time to convince 'em to let Lily go for a while."

"May I ask why that might be?"

"My fatha' doesn't know that Lily can play piano, nor does he know about what I'm askin' of you here today, and he doesn't take the matta' of his property lightly. You'd swear he paid a million dolla's for every slave on that plantation and *five* million for Lily. So long as he's alive, he'd neva' let 'er set one foot off that farm."

"And so just how were you planning to convince him to let you take her on the road with you when you went on your medical journey?"

121

"Just like how I plan to get 'er here ... by any means necessary."

Loving James's tenacity, William smiled, nodded, and gave his shoulder a squeeze. "Sounds like a brilliant plan to me, young man!" He then began escorting James toward the front door. "Are you sure I can't offer you something to eat? You could have dinner and stay the night if you'd like and have breakfast in the morning before your departure. I know you have a rather long journey ahead of you. It might be best to go about it on a full stomach and well rested," William offered, as they walked down the long hallway toward the foyer.

"Thank you, but I'm eaga' to get back on the road."

"I understand. Well, at least wait here and let me have Anna Mae prepare you a bowlful of her famous chicken and dumplings to take along with you. You'll thank me for it later!" William smiled.

"I'd appreciate that." James waited by the door until William returned with more than enough food to last him on his journey. "Thank you for your hospitality, Mr. Werthington. You're incredibly kind. And again, I thank you in advance for your willingness to help Lily."

"You're quite welcome, but I almost feel as though I should be thanking *you*. I now find myself very much looking forward to meeting this lovely young lady you speak of." He shook James's hand again after they stepped out onto the porch. "It was truly a pleasure to meet you, Mr. Adams."

"The pleasure was all mine. I look forward to seein' you again soon." James walked away and was about to proceed down the porch steps but then stopped. "Oh, and one otha' thing. Please don't mention anything to Lily about what we're tryna accomplish when she gets here. I don't know how any 'a this is gonna work out, and I don't wanna get 'er hopes up for now. I'd just prefer to speak to 'er about things when I feel the time is right."

"As you wish. But a little optimism will take us far, don't you think?"

"I am optimistic, but also realistic. I know this won't be easy."

"Agreed."

"Good day, Mr. Werthington." With that, James put his Stetson hat back on and trotted down the porch steps.

"Mr. Adams!" William called out before he reached his wagon.

James stopped, turned around, and looked up at William.

"Are you certain that it was *just* your need for an assistant that prompted you to want to take Lily along with you on the road?" William asked curiously.

James said not a word. Only the musical sound of birds chirping around them could be heard. His eyes momentarily drifted to the grass and then back up at William with a sudden childlike innocence present in them.

"Forget I asked," William said, after the look on James's face answered his question with more clarity than he felt his words ever could. It was an answer William presumed may have had a lot to do with why James had avoided his own home for six long years. "Have a safe journey back home to get your Lily, Mr. Adams."

James tipped his hat, climbed into his wagon, and went on his way.

William stood on the porch watching James ride off his property. "Something tells me that it was far more than a rumor that inspired you to be a great man for all these years, Mr. Adams. Something so powerful that I doubt you ever really needed to hear a story like mine at all," William whispered to himself.

That one-hour meeting had William completely riveted. It left him eagerly anticipating the arrival of the woman who had motivated a complete stranger to travel two days to passionately bare his soul. James was just as eager for William to meet Lily too. He truly hoped that there was some way that William could help her begin a career in music. However, he was not ignorant about the risks they were taking by helping a Negro. In fact, he feared that he may be putting William in harm's way. But James was convinced that Lily's existence had a purpose far beyond that of being a slave. Through her very fingertips, he believed that Lily had the potential to help subdue the ill-fated morals that had severed society. He heard a constant inner voice telling him that Lily simply had to be heard and that the reward would greatly supersede any and all risks. And after just *one* piano session with Lily, William, too, was instantly convinced that it was not only the world of music that she had the potential to impact, but the very world itself.

The afternoon following his only piano session with Lily, William had set out with James to carry out the "business" that Lily was unnecessarily concerned over. "Business" turned out to be William and James trying desperately to find her adequate work. They spent all day traveling to different towns to speak with William's old acquaintances to see if any of them would be willing to use Lily as a pianist in their orchestras. With no luck there, they resorted to asking owners of taverns and pubs to see if perhaps they would like to use Lily as an entertainer. They, too, all declined often in the cruelest of ways upon hearing of Lily's race.

At the same point in time that Lily had finally gathered the strength to venture out of her room, James and William were pressing on in her honor. After three days of traveling countless miles with grim results, the duo was exhausted. Despite that, though, they carried on with cautious optimism and eventually found themselves in a very familiar place. At the very moment that Lily had stepped out of William's home into the sunlight, the hopeful duo stepped through the front doors of the very building that William had retired from two years prior. It was also the very place that James had hidden himself away for six years during his quest to become a doctor. They walked onto the Ohio University campus to speak to Richard Wells. For nearly a decade, Richard had been a part of William's orchestra. William still considered him as a close friend. He had even personally recommended Richard to be his successor when he retired. Because of that recommendation, Richard now held the title of music director in the prestigious school. Considering their history, William was confident that Richard would be willing to help. He was so confident, in fact, that he cursed himself for having not started their search with Richard.

William and James approached the orchestra room and could hear the starting and stopping of a classical arrangement. They peered through the door and could see Richard standing at the podium, lecturing the brass section on how to improve the portion of the piece they were working on. The sight of the podium, the classroom, the sound of the instruments, and even the scent in the hallway all brought back fond memories for William. It cast him into a trance of sorts. Moments later, he was suddenly shaken back to the present when the students began to file out of the classroom, filling the hallways with their chatter. When the last student left, William made his way into his old music room with James by his side.

"You have them playing that piece in the wrong key, you know? Sounds dreadful, I tell you," William teased.

Startled, Richard stopped scribbling notes on his music sheet and turned toward his old friend. "William Werthington! You bloody bastard!" he blurted in a British accent similar to William's. "So good to see you!" he said as they shook hands.

"Good to see you again too, old friend. This here is a friend of mine, Dr. James Adams. James, this is Richard Wells."

"Pleased to meet you, Mr. Wells," James responded while shaking his hand.

"Likewise, Dr. Adams." Richard turned his attention back to William after releasing James's hand. "Well now, I was certain I wouldn't be seeing you again until the fundraising gala for the music department at your home in a few weeks. Seems the only time of year I can catch a glimpse of the elusive William Werthington. Lord knows, it's not often that you emerge from that palace of yours anymore these days," he joked. "So, to what do I owe the honor of your visit?" he asked as they all filed into his office.

"A favor actually."

"The great and powerful William Werthington in need of a favor? Say it isn't so," Richard replied sarcastically as he took a seat at his desk. "After all you've done to get me here, I'd be glad to do what I can for you."

"That's encouraging to hear."

"Oh, come now, how could you expect to hear anything less? Just name it, and I'll do all I can to help."

"Well, I have a friend who is in need of work."

"Let me guess, his name is James?" Richard joked, laughing at his own sarcasm.

"No, Lily, actually."

"Ooohh, a lady." Richard raised a single eyebrow. "Now I'm *really* eager to assist," he joked again.

"Yes, she's a pianist ... one hell of a pianist actually. Without question, she's far better than anyone I've ever heard ... myself included."

Richard folded his arms and raised his eyebrow again, but this time in disbelief. "Really?" he asked with seriousness finally evident in his tone.

"Yes, it's true. And you know that I'd never admit to such a thing lightly."

"Oh, trust me, I know," Richard replied quickly.

"She has perfect pitch, Richard."

Richard sat up straight in his seat with a curious look on his face. "You're certain?"

"I've witnessed it with my very own eyes. Tested her myself."

"That's truly a rare gift … a gift that some claim is just an old wives' tale."

"Well, I can assure you this is no wives' tale. Not in my whole life did I ever think I'd meet someone of her caliber, especially with the few years I have left. Hell, even if I lived another five lifetimes, I don't think I'd ever be fortunate enough to meet another like her. I'm telling you, Richard, she's truly one in a million."

"In all the years I've known you, William, I have never recalled you carrying on so passionately about a musician in this manner."

"I can't seem to help it. It's just that, what I saw…" He thought back to the few hours he had spent playing with Lily. "Richard, it was incredible. She also has a memory so precise that it made me question my own sanity. It was a feat I didn't even know humans were capable of. She absorbed and replayed an entire song after I played it only once." He held a finger up. "One damn time!" he expressed, still in disbelief over the matter.

Richard turned toward James with an inquisitive look on his face, seeking confirmation about a story that seemed like an impossibility. James affirmed with a nod.

William ignored Richard's doubt-filled glance and carried on talking about Lily. "Her theatrics, and the speed and agility with which she was able to play the song back, it was all just…" He shook his head. "Absolutely astonishing." William stared blankly at Richard as he continued to think of her. "The most incredible part of all is that every element of what Lily can do is simply God-given talent. She's never once had a lesson. Everything she knows, every instinct, she learned on her own."

"Good heavens," Richard whispered, a look of shock on his face as he tried to conceive of this mysterious young lady's capabilities. "I've only heard rumors of such people before now. I was beginning to think that no one like that really existed, much less that I would ever be offered the opportunity to actually meet someone like that in person."

"Well, meeting her will change you in some way. I can promise you that."

James nodded in agreement.

"Hearing you speak of another musician with this kind of passion, I'm forced to believe you. I find myself suddenly wishing that you would have brought her along with you today, so that I have the honor of becoming acquainted with this young lady as soon as humanly possible. I'm *definitely* eager to assist now more than ever. So, tell me, how exactly can I help you where she is concerned?"

"Well, I know sometimes the students are seeking tutoring and mentoring for their music. So, I thought perhaps Lily could be of assistance here in your department as a tutor."

"That's all?"

"Yes."

"Well, as I'm sure you already know, we can always use extra tutors for the students. So, of course, that wouldn't be a problem at all."

"That's wonderful!" William exclaimed, turning to look at James, who nodded again in agreement.

"But if that's all you want, then there's something I just don't understand."

"And what's that?"

"Well, you've come here claiming that this young woman is a far greater pianist than yourself, going on and on about all of these incredible gifts she's been born with, but yet you want to reduce her to a simple music tutor? Doesn't make any sense to me."

William's excitement waned upon remembering that he had yet to mention the most important element of the favor he needed to be fulfilled. "Well, we were hoping that this would only be a temporary way for her to earn some money until we can find her some permanent work with an orchestra. Trust me, she is certainly worthy of playing for one. She is truly brilliant, undoubtedly every definition of a genius, but…"

"But what?"

William looked over at James, suddenly understanding how embarrassing it was for him to have to admit to what he was about to say. "She, umm … She was once a slave," he confessed, lying about the fact that she technically still was.

Richard stared at William in silence for a moment and then began to laugh uncontrollably. James and William could both feel their optimism start to melt the longer Richard laughed. "Y-you're joking, right?" he asked after his laughter subsided.

"Of course, I'm not joking!" William fired back through tightly pursed lips. The tone of his voice easily revealed his irritation.

"You know, rumor has it that you retired because you had lost a marble or two upstairs," Richard replied, swirling his finger around his ear. "I didn't very well believe it until now, though," he laughed again.

"Enough of the jokes! Are you going to allow her to work here or not?!"

"Oh, come on, William! You didn't really expect that I'd allow a *Negro* to work with my students, did you?" Richard asked, finally sounding serious.

"And why not?"

"William, how is some former slave, who has no formal education, supposed to tutor anyone?"

"I could train her myself how to go about it. She's brilliant. Absorbs everything like a sponge."

"A *sponge!* Now there's something I would gladly give her, because I'm certain that the only thing a former slave would ever be able to *absorb* is the filth off the floors around here. I simply refuse to believe that a Negro has the capacity to learn things of such complexity."

"Are you really that dense?! I just told you that she's a gifted, brilliant pianist, who possesses skills you and I could only ever dream of!"

"Well, even in the rare circumstance that she does have the capacity to learn enough to teach, which I doubt very seriously, I don't think my students would be very receptive or welcoming to a person of her *hue*. She'd be nothing but a distraction in my classroom!"

"That's a ridiculous excuse, Richard! Eventually, they won't give a damn about her complexion once you show them that you've accepted her. It's not always about *what* you know, or *who* you are, or what *credentials* you have. It's sometimes *who you know* that has the greater influence. You of all people should know that!"

Richard slammed his hands on the desk and rose from his seat. "Don't you dare throw that in my face! I don't give a damn who you are, or what you've done for me!" He pointed at William. "You have most certainly come to the wrong place if you are expecting any *influence* from *me* to help with a lowly *Negro!* You truly *have* lost your marbles if you think I'd be willing to defame the legacy I'm trying to build here by disgracing the walls of this place by doing such a thing!"

James tensed and took a step forward, but William grabbed him by the arm before he could make another move. "Don't trouble yourself over him, James. I'm sure he'll soon be regretting his moronic words and his foolish actions," he said, staring his *former* friend down. "Let's go."

"Yes, do as you're told," Richard replied, dismissively waving his hand at James. "Saves me the trouble of throwing you out."

James clenched his jaw tight to keep from verbally erupting. He clenched his fists even tighter to keep from reaching over and snatching Richard from behind the desk. With William still gripping him tightly around the arm, they both turned and stormed angrily from Richard's office without another word.

Unfortunately, the way that meeting had ended was something that William and James had quickly become accustomed to in the three days they had ventured together. Infuriating rounds of ridicule, sarcasm, and laughter seemed to be a recurring theme with everyone they had crossed paths with. In every instance, it revealed the nastiness and ignorance of people that William had once considered as dear friends. The annoying, predictable cycle left both men feeling utterly frustrated as they left their old university.

While their meeting with Richard had plunged the pair into a temporary darkness, Lily had been slowly rising from her internal abyss toward the light after walking the grounds of William's estate. As both men made their way back home in silence, Lily had just made her way into the kitchen and was already seated listening to Anna Mae and Benjamin tell the emotional tale about the day William had set them free. Just as their emotional story ended, James and William had also ended their emotional journey back to the estate.

After riding in silence the entire way, William halted the carriage on the estate grounds, eager to share a suggestion that had been on his mind. "James, perhaps I can find Lily some other sort of work in the meantime while…"

"*What?!*" James snapped, instantly offended by the notion. "Are you givin' up already?!"

"No, I was just…"

"It sure as hell sounds like it to me!"

"I just thought that maybe while we searched, Lily could earn some money…"

"Doin' what sort 'a work?!" James threw his hands up. "Workin' as a seamstress?! Cookin' somebody's goddamn meals?! Takin' care 'a somebody else's children?!" His face was red with anger. "Don't you get it?! I don't want Lily doin' the sort 'a work that reminds her of…"

"Being a slave," William finished calmly, completely unfazed by his companion's sudden outburst. He quickly understood why James was so upset and felt that he was right. Lily deserved far better than that.

After listening to Anna Mae and Benjamin's emotional story, Lily had gone to the kitchen window and watched as James climbed down from the carriage right after his outburst. She stared at him as he marched toward the house, thinking about how much William's story had reminded her of James during his teen years. For eight years, she assumed that that compassionate young man no longer existed. But after the revelations of that day, Lily was beginning to realize that perhaps her assumptions had been wrong. At that moment, though, James had stormed into the house with an attitude, breezed by her without a word, and slammed his bedroom door. His actions allowed the doubt about the man James *really* was to linger in Lily's mind just a while longer, before she confronted him on the porch later that evening with the true details of William's rumored story.

Just before Lily had joined them on the porch at dinner, William felt the need to make amends with James for their misunderstanding. He genuinely felt sorry for sounding defeated in the carriage earlier in the day. "James, I'm sorry about what I suggested earlier. I was only trying to help, but I completely understand why you were so upset. I assure you, though, that I haven't given up."

"No, I'm the one who needs to apologize. You're doin' so much for Lily, and I acted like a complete ass."

"Actually, you were acting like a man who cares a great deal about someone. Maybe more than he's willing to outwardly admit." Much like the moment William questioned him about Lily before leaving his home the first time, James did not verbally respond, but his eyes spoke for him yet again. And just like that last time, William let him off the hook and changed the subject. "Anyhow, I just want you to know that I stand united with you and your dream for Lily."

"I know, William. And despite what my temper may have made you think, I truly do appreciate it."

"Actually, your temper only further helps me understand how important this is to you."

"It really is."

"It is to me too, which is why I wanted to speak to you about a potential idea."

"Idea?"

"Yes, a plan that I think might help to move things along for Lily, if all else fails."

"I'm willin' to do whateva' it takes. I'm listenin'."

Before William could begin to explain, however, he ceased the conversation with a smile when he caught sight of Lily emerging from the front door to willingly join them for dinner. Their conversation halted at that moment, but the following day William laid out his back-up plan to James. From then on, they both methodically began to put all its elements into action.

Chapter Eight

Stripes:

A forceful stroke on bare skin from a whip, rod,
or cane that oftentimes leads to stripe-like scarring.

Slave Code
Article II Section X

Persons willingly entertaining slaves, unlawfully absenting, or permitting them
to be about their houses or plantations for one hour or longer shall forfeit one
hundred pounds of tobacco for each hour or pay a monetary penalty equal to the
cost of the forementioned goods. Free Negroes so offending shall be whipped; not
to exceed thirty-nine stripes.

Saturday
February 12, 1859
Ohio University music department
annual fundraising gala

Lily kept her head down staring at the piano keys. She was afraid to look up and face all of the eyes that were pasted on her, as she sat at the grand piano *alone* in the middle of all the guests that had collected in William's library during his annual fundraising gala. The sound of meaningless chatter, the shuffling of footsteps, and the clinking of wine glasses had immediately ceased while watching her performance. No one was quite sure how they were supposed to respond after her last note rippled through the air. The other festivities were easily forgettable compared to the brief mystifying show that Lily had just put on. But because of who she was, complete silence was the only reaction, until a spellbound man in the crowd finally emerged from his trance enough to speak. "Who the hell is this woman?" he asked, his eyes glued on Lily.

"They say ol' William been trainin' nigga's here for years! Looks like he done taught 'emself anotha' monkey!" Tucker McCormick replied, his speech slurred from his drunken state. He slapped his hand to his knee and gave a hearty laugh after rudely reminding everyone of the rumors that had circulated about William for years. Tucker was never one to bite his tongue, especially if it meant he had the opportunity to degrade someone. But no one other than him found his joke amusing, especially James, who suddenly jumped in his face out of nowhere.

"Mind your fuckin' mouth!" James snapped, the fury in his tone seemed to instantly sober the heckling drunk.

Lily finally raised her head from the piano keys after hearing James snap at Tucker. She was shocked that James had bothered to come to her defense when the deputy disrespected her while on their journey to William's home. She was even more stunned this time around, considering that James had done so in front of a large crowd. The ferocity of his protective nature had warmth running through Lily as she gazed at him. But James never noticed her eyes on him nor her expression of gratitude; he was still too busy trying to stare a hole into Tucker's face.

James's bold reaction made it obvious that Tucker was not the only one who had had too much to drink that night. James had certainly had his fill. Not only was he tipsy, he was aggravated by something that he had witnessed prior to Lily's performance. It left him eager to pounce on anybody who crossed him, a fact that Tucker realized after spitting out his nasty words.

James had tried, but he could not seem to depart from the uproar of emotions that began in the earlier part of the day with the arrival of Anna Mae and Ben's two children, Isabel and Elijah. They had both returned to help with William's fundraiser. Their oldest, Elijah, had taken immediate notice of Lily and had not ventured far from her side from the moment he laid eyes on her. James was there when Elijah first got a glimpse of her in the kitchen. He saw the way that Elijah's eyes lit up and slowly careened up and down Lily's body the very second he spotted her. He saw the look of awe on Elijah's face as he then approached Lily and introduced himself. James's eyes homed in on the way Elijah let his hand linger in Lily's for the longest time while he gently shook it. An irrational urge to pry Elijah off of her began building with intensity inside James for every second he held her hand. His strong desire to intervene grew as he continued to watch the way Elijah gazed at Lily with lust in his eyes while engrossed in conversation with her. But what James had hated more than anything was the double take that he saw Lily give to Elijah when he first entered the kitchen.

When Elijah walked in to greet his parents, Lily had instinctively turned toward the sound of the deep, unfamiliar voice to find a man standing there, who was equal to James in size and height. His extraordinary handsomeness caused Lily to do a double take. Upon glancing back, Elijah flashed a smile at her, illuminating brilliant white teeth that stood out against his chocolate brown skin. Lily, too, seemed not to be able to turn away as she noted Elijah's sculpted body; it was outlined well underneath a pair of gray trousers, a white long-sleeved shirt, and black suspenders that clung to his muscular frame. His ensemble was topped off by a single-brimmed gray cloth hat, covering his tightly cropped Afro. Elijah was so well put together that even James had to admit to himself that he was worthy of Lily's double take. But capturing a glimpse of the sensual smile that accompanied Lily's glance was the beginning of the deterioration of James's night. After seeing that she had a mutual attraction to Elijah, James suddenly found it difficult to focus on the importance of the plan that he and William had laid out for the evening.

After the disastrous meeting with Richard Wells, William conceded to the fact that his words alone would never be enough to find Lily work as a musician. He realized that her abilities had to speak for her. William felt that his fundraising gala would be the perfect opportunity to give Lily a chance to showcase her talent and prove that she was worthy of working as an entertainer. As part of William's scheme, he was sure to invite everyone to the fundraiser who was affiliated with an orchestra, pub, or tavern, including the ones who were unwilling to hire Lily. Despite the ugly ending to their meeting, Richard was also among the attendees, since the money being generated was specifically for the Ohio University music department. In attendance as well was Tucker McCormick, a tavern owner, who had stood amongst the many guests in the library rudely letting words fly uninhibited from his intoxicated mouth.

To ensure that their plan continued to run smoothly, William had worked feverishly during the party, talking to all of the prospects who could potentially be of help to Lily. James was supposed to be doing the same, but instead, he was standing in the corner of the room drinking one glass of whiskey after another, watching Elijah interact with Lily throughout the night. While James was scrutinizing the pair, all the young ladies at the party were scrutinizing *him*. His neatly sculpted hair, freshly groomed face, and tailored suit further added to his natural stunning good looks. The design of his expensive attire accentuated his physique in a way that commanded the eyes of every young lady in the room, many of whom sashayed by him in hopes of winning his affections. But for James, they were just an endless stream of blank faces who failed to win his attention, let alone his affections. He was way too focused on Elijah, who was stealing every moment he could to whisper in Lily's ear, which James noticed never failed to make her laugh or smile. And with every smile that Elijah put on Lily's face, the heat in James's veins went up another degree.

James had secretly been with several women while living in Athens, but they were never anything more than a means of satisfying his natural urges. When it came to the women from his past, he was never once tickled by jealousy. But on this night, watching Lily smile at Elijah's playfulness, jealousy had run James over like a freight train. After six years of being away from Lily, James thought that he would be able to continue suppressing the feelings he had for her. But he realized how wrong he was the very instant he saw her angelic face sitting at his mother's piano. Since then, he kept trying to convince himself that being with Lily would never be right, that he could never give her all that a woman deserved, and that she was *not* the woman for him. Excuse after excuse he tried to create, but his body, his heart, and even his dreams always contradicted the lies he tried to *force* himself to believe. Deep down, he knew those lies stemmed from the ignorant beliefs of people like his father, who could never see past one's race or status in life.

James saw so much more in Lily than just a colored slave girl; her uniqueness made all other women seem so subpar to him in comparison, including the ones he had lain with. Unlike the women he used, Lily was far more to James than just a warm body he desired to be one with. Through Lily he learned that judging someone by their appearance was foolish, that there could be more to a person than what the eyes could see, a fact further proven by her prodigal abilities. Lily taught him about the inner and outer strengths of a woman, about perseverance, the true meaning of beauty, the definition of a best friend, and about how laughter could lift a heavy heart. Many nights, James even had vivid dreams that convinced him that Lily was the *only* woman capable of defining to him the true meaning of passion and lovemaking. His intimate encounters with other women supported that notion. Those encounters were always so empty and meaningless. Most were alcohol-driven attempts at forgetting about Lily, which hopelessly failed. In fact, it was Lily's face and body that *always* came to James's mind the very instant he slid inside of a woman. Beautiful fantasies of Lily had passionately propelled every stroke, igniting intense climaxes that further proved how much he longed to be one with her. Returning from his fantasy and opening his eyes to the sight of some other woman lying beneath him always caused the feeling of guilt and betrayal to ravage his body with more intensity than a climax ever could.

With all his true feelings having quickly resurfaced, it was crushing James to endure the sight of Elijah making his interest in Lily known, very loud and excruciatingly clear. Since he was a teenager, James was thoroughly convinced that no other man would ever hold Lily as sacred to his heart as him, yet there Elijah stood trying to prove that notion wrong. The sight of it drove James to drink like a madman who was trying to extinguish the jealousy-fueled fire raging within him. Sweat was quickly accumulating on James's brow while watching Elijah try to win the affections of a woman who was extraordinarily precious to him. Minute by minute, his appetite was decreasing. Second by second, his irritation was rising, along with the alcohol in his veins. James longed to be the one whispering in Lily's ear in place of Elijah. He was desperate to be the one evoking her laughter and putting a smile on her face, something he had failed to do for her in years. Graphic visions of Elijah and Lily intimately entangled together began erupting in James's inebriated mind, tying his stomach in knots, and causing his heart to beat a song of pain. Imagining just the small possibility that Lily could end up lying in Elijah's arms at the end of the night had James ready to dive headfirst over the edge of insanity.

James suddenly threw the last bit of whiskey in his glass straight to the back of his throat, ignoring the fire that erupted in his chest shortly thereafter. He slammed his glass down on the table beside him and began weaving his way through the crowd toward the corner where Elijah and Lily stood speaking to each other. He passed by several ladies, who hoped that they were the reason he seemed so desperate to make his way through the maze of people. But each would end up watching the backside of his tailored suit in disappointment after he brushed by their unmemorable faces.

"It's time!" William exclaimed, placing a firm hand on James's shoulder, suddenly stopping him in his tracks.

"What?!" James snapped, staring at the hand on his shoulder that had the audacity to impede his onslaught. Fate had intervened on his march into battle and grabbed him just as he was about to put his foot over the edge of insanity.

"It's time!" William excitedly announced again, oblivious to James's frustration.

"*Time?!*" James replied, sounding irritated and confused. "Time for *what?!*"

"Our plan!" William reminded him, still ignoring James's odd behavior.

"Oh, umm, yes … Yes, of course," James said, finally clearing his mind enough to make sense out of what William was talking about. "You found someone to play an original song then?"

"Yes, yes," William whispered. "Richard, of all people. I didn't much enjoy having to speak to him again after our debacle in his office. But he has a new piano piece that I talked him into playing, which didn't take much. I still know the old bastard well. A few glasses of Scotch and he's always ready to be the center of attention. Bring Lily along quickly. This will be our opportunity."

"Will do. Try to stall a moment until we get there."

"I will," William replied. He then headed to the library.

James definitely welcomed any excuse to get Lily away from Elijah. Fortunately, the brief interaction with William had allowed James's mind and body time to cool down a few degrees to retrieve Lily without resorting to the drunken brawl that likely would have ensued otherwise.

"Lily, William would like to see you in the library," James said while glaring at Elijah in a way that neutralized the smile on his face.

"Yessa'," she said, sitting her service tray down.

James gently took her arm and guided her through the crowd, glancing over his shoulder at Elijah with a look of disgust on his face. They arrived together in the library just in time for the mini concert Richard was about to bestow upon the awaiting guests. The song Richard planned to play began the sequence of events that would soon have Lily parked at the piano bench, bringing the room to silence, and prompting Tucker McCormick to make his rude drunken statement.

Despite the numerous glasses of Scotch that William had drowned Richard with, he was able to play his new piano piece quite skillfully, and there was a round of applause upon its completion. William then stepped forward to say a few words to his delighted guests. All his years of playing centerstage gave him a certain professional tone in his voice whenever he addressed a crowd. "For those of you who don't already know, this fine composer and dear friend of mine is Richard Wells. He is the director of the music department at Ohio University. It is a department that my lovely wife began raising money for many years ago with this very event while I was the director there. Emma began the fundraising efforts because, unfortunately, music is one of a few departments that receives very little money throughout the fiscal year. So, your donations here tonight will help to ensure that music will always be a part of Ohio University's curriculum. Every dime will be greatly appreciated by the school, by Richard, and of course, by all of the wonderful students, whose lives your money will directly impact."

The audience gave a brief applause in response.

"Speaking of Richard and all the students he has so brilliantly trained," William continued, waving his arm toward all of them. "If you find yourself in the mood for fine music, and you've never been to one of the many shows they put on throughout the year, I highly

141

suggest it. Richard has just given a small sample of one of the incredible pieces you might have the luxury of hearing while in attendance." William then glanced over at James, who gave a discreet nod in his direction, signaling that he and Lily had been present for Richard's entire song. William then returned to addressing the crowd. "The song Richard just played was quite splendid, wouldn't you all agree?"

Everyone in the room gave another round of applause. "Simply beautiful," an older lady from the crowd professed.

"Yes, simply beautiful indeed," William concurred. "Such a magnificent piece is certainly worthy of another listen, don't you think?"

"I'd be glad to play it again," Richard replied, still eager to be the center of attention.

"Ahh, no need," William replied, dismissing him with a wave of his hand. "I have a very special guest here tonight, and I'd much rather hear her rendition of your beautiful piece." He then turned toward his *special guest*. "Lily," William smiled. "Would you be kind enough to grace our ears with Richard's delightful song again this evening?"

Lily's mouth fell open but not a single word escaped. She knew nothing about this ploy and was never told in advance to be prepared for such a thing. Her heart immediately began to gallop as all eyes turned in her direction to scrutinize the face of the insignificant slave that they had looked right through all evening. Lily's eyes slowly surveyed the crowd in return as they began to whisper to each other about her. She assumed that they were probably criticizing the term that William had used to describe her. She had always felt that every man of William's status had not even considered her as human, let alone a *special guest*, especially at such an esteemed event. At all other gatherings, she was only ever used to being as transparent as the very wine glasses she was expected to keep filled. It was, therefore, instantaneously paralyzing to consider the prospect of being the center of attention.

James stood shoulder to shoulder with Lily in the tightly packed room and could feel her start to tremble as a bout of nervousness began ricocheting through her body. Without her needing to say a word, James gave her the reassurance she was looking for. He gently caressed her back and leaned in close to her ear. "It'll be alright, Lily. You can do this." She turned to look at him, and he could see the fear in her eyes. "I believe in you," James whispered, stroking the side of her arm softly.

Lily continued looking into James's eyes for a moment longer as she absorbed his words. She then nervously surveyed the crowd again, and finally turned toward William.

"Come, come, Lily. It'll be alright," William reassured her as he extended his hand toward her. James then parted the crowd with his arm so that she could step through more easily. William smiled at her as she began to weave through the crowd toward him. He took her by the hand once she was standing next to the piano. "Everyone this is…"

"Is this the *Negro girl* you told me about?" Richard asked, rudely interrupting.

William was instantly aggravated by the demeaning way in which the word *girl* rolled off of Richard's tongue. "Yes, this is *Lily*, the *young lady* I spoke to you about."

"Oh, come on, William! You don't really expect *her* to replay this piece, do you?" Richard fired back, a snobbish sneer on his face as he looked at Lily with disgust.

"Well, yes and no," William answered.

"What in the devil is that supposed to mean? Either she will or she won't," Richard scoffed, in his snotty proper dialect.

Despite their longtime friendship, William was always annoyed by the arrogance in Richard's tone. "Well, I don't think that's anything I can explain," William replied, glaring at Richard with equal disgust. William then turned to look at Lily and gestured with his hand toward the piano bench, inviting her to sit down. "Lily, the floor is yours," he said, wanting her to explain exactly what he meant, in a way that his words could not.

Lily sat down slowly while her eyes drifted across the sea of faces staring coldly back at her. She thought that she would never be able to focus on such an insurmountable task while sitting in the center of the room alone, feeling like a sheep surrounded by lions. But she suddenly found a pair of striking blue eyes in the crowd that were tenderly gazing at her. As always, James's gaze instantly gave her the comfort and peace that she needed. And, as always, she found it nearly impossible to turn away from him. *I believe in you*, she could hear him saying again in her mind as she gazed back at him. Those four words had resonated far deeper in her than he probably realized. The impact suddenly made her feel as though she was born to command crowds with the grand instrument before her.

James nodded at Lily as another small gesture of his support. His nod finally broke her trance. Lily nodded back and then exhaled. With her body and mind now relaxed, she closed her eyes and began. From the very first strike of the piano keys, the submissive mannerisms typical of a slave faded away from Lily and gave way to the elegant dances of a woman who had just been freed. Gracefully, she swayed through the delicate notes of the song. Harshly, she pounded the keys through the portions that were more aggressive. Her theatrics made it seem as though Lily had morphed into another person altogether. Her closed eyes and the expressions on her face made it clear that she had mentally transported herself into another world. Her mental world was far more beautiful than the one in which Richard was currently glaring at her with disgust and envy for the way she was easily replicating his song in her own unique way. William snickered at the look on Richard's face, then turned and smiled proudly at Lily, just as James was currently doing. In fact, James could not bear to take his eyes off of her, much like everyone else in the room.

The precision of Lily's memory proved to be uncanny, as usual. She could have easily replayed Richard's complicated song note for note. But her musical instincts naturally motivated her to infuse an array of beautiful runs into the dull portions of his piece, bringing life to the blander verses. Her manipulation of the song created a sound that was uncommon to classical music. Eyes were unblinking, and mouths were agape as the crowd listened intently to a rhythm that was so foreign to the era. They seemed utterly hypnotized by not only her ability to mimic but by her spontaneous creativity and brilliance. It was that particular authenticity that gave clarity to Richard's question in a way that William felt his words could not. It was also the sole quality that William had hoped Lily would share with all the men who had denied her the opportunity to work for them as a musician.

William proved to everyone how easily Lily could replay a piece she had never heard, but he also knew that she was not just restricted to copying the play of others. It had recently become William's ritual to play piano with Lily every morning. He had since learned that dozens of songs were alive in Lily's genius mind. Many of her songs were born from a wide array of her life experiences, from the sweet memory of her little turtle, to the simple light and airy emotions she felt when listening to birds sing, to deep and heartfelt arrangements inspired by the trauma of past pains. William was well aware of that side of Lily's talent but wanted to bring that to light later when he felt it was more necessary. For now, he wanted to win over his former colleagues with her innate ability to memorize, improvise, and manipulate the most difficult arrangements, as if it were child's play. However, he would be forced to wait and see in the days that followed whether or not her crowd-silencing, flawless performance had done just that.

Chapter Nine

Slave Code
Article V Section II
Any free Negro intermarrying with any white person shall become a slave for life, and any white man or woman intermarrying with any Negro shall become a servant for seven years, to be disposed of at the discretion of the court.

William sat in his den with his hands clasped together on top of his desk. He was as still as a stone statue, staring blankly across the room at nothing in particular. His frustrations were rampant on his mind and had cast him into a hypnotic trance of sorts. He had not even gotten up the energy to play piano alongside Lily this particular morning, which was something they had both come to look forward to on a daily basis.

"William, you alright?" James asked, after stepping into his den unannounced. The fact that he just woke up was apparent by his scratchy voice and his disheveled hair. He had not been awakened early by the sound of piano music as he had in the previous weeks. "I saw Lily in the kitchen a moment ago, but she said she hadn't seen you this mornin'."

William was still silent and continued staring blankly at nothing. By his lack of reaction, James wondered if he had even heard him at all. Out of the blue, William finally spoke, but it was like he was talking to an imaginary person in the room. "Why does it matter so much to people?" he asked, still not bothering to look in James's vicinity.

James was confused for a moment but then realized that William was not replying to his question. "Why does what matta'?"

"*Who* we are? I just don't understand it. Why does it matter so much to people?" William finally blinked for the first time since James entered the room. He then turned to look at James with puzzled eyes, like he hoped that he really did hold the answer to his question.

"William, I'm sorry, but I'm not followin' you," James replied, trying to make his groggy mind comprehend where he was going with the statement.

William got up from his chair and walked over to a wall that had a portrait of his deceased wife hanging on it. When he looked at her, images of his wedding day began erupting in his mind. He suddenly closed his eyes to see it more vividly, hoping to feel like he was reliving the day all over again. He opened his eyes when the imagery faded and said with great reluctance, "Let's face it, James, nobody is going to be bold enough to pay to see a Negro woman perform." William still did not dare to remove his eyes from his beautiful wife's picture. "It doesn't matter how phenomenal she is, all people will ever care about is *who* Lily is."

William's natural jubilant outlook was undoubtedly absent. It was the first time that James had ever heard defeat in his voice. He suddenly worried that William was truly on the verge of giving up for good this time. Giving up easily was something he never would have expected from a man like William; however, James understood where his doubts were coming from. It had been well over a week, and not one single guest from the fundraiser had bothered to offer Lily a chance to breathe life into their venues, the way William was confident she could. Despite her talent, it seemed that nobody was willing to overlook *who* she was.

"But..." William began.

"But what?" James replied.

"There is something in me that just won't allow me to give up," William confessed, his eyes still transfixed on his wife.

His words were something James understood all too well. That same unexplainable *something* had been swirling inside of him since the moment he found out that Lily could play. "I know exactly how you feel. But what do we do now?"

"Since the bigger concern for people is about *who* they are paying to see perform, I do have another idea," William continued.

It was then that James finally felt himself awaken fully. William may have sounded down, but James appreciated that his willpower to help Lily was still thriving.

"Will you talk to Lily about something for me?" William asked.

"Sure, of course. Anything."

William asked James to close the door and then proceeded to explain what he had in mind.

* * * *

Not long after his conversation with James, William sat down near the tombstone of his beloved wife, Emma. He had buried her on his estate next to her cherished garden, so that she would never be too far away from him. When she was alive, Emma had truly been William's best friend and most loyal confidant. They told each other everything, never holding back about even the darkest of secrets. Even after her death, confiding in his wife was a ritual that William refused to part ways with. Every Sunday, he would sit on a stone bench near her tombstone and talk aloud to her about everything on his mind. This particular Sunday, he admitted being angry about the fact that the color of skin was superseding the talents of a woman whom he felt was far superior to him on the piano.

The fact that William was one-of-a-kind in a world that judged heavily on complexion and status was the quality that Emma found the most endearing about him when they first met. William's efforts to abolish slavery, and his compassion for people from all walks of life, immediately earned her love and respect, especially since his passions, beliefs, and desires were similar to hers. As a united front, they worked together to help obliterate popular degrading immoral practices in America. Their philanthropic quest strengthened their bond and ignited a blissful romance that led to marriage and the birth of their two sons.

After thirty-five years of marriage, Emma became seriously ill. It was then that William retired from Ohio University. He wanted to spend every day by his wife's side, trying all that he could to get her well. But his efforts were in vain. For two years, he watched as a bizarre illness slowly withered the love of his life away into only a shell of a person. But day after day, William was there to tend to her needs and talk with her about the most memorable moments of their lives. Despite him sharing such beautiful stories, the memories of the life they had built together faded away from Emma's mind completely, along with the mental burdens of the dark secrets in her life that she had openly shared with William throughout the years. It was a painful thing for him to witness and even harder for him to accept. But, at the very moment that Emma drew her last breath, William was there holding her hand, tearfully telling her how much he loved her, and thanking her for all the years of joy she had brought into his life.

Even after two years, the death of his beloved wife was still just as fresh to William as the day she passed away. It caused him to lose his zest for life and destroyed his desire to write, play, and even listen to music. It was the sole reason why William was so reluctant to assist when James first approached him for help. But the passion with which James spoke about Lily quickly changed his mind. It reminded him of the passion that he always exuded whenever he talked about Emma. That factor alone persuaded him to find the strength to assist a young lady who sparked such emotion from a man.

The morning after Lily's arrival was William's very first day back on the piano since his wife's passing. At the time, he felt like he had to push himself to strike every key. But it was not long after working with Lily that he found that dark hole between music and his desire to play starting to fill itself. As the hole began to fill, William was suddenly overcome by the feeling that everything that had happened in his life was for a much grander reason. He began to believe that his musical ability, his job at Ohio University, and his unique marriage had all finally led him to his ultimate purpose: dedicating the last years of his life to helping present one of God's precious gifts to the world. If Lily so chose, William was suddenly willing to risk all that he had, including his life, to do just that.

In many ways, William felt that helping Lily would be a way to honor his wife and her strong opposition to slavery. He truly believed that it would be people like Lily that could lead the misguided to see that Negros were worthy of far more than a life of oppression, that it would be people like her that would slowly drive the world to be a place where no other human would have to be ashamed of the skin they were born in, the way Emma had always dreamed. William was not foolish enough to think that Lily would single-handedly put an end to hatred or slavery, but he certainly believed, much like James, that people were not handed special gifts from God without purpose. He believed that Lily was one of many special humans that God would send in His good name to assist in mending a broken society. Simply put, William was convinced that Lily and her unique gifts were invaluable to the world. So, despite the current frustrations that he was sharing with his beautiful wife, there was not an ounce of him that thought to give up. In William's mind, doing so would be parallel to giving up on God's request for his help.

It was all of those matters that William sat speaking to his wife about on this Sunday to help ease his mind. And ease him it did, but more so because of how strongly he always felt the presence of Emma's spirit there with him in the midst of her extravagant flower garden. William could easily sit there with her for hours and even then find it nearly impossible to walk away. Before summoning the strength to leave, he would always place a handful of fresh, pure white *lilies*—Emma's favorite flower—in a marble vase near her headstone. In William's mind, the coincidence of the name of his wife's favorite flower was yet another sign that helping *Lily* was truly a part of his destiny. After arranging the bouquet neatly, William kissed his hand and touched it to his wife's tombstone. "I love you, Em," he whispered as his tears dripped down onto one of her precious *lilies*.

* * * *

"I hate to break it to ya', but you won't find Wilbur anywhere out here," James said to Lily, picking up a rock and skipping it across the lake on William's plantation. He had quietly walked up behind her as she stood there alone staring out at the water. He had not startled her, though; she had sensed his presence long before he said a word.

"Ol' Wilbur. World's fattest turtle," Lily replied, a smile creeping onto her face.

"What did you expect? You gave that turtle more crickets in a day than he could eat in a lifetime," James reminded her.

"I can't help that I's always betta' at catchin' crickets than you," she teased. "You still had a small hand in fattenin' 'em up too, ya' know … *very* small, I might add."

"I admit, I could neva' hold a candle to the greatest cricket catcher alive."

They both laughed lightly afterwards. Their lighthearted banter made James realize how much he had missed this playful side of Lily.

James's silence in the previous weeks was partly due to his effort to keep the secret about the true mission of their journey. But majority of it had to do with him feeling overwhelmed with where to begin again with Lily after so many rocky years between them. He could easily sense Lily's discomfort whenever she was in his presence; it made him even more anxious about what he could possibly say that would ease the tension between them. He was, therefore, glad that William had requested for him to speak to Lily. It finally gave him a good reason to force himself to overcome his apprehension and approach her. So far it seemed that he had chosen the right topic to begin with. He was happy to see how receptive Lily was to his initial comment about Wilbur and even happier to know that he, for once, had given her a reason to smile. Such a simple thing had instantly uplifted him and eased his nervousness.

But Lily's smile would not last for long. She turned back toward the water and folded her arms across her chest after their shared memory. "May sound strange, but I sho' do miss my ol' friend," she said, continuing to stare out into the water. The smile faded from her face, and she was serious all over again. Her tone of voice and her body language told James that she had put the brick back into place that he had just taken down from the protective emotional wall she had erected around herself.

James slid his hands into his pockets, the way he always did when he felt uneasy. He was silent for a moment while he stared at the profile of Lily's face. "Me too," he admitted, knowing full well they were no longer speaking about their old turtle.

The sound of Lily's voice, her laughter, and the sight of her smile were things that had not faded from James's memory while he was away at school. Their playful banter immediately reminded him why he had desperately missed such small sentimental things while they were apart. It further motivated him to finally put an end to this extreme awkwardness between them. One by one, he was ready to carefully begin removing the bricks from Lily's protective emotional wall. He quickly thought of something to say before the cement cured around the brick she had just put back into place. "This is the second time I've seen you standin' here at the lake this week. Where's your mind run off to when you're out here all by yourself?" he asked, turning to stare out at the lake along with her.

Lily was surprised that James actually had an interest in her thoughts. It caught her a little off guard and made her hesitant to speak at first. She bought a little time for herself by wandering over and plucking a leaf off of a nearby tree. "You'd just laugh if I told ya'," she finally thought to say.

"Try me."

Again, Lily hesitated. "Well, wheneva' I'm tryna let my mind escape from my troubles, I always daydream about what it'd be like to..." She stopped, suddenly feeling that maybe her intimate thoughts were not something she should share, especially with James.

"To what? Please, go on."

"I-I ain't neva' said these things out loud before. Don't know how foolish it might sound."

"Your innermost thoughts and secrets are safe with me."

"Promise you won't laugh?"

"You have my word, Miss Lily."

There was something endearing about the way James added "Miss" to her name. She liked it. Lily looked over at him a moment, hesitated again, but then decided she would trust him with her thoughts on this occasion. She was too nervous to gaze at him while speaking, though, so she turned back toward the water. "Well, I daydream about what it'd be like to walk into town wearin' one 'a them real pretty summa' dresses, totin' me a purse. Nothin' fancy, ya' know, just be nice to have one to carry my things," she said, nervously fiddling with the leaf in her hand. "Anyway, I walks into one 'a the stores to buy me some groceries, and some 'a the town's white folks are in there, and they actually smile at me when I walk past 'em. Some of 'em even stop and talk to me 'bout things goin' on in they lives and such. Even the clerk asks me how I been doin' when I get to the counta' and hand 'em my money. We chat for a moment, then he smiles and wishes me well. He even tells me to come back soon when he gets done givin' me my change.

"I walk outside in the fresh air afta'wards and start makin' my way back home. I look up and it ain't a cloud in the sky. It ain't too hot and it ain't too cold, so I decide to take my time walkin'. All the way home, I'm passin' one white person afta' anotha', but they don't run off and find the sheriff, they don't ask to see my papers, they don't sic no dogs on me, or look around to see if my masta' is nearby keepin' watch ova' me. They simply wave, or smile, or ask, 'how do you do?' like it ain't nothin' to see a Negro woman walkin' down the road in a summa' dress, totin' a purse, and an arm full 'a groceries.

"Then I finally get back to my house. It ain't a big house … but it's *home*. I get my groceries out and start fixin' dinna'. By the time I get finished I…" she paused, feeling a little embarrassed to continue.

"Go on. Then what?" James asked, truly eager to hear what was hidden in her thoughts.

Lily nervously fiddled with the leaf in her hand again. "Then I hear my husband comin' up to the house on his horse," she continued, smiling sheepishly. "I walks on outside and wait for 'em on the porch. He gets off his horse, walks up the steps, and hugs and kisses me like he ain't seen me in years, even though he only been off workin' for a few hours." Her smile broadened like she could feel his arms around her. "I pour 'em some lemonade that I just made fresh, and then he sits on the porch swing with me, wraps his arm around me, and asks me 'bout my day. I tell 'em how I been into town, and 'bout all the folks I seen and talked to, and how nice everybody was to me. We sit there talkin' and laughin' 'til we see our children runnin' home in the distance. We stand up and watch 'em racin' each otha' down the dirt path. But they ain't runnin' away from no dogs, or no evil men chasin' 'em, or worried 'bout a sheriff gettin' 'em … 'cause the day I brought 'em into the world, they was free. Me and my children ... we *free*. They don't know nothin' about chains, and auction blocks, o-or worryin' 'bout bein' sold away from they family, or runnin' for they lives. They's just runnin' home from the schoolhouse as fast as they little legs'll carry 'em, 'cause they miss they mama and daddy ... And that's the *only* worry they eva' known in they little lives."

James was totally silent when Lily finished. There was nothing but the sound of leaves in the surrounding trees rustling in the wind for what felt like an eternity to Lily.

"Foolish thinkin', ain't it?" Lily asked, feeling uncomfortable with the silence.

James could not look at her for fear that the tears her story had stirred in him might actually fall. "Not in the least, Miss Lily. Not in the least."

After listening to Lily, James found himself viewing the world from a different perspective, just as he had so many times in the past. It gave him such insight, not only into her mind, but into the mind of a slave and how something so simple could mean so much to them. James's tears had begun to surface knowing that the pretty dress, the simple purse, and even the home were things he could easily pay to give Lily. But a Negro walking down a road free of chains and being greeted by *every* white person with a smile or a 'how do you do?' had a price tag labeled IMPOSSIBLE! It bothered James deeply to know that it was a luxury he could never afford to give Lily. Not only that, but he knew that her freedom rested in the hands of a man who would surely die first before allowing her to have such a thing.

Despite the reality of how sad the story was, James still admired the simplicity of Lily's dreams, and that she was a woman who was never impressed by extravagance. She had not daydreamed of a faraway vacation, a trip to a stage play, or even a lavish home. She simply wanted to go to a store alone in town and be greeted with kindness and return to her simple home to prepare an intimate meal for the family she loved.

Although he could not empathize with Lily about how grand it would be to walk to a store, James certainly understood and shared the part of her dream about having a family to come home to. In his dream, Lily was the *only* woman he had ever imagined as his wife and the mother of the children he desperately wanted with her. Quite often, he had envisioned their little ones with dark curly hair, their mother's lovely skin tone, and her beautiful sparkling eyes. His dreams lived on despite learning that not only did his father forbid such unions, but so too did the laws. So, while listening to Lily's story, James could not help but wonder the identity of the man who had the honor of calling himself her husband and the father of her children. The thoughts were starting to weigh him down. He wanted to change the subject and think no more about the complexities that stood as an enormous wall between himself and a woman who unknowingly owned all of his heart, a woman that he had no regrets about giving it to either, despite what his father and any unjust laws had to say about it.

James cleared his throat before speaking again to be sure that Lily did not hear any emotional breaks in his voice. "The piano. I assume you escape there too in times that you're feelin' down?" he asked her, trying to steer the conversation in another direction.

Lily nodded. "I don't know what I'd've done without it all these years. All my tears, my worries, my fears, and my pain, I lock 'em all up in songs to help ease my troubled mind. Just don't know what I'd've done without it," she reiterated, her voice trailing off as she dug deep in her mind for what the alternatives may have been.

"I don't know how you do it. Don't matta' how much time my mama spent trainin' me on that thing, I ain't neva' see that piano 'a hers as nothin' more than a pine box with ivory keys. It ain't neva' make any sense to me. None whatsoeva'."

"So many things in the world don't make no sense to me. Don't make no sense how I can be a human who thinks, talks, senses, feels, and even loves, just like everybody else. But just 'cause I's born in a darker wrapper than white folks, I'm treated like an animal. Long as I live, I'll neva' unda'stand that. The only thing in my whole life that's eva' made complete sense to me is the piano. It ain't nothin' I can explain." Lily shrugged her shoulders. "Somehow it just does."

Again, Lily had infused James's mind with a different point of view. He had never even considered that a slave would think of themselves on the level of an animal. At times, he found it too difficult to hear of such things, especially after the way he had treated Lily before departing for Ohio University. He was not yet ready to face all that he had done, so he was sure to continue steering the conversation into safer territory. "So, how did it feel? The otha' night, I mean, playin' in front 'a all those people?"

"I love playin' the piano and all, and I usually feel so at peace, but that night I ain't neva' felt so terrified in all my life with all them people lookin' at me. There wasn't nothin' peaceful about it. Thought my heart was gonna beat its way outta my chest. But then…" she paused, remembering what James had said to her before she sat down to play. "Somehow I found the strength to get through it. But when it was all ova' and wasn't nobody clappin' like they was for that Richard fella', I-I didn't really know what to think. But even if nobody else cared for it, I's proud 'a myself, 'cause I knew I put all my heart into that song," she admitted, once again remembering the four words that James had whispered to her that ignited such motivation.

"Well, I'm quite certain the reason they didn't react had nothin' to do with you playin' badly. I think they just couldn't make any sense of it, Lily. I know I couldn't at first and neitha' could William. Hell, I think most folks would have to live four lifetimes 'fore they eva' meet somebody again who's capable of what you do. So, I don't think you can blame everybody for bein' in a state 'a shock. Personally, I think everybody was amazed by you, but they just didn't know how to show it, or maybe they were just flat out afraid."

"I guess that makes sense."

James picked up a rock. "That audience may have been hesitant, but there's certainly one person who ain't afraid to tell me how he feels about you," he said, skipping the rock across the lake.

"Who's that?"

"William. He's mighty fond 'a you, ya' know? You're all he eva' talks about. He goes on and on for hours about you sometimes."

Lily smiled. She had grown close to William rather quickly during their morning piano sessions. "I really like Mr. William too. He's been awfully kind to me. I bet all his students at that fancy school really loved 'em too. You just can't help but love a man like him."

Hearing how Lily felt about William, James turned toward her, finally feeling ready to ask what William had sent him there for. "Lily, I need to ask you somethin'," he said, suddenly sounding very serious.

The way James was looking at her suddenly made her nervous. "Is something wrong?"

"No. Not at all. You rememba' Anna Mae and Ben tellin' you about William bein' an orchestra conducta' and composa', and about how he's performed all ova' the United States?"

"Of course."

"Well, William told me today that, for the first time in years, he's wantin' to put on anotha' concert. He misses bein' onstage a lot, and well…" James paused a moment to be sure that the next thing he was about to say came out the way he wanted. "Well, he was wonderin' how you'd feel about lettin' 'em use your music for his show? He said he'd write all the accompaniment for the rest 'a the orchestra and conduct the show, but he wants every song that's played to stem from your personal collection."

Lily's astonishment was apparent by the look on her face. She was stunned that a man of William's caliber would ever consider using her material. "He wants to use *my* music?" she asked in disbelief.

"He sure does. He thinks many 'a the arrangements he's already heard you play are phenomenal. He's confident that everyone else would say so too. So, what do ya' think?"

"I think I..." Lily's bewilderment caused her words to get lost in her mind. "I think I find that nearly impossible to believe."

"Believe it. He asked me to ask you just this mornin'."

"B-but I don't know how to write the music I hear in my mind. I only know how to play it," she replied, feeling a bit embarrassed about that fact. She sheepishly turned to stare out at the water again, wondering how she would ever pull off such a feat.

"Well, you wouldn't have to worry about that."

"I wouldn't?"

"No," James assured her.

"Well, why not?"

James walked in front of Lily and blocked her view of the lake to be sure it was he who held her attention. "Because it's *you* that he wants to play the piano durin' the entire show."

Lily's heart immediately began to pound mercilessly against her chest, pumping fear into every inch of her body. "*Me?* H-how would I eva' be able to do that? Wouldn't nobody eva' let somebody like me play in a..."

"Don't you worry about that, eitha'," James interrupted, already knowing exactly what she was thinking. "William has a way."

"But how? Th-this wouldn't just be some gala in the middle 'a William's library. I mean, th-this would surely be a huge audience, right? In an elaborate theata'? I-I just, I don't unda'stand how it would eva' be possible," she rambled, trying to spit out every question that had overtaken her mind all at once. "Is he certain this is what he'd wanna do?"

"I unda'stand that you probably have a million questions, but the only thing you need to worry yourself about for now is whetha' or not you're willin' to play by William's side. Let William handle the rest."

Lily's mind continued racing, and her eyes were darting nervously from place to place, as if she would somehow find the answers lying in front of her. Recalling Tucker McCormick's rude statements and everyone else's lackadaisical response after her performance suddenly had her doubting herself. "I-I just don't know about this. M-maybe William should get someone else. I don't think I can…"

"Lily, wait, please just listen to me a moment," James interrupted, wanting to stop her before she could continue to talk herself out of it. He then took her gently by the shoulders to help calm her. "Lily, please look at me." He proceeded to talk again when she finally relaxed enough to look at him. "William couldn't possibly conceive of anotha' person he'd ratha' have the honor of sharin' the stage with," he explained. "Because it was *you* who inspired him to perform again."

Lily did not respond at first, but her face certainly expressed how moved she was by his statement. She slowly pulled away from James's grip and turned toward the lake again, feeling the sudden need to be comforted by the glistening waters, just as she always had been as a child.

"Trust me," James said, walking up behind her. "If you say yes to this, it would mean the world to William."

"Forgive me if I'm outta place for sayin' this, but I know the fact that you brought me here to meet William, and everything else that's been happenin', ain't all been some kinda coincidence. I just … I don't unda'stand. Why you doin' this for me?" she asked softly, a little fearful of his answer.

160

James stepped in front of her, blocked her view of the lake again, and waited for her to look at him. Lily was slow in doing so, but when she did, he answered with the sincerest tone in his voice. "'Cause I've been inspired by you too, Lily. Have been since the day I heard you playin' my mama's piano," he admitted. "The way you play and seein' all that you're capable of without eva' havin' had help from anyone … It's truly remarkable."

Feeling moved yet again by his words, Lily closed her eyes and said nothing in return. She just wanted to hear it echoing again in her mind.

"Listen, I know all 'a this may seem surreal, and maybe you're a little afraid. I can unda'stand that," James continued. "So whetha' you decide to play with William or not is completely up to you of course, but…"

"But what?"

"I'd give everything I have to see you up there on that stage with William. You're amazin' Lily. And if you decide this is what you wanna do, come hell or high wata', I'll be damned if I eva' miss a minute."

After having lost her belief in James's ability to say anything kind to her, Lily stood there speechless again. She assumed that she was bound to wake up at any moment, that the things she was hearing were only possible in her dreams.

"But ultimately, it's all up to you," James continued.

"I thank you kindly for your words, I really do. It means more to me than you'll eva' know," Lily finally managed to say, staring at James as if the man she knew him to be years ago had finally reappeared before her very eyes. "But this is all so unexpected, and I really don't know what to say."

"I see," James replied, a twinge of disappointment evident in his tone. "I completely unda'stand your reservations. But will you at least take the time to think about it a while before you make a permanent decision, and then let us know?"

"Yes. I promise I will."

"Take your time, okay?"

"Okay."

Despite his overwhelming desire to spend the rest of the day by Lily's side, talking and rebuilding the broken bridge between them, James figured it would be best to give her time to think things through alone. So, he forced himself to walk away, leaving Lily to contemplate the outcome of her future for the first time in her life.

As James walked away, Lily thought about the fact that Auntie was the only person who had ever heard her play piano up until a few weeks ago. For Lily, music had been a simple thing that brought her comfort, joy, and a means of escape. But now, here her music was being praised by one of the world's finest composers, with the chance to be unburied from the secret world of her mind and heard by thousands. Lily had never once given thought to the idea of that level of vulnerability, nor considered the impact, or how it might make her feel. Contemplating it all had momentarily ceased her ability to give even the simplest reply, until one thing came rushing back to her mind. "James!" she called out before he had gotten too far.

He stopped immediately and turned around. "Yes?"

Lily took a moment before she spoke again. "Do you really believe in me?" she finally asked, staring nervously at the little leaf she still held in her hand.

James walked back over and stood in front of her once again. This time, he placed his hand underneath her chin and gently raised her head toward him. "With all my heart," he replied, gazing deep into her eyes.

That was all Lily needed to hear.

Chapter Ten

Slave Code
Article II Section XII

Any person convicted of assisting a slave by advice, donation, transportation, loan, or otherwise in any way cause them to be deprived from their master, shall pay damages to said master to be adjudged by the justices of the provincial court or shall spend up to one year in jail.

William had been certain after his wife's death that he would never again return to playing the piano, let alone the stage. But in this special instance, he felt as though his return would serve a very prodigious purpose. If people were not motivated to come and see a Negro woman play, who ironically surpassed his capabilities, then his belief was that perhaps they would flock to see William Werthington's grand return to the stage. William was not the arrogant type, but after decades of being regarded as one of the world's greatest classical musicians, he knew that his name alone held lots of power. During his years on the circuit, William had never played to anything less than packed theaters, which often had to add shows just to accommodate the demands to see him. He was such a well-respected composer that his sheet music remained in high demand, well after his retirement. It was even a main staple in many schools and was played a world over by other professional orchestras. Knowing those facts, William wanted to take advantage of his fame and the revered

Werthington name, in hopes of convincing people to see a show that in actuality belonged to an indentured woman.

But using the famous Werthington name to attract an audience only resolved one of a few problems that William and James felt they had. During his discussion with James in his den, William realized the grave mistake he was making where Lily was concerned. He and James both had this magnificent dream for her to become a professional pianist, but they never once bothered to ask her what musical aspirations she had, if any. James and William both agreed that putting Lily on the spot at the gala without her permission was wrong. They now realized that forcing her to play piano in a show was no different than them playing her master and continuing to make her submit to them as their slave, which, ironically, was the role that James had literally gone out of his way to remove her from.

To begin trying to atone for his mistakes, William wanted to first find out what Lily's musical desires were. He wanted to know if she would allow *him* the honor of sharing the stage with *her*. He wanted that decision to be hers alone and not something she ever felt forced into doing. If she had no interest in performing, William was ready to humbly accept her decision and simply live with the honor of having met a woman of her brilliance. But if Lily desired to share her musical talent with the world, then it was *he* who was ready to submit himself to *her*.

With that knowledge, James had set out to speak to Lily about the prospect of performing her music with William live onstage. With the news James delivered to him later that evening, William was pleased to hear that he would indeed have the honor of helping Lily carry her musical dreams to any place in the world she wished. He silently pledged his devotion to her dreams for as long as there was still air in his lungs.

The second problem William faced was that he had no orchestra to play the accompaniment for Lily's symphony. So, he set out to resolve that matter by returning to Ohio University. This time, however, it was not Richard he wished to speak with. William had only retired a few years prior, so he was certain that many of the students he taught still remained at the school. He went in search of his best musicians and found eighteen of them. Knowing that students often struggled with finances and food, he took them all out to dinner. As they ate, he explained his current musical plight. All was received well by the hungry brood until William mentioned Lily, whom they all remembered from the fundraising gala. When William heard the students' predicted reluctance, he quickly mentioned the substantial amount of money he was willing to pay them for their assistance. For the band of impoverished students, suddenly, reluctance was no longer an issue. After they all agreed to participate, William insisted that they whisper nothing about the show to anyone. He gave them each a small down payment to ensure their silence and assured them that they would receive the rest of the money upon completion of the show.

With Lily and her orchestra secured, the only matter that remained for William was ensuring that he had a suitable venue for them to perform in. But he was confident that the solution to that problem would soon be arriving at his home.

Chapter Eleven

Slave Code
Section V Article XII

Be it enacted that slaves and free Negroes are exempt from the right to dispense medication. Selling, preparing, and/or administering medicine shall result in a public whipping, not to exceed twenty stripes.

James stormed into the kitchen frantically opening and slamming kitchen drawers without saying a word. Lily stopped preparing lunch and looked at him like he had lost his mind. "What on God's green Earth is wrong with you?"

"Nothin'!" James spat. He had his hand balled up in a fist, clutching it to his chest.

Lily looked down and saw blood collecting on his shirt. "Lemme see." She stopped him, turned his hand over, and gasped. "That sho' don't look like *nothin'* to me! You done just about sliced your hand off!" she exclaimed, after seeing the gaping wound he had accidentally sustained while handling a splintered piece of wood.

"It's not that bad!" James retaliated, trying to convince himself of that.

"Sit yo'self down!" Lily commanded, shoving him into a chair.

James was calm while Lily searched for some first aid products, but then lost his wits again when he saw what she put on the table. "I don't need that!" he objected, nearly falling out of his seat as he quickly

166

backed away from the table. He was referring to a bottle of the same solution that he had used on Lily's knee after she had fallen from their old tree as a kid. James had always hated the sting and the burn that lasted long after it was applied.

"I do believe it was *you* who once insisted that this was necessary to keep from gettin' infections," Lily reminded him as she shook the bottle up.

Knowing he had no argument against her, James blew out a breath of frustration and pouted like a spoiled child.

"You always were like a scared little cat when it came to this stuff. Your mama would find you halfway up a tree by the time she caught you to put it on," Lily teased.

"Well, I's just a kid then," James replied, yanking his hand away when Lily tried to grab it.

She rolled her eyes. "Mm-hmm, I can see how much things have changed," she said sarcastically, trying to stop his hand from moving.

"Well, I ain't up a tree," James pointed out, trying desperately to defend his cowardice.

"Not *yet* anyway," Lily joked. She finally grabbed a firm hold on his hand and used a pair of tweezers to pull out the large shards of wood that were still lodged in the wound.

"Ow!" James kept grunting as each piece came out.

"What in the world y'all doin' out there anyway?" Lily asked, referring to all the men she had seen hammering away at the wagonload of wood James had brought onto the plantation earlier in the morning.

"William hasn't told you yet?"

"Naw, he ain't said a word. We've been workin' nonstop on my music pieces."

"Well … Ow!" James yelled and flinched again. "Let's just say, I hope it's sturdy enough for your piano."

Lily suddenly stopped tending to James's hand and looked up at him with an expression on her face that he had a hard time reading. "You mean, y'all buildin' a stage?"

"We are."

For days, Lily had wondered what theater was ever going to let her be a part of a show along with someone as prominent as William. She now had her answer. "William wants the show to be here?" she asked.

"Right here on this very land," James replied.

Lily let go of his hand, stood up, and stared out the window. "Won't no otha' place be willin' to let me play, will they?" she asked, suddenly feeling like more of a burden than anything else. "He has to do it this way 'cause 'a me, don't he?"

"Lily," James said, trying to get her attention, but she still continued to look out the window. "Lily, look at me, please." When she finally turned toward him, he could tell by her expression that she felt horrible about all the extremes William was going through on the count of her. "William *wants* to do this," he emphasized. "And don't you believe anything else, ya' hear?"

"He's right," William said, appearing in the kitchen doorway, startling them both. He approached Lily and held both of her hands. "And I'd have them build ten stages if that's what it took to have the honor of standing up there alongside you."

"William," Lily whispered appreciatively. It was the only word she could seem to find after being touched by his. The rest of her reply was in a single tear trickling down her face.

"But not eleven stages, though!" William suddenly joked, a silly tone in his British accent. "No, no, I'm afraid you aren't worth that many!" he teased, as he so often did with Lily. He instantly turned her tears into a burst of laughter the way he had hoped. His joke was actually more of an effort to halt his own tears. But Lily suddenly hugged him tight, making the fight to hold his tears back just a little harder.

William pulled back from Lily's hug, smiled, and wiped away her remaining tears. "I don't need you to worry yourself over these trivial matters. I need only for you to bring your heart onto the stage that this young man is building for you," he said, glancing over at James, winking, and then turning his attention back to Lily. "Okay, my dear?"

Lily nodded. William then cleared the rest of her tears and left her and James alone again. When he was gone, Lily turned again to stare out the window in amazement at all the men busy hammering away at wood. She truly had no words to describe how she was feeling over what William was doing for her and for the fact that James had brought her there in the first place. She was so overwhelmed, she did not know where to begin in thanking them for gifts and opportunities she felt she could never match in return. Her music was all she had to give. She only hoped that within every note she played they would hear the depths of her immeasurable gratitude for the kindness they were bestowing upon her.

While Lily was pasted to the window watching the workers, James took the opportunity to weasel his way out of having his hand further tended to, in hopes he could avoid the solution he detested so much. "If we're gonna finish that stage on time, I need to get back out there," he said, turning to leave.

Lily quickly grabbed his arm. "I ain't nowhere near finished with you yet!" She shoved James back in his seat and sat down across from him. She grabbed the solution, dabbed it on the wound, and was surprised at how relatively calm he was in the process. She was even more shocked that he did not once flinch as she stitched the wound closed.

Calmness had quickly come over James when his attention drifted from his injury to Lily's angelic face while she diligently worked to mend his hand. Lost in a world of lovely thoughts about her, he was completely oblivious to pain. Lily looked up when she was finished and met his unblinking eyes. There was an intensity in the way James stared at her that ignited all of her nerve endings. The feeling was so intense that she could only hold a return gaze for a few seconds before she needed to escape. She jumped up abruptly and began digging around in a kitchen drawer to help ease the way she was feeling inside.

"Umm, m-maybe you should use these," she said, after finding a pair of gloves for James to use. She hoped that by the time she turned around, he had freed her from his sight. But she turned to find that she was still his visual prisoner. The way he gazed at her raised the heat within her another degree. She slowly walked back toward him, finally gathering the courage to fearlessly gaze at him in return.

James stood as Lily approached. Still gazing hypnotically at her, he reached for the gloves with one hand, while simultaneously taking hold of her wrist with the other. "Thank you," he said, never letting his eyes waver from her face. After snapping out of his trance, he finally let her hand go and proceeded to head back out to the field.

With his eyes off of her, Lily finally felt like she could breathe again. "James," she called out before he exited. He turned and enjoyed finding that he was still trapped in her sights. "Be careful, okay?"

"I will," James replied. He stared at Lily a moment longer before proceeding back out to the area of the field where he would soon have the chance to be entranced by her beauty yet again, but instead, while she was perched high above an audience, seated behind a grand piano, on a stage that he took great pride in building for her.

With the construction of the stage underway, the third and final problem on William's list had been resolved. If nobody would have Lily in their venues, then William simply wanted to build her one. He and James had worked together to design a beautiful outdoor amphitheater with the acoustic structure necessary for the music of an orchestra in mind. It would all be situated on the sprawling land of William's estate. The wood, the labor, the seats, the décor, the paint, and any other costs incurred were coming directly from William's very own pocket. Fortunately, the price tag for the project would do little to dent the enormity of his wealth. To the average person, it would have been an expensive undertaking, especially considering that William did not plan to charge a fee, at first, to any of the patrons who attended. Being able to help a woman of Lily's caliber, with the creation of a show that was all her own, was payment enough for William Werthington.

Chapter Twelve

Slave Code
Article I Section VI

Be it enacted, that any person whatsoever, who shall hereafter teach or cause
any slave or slaves to be taught to read or write, or shall use or employ any slave
as a scribe, in any manner of writing whatsoever, shall for every such offense,
forfeit the sum of one hundred pounds, current money.

March 1859

The preparations for the fundraising gala paled in comparison to
the efforts needed to prepare for Lily's upcoming musical
spectacular, which was set to be held at the very end of William's
Spring Extravaganza. The event was once another one of Emma's
favorite traditions. She used to invite families from all over Athens,
disguising the party as the welcoming of spring weather and the
coming of Easter. In actuality, it was her clever way of forcing people
from all walks of life to mix and mingle with one another, especially
children. It was Emma's lifelong passion to break down the invisible
social barriers in between class and race; she felt there was no better
way to achieve that than by luring a variety of colored faces to her
spring affair with music, games, food, and fine wine. After her death,
however, William had ceased the tradition; it was too massive an
undertaking for his broken heart to handle. But with a very specific
purpose in mind, William found the strength to revive the highly
anticipated event. There were now exactly three weeks left before that
beautiful celebration was to resume. Normally, that would have been

plenty of time for William and his pseudo family to prepare, but with the added element of Lily's show everyone was putting in overtime to meet the deadline. For weeks, everyone assisting knew nothing but long work hours, brief dinners, and very little sleep. The resulting exhaustion was evident on everyone's faces by the end of each day. But knowing the amazing feat they were trying to accomplish, there was not a single person who complained about the intense labor.

Typically, William was responsible for collecting wine, food, and setting up games, but this year Anna Mae and Ben took over his tedious to-do list since nearly all of William's time was dedicated to working with Lily. After having Lily choose eight songs from her mental archives to use in the performance, William taught her to read and write music. He also showed her the instruments that would be accompanying her piano melodies. He then taught her the basics of playing each. Lily quickly absorbed the knowledge with ease, far surpassing what he expected of someone after just a few weeks of lessons, or even years for that matter. In fact, Lily's musical instincts were unlike any other William had ever known, including himself. All aspects of music came as naturally to Lily as a baby's ability to suckle, further proving to William that music was clearly what she was born to do.

William and Lily had initially collaborated to create the background sounds that would enhance her piano melodies, but soon William was afforded the luxury of reveling in her accomplishments from afar. In a short amount of time, Lily had learned enough to write the majority of the accompanying pieces on her own. She was soaring under William's wing, not only because of the clarity of his instruction but also because of the way he caressed her spirit with fatherly affections.

James did not know much about music and could not offer Lily any assistance in that area of her life, but he took a great deal of pride in contributing to her grand cause by creating a masterpiece in the middle of William's land with his very hands. Even the serious injury

Lily had stitched did not stop him from working until his body nearly gave out at the end of every evening. He wanted to ensure that Lily's amphitheater was ready on time and done with artistic perfection.

Unbeknownst to James, the diligence of his efforts did not go unnoticed. Lily happened to glance out the window one afternoon while pouring herself a glass of lemonade. What she saw stole her attention to the point that she overfilled her glass. The mesmerizing visual kept her coming back to that window every afternoon since. Lily was drawn to the kitchen window for one thing only, or rather, one *man* only. Every afternoon, she hypnotically gazed at James as he worked without a shirt during the hottest part of the day. She was amazed to see that nothing more remained of his boyish body. His chiseled chest and abdominal muscles and well-defined arms were a sight she struggled to pull her eyes away from. Since the day she had taken notice, she had been creating new excuses during her rehearsal time with William to escape for short periods of time to watch James work. Some days her excuse was laundry, other days it was food or extended bathroom breaks. Lily was using any reason she could to delight her eyes with the sight of such a ruggedly handsome man.

Today, Lily's lie to William was thirst. As far as William knew, she had gone into the kitchen to pour herself some water. Instead of filling a glass, though, she was filling her eyes with the view on the other side of the window, where James and another man were carrying a large piece of plywood.

"Now I see why you were so thirsty," William teased, startling Lily, after he had quietly peered over her shoulder and saw why she was pasted to the window in a wide-eyed trance.

"Oh my God! Williaaam!" Lily smiled sheepishly. She then buried her face in her hands to hide cheeks that had flushed red with embarrassment. William put his arm around her and she laid her head on his shoulder as they laughed.

Moments after William and Lily headed back to the library, James stepped inside for a drink. He walked around the corner to see why the pair were giggling like school children, but they had returned to the song they were working on by the time he peeked in on them. James stood there recalling how Lily had sat looking dejected at his mother's piano just a few weeks prior, her tears coursing down onto the keys. Her emotional transition since then now made James the one who felt a need to shed a tear. James noticed that Lily always had a smile on her face whenever she was playing alongside her new mentor. He could hear the immense joy in her voice each time she spoke about the new ideas that she and William were considering for the show. Just hearing Lily's constant laughter as of late had made James's journey to find William so worth it. Her extreme jubilance made every blistering hot day and every aching muscle James endured while building her stage worth it as well. Her excitement fueled his strength to work from sunup to sundown. James was willing to do anything to see to it that this happy side of Lily never vanished again. And as James stood there secretly watching William interact with Lily now, he was convinced that William, too, would always go above and beyond to contribute to her joy.

"Thank you, William," James whispered softly, still peeking around the corner as Lily played with her smile firmly in place. James's words of gratitude were for the way that William treated Lily more like his daughter than just an ordinary friend. James felt forever in William's debt for allowing Lily to experience that sort of special affection for the first time in her life.

Ironically, though, the fatherly love and affection that William showered Lily with had assisted in creating a problem. Lily was living in a bubble of isolation, surrounded by people whose eyes did not seem to see in color. The warmth exuded from those around her began to give her a false sense of reality about how she might be perceived during the show. But she was soon about to be placed in a situation that would quickly readjust her perspective.

For the past few weeks, the student orchestra had worked separately on the pieces that Lily had written. Today, though, they arrived at William's home for their first rehearsal together. Lily had greeted them all at the door with enthusiasm, but the student's reception was nowhere near as warm. They chose not to shake her hand nor even give their names after she introduced herself. They left her standing in the foyer feeling foolish, quickly reminding her of how people from the outside world truly viewed her.

While waiting for William to return home from running an errand, Lily and the students all gathered in the library. They all sat quietly surrounding Lily at the piano like she was their prey. To Lily, their eyes felt like cold shards of ice burrowing holes into her skin, making the climate in the room feel like winter in the midst of the warm spring weather. However, when William finally arrived, their demeanors changed. Like a sergeant walking into the barracks of his misbehaving soldiers, William's presence instantly cured their nasty attitudes. From then on, the students all worked cooperatively for an hour or so. But the frigid winter conditions returned when William was called away briefly to tend to an issue in the house.

"Alright everybody," Lily commanded. "While William's out, let's just go ova' bar two on the third page right quick."

"We don't take no goddamn orda's from nigga's," Austin said, glaring at Lily while he twirled his timpani baton.

Lily just turned and stared back at the arrogant percussionist. She had already accepted that none of the student orchestra liked her, but she was hoping that they would all just continue to do as they had been paid to do ... in silence. She was already overwhelmed with show preparations, and she was not in the mood to deal with anyone's abhorrent behavior.

When Austin did not get the reaction out of Lily that he wanted, he continued pestering her. "I rememba' you from the fundraisin' gala, sittin' in here mimicin' Mr. Well's music like the little monkey you are."

Lily looked Austin up and down and scoffed. In her opinion, there was something about him that reeked of the need to feel superior over someone ... *anyone*. But Lily felt an equal need to let Austin know that that *someone* would not be her, not now ... not *ever*. She decided right then and there that she would not tolerate any disrespect from him, or anyone else in their group, without defending herself, despite any consequences.

"That was reeeal original." Lily squinted her eyes at Austin. "I bet you proud 'a yo'self for that one, ain't ya'? Go on and give yo'self a pat on the back, and when you're done, turn to page three," she demanded, her words briefly revealing the strong woman Lily truly was inside. Her true self had peeked through the crack in the cloak of meekness society had forced her to wear.

Lily's words instantly roused Austin from his cocky relaxed stance against the timpani. He stood tall with his chest out, ready to fire back. "Just 'cause y'ur workin' with someone like William, you think you can talk to a white man any kinda way now, do ya'?!"

Lily refused to respond, but Austin was relentless.

"How is it y'ur payin' William to teach ya' anyway, huh? You know you ain't got no goddamn money. So, go on and tell us..." Austin looked at Lily with scathing eyes and stepped closer. "Just how many times did you have to get down on y'ur knees and wrap those nigga' lips around William's cock to earn y'ur way?" he smirked.

Lily lowered her eyelids, rose from the piano bench, and fearlessly took two steps toward Austin too. "Far fewa' times than it's taken you to run through this song without messin' it up for everybody," she said, pure ice in her tone. Everybody in the room began to snicker at how slyly she had exposed the truth about him being their weakest link. He was the main reason they had been stuck rehearsing the same song for the last hour.

Lily's response wiped the smirk clean off Austin's face. "What the hell are all 'a y'all laughin' at?!" he fired at his bandmates. His face was red, and his hands suddenly gripped his batons tight. He and Lily stared each other down until William and James entered seconds later and instantly restored civility to the situation. William seemed oblivious to the climate in the room, but James immediately sensed the chill.

It had become James's routine to spend his lunch break in the library watching Lily and William rehearse together. Lily's childlike effervescence always refueled his energy. But with the presence of the orchestra, the stark change in Lily's demeanor was draining him instead. Sweat began to bead on James's forehead when he noticed that Lily's laughter no longer enveloped the room. The smile he looked forward to seeing was missing. Even the way Lily played her music told him immediately that something was wrong. When James read the expression on her face, his stomach clenched, and he set his plate aside, suddenly no longer interested in his meal. After continuing to watch for a while, the sick feeling in his stomach began to fester, until he could no longer handle sitting idly by. "Lily!?" he suddenly snapped. The way he barked her name caused everyone in the room to stop playing and turn in his direction. "Can I see you for a minute?"

Lily nervously looked around and then over at James. "Yessa'," she replied.

James cringed every time Lily referred to him as "sir," but even more so when she said it in front of others. For the moment, though, he did not correct her use of the word. He was too busy staring at the way she briefly locked eyes with Austin before she headed out into the hallway. Though brief as it was, their exchange spoke volumes to James. He glared at the troublemaking percussionist with questioning eyes as he held the door open for Lily and then stepped out into the hallway with her.

"Lily, what is it?" James asked her after closing the double doors.

"What do you mean?"

"Somethin's botherin' you. I ain't seen you like this in days. Now, tell me what the hell's goin' on in there."

"I don't know what you're talkin' about." She folded her arms up and looked away as she told her lie. "Ain't nothin' botherin' me." Her body language and the way she turned away confessed otherwise.

Even before Lily's silent confession, though, James was convinced that it was the percussionist who had upset her. But he was only partially right. It had not been Austin's words that directly affected her. Lily suddenly had the realization that Austin's thoughts would reflect the sea of people she was soon to sit centerstage in front of. Austin's words and actions had quickly forced her to remember that not everybody would be as warm as William. The whole ordeal made her realize that she somehow had to strengthen herself emotionally to prepare for the judgment and ridicule that were sure to go hand in hand with such a huge undertaking. The negative effect of that emotional preparation was written all over her face and was very easily read by James as he sat in the library. It was even more obvious to him now while standing only feet away from her. "You're not bein' forthcomin'," he said to her. "I know somethin' or *someone* is botherin' you!"

"I'm tellin' you the truth. I'm fine!"

"Are you sure? Because it doesn't look that way to me."

Lily thought for a moment to tell him her troubles, but with all that he and William had already done for her, she did not wish to burden them with small things. "I'm just tired is all. We've been workin' awful long hours to prepare."

"*Tired?* You're certain that's all it is?"

"Yessa'." She looked up at James and then quickly looked away again. "I-I'm certain," she lied.

James was ready to set Austin straight, and anybody else, if need be. But he did not press Lily any further for fear of upsetting her even more. "Well, listen, if you feel you need a break, don't be afraid to speak up, okay?"

"Yessa'. Thank you. I promise I will."

"Good."

"Well, everyone is waitin' for me, so I betta' get on back."

James nodded, and she proceeded to walk past him.

"And Lily…"

She stopped and turned back around.

"*James* … Please, I'd really like it if you'd only call me James from now on. No more 'a this *yessa'* and *no sa'* nonsense. It's not necessary, okay?" Although she had dropped the "master" and "sir" from time to time, he wanted to be sure it was permanent.

"Okay, I'll rememba' that." Despite how Lily was feeling inside at that moment, she forced a brief smile in appreciation for another one of James's wonderful gestures.

Lily's focus then quickly returned to the fact that she had to walk back into the library and sit amongst the wolves that had devoured her jubilant mood. When she returned, though, she felt an even greater tension in the room than before. Everyone, including William, stopped talking and stared at her. She lingered in the doorway, afraid to ask what she had just walked in on. She somehow knew from the lack of warmth in William's expression that something was seriously wrong. James walked up behind her just in time for both of them to hear the end of the heated conversation that had just taken place while they were absent.

"Figure it out, William! Or we walk!" Austin left William with those final words before he and the other students began packing their instruments to leave for the day, two hours before rehearsals were due to end. For the few minutes that she had stepped away, Lily's arch nemesis had finally found the position of superiority he was seeking. Austin had led the charge that caused every member of the orchestra to stomp out of the library. They all glared nastily at Lily on their way out.

"DAMN IT!" William yelled, slamming his hand on his grand piano, causing Lily to jump.

"What the hell just happened in here?!" James asked after everyone had filed out.

William had taken his spectacles off and was vigorously rubbing his eyes to soothe himself. "Lily, do you mind if I speak to James alone for a moment?" he asked, trying to sound like his usual gentle self, but she could easily hear the anger in his tone.

"Please, if you don't mind, I wanna know what's goin' on."

"Please, I really don't want to trouble you with such trivial things."

"I don't mean to ova'step my boundaries, but judgin' from what I just seen, it doesn't seem trivial at all. Please, I'm just as much a part 'a this as the both 'a you and I'd really like to know the truth," she said, wanting to strengthen her mind to the future harshness she was soon to endure.

William realized that Lily was right and that it was not wise to always shelter her from the cruelty of society. So, in honoring her wishes, he began to explain a more subtle version of how he had been blindsided by Austin with news that threatened to put an end to their chances of opening the show during the Spring Extravaganza as scheduled, or perhaps even at all.

"Well, before I even begin, let me apologize to you, Lily. It's so hard for me to say these things in front of you, but just know that they don't remotely reflect any of my beliefs."

"Of course, I know betta' than that."

With solemn eyes, William glanced at Lily again and then hung his head. He could not bear to look her in the eyes as he recounted what happened. "Well, if you must know, the students admitted to me that finally being here in the reality of this situation has opened their eyes to what they may be getting themselves into. They said they had not carefully considered all the risks that they were taking by performing with a Negro woman. They don't feel that any amount of money is worth bringing embarrassment or shame to themselves or their families by playing background to someone who was once enslaved. They told me that I needed to find a way for them to remain anonymous during the performance or that they would take the money I've already given them, yet not bother to fulfill the rest of their agreement." William spoke the whole time shamefully staring down at his desk.

Lily stood across the room expressionless and numb. She tried to repress it, but the feeling of being a burden began to weigh heavily on her again.

William suddenly began pacing around the room, aggravation apparent in his strides. "A symphony is not only about the music!" he erupted. "It's about the artistry of the instruments and performers dancing and swaying in unison! Taking that away destroys the visual appeal of the show. I know Lily is capable of extraordinary things, but the stage will seem empty and lifeless without the orchestra's visual participation. How am I to proceed without such a thing?!"

"You paid them! They agreed to this! They can't back out now!" James spat, anger drenching his tone. "We've been advertisin' for weeks and invitin' people from all ova' to see this! We can't possibly push this back to find a whole new orchestra now! What the hell do they expect us to do?!"

"They've asked for us to redesign the stage and possibly create some sort of barrier or simply add a curtain for them to sit behind. Of course, it can be done. But again, a symphony loses its elegance without their visual participation."

William and James continued to bicker about what to do. James had yet to lower his voice as he spoke of forcing the students to do as they agreed. William, in turn, paced back and forth in frustration, trying not to let the feeling of defeat settle upon him. But the one who should be most upset had calmly walked over to the window. She quietly stared out at the lake in the distance, longing to be near it. Lily wanted to stand on its shores and drift into a fantasy world or think back to happy childhood memories, the way the sparkling water always relaxed her enough to do.

"Please, just let 'em be." Lily's fragile voice penetrated James and William's angry banter and brought a sudden peace to the atmosphere in the room. They both ceased their conversation and turned to find Lily with her back to them, still gazing out the window. She did not want to argue with the students, force them, or fight with them as James was suggesting. Pushing against one's will was something she was painfully familiar with. She wished it on no one, including those who held unnecessary ill will against her. "If that's the way the students want it, then so be it. But please … please, just let 'em be," she continued softly. "Besides, I think I have a way to give 'em what they want and still have the kind 'a show you're talkin' about, William."

William walked over to her, gently turned her toward him, and then held both of her hands. "You need only speak it, and I will see it done."

"But with only three weeks left, I just don't know if we could eva' make it happen."

183

"Lily, I *will* see it done."

With his insistence, Lily proceeded to explain what she knew would give the student orchestra the anonymity they had requested, and what she hoped would give the audience a show that would truly be unforgettable.

* * * *

"Beautiful day isn't it?" James asked, walking up beside Lily, holding two fishing rods.

"Sho' is." Lily had finally made her way out to her favorite spot on the lake. She was in dire need of a way to mentally escape after the earlier rehearsal disaster.

"I'd love to relax my mind by doin' a little fishin' right about now. But seein' as how it's been pointed out to me that I ain't so good at catchin' bait, I sure could use me some help from an ol' pro," James teased.

"I don't see the point. I could dig you up a whole bucket full 'a worms, but you couldn't catch a fish if it jumped in your lap," Lily smiled.

The origin of her joke flashed instantly in James's mind. As kids, he and Lily had set out together one Sunday in his tiny fishing boat in their childhood paradise creek. After casting their lines, James was startled by a fish that leaped out of the water into his lap. Frightened, he jumped up and started dancing around to get away from it. He lost his balance and fell out of the boat with his arms flailing, screaming like a little girl. The sight of it had Lily bent over howling with laughter.

"Guess I'll neva' live that one down, will I?" James laughed after recalling the embarrassing moment.

"Nope, 'fraid not … nor the fact that I's always a much betta' fisha'*woman* than you," Lily reminded him.

"Now, that part seems to have slipped my memory. You'll have to prove it to me. I've got two fishin' poles here." James held them up. "And there's a rowboat ova' yonda'," he said, motioning his head toward it.

Lily looked in the direction of the boat, contemplated a moment, but then declined. "Naw, that's alright, you can go on without me."

James felt his heart sink a little. He had no desire to fish without her. "C'mon, now. A little lazy fishin'll get your mind off things for a while. Besides…" He rubbed his temples and closed his eyes. "Umm, geez, I just can't quite rememba' you bein' all that great of a fisha'man."

"Fisha'*woman!*"

"Oh, excuse me! I stand corrected. Well, I'm gonna need you to jog my memory on how great of a fisha'*woman* you truly are, 'cause I have an awfully hard time believin' that." The Lily James knew as a boy never backed down from challenges. He figured he would try the old tactic on her and see how well it worked nearly ten years later.

"Well…" she started.

"Well, what?"

"Well, you'll have to make it worth my while."

"Oh." James raised an eyebrow. "How so?"

"If I catch more fish than you, then Anna Mae and I get to watch you cook dinna' for the rest of us tonight."

"Well, what do I get if I win?"

"The simple honor of finally havin' caught more fish than me for the first time in your life!" she answered, snatching one of the poles and giving him a smile dripping with playful arrogance.

"You got yourself a bet!" James smiled in return. "But it doesn't count 'til we shake on it."

Lily looked him in his eyes and reluctantly extended her hand. James took it gently into his, barely shaking it all, concerning himself more with the softness and warmth of her skin. Lily was not oblivious to the way his facial expression changed when he touched her. It was subtle, but she read it well. "Now, it's official," she said, creating an excuse to take her hand out of his and settle the rapid beating she suddenly felt in her chest after the way he had just looked at her.

James gestured his hand toward the boat and allowed her to walk ahead of him. Shortly thereafter, he rowed them out into the middle of the lake. Lily let her eyes roam everywhere except for on James. She could feel him looking at her, but she did not want to reciprocate. When they reached the deepest part of the water, James continued to watch her bait her hook with worms and cast her line out as if she had done it just the day before, and not years. While gazing at her, James was thinking about the fact that Lily only allowed him short glimpses of her old self before quietly slipping back behind her carefully crafted wall and shutting him out. Even while they were just feet apart, she sat staring at her fishing line, having yet to say another word since their interaction on the shore. "What's on your mind, Miss Lily?" James asked, in hopes that she would give him another glimpse of her old self for a while.

It had been so many years since James had concerned himself with Lily's emotional state. Over the last few weeks, she realized that it was a lot more challenging to adjust to his kindness than she had anticipated. After everything that had happened between them in the past, she kept telling herself that it made more sense to keep her private thoughts as just that. But there was something about the way James spoke to her lately, in such a gentle tone, that was slowly making her want to open up to him just as she had in her youth. Lily often wondered, though, if she would regret unlocking the entrance to her protective wall and allowing him in, even if only for short periods of time. Despite her fears, she let him in again, but proceeded with great caution. "Well, I been wantin' to tell you how sorry I am about rehearsals today. I…"

"No! No! No!" James replied, cutting her off and startling her.

"What?!" Lily jumped, thinking it had something to do with his fishing line. "What is it?"

"You don't owe anyone any apologies, ya' hear?! If anything, those little rats should be apologizin' to you! I don't appreciate the little stunt they pulled today! And I'll tell you right here, and right now, if any one 'a them personally gives you a problem, you let me know," he demanded, recalling the cold glance between her and Austin. "Alright?!"

Lily just stared at him a moment, surprised at his instantaneous hostility and his genuine desire to be protective.

"*Alright?*" James insisted again.

"Alright," Lily finally replied. "I'll rememba' that. But I hope maybe we can get the changes done on time and everything will be fine," she said calmly, attempting to settle James down.

"Me too, but it neva' should've come to this. They…"

"They what?"

"Neva'mind," he said, running his hands through his hair and blowing out a breath to calm himself. "Listen, we're not s'pposed to be thinkin' or talkin' about anything like that while we're out here, don't you rememba'?"

"Rememba' what?" Lily asked, looking confused.

"Surely you rememba'," he said, calmness finally having returned to his voice. He took a second to reflect before diving back into a moment of nostalgia. "It was the summa' right afta' Auntie passed away and my parents were about to send me and my brotha's away for a couple 'a weeks to stay with my uncle and cousins for a while." He continued talking as he baited his fishing line. "Rememba' we were both feelin' mighty down about everything? So that Sunday, we decided we's gonna do a little fishin' before I's due to leave. But before we left the shore, we promised each otha' that wheneva' we was floatin' out in the middle 'a the wata', just like we are now, that we'd always pretend like we's in anotha' world, in a world where no troubles could touch us, where we talked about nothin' but happy things." He turned to look at the profile of Lily's face. "Don't tell me you've forgotten?"

Lily turned and looked him in the eyes. She was instantly warmed by the fact that he had recalled something that meant so much to her at the time. "How could I eva' forget somethin' like that?" she smiled, feeling comforted by the memory. "I guess I'm just surprised that you haven't forgotten eitha'."

"You ain't the only one here with an amazin' memory," James boasted, poking his chest out, feigning arrogance.

Lily tried not to smile at his playfulness, but she could not help herself.

"Ya' know, speakin' 'a my cousins, that reminds me," James said, finally casting out his fishing line.

"Reminds you of what?"

"I neva' did get around to thankin' you way back then," he said, as they both turned to focus on their fishing lines.

"Thankin' me for what?"

"Back when my uncle had sent my cousins to stay with us for a change, I remema' us boys decided we's gon' try to make a tent usin' some 'a my mama's dresses. Wasn't too bright of an idea, but we was just a bunch 'a dumb little boys."

"I can't argue with that!" Lily teased.

"Wasn't long 'fore we ended up rippin' a hole in two 'a her favorite dresses, not to mention all the dirt stains we'd gotten all ova' 'em. I rememba' I tried to hide 'em, thinkin' maybe she wouldn't find 'em. But the oddest thing happened…"

"And what might that be?"

"Three days lata', mama was dressed for church in one 'a the dresses we tore up. I saw 'er walkin' toward me in that thang, and I swore she was comin' to grab me by my scrawny little neck. But she walked right on past me with her dress flowin' in pristine condition. She must 'a thought I's half outta my mind the way I circled 'round her two or three times lookin' for that big ol' hole that I's certain I'd put in the backside 'a that dress. But magically…" He waved his hand in the air. "It was nowhere to be found, nor were the stains," James recounted, in a hypnotic voice.

"Ya' don't saaay!" Lily replied sarcastically.

"Can you believe that?" James smiled, sounding just as sarcastic.

"Simply amazin'!" Lily smiled back. "But, I'll let you in on a little secret." Lily looked around as if somebody was going to overhear her. She then leaned in close to James. "You don't have me to thank for that."

"No, well who else could it've been? I know good 'n well my fatha' and brotha's can't sew worth nothin'."

"Shh, this is a well-kept secret amongst all us slaves." She looked around once more and whispered, "it was The Sewin' Fairies who fixed your mama's dresses."

"The who?!"

"Shh! Keep your voice down!" Lily insisted, looking around again. "The Sewin' Fairies."

"The *who*?!"

"You mean you ain't neva' heard 'a them?"

James just kept looking at Lily like she had lost her mind.

"I just don't know what we'd do without The Sewin' Fairies. See, they float around at night searchin' for clothes that dumb little boys done tore up tryna build tents … tents that actually look more like flags blowin' in the wind," she sarcastically pointed out. "Then when they spot 'em all balled up in the back 'a the closet … where any blind man could find 'em!" she teased again. "They swoop down outta the sky, wash 'em up, sprinkle a little mendin' dust on 'em to make 'em good as new, and hang 'em back on the rack 'fore anybody eva' notices a thang."

This time around, floating out in their fantasy world of happiness, drifting far away from the reality of their troubles, it was James who sat in the fishing boat laughing uncontrollably at Lily.

"I can't believe you's laughin' at The Sewin' Fairies afta' they saved your little scrawny behind all them years ago. You should be 'shamed 'a yo'self," she joked, fighting to hold back her laughter until she finally lost it too.

When they regained their composure, James was quiet for a moment while he reflected on the flash of many memories from his youth that were the most precious to him. In every single one of them, he realized that Lily was always there by his side. "Thank you, Lily," he suddenly said, seriousness now in his tone.

"I already told you it wasn't me," she teased again.

"No, I really mean it … *Thank you*," James said again, turning toward her this time.

Lily looked at him with inquisitive eyes.

"For helpin' to give me a childhood full 'a unforgettable memories," James continued.

Lily could feel her cheeks flushing red as he stared at her in a way that conveyed his sincerity. "Thank you too, James."

"For what?"

"For givin' me a childhood at all."

Chapter Thirteen

Slave Code
Article VIII Section XI
No slave is permitted to work for pay, or to keep horses; or to own a wagon
or carriage; or to buy or wear clothes finer than "Negro cloth."

Saturday
April 15, 1859
Annual Spring Extravaganza
and
"The Return of William Werthington"

William had never known what it meant to be nervous or anxious about a performance, until this very moment. Not being able to foretell the future had his stomach in knots, his heart racing, and sweat threatening to seep through his clothing. The stage was normally like his second home. But now, here William was, sitting at the piano in front of a lawn full of people, about to strike the keys to begin a show that would undoubtedly be epic, in the most magnificent of ways ... or in the most disastrous. Such immeasurable pressure had William experiencing a feeling that had always been foreign to him. Before he began, he silently prayed that the end result of the night's events would be worth crying tears of joy and not tears of heartbreak. But it was not himself that he sent that prayer for. He wanted the night to be spectacular ... for Lily. Anything less than that would have devastated him.

Even in the hours before William took his seat at the piano, it was apparent that he wanted nothing but the best for Lily. Not wanting nerves to affect her leading up to the show, William expressed to James that Lily would more than likely benefit by having her mind and body far away from the night's approaching events. He explained that drowning one's thoughts in every detail of the show just hours before could be detrimental to the outcome. After that advice, Lily had been awakened that morning by Anna Mae and her daughter, Isabel. "Wake up, sunshine," Anna Mae said to Lily as Isabel drew back the curtains, letting in the beautiful spring sunlight.

"What time is it?" Lily asked, rubbing her pasty eyes.

"A little afta' nine o'clock. You's the only one still asleep in the whole house."

"Nine o'clock!" Lily shrieked, throwing the covers off herself in a panic. By this time, she was usually wide-awake, helping Anna Mae prepare breakfast for everyone. "Why didn't anyone wake me?" she asked, scurrying to get out of bed.

"Whoa, whoa, lay down chil'! Just relax," Anna Mae said, stopping her. "Everything's fine. We all wanted you to rest before your big performance tonight. We figured it'd do ya' good to let you sleep in for a change."

"Oh, thank you," Lily replied. She quickly settled down, leaned back on the headboard, and yawned. "I didn't fall asleep 'til well afta' midnight," she admitted.

"No worries baby. That's all the more reason for us to pamper you and help you relax a little before tonight," Anna Mae smiled. "We don't want you liftin' a finga' 'til then."

"*Pamper* me?"

"That's right!" Isabel smiled. "And you can start with breakfast in bed!"

"Breakfast? Sittin' in bed?"

"Well, yes! Ain't you eva' had breakfast in bed?" Isabel asked, looking bewildered. Anna Mae nudged her spoiled daughter. She had led a privileged life thanks to William. She was only six when he bought her at auction. She hardly remembered what being a slave was like. Isabel was now in her twenties, but often still acted much like a mindless teenager, despite her sweet disposition and good intentions. "Me and Elijah used to make mama and daddy breakfast in bed nearly every Sunday," she continued, despite her mother trying to get her to be quiet.

"Ain't nobody eva' served me nothin', 'specially not while in a *bed*," Lily laughed, finding the thought of such a thing amusing.

"Well, there's a first time for everything!" Isabel squealed, sounding like an excited schoolgirl. She then handed Lily a tray filled with eggs, biscuits, bacon, fruit, oatmeal, and a glass of freshly squeezed orange juice.

"Thank you. This is mighty kind 'a you ladies to go outta y'all's way like this," Lily said before she dug into her breakfast. She was appreciative of Anna Mae and Isabel's efforts, but still felt a bit strange about someone bringing her food and then eating it in a bed. She did her best to adjust and enjoy such a rare pleasure though.

Breakfast was only the beginning of Anna Mae and Isabel's efforts to treat Lily like a pampered princess. While she finished eating, Anna Mae stepped out of the room for a moment. Isabel then sat on the edge of the bed and chattered on and on about all the latest gossip that had gone on in her life since the last she had seen Lily at William's gala. When the pair first met that day, they had an instant sisterly connection. That night, Isabel talked so much that Lily could hardly get a word in edgewise; the same held true this time around. Lily did not mind it, though. She was always thoroughly entertained by Isabel's stories and found her bizarre unfiltered comments amusing. She was fascinated by the ignorant bliss that Isabel's mind seemed to wallow in. She also thought it was adorable that she always went on and on talking about Elijah, her parents, or her latest beau, jumping from one story to the next without a breath in between.

"Maaama! Is it ready yet?" Isabel suddenly screamed while slap in the middle of a story. She then sporadically jumped out of bed like a hyper two-year-old and peeked her head out the door.

"Is what ready?" Lily asked her.

"Your bath wata', silly," Isabel replied, like the answer was obvious.

"Bath wata'?"

"Don't tell me you ain't neva' had one 'a them eitha'?" Isabel asked, putting her hands on her hips, not realizing how offensive she was being, as usual.

"Naw, it ain't that. I've had plenty since I been here in William's house. Truth be told, I done had more here than in my whole life." Lily rubbed her arm, feeling the dramatic change in her skin's softness in the previous weeks. "It's just that I ain't neva' had nobody draw up the wata' for me."

"Oh, you'll love it! Mama always used to make my baths when I's just a girl. She adds in a little honey and milk and some 'a the finest fragrances. And she always knows how to make the temperature just right! Now come on and get them clothes off!" she smiled, pulling Lily's arm to get her out of bed.

Lily followed along with Isabel's wishes. She went down the hall to soak in the warmth of the bubble-filled bath water while Isabel and Anna Mae washed her hair. She found it hard to sit still and let them do all the work, though. It was normally she who was in such a position, so it was difficult for her to make the adjustment.

"I didn't know you was hidin' all this hair unda' yo' scarf. Sho' wish my hair was this long and soft," Isabel confessed. "Me and mama gonna have a fine time fixin' it up."

195

"Y'all gonna do my hair too?"

"Nails, make-up, and all!" Isabel told her.

"Y'all bein' so kind to me. I-I really can't thank ya' enough. I wouldn't know what in the world to do without the both of ya'. I ain't neva' wore make-up in all my life," Lily laughed. "Come to think of it, I ain't neva' really done my hair eitha'."

"Well believe me, when we finished with you Elijah gon' be sorry he couldn't be here to see you again tonight," Isabel blurted. Her mother nudged her again. "What Mama?! It's true! Elijah told me how pretty he thinks she is."

"Hush up girl! Quit tellin' business that ain't yours to be told."

"Yes, Mama."

"It's okay, Ms. Anna Mae, the feelin's mutual. I must admit, you and Mr. Ben make fine lookin' children. Isabel's so beautiful and Elijah is awfully handsome."

"Well, thank you baby. But Isabel still needs to learn how to hold 'er tongue sometimes."

Isabel was not saying something that Lily did not already assume about Elijah. His attraction to her was blatantly obvious in the lustful way he gazed at her. The attraction was mutual. Lily found Elijah's chocolate-colored smooth skin, his tall muscular frame, and his smile difficult to turn away from. But oddly, Isabel's mention of her brother suddenly made Lily curious about what a certain someone else would think of her with make-up and a new hair style. Lily let her mind drift away as she leaned back with her eyes closed in the enormous garden tub, washing herself slowly with a loofah. Suddenly forgetting that there were two other people there with her, she began pretending that her hands belonged to the man whose face and shirtless body she saw in vivid detail behind her lowered eyelids.

Lily then began reflecting on the weeks since her and James had fished together. From that day forward, the awkwardness they once felt around each other quickly faded away. It was replaced by a familiar ease and comfort. More and more, Lily found herself *wanting* to speak to James when the small windows of opportunity would arise. James relished every second of those precious moments with Lily. Their meetings were always playful and silly and were the escape they needed from their daunting show preparation. Each time, though, they were always called back to their duties sooner than either of them wanted. Every conversation was left lingering, leaving them both eagerly awaiting the next time they could exchange a few words. Lily walked away from every encounter with a crack in the wall that she had erected to keep James from trampling on her emotions. However, she still remembered to proceed with great caution while allowing him temporary access to her vulnerability.

Lily was so absorbed in her thoughts and at ease in the warm water that she did not want to get out when Anna Mae and Isabel finished washing her hair. With reluctance, she emerged from the wonders of her soothing bath and wandered back into her room with them and locked the door. After drying off, Anna Mae gave her a bottle of the homemade lotion that she had been making for decades. Anna Mae swore every woman needed to use her secret formula if they were going to keep their skin looking youthful and feeling soft. Anna Mae's supple skin was silky smooth proof. She looked nowhere near her actual age.

As Lily applied her new lotion, she once again imagined that it was a set of strong hands gliding down the length of her legs, across her abdomen, up her arms, and into a light massage of her shoulders. She literally had to shake herself from the image to stop her body from reacting to the mere fantasy of it all. She then suddenly tried to hand the lotion back to Anna Mae, feeling as though getting rid of it was the only way to put an end to her erotic visions.

"Naw, baby, you keep that," Anna Mae told her. "That's my gift to you in celebration of your first show."

"Thank you, Ms. Anna Mae," Lily replied, sounding truly appreciative. When Anna Mae stepped away, Lily looked at the bottle again and smiled devilishly while imagining all its pleasureful uses.

Isabel stepped up beside Lily and snapped her out of her trance. "Now yo' skin gon' be nice and soft unda'neath yo' new dress!"

"New dress?" Lily replied, surprise evident in her tone.

"Yeah! You didn't think we's gon' let you wanda' up on that stage wearin' this ol' rag, did ya'?" Isabel asked, holding up the dress she wore daily.

Anna Mae rolled her eyes and let out an exasperated breath, wondering how to fix her absent-minded daughter. She was convinced that her mindlessness was a trait she had inherited from Benjamin's side of the family.

Still oblivious to her insulting comment, Isabel wandered happily over to the closet and pulled out the dress she was excited to show Lily. Knowing the laws about the sort of generic fabric that slaves were limited to wearing, Lily assumed that her new dress would not be too far different from the one James had given her on the journey to Ohio. What Isabel revealed, though, completely obliterated her expectations. "Oh my," Lily gasped, unable to take her eyes off the beautiful gown. She stepped closer to it and reached out to feel the sort of fabric a slave would normally never be allowed to wear. "This can't possibly be mine."

"Well, sho' it is!" Isabel assured her. "You like it, don't ya'?"

"*Like* it? *Like* ain't the right word. It's the most gorgeous dress I've eva' laid my eyes on!" Lily took it and walked over to the mirror and placed it in front of herself, trying to imagine what it would look like when it was finally on her body. She got just as giddy as Isabel at the prospect of being allowed the honor of wearing such a beautiful piece of clothing. "Oh, I love it!" She turned and hugged Isabel. "Thank you both so much!"

"Don't thank us!"

"No, well, who else then?"

"James!" Isabel said excitedly.

"Good lawd," Anna Mae mumbled, shaking her head again at her silly daughter. Isabel was not supposed to tell Lily about the hand that James had in any of their affairs that morning.

"*James?*" Lily asked curiously.

"Yeah!" Isabel confirmed. "He say he knows red's yo' favorite color. He brought us the fabric and asked if we could fix you up a real nice dress. He gave us a catalog filled with all kinda pictures 'a fancy dresses in it, so we could pick the one we liked best! He sho' do want you to look pretty!"

In fact, all the morning's events were requests that had come from James. Even if William had not told him about the powers of relaxation, James planned to bombard Lily with an array of pleasantries to help ease any lingering fears or worries leading up to her performance. William's words of wisdom simply confirmed that it was a wonderful idea. However, James knew nothing about primping and styling a woman. For that, he had called on Anna Mae and Isabel to meet the call of duty, feeling that women would be more suited to handle all of Lily's personal needs. After mother and daughter happily obliged, James gave them money and a list of things that Lily might like. He then swore them to secrecy about the hand he had in their arrangement. He wanted it to seem like a genuine gesture from Anna Mae and Isabel, rather than making Lily feel as if it was just another chore he had added to their to-do list. After sworn silence from both ladies, James handed them the insurmountable task of distracting Lily's mind from the night's coming events.

"That dress is gonna look even more beautiful when we get it on ya'," Anna Mae told Lily after joining her and Isabel in front of the mirror. "Go ahead and try it on, so I can see if I'm needin' to take it in an inch or two."

While Anna Mae worked on fine-tuning the dress, Isabel started working on styling Lily's hair. In the process, Lily asked to hear stories of what it was like living with William for all the years that they had. Anna Mae took the opportunity to inundate her with embarrassing and funny tales of her children, especially stories about Isabel; it was her way to retaliate for all of Isabel's unintended rude comments. In between stories, wild outbursts of laughter, and working on the fine details of Lily's makeover, Isabel would sneak food and wine in from the kitchen to help further relax them all. The scene was less like the preparation for a major show and more like that of a mother enjoying the simple pleasures of having two daughters. It was exactly the sort of escape that James was hoping Isabel and Anna Mae would provide for Lily.

For James, however, the morning had been a far cry from relaxing baths, pampering, and pleasantries. From the moment he woke up, he had been going full steam to finish every last-minute detail for the show. With a little over an hour left before the show was set to begin, he finally had a chance to shave, cut his hair, take a much-needed bath, and get into his new suit, in preparation for the few minutes that he would be onstage. When he was finished, James glanced out the window and watched Benjamin and some hired helpers guiding anxious audience members from their carriages to their seats. Parades of people in flowing dresses, fancy hats, and expensive attire began quickly filling the freshly finished amphitheater seats. James stood there for a moment to admire his work of art. Before long, though, his nerves began to toy with him again. He had already been incapable of eating, and despite how tired he was after weeks of labor, he had gotten very little sleep the night before. His worries had nothing to do with his own well-being, but with that of Lily's. Since he and William had been so busy, he had not seen Lily all day, which left him worrying obsessively over the state of mind she might be in. After making a few minor adjustments to his hair and his attire, he planned to finally head to her room, hoping to learn that she was doing much better than he was at that moment.

As James was leaving his room, William had just come in from backstage to retrieve something from his desk. William took the free moment away from the madness to collect himself. He paced nervously in his den, stopping to look out the window every so often at the crowd that steadily gathered. For the three weeks since the debacle with his students, William had been highly stressed while expending all his efforts to make the necessary changes to bring Lily's show idea to life. It had taken twelve-hour days, and damn near an act of God, to turn something relatively simple into something that was now going to be extremely elaborate. Where Lily was concerned, William was not surprised at her level of creativity and innovation. But he was surprised, however, that they had pulled off her extravagant idea in as little time as they had. With everything completed on schedule, William's stress and worry had now shifted to the unpredictability of the audience and their reaction to what they were about to see.

As William was pacing in his den, he heard footsteps coming down the hallway. He peeked his head out and startled James, who was in a hurry to see Lily. "H-how is Lily? Is she alright?" William asked, talking fast and fidgeting with his spectacles. "I haven't bothered to go up and see her. I'm a nervous wreck, and I was afraid I would just end up stressing her."

James was surprised at William's demeanor. He was used to seeing him so calm and collected. "I tried to go up and see her earlier, but Anna Mae caught me in the hallway and shooed me off. She assured me Lily was fine, though. I'm headed back up there again now. I'm sure Lily's dressed by now."

"Perfect. It's less than an hour before showtime. She'll need to warm up a bit," William explained, rubbing his sweaty palms together. "Everything from the list I gave you this morning is prepared and ready, correct?"

"Yes, William, everything is in place." James noticed the jittery sound in William's voice and the way he was continuously smoothing his hands over his clothes and looking everywhere but at him. "Listen, are you gonna be alright?"

"I just ... I just hope I've done enough."

James realized that William was beyond being just a nervous wreck. He was in a state of panic. James pulled him into the den and shut the door, hoping to say a few words to him in private to help calm his nerves. "You hope you've done enough?" James reiterated. "My God, William, the only thing you've yet to do for Lily is snatch the moon down from the sky so she can have a betta' look. You've done so much for her that I don't even know where to begin thankin' you for all 'a this. When I brought Lily to you, I certainly didn't expect it to escalate to all 'a this."

"Be honest with me, though, James. Do you think Lily's truly ready for this? O-or do you think we've pushed her too hard?"

"I assure you, William, Lily's more than ready for this. I have no doubt about that. This show is all she eva' talks about now. Besides, I've known Lily nearly all my life, and she's, honest to God, the strongest woman I know. So, no matta' what her demeanor may show, I know that when the moment comes for her to show 'er strength, she will." James really believed that despite how worried he was feeling on the inside as well.

"I just want this to be perfect for her, James ... I really do," William said, walking over to stare out the window again at the artistically crafted amphitheater sitting in his yard.

"If there's anybody in this world who knows that already, William, it's definitely me. It's one 'a the many reasons I appreciate you as much as I do." James walked up behind William and put his hand on his shoulder as a gesture of his sincerity. They were both silent afterward while they continued to stare out into the fields at the grand open-air amphitheater.

"The amphitheater, James. It's just marvelous. Even better than I imagined it would be. For all your labor, I truly thank you."

James simply nodded and took in his compliment with silent gratitude and pride.

"Well, I'm headed backstage to be sure everyone is ready and in place," William said, sounding much calmer. "I assume you're headed to fetch Lily now."

"Yes, we'll be there shortly."

After William departed from the den, James's feet immediately began carrying him toward the only person whose company he had wanted throughout the day. He ascended the stairs two at a time, feeling like a child anticipating the opening of a birthday gift. He was eager to see the fruits of Anna Mae and Isabel's labor. But most importantly, he was hoping to find that Lily was doing fine emotionally. He checked his hair and straightened his bow tie in the mirror at the top of the stairs before he proceeded to knock gently on her bedroom door. Isabel opened it slightly and peeked her head out.

"Hey, Isabel. You ladies decent?"

"Yeah, come on in," she smiled, stepping aside and opening the door all the way. "Mama's just about finished."

Lily was sitting at a vanity table in the corner with her back to James while Anna Mae finished making a few adjustments to her hair. James looked in Lily's direction, and his eyes immediately fixated on the length of her hair and the way it fell in long spiral curls down her back. James then realized that they were still children the last time he saw her without her hair wrapped neatly in a scarf or bonnet. Underneath Lily's long curls, James could see a few of the silky white drawstrings that held her brand-new handmade dress firmly in place. Just seeing these small details of her transformation had James's heart pounding with anticipation.

Anna Mae stepped back and smiled at all of her hard work when she was done. "All finished!" she said, a look of pride on her face.

Lily took a moment to look at herself in the mirror, turning her head from side to side and touching her hair. She found it hard to believe it was her own reflection she was looking at. She then stood up and looked at herself from head to toe in the floor-length mirror nearby. Once she absorbed the fact that it was indeed her own reflection, Lily smiled and held back the urge to cry. Nervously, she then turned around for Isabel and James to finally see her for the first time ever with her hair neatly styled, in make-up, and adorned in her beautiful, floor-length, red Victorian dress. The exquisite flowing gown hugged Lily's waist tight and hung like the shape of a small bell from her hips down. It highlighted the sultry curves of her body that were typically hidden underneath her usual plain attire. Aside from a few wispy bangs hanging neatly across her forehead, the top portion of Lily's hair was pulled back out of her face and styled decoratively on top, while the rest of it fell in perfect spirals around her shoulders and down her back. She wore eye shadow that matched her dress and thick black mascara that accentuated each one of her long, dark eyelashes. A light application of foundation gave her face a soft glow. Anna Mae added just a hint of shiny color to her lips that easily brought attention to the sensuality of their illustrious shape.

James drank in the sight before him. Lily's lips, her lines, her curves, her hair, the sparkle in her eyes, all of her accentuated beauty overloaded his mind and temporarily rendered him speechless. The mass amounts of adrenaline coursing through his body had genuinely taken its toll on him. He began sweating, his mouth had gone dry, and his mind remained blank. Lily had always been beautiful to James, but at that moment, her beauty had reduced him to a nervous schoolboy with a crush. He just stood there unable to take his eyes off her, struggling to find words that were worthy of expressing how phenomenal she looked in his eyes.

Lily smoothed her hands down the sides of her dress, suddenly feeling nervous herself. The fact that James had yet to say a word was making her question her transformation. "I-I ain't neva' had my hair done before," she said nervously, not knowing what else to say to fill the silence.

With a look of awe on his face, James's eyes panned slowly up her entire body again. When he reached her face, he gazed into her eyes. "My God, Lily. You ... Are ... *Stunning*," he said, after finally remembering how to string a few words together. "Absolutely stunning." He had yet to even blink, for fear of interrupting his view. Isabel gave a girlish giggle, but he did not even hear her. To James, nothing else in the room existed except for Lily, whose brilliant smile lit up the room after his compliment.

"I certainly agree with that," Anna Mae said, smiling and stepping up beside Lily.

James's body certainly agreed too. Having forgotten that there were two others in the room, it had instinctively reacted to what he was seeing. He cleared his throat, looked around, and suddenly remembered that there was a need to gather his composure before he embarrassed himself any further.

"C'mon, Isabel. Let's you and me go on down to our seats," Anna Mae said, wanting to give James and Lily a moment alone.

"Okay, mama."

"I just know you's gon' be incredible tonight," Anna Mae told Lily as she gave her a hug.

"Thank you for everything today, Ms. Anna Mae, and you too, Isabel."

"No problem," Isabel replied from the doorway. "And good luck tonight!"

"Thanks, Isabel."

"I'm glad to help suga'," Anna Mae told her. "Now, you go on up there and show them folks how piano playin' is really done, ya' hear?"

"Yes ma'am," Lily answered with a smile.

Anna Mae kissed her on the cheek, and she and Isabel departed from the room, finally leaving Lily and James alone. Lily watched the door close and then turned to look at James, who had still yet to remove his eyes from her. They stood there quietly for a second, staring at one another. While they were dressed as elegantly as ever, they both found it hard to turn away, especially in the absence of other people.

Lily suddenly smiled nervously when she began to feel self-conscious. When she did, James's demeanor quickly changed, like he had finally snapped out of a trance. He stepped closer to Lily, wanting to be nearer to the intoxicating scent he smelled on her. "You really do look phenomenal, Lily," he could not help but tell her again, still helplessly absorbing every inch of her.

"Thank you, James. That's awful sweet 'a you," Lily replied shyly, blushing a little. "Y-you look wonderful too." She had certainly noticed how his rugged features of the past few weeks had been traded for a fresh, clean-cut look. Whether dressed in fine linens or shirtless, clean-shaven or with facial hair, Lily was impressed by James's strapping good looks in all cases.

"So, umm, how're you holdin' up?" James finally asked her, in a desperate attempt to turn off a certain part of his body. "Much betta' than last night, I hope," he added, referring to an unintended encounter they had the previous night ...

After several weeks of draining work in the fields, James had gone a lengthy amount of time without being awakened by the ghastly reoccurring nightmare that had become an unfortunate part of his life. His streak, however, had ended the night before. As usual, he found himself wandering into Lily's room to check on her. He had walked in quietly, not planning to stay long. After a few minutes, he opened the door to leave until he heard Lily's voice call out to him in the darkness. "Please don't leave," she had said.

James stopped and turned around, his heart pounding, quickly spreading the heat of embarrassment throughout his entire body. "I-I'm sorry, I w-was just…"

"Please stay," Lily requested again.

"A-are you sure?"

"Yes, please. I can't sleep, and I really don't wanna be alone."

Without contemplating it any further, James happily fulfilled Lily's request. He closed the door back softly and pulled a nearby armchair closer to her bed to sit in. "Bein' wide awake this time 'a night doesn't seem like you at all. You usually sleep like a baby … I-I assume," he added, not wanting her to know that he had visited her while sleeping on multiple occasions.

Lily sat up and lit the oil lamp on the nightstand. "I know, but … It's just…" she sighed. "I know it may sound childish, but I'm a little scared."

"Scared 'a what?"

"Tomorrow night," she replied.

"The show?"

"Yeah."

"Well, from what I've seen, you and William have prepared well. So why the fears?"

"It's not that at all. I feel like we're well-prepared despite all the last-minute changes."

"Then what's botherin' ya'?"

Lily leaned back against the headboard and drew her knees up to her chest. "It's just that ... Well, all my life most people ain't neva' bothered to look at me for more than two seconds. It seems like most folks don't even really see *me*. It's like they's lookin' right through me or somethin'. I dunno, it's hard to explain, but it's almost like I don't even exist to most of 'em."

After all James had put Lily through, he hoped that she had not grown to feel that he viewed her that way as well, but he figured she would certainly be justified if she did.

"But tomorrow," Lily continued. "A whole audience full 'a people gon' finally *see* me. Not the servant that most folks look right through. They gon' see, *Lily* ... And that scares the hell outta me."

After many years of repressing it, James's instinct to comfort Lily finally resurfaced. He suddenly took her hand into his without any hesitation. "Lily," he began. She looked down at his hand covering hers as he continued. "Anybody who doesn't love who you are afta' they come to know you is a damn fool. Let those who choose not to love you wallow in their stupidity and neva' worry yourself ova' their foolishness. You need only to sit at that piano and pour your heart out onto those keys, just the way you always do. You shouldn't concern yourself with anything more than that, ya' hear?"

James's words immediately struck a chord in Lily and calmed her racing thoughts. She said nothing in return at first, though. She simply sat quietly for a moment, enjoying the feel of her hand in his. His words and the simple gesture had quickly evaporated all of her reservations and suddenly fueled her desire to share her current intimate thoughts. "More nights than I can rememba', I've dreamt 'a you sittin' quietly at my bedside." She finally looked over at James. "In those dreams, your presence always brought me so much comfort…" Lily suddenly paused and closed her eyes when she felt him begin to caress her hand. "But even more so in reality."

James was astounded by Lily's confession, but it also made him wonder if her dreams were not really the place she had seen him. He thought perhaps this was not the first night she had caught him there at her bedside. That possibility initially made him feel a hint of embarrassment, but knowing that it was a comfort to her quickly settled him.

"Will you stay with me a while?" Lily asked. "Jus' 'til I fall asleep."

"Of course. I'll stay here as long as you need me to." He took her covers and lifted them up with his free hand. "C'mon, lay back down. You need your rest."

Lily slid under the covers, arranging herself in a way that she did not have to let go of James's hand. "Thank you, James," she said yawning, her body already giving in to sleep.

"You're welcome." When Lily closed her eyes, James blew out the oil lamp and stayed there holding her hand until it grew limp and he was certain that she had drifted off into a deep sleep.

… Lily was truly appreciative that James was willing to stay by her side for as long as he did. And now, as she stood in the middle of her room alone with him, she wanted to be sure that she expressed that sentiment. "Thank you for stayin' with me last night. I thought I's gon' be up 'til mornin', but your kind words put me so at peace. I slept well and I owe that to you."

So did I, James thought to himself, suddenly feeling that *he* was the one who should be thanking *her* for all the nights of peaceful sleep. But he kept that to himself for the time being. "Anytime, Lily ... Anytime," he replied, holding back the desire to touch her face.

"Well, I betta' get down to the amphitheata'," Lily said, trying to find a way to get James to stop looking at her in that certain way that always ignited her insides. "I'm sure William's probably worried to death about startin' on time."

"Yes, you're right, I guess we should get goin'," James replied, shaking himself from his fantasies and remembering there was a show to do. "May I have the honor of escortin' you?" he asked, extending his arm.

"But of course," Lily smiled as she slid her arm into the crook of his elbow.

James felt a sense of pride having a woman of Lily's caliber on his arm. He walked in a way that exuded that fact as he began to guide her out of the room like an upstanding gentleman. Lily, too, walked tall and confidently on his arm down the grand staircase, suddenly feeling like a princess on the arm of a prince as they made their descent. James stole glances at her while she walked alongside him. He did not see or feel an ounce of nervousness in her at all, which consequently relaxed him. To James, Lily seemed like a completely different woman than the one he had spoken to the night before, who lay awake well after midnight drenched in fear. He hoped that fact could be attributed to her growing confidence, as well as the pleasantries of her day.

Before heading backstage, Lily stopped in the library so that she could warm up on the piano for a few minutes. James watched on, unexpectedly becoming emotional while thinking of what Lily was about to accomplish in front of a crowd full of people. When her warm-up drills were complete, James offered a hand to help her stand. He smiled at her as she rose from her seat, still thoroughly entranced by her beauty. He then continued guiding her like a gentleman out of the house and through a long makeshift tent that led from the porch to the backstage area of the amphitheater. When they made it to the staging area, they both stopped and watched as William ushered everyone to their positions and gave last minute instructions.

James turned to Lily. "You ready for this?"

She truly felt calm and collected, especially while he stood there beside her. She took a deep breath and exhaled. "Ready as I'll eva' be, I s'ppose."

In the chaos of trying to get everyone in place, William turned and caught sight of Lily and immediately froze. Wondering what it was that stole his attention, one-by-one, everyone in his vicinity began to turn in Lily's direction as well. Even Austin, the scheming percussionist, did a double take when he saw her. When all eyes were finally on Lily, complete silence came over the room.

William instantly abandoned everything he was doing and made his way toward Lily with a smile creeping onto his face. His eyes began to mist with the reflection of her beauty dancing in them. When he reached her, he took both of her hands into his. His smile was so wide his kind green eyes had nearly squinted shut. "My darling, you are truly a vision."

Lily's cheeks flushed red. "Thank you, William." She smiled and gave him a warm embrace.

Like everyone in the room—including Austin—James still struggled to take his eyes off Lily while they embraced. James wanted to be sure that every detail of the night, especially Lily's beauty, stayed locked away in his memory forever. When William finally released her, James then took Lily by the hand, wanting to say a few words before he departed. "I can hardly wait to see you up there. You're gonna be amazin' tonight. I really do believe that," he said, finding it hard to fend off his desire to kiss her, even as everyone watched. "Good luck."

"Thank you," Lily replied, her face lighting up in a smile filled with appreciation.

"Come now, James, time is of the essence," William interrupted. "I promise you're leaving her in good hands."

"I have no doubt about that," James replied, placing a firm hand on William's shoulder. "Good luck to you too."

"Thank you. Now get going, my boy. We have only moments to spare." With that, James headed toward the stage, checking first to be sure that all the other performers had already settled into their positions.

After James left, William once again turned his attention back to Lily. He raised one of her hands and kissed the back of it. "I have all the confidence in the world that you will be stellar tonight," he told her, caressing her with uplifting words as he so often did.

"Thank you, William." The smile had yet to fade from Lily's face. It was a symbol of how wonderful she was feeling, inside and out. All of the rare opportunities that William and James had blessed Lily with in the past few weeks suddenly brought forth another surge of unadulterated joy within her. *This*, however, was an opportunity unlike any other. Her two leading men had given her a chance to do something that no other Negro, slave or not, had ever been afforded the luxury of doing. Lily felt humbled and honored by that fact, and she wanted to perform in a way that proved she was worthy of setting such a monumental precedent. But more than anything, she wanted every note on this epic eve to convey to James and William that all of their efforts were not in vain. "I promise you that I'm gonna give it my all tonight, William. But no matta' how tonight ends, I just want you to know how truly grateful I am to you for all 'a this." Her voice cracked as her emotions began to rise. "I don't think there are words to describe how much this all means to me."

"No worries, my dear." William moved his hands to the sides of Lily's face. "Sometimes words are not necessary to convey one's sentiments. Trust that I have felt the sincerity of your gratefulness and the depths of what this means to you long before you ever whispered it. And tonight, I know this audience will feel it too."

Lily gave William a final hug and fought the urge to cry again, not wanting to ruin the make-up that Anna Mae and Isabel had worked nearly an hour to put in place.

"Now then," William said, pulling back to look at Lily once more. "Are you ready to begin your journey?" he asked, extending his elbow.

Lily interlocked her elbow with his. "With all that you've instilled in me, I feel like I'm ready for anything."

Arm in arm, the pair then made their way to their places onstage.

* * * *

The remaining sliver of the sun cast an orange glow on the horizon just behind the massive audience awaiting "The Return of William Werthington." With the sun in perfect position, James knew it was now the precise moment to make his way out in front of the packed amphitheater. Many women, old and young, sat up tall in their seats when he finally stood at the forefront of the stage with the remainder of sunlight bouncing off him at all the right angles. Their colorfully decorated hand fans began to pick up speed as thoughts about him began to dance in their minds, thoughts that those with husbands would certainly deem as inappropriate. When the chatter and fidgeting stopped, and James had everyone's attention, he began the show with the brief and simple introduction that William had requested. "Ladies and gentleman, afta' ova' ten years away from the stage, I give you the world-renowned..." He waved his arm to the right. "William Werthington." James then abruptly took his seat in the front row. He had not yet seen the finalized version of their show, wanting to be just as surprised by it as the rest of the audience.

Walking with the confidence of a polished professional, William made his way on stage. The very moment he was visible, the entire audience stood and applauded to show their appreciation of his much anticipated return. William stopped and stood just in front of his grand piano and took in the applause with gratitude. He then bowed, tossed his short gray coattails out behind him, and sat down on the piano bench. It was at this very moment that William's nerves hit him full force and he said his brief prayer for Lily. After begging God to shower her with a wealth of blessings, he gracefully struck the keys to officially begin the show. Everyone instantly recognized the well-known tune he began to play and roared into another round of applause. William could feel that he was already starting to draw them in the way that he needed to. Lily recommended the clever song choice to start the show, figuring it would instantly remind people of why William and his music had become such a worldwide sensation. He was playing a solo piece that he had originally composed as a boy before he had learned to incorporate the harmonies of accompanying instruments. It was by far Lily's favorite song to hear him play and still remained a popular tune that was performed by no other the way William was capable. After decades of playing this particular number, his fingers automatically danced in a beautiful, elegant cadence. Although on this occasion, unlike in times past, William intentionally paced the song slowly, wanting the ending to coincide with the exact moment that the sun dropped completely out of the sky.

The very minute the sun sank below the horizon, William's melody suddenly transitioned into one that was just as dark as the night sky had quickly become. A large red curtain then began to sweep slowly from the left side of the stage. By the time it passed William completely, he and his piano were gone. As soon as he disappeared, the fire in the tiki torches at the end of every aisle snuffed out in unison, causing the audience to gasp. Now engulfed in pure darkness, the crowd was left only able to hear the extreme musical mood change being played by the seemingly invisible William.

When the night sky became even more prevalent, the deep acoustic sounds of the cello began accompanying William's sullen melody, followed shortly thereafter by the soft tap of the timpani. The violins, French horns, oboes, and all other woodwinds softly joined in, cuing the percussion to begin a long-drawn-out ascent of power and intensity. In the midst of the timpani's rising reverberation, a sudden flash of light appeared and faded away onstage in the background. It appeared like lightning with the powerful sound of the percussion as its rumbling thunder. With every other beat, the sudden flash of light illuminated and faded away quickly, each time revealing a sheer satin sheath that hung like an enormous curtain from the top of the rafters clear down to the floor. It stretched from one end of the stage to the other, just behind where William's piano once stood.

As the brooding piano music continued and the power of the timpani was nearing its peak, another flash of light appeared. But this time, the dark silhouette of a man holding a sword high above his head was cast onto the thin, curtain-like sheath. Before being drowned by darkness, the audience reacted audibly again to the sudden appearance of the shadowed knight. As the booming bass sounds of the percussion continued, the light appeared briefly again and unveiled the silhouette of a woman on a makeshift mountain, clinging to a child. When the light faded out again, the mysterious music began to gather speed. Together, with the intensity of the rolling timpani, the entire orchestra roared into a sensational climax, meeting the exact moment that an explosive burst of flames erupted on both sides of the stage. Simultaneously, the white sheath lit up in full brilliance, revealing the dark shadow of a fire-breathing dragon, standing between the damsel on the mountain and the armored knight. With a constant beam of light now shining behind them, their large dreamlike images were all etched in permanence onto the sheer sheath. Just then, a mighty duel commenced between the dragon and the knight.

After the very first shadowy fireball erupted, William began pounding away at the keys, unleashing sinister sounds that coincided with the movements of the dragon. As soon as the knight took his first swing, ominous chords of music from a second piano became intertwined with the movements of the knight, as he began jousting to take down the looming dragon. Hidden behind the scenes, Lily had watched and waited patiently for her cue to begin a musical duel with her very own mentor. While the dreamlike shadows were locked in war, Lily and William were in a musical fight of their own, even playfully exchanging mean glares with one another as they battled each other with their menacing melodies.

Lily's playfulness proved that she was confident, relaxed, and completely lost in the moment the way she needed to be. Her calm demeanor was attributed to the warmth of James's words from the night before still caressing her soul. James, on the other hand, was anything but calm. His excitement was at immeasurable levels. The moment he heard Lily join in the battling duet, his face lit up just as bright as the amphitheater lighting. He, along with the rest of the audience, watched the elegant dance between blade and flame in awe, completely enraptured by every note that Lily had composed. The continuous discharge of flames on either side of the stage had everyone physically reacting every time the dragon hurled shadowed fireballs toward the knight's shield. Having never seen imagery of the sort, the audience fought the urge to blink, not wanting to miss a second of the poetic silhouette movements of the armored hero wielding his sword to strike down the fire-breathing beast.

While riding on a confident high, Lily continued delicately trotting across the keys, playing musically in sync with her knight. Not long into the battle, William's melody began to chop, slow, and fade, along with the life of the wounded dragon that his fingers were representing. When the dragon began to falter, the knight hurled his sword end over end in its direction. Just before the blade reached the creature, the light and all music ceased, leaving the audience with sudden silence and darkness. After a few moments of suspense, muted sound, and blindness, the timpani rolled into ascension, joined shortly thereafter by the entire orchestra, just as the bright and beautiful light source returned. At the peak of the orchestra's crescendo, a magnificent display of fireworks was set off into the sky in celebration of the heroic knight, whose larger-than-life shadow now stood with the slain dragon lying near his feet. He then pulled his sword from inside the beast and raised it in victory, invoking massive cheers from the delighted spectators. Fireworks continued to rain colorful sparkles into the star-filled night sky, in time with tickling piano notes that were equally as beautiful as the silhouette of the knight embracing his rescued family.

When the fireworks trickled away, and the applause finally settled, every member of the symphony returned to play for the next song, except for William. With the slaying of the dragon, he had playfully placed his hand over his heart and pretended to pass away along with the beast, causing Lily to giggle. William then got up from his piano bench, smiled, and bowed toward Lily with pride. Lily smiled back as he waved his hand toward her, symbolizing that he was now passing the piano reins solely to her for the remainder of the show. After playing just two songs, William returned to his role as the orchestra's conductor, feeling as though he had fulfilled his obligation to give the audience what they had initially come to see.

After proudly taking the reins William had handed her, Lily began the next music-infused, dreamlike story. The melody Lily played for this occasion was light and uplifting and was, once again, intertwined with the movements and emotions of all the shadowed characters. It began with the prince and his child after they had returned home to their castle. The prince left his armor and savage side behind and let loose his gentler side. His shadow tossed his young daughter into the air, read her stories, and taught her songs on the piano. Each time the little girl sat at the piano with her father, the stage would fade into darkness and light up again to reveal the prince sitting next to an older child. The little girl grew and grew until the lights faded in for a final time with the prince's daughter now sitting alone at the piano, surrounded by a symphony of violins, cellos, and soft harps while her father watched on from afar. For the first time in the show, it was Lily who sat in front of the projection of light with her dreamlike silhouette cast out to the audience onto the sheer sheath that protected her identity. She was portraying the prince's adult child while the student orchestra swayed eloquently as shadowed figures by her side. The crowd, none the wiser to who she was, applauded in grand fashion when she softly completed the piece and the light slowly faded away.

Lily looked over at William when that song was over. He gazed back and gave a proud smile, but she did not hold his gaze for long for fear that she would cry. Lily had not told William, but the shadowed story about the knight, as well as that particular song, had been inspired by simply knowing him. Lily wished that she had been rescued by William along with Anna Mae and her children. Many times, she had fantasized about William nurturing her until adulthood, passing his fatherly love, guidance, and knowledge down to her. The imagery of the prince with his child was the fairytale version of the way she had always imagined it would be while she stood alone at William's lake some days letting her imagination run free.

For a little over an hour, Lily and the student orchestra played seven more glorious songs in conjunction with actors and dancers, who portrayed stories as silhouette shadows on the specially designed material that spanned across the stage. The stories ranged from silly satires to simple dances to very deep and emotional. But most importantly, as requested, not once was there a single face of the orchestra, or other participants, revealed to the crowd, that is … until the very last song.

Before the final song was to begin, William made his way to the forefront of the stage to the applause of the awaiting audience. "Have you all enjoyed tonight's show thus far?" he asked once everyone had settled.

Everyone applauded in affirmation of his question.

When all was quiet, William took a deep breath to calm himself and clasped his hands together behind him. "Well, I must confess, I cannot take all the credit for tonight's incredible showing," he admitted. The very second he made his confession, his paranoia raced to a new high and sweat began to quickly accumulate on his brow. He then nervously cleared his throat before he continued. "You see, I had the honor of collaborating with a rather extraordinary young lady, who at the age of ten-years-old, despite incredible odds, taught herself to play the piano. In fact, most everything you have seen and heard tonight has come from the creativity and imagination of her ingenious mind. And so, it is not I alone that you owe your appreciation of this evening's entertainment." People in the audience began to turn and look at each other with questioning eyes, but William was not deterred. He took another deep breath and proceeded. "So, ladies and gentlemen, I would like to proudly present to you the true mastermind behind tonight's mystifying show." With the wave of his arm, the stage was overcome by darkness. When William disappeared once more, a solo piece from the piano began to play softly and the white sheath illuminated, displaying the first of a series of sentences upon it:

I lost my mother 14 years and 4 months ago...

The sentence faded away and another illuminated. Every line thereafter continued in the same fashion:

But she did not pass away

Nor did she abandon me

In front of her very eyes

I was stolen from her

All that I have left of her now

Is the distant memory of her face

And this very song that I play

A song that keeps her alive in my mind

Along with the belief that one day
I WILL see her again...

When the words concluded, the stage remained enveloped in darkness until Lily's solo climaxed and transitioned into a melody of anguish. It was then that ballet dancers took to the stage behind the screen with graceful movements in front of the light. Their silhouettes appeared to float from place to place as they began the final dream story with the ugly scene of a child being pulled away from her mother. The child's distress was apparent by the way she was carried away kicking and reaching out for her mother, who was being held back by two large men. Their shadowed movements were silent, but the desperation in their body language and the pain in the music spoke loudly for them.

In the scene that followed, the young girl was perched on an auction block as shadows danced violently around her in unison. They circled her like ravenous lions around their prey, throwing their hands up in rhythm with the melody. From high to low, Lily's music sank into a dismal plethora of notes that mirrored the confused mind of the child, who stood as prey to the animalistic men surrounding her. Much like the young girl, every note seemed to be crying, while the sullen sound of the strings added to the heaviness of her ordeal. With the conclusion of their predatory dance, all the greedy men, except one, hung their heads low and rhythmically took slow steps away from the auction block. The one man remaining crept slowly in sync with the beat toward the vulnerable child, proudly displaying chains high above his head. When he reached her, all music and lighting ceased.

When next the little girl's silhouette appeared, she knelt alone, scrubbing a floor in a tattered dress, her arms sweeping side to side to the softness of nothing but violins. The piano then began to tiptoe in to join them, along with a little boy who quietly appeared behind the little girl. He curiously watched her from afar but then quickly disappeared when the little girl felt his presence and turned to see who was there. She stood slowly and gallivanted across the stage alone with her dress flowing behind her, being just as playful as any child would. Suddenly, though, she stopped to tinker with a piano. She then danced and twirled around it with ballet-style pirouettes and leaps as she neglected her duties, until colliding unexpectedly with the evil man who once held the chains. He angrily waved his finger in her face. She hung her head in shame, dropped back to her knees, and continued scrubbing and swaying in time with the soft violins as the light faded out.

When the sheer sheath brightened again and represented a new day, the young girl in her tattered garments rose from a stack of hay. In sneaky fashion, she proceeded to leave her resting place, escaping to an outdoor place that only a child could see as a world of wonderment. As the little girl carried on in her wooded playland, the music suddenly began to float as beautifully as the butterflies and birds that surrounded her. She then picked up a turtle and twirled him around, but she would soon learn that she was not alone. The little boy, who had curiously watched her earlier, peered at her now from behind a tree and was forced to reveal himself when he tripped and fell from behind it. The music momentarily ceased as the young boy and girl stared at one another. In dramatic fashion, they slowly approached each other, their footsteps represented by the light touch of the highest key on the piano. When they reached one another, together, they held the turtle high in the air, and the entire symphony crescendoed once again. With happy and uplifting notes as their guide, the two children sat their turtle down and suddenly danced playfully in unison, chasing the butterflies and the birds above them. The ease of their beautiful bond brought an instant smile to every audience member's face.

With each new day that passed, the two young children continued their adventures together, fishing, climbing trees, and reading books together. Their friendship was acted out through elegant artistic dances, making it clear that the strength of their relationship continued to grow along with the size of their dreamlike images. The entire visual reflected the passing of years, all while Lily and the orchestra captured the emotion of their journey through her carefully crafted ensemble.

It was clear to the audience that this last shadowed story was about a slave. A few, who had attended William's gala, surmised that it was the same young lady they had seen play there. But that did not seem to matter to anyone this time. Only seeing the shadow of a child, with no true color or identity, managed to quickly turn off everyone's prejudices, allowing her story to resonate with them in a truly profound way. The music and stunning visuals further penetrated their emotions, making it nearly impossible for them to pull their eyes away as the story continued to unfold of a unique friendship between a young white man and a young lady, who was undeniably a *slave*.

And so, as the young twosome gallivanted fluently across the satin sheet, the audience remained awestruck by the beauty of their innocent dance as it slowly flourished into one filled with deep emotion. But just as the crowd began to feel the intensity of the pair's connection, the graceful dance between them was interrupted by the appearance of the villain who once held the chains. He danced onto the stage in a manner all his own, to notes now filled with anger. Suddenly, the two dear friends no longer danced as one. Slowly, they drifted apart. Closer and closer, the young man pranced toward the villain, gradually adopting his soldier-like moves and dancing in step with him instead. He and the villain then quickly disappeared from view, leaving the young lady to dance in solitude to the now weeping melody of Lily's piano until the light melted away.

When the light illuminated again, the story began to show the passing of years. The young lady's age and loneliness were reflected by the sorrow in the music and the slow emptiness of her movements. Her unique friend and the birds, butterflies, piano, and books they beautifully danced around, she now only experienced in her dreams. Every night as she slept, they all appeared as elusive illusions, bringing temporary joy back to her life and into the beautiful piano music that accompanied them. Sadly, though, the aging woman awakened each morning to the misery of an empty room, left only with the monotony of scrubbing kitchen floors all alone, year after painful year.

As the emotional music continued, the light soon revealed the silhouette of the once youthful girl as an old woman, hunched over, clenching tight to a walking cane, unable to move as gracefully as she once had. With Lily's symphonic music guiding her, the old slave lady hobbled over to the piano that she once drifted around as a child and touched it gently. She then painstakingly made her way out to visit the tree that she once climbed with her friend. She looked up at it and let the precious memories it held prance in her mind. Afterward, she crept back to the haystack that had been her lifelong resting place. She slowly sat down and laid her walking cane next to her. From a hidden compartment, she then pulled out the book that her old friend had once shared with her during happier years. She opened it and ran her fingers slowly down the page before lying back and placing the book upon her chest. On this night, when she finally drifted off to sleep, her dream was unlike all the others in the previous nights, and so, too, was the sorrow in the music that Lily's orchestra now played. This time, there were no mystical visions of butterflies fluttering randomly from place to place, and no birds to chase. Her dreams did not show her the tree that she once loved to climb or the face of her dear friend. Instead, drifting high above where her motionless body lay, she was graced with the image of someone she had not seen since her childhood.

The soft hymns of a choir suddenly joined in with the harps, other strings, and the piano of Lily's orchestra. When the harmony began, an apparition adorned in a flowing robe, floating above the old lady's bed, suddenly spread its wings far and wide. The girl who had spent her life enslaved had laid for the last time on her makeshift hay bed.

Her shadowy soul began to rise from her lifeless body toward her angelic mother as she awaited her daughter in the sky with her wings lovingly outstretched, ready to finally set her only child free. As her soul rose toward her angelic mother in the sky, so too did Lily, along with the grand piano she sat playing. She rose slowly into the view of the crowd from the pit beneath the stage that William had been lowered into during his act of illusion. Throughout her ascent, Lily felt her heart in her throat and her nerves beginning to attack. But despite it, she kept the ultimate composure. Fully prepared for the serious risk, she reached the top of the stage. Alone, she played stoically in front of everyone, figuratively naked, with no sheer curtains, nothing to hide her true identity, putting an end to the mystery of the show's actual creator. As soon as Lily was in full view, the harmonies from the choir deepened and radiated out into the field. At that very moment, the angelic mother, floating high above everyone, wrapped her wings warmly around her daughter's spirit, embracing her for the first time since she was stolen away from her as a child.

It could be visibly seen in every patron's face that the power of the intense music and the heavenly scene had completely captivated them all. Before the orchestra and the choir delivered the last of the emotional notes, every member of the audience was on its feet, and a standing ovation ensued. Enthralled by the touching story and the heartwarming music that coincided, ladies started dabbing dainty cloth towelettes to their eyes, while the men next to them did their best to hide the effects of a truly grand finale.

After the last of the piano melody rippled out into the night air, Lily stood with great poise in her beautifully designed handmade red gown to the overwhelming applause of the audience. She stood there silently a moment and absorbed their warmth with extreme gratitude. With the way her piano was situated onstage, William was the first person she saw when she stood. He was in the wings beaming at her with pride as he applauded with the rest of the crowd. Her first emotional instinct was to walk over and hug him, but he prompted her to walk forward, wanting the celebratory moment to be hers and hers alone. Lily nodded and bravely took her first steps toward the audience. With every step, the sound of the reception grew louder, and William's strength to hold back his tears grew weaker.

As Lily continued moving forward in her beautiful gown, she looked to her right and caught a glimpse of the student orchestra, hidden on the other side of the stage. Ironically, they were a group that she owed a portion of this unforgettable moment too. Aside from their musical accompaniment, it was their malicious act of cruelty and attempt to diminish the quality of her show that catapulted her creativity to new heights. That very day, Lily had explained to William her desire to create a show that depicted the shadowed imagery in her mind when her songs were born, and that she wanted to combine it with his love for pyrotechnics. William spared no expense and had completely exhausted himself to ensure that every element of her wishes would be fulfilled exactly how she had envisioned. To do so, he turned to the technology of gas light projectors, which had been in its infancy during his days as a performer. He remembered how the machines had drastically changed the power to control the intensity and operation of light in theaters. He took something that had simply been used to illuminate the halls and walls of theaters and used it to breathe life into Lily's ingenious ideas in a way that had never been done before. At the same time, Lily's idea ultimately gave all the other performers the anonymity they had requested.

With the control of light, Lily was able to visually share her happiness, pain, sorrow, and all of the memories from her life that ignited such passion in her music, through silhouettes. As a result, her race and status became irrelevant in the span of the hour and a half that she presented her art. She had simply become a human being, who had grasped the heart of every person watching her visions come to life as elegant shadows. She had uplifted and inspired them all and had unexpectedly brought many of them to tears. Lily had become extremely vulnerable, embracing her audience with open arms while allowing them inside the brilliance of her mind. And now, they all stood on their feet embracing her warmly in return.

No one, however, was touched by the evening's performance more so than James Adams, whose happy childhood years with Lily had just played out in front of him in such a magnificent manner. It left him emotionally riveted. James recognized the final song as a modified version of the one Lily had played upon his return home from school. He had heard Lily explain to William that the images in the show would be reflections of her thoughts as she created her music. He now understood the reason for her tears while she played that particular song that day. Not knowing entirely what to expect from the show, James had sat amongst the audience watching the moment that he had abandoned Lily come to life. And as painful as it was, he was then forced to see the loneliness she had suffered through in the years afterward. The misery he had caused her was the reason he could not stop the tidal wave that rolled out of his eyes during the final moments of the finale. At the same time, though, he recognized the brilliance of Lily's performance as well as the overall visual show. He, therefore, allowed that to overshadow what he was feeling, wanting to celebrate Lily as she undoubtedly deserved, instead of dwelling on the upheaval of emotions that had migrated into every corner of his body.

Feeling as if she was living in the most surreal dream, Lily had slowly made her way to the forefront of the handcrafted amphitheater stage as everyone continued to applaud. Only joyful and tear-filled faces greeted her as she stood there, proving the sincerity of their reception. But more important to her than all of the pomp and circumstance was a particular face that she was eager to find in the crowd. She looked sporadically from place to place out into the sea of people. In the very center of the front row, she finally spotted the man who had inspired many of the portions of her show. As soon as she laid eyes on James, Lily's smile illuminated to full brilliance and so, too, did his. With that, the tears that she had held back during the show finally overflowed down her cheeks.

After a few minutes, William finally made his way out from behind the scenes. When he reached Lily, he took her hand in his and kissed it. With his other hand over his heart, he then took a graceful bow toward her. As Lily's tears continued to flow, together, her and William turned and bowed in unison to the delight of their grateful audience.

Chapter Fourteen

Slave Code
Article II Section VIII

*It is required that any runaway slave, committed to the custody of any
respective Sheriff, be advertised in a public newspaper, making particular their
whereabouts, description of clothing, and any bodily marks of such runaway.*

Saturday
June 4, 1859

The immense success of Lily's first show was undeniable. But
despite that fact, there was no critical acclaim printed in any
headlines to commemorate that precedent-setting evening. Even
in the free state of Ohio, newspapers were still reluctant to write a
story about a Negro, unless they were wanted by the law or being listed
as a runaway. Since Lily, fortunately, did not fall into either of those
categories, there was not a single word printed about her grand
achievement during William's Spring Extravaganza. But, amazingly,
that did not stop the news about her show from spreading by word of
mouth with the ferocity of a wildfire.

The disclosure of Lily's identity during her first grand finale did
absolutely nothing to diminish people's love of her show. In fact, the
demand for more shows was overwhelming. Lily was astounded by
people's wishes to see her show again, and she was more than happy
to fulfill their requests. For two straight months, she began putting on
shows every Friday, Saturday, and Sunday night. She could have easily

done shows seven days a week and never once have had an empty seat in the amphitheater. Caucasians and Negroes, the rich and the poor, the young and the old were flocking in droves, sitting side by side, to see a blend of shadowed artistry and music that they knew full well was composed and choreographed by a Negro. Many were even traveling from places far off to witness what had finally been named *The Dream Symphony*.

Admittance was free during the first week of The Dream Symphony. During that time, seats were filled in the amphitheater two or three hours before showtime. After the first week, William began charging an entrance fee. Even then, the demands to see the show continued to escalate. In fact, even after all the amphitheater seats were sold-out, people still insisted on paying to get through the gates. Spectators were happily willing to sit on blankets in the grass to satisfy their curiosity about a show that had stirred up a great amount of gossip and controversy. Most covered up their curiosity by telling others that they were only attending in order to protest William's antics. In the end, though, they would only leave with a true understanding of the passionate enthusiasm of those who had already fallen in love with the exhilarating spectacle.

A month after the shows began, William held an after-party to fulfill the desires of those who had requested to meet Lily following her show. For once at a gathering, Lily was not dressed in attire that prompted demands from the hungry or the thirsty, nor was she expected to just linger in the shadows. Instead, Lily stood as the center of attention in William's library, wearing yet another one of Anna Mae's elegantly designed gowns, as streams of people approached to ask questions and shower her with an array of compliments. All the while, James was by her side with his pistol visible on his hip, leery of everyone and watching carefully for anyone who might dare to make any violent advances.

Much to James's dismay, though, his position of authority by Lily's side also accomplished the goal of appearing as her rightful owner. He hated such a degrading visual facade. But the way the laws were written, he knew that even in a free state Lily could be hauled off to jail without the appropriate paperwork, or without her master nearby keeping watch over her. James, therefore, played his protective and authoritative role to perfection. The potential grim consequences of breaking character became equally as terrifying for him as his night terrors.

James even wanted to protect Lily from the stream of hate letters and threats that had made their way into William's mailbox and even onto his front porch. After reading the first batch, James questioned whether or not he should let Lily proceed with further shows, but the excitement she exuded after her performances always answered that question. He simply could not bear the thought of bringing rain and hail to the sunlight that had been shining on Lily in the weeks since her show began. In fact, James was so adamant about letting Lily float in an ignorant bliss that he and William embellished the truth as to why they had suddenly hired a security team. Lily was naturally curious as to the need for the barrage of men she had seen standing at the front gates with rifles and those on horseback with six-shooters keeping watch over the plantation and the crowds at her show. James explained to her that they were just for precaution. He was simply not willing to share with her the real, unspeakably cruel reasons why it was a necessity to have the men standing guard twenty-four hours a day.

William had hired the sort of men that he knew always worked best for security detail: half-crazy, bloodthirsty, and loyal to those who employed them. Up to that point, William's choices had been worth it. The first few weeks on the job, the team of unkempt bandits had yet to allow any gruesome threats to come to fruition. The amount of money that William was paying the loyal band of misfits was an excellent incentive to assure that things remained that way. But even without the hefty paycheck, the filthy bandits were just naturally the sort of men that would have loved to blow a man's head off his shoulders, simply for the pleasure of doing it. The proof of that was evident on this particular Saturday afternoon when a man they did not recognize approached the entrance to William's estate. The bandits had not been made aware of any scheduled visitors for the day, so the unfamiliar face was greeted by the barrel of four pistols, held by two scraggly men with a multitude of missing teeth, who were in desperate need of bathing. They asked the unwelcomed visitor to state his business. When he claimed to be an old friend of William's, he was escorted to the front door like a criminal being marched to his chambers, with a cocked six-shooter not far from his head.

Tucker McCormick was the man in question. He was hardly someone that William considered as a friend, especially after his rude drunken comments about Lily at the fundraising gala. Although William was not fond of him, he had gone to speak with Tucker during the period when he and James were searching for work for Lily. They had hoped Tucker would hire Lily as an entertainer at "McCormick's," a tavern that Tucker owned. McCormick's was once a pristine bar and restaurant with a decent sized theater room, where highly entertaining shows were held. In its prime, it was considered as a fine establishment and a popular place to be for late night entertainment, drinks, and food. Tucker's successful bustling business had initially earned him lots of respect as a prominent man in the community. However, he lost that title when his wife divorced him and took their children as a result of his numerous bold and much talked about affairs with his employees and clientele.

After the loss of Tucker's family *and* his many mistresses, he took to heavily drinking his own supply of liquor. The more he drank, the less he seemed to care about the success of his business. McCormick's slowly began to lack theatrical bartenders, outstanding service from beautiful women, and the exciting entertainment it was once known for. After all the unique nuances of the fancy establishment began to fade away, so too did the willingness of patrons to spend their money there. It left the once thriving bar financially dangling by a thread and propped the door wide open for a pub called "Buck's Tavern" to become the preferred venue for food, fine wine, and spirits. As a final blow to Tucker's ego, everyone in Athens began labeling him as a laughingstock, an entrepreneurial failure, and an alcoholic outcast.

The town's constant snickering behind Tucker's back turned him into a man who was bitter, cold, and liable to bite the heads off of anybody who whispered anything he did not like. But despite the way the town treated him, Tucker continued to hang around at gatherings, always slithering his way into social events without an invitation—especially William's massive parties—just to torment people with his presence for betraying him and his establishment during a rough time in his life. But most had simply come to expect his foolish antics. They either ignored Tucker's nastiness or resorted to using his attendance as a source of humor.

Despite the town's distaste for Tucker, William and James had approached him months earlier with the angle that Lily might have the ability to breathe life back into his dying business. But despite the dire situation of McCormick's, and the financial ruin he was facing, Tucker still refused to let an extremely talented Negro set foot on his stage. But now, here Tucker stood, quaking in his beat-up dress shoes with a pistol near his skull, suddenly wishing to speak to *William* about something. Tucker had actually hoped to talk to him during *The Dream Symphony* post-show party, but the constant presence of James, with a pistol on his hip, made Tucker change his mind. He still recalled the way that James had snapped at him during the fundraising gala for calling Lily a monkey. But now, after seeing James at a store in town, Tucker decided to take advantage of the opportunity and finally drop by—uninvited as usual—to speak to William in private, hoping for a rather calm interaction in the absence of James. It was a cowardly maneuver that everyone in town would have expected of Tucker.

"Excuse me, William. Tucker McCormick is here to see you," Benjamin informed him after stepping inside his den.

William paused in the midst of writing a letter and looked at Ben over the top of his spectacles. He immediately thought back to the nasty way in which Tucker had turned him and James down when they asked him to help Lily. After such a disastrous meeting, William could not help but wonder why the town reject would now have the audacity to show up at his home again, unannounced at that. "Did he say why he was here?" William asked.

Ben shook his head. "Just said he wanted to speak with you."

"Well, let him in I suppose," William said, even though his first instinct was to have the bandits throw him off the property. He figured he would at least give the babbling old drunk a brief opportunity to state his business, hoping it included an apology for the nasty things he had said to Lily during the fundraiser.

After William gave the okay, Tucker was handed off to Benjamin by Samuel, the mustiest and filthiest goober on the security bandit team. Samuel had patiently watched over his prisoner on the porch, never once pulling his gun away from Tucker's skull. He had stood there with his pistol cocked and a smile on his toothless face, feeling giddy about the opportunity to take Tucker out if need be. While Tucker waited with the bloodthirsty bandit, he had sweated profusely through two layers of clothing. When Benjamin returned for him, he scurried into the house like a wet, hungry kitten, eager to get away from the man who would have been more than happy to rid him of his brain and then receive a bonus check for doing so.

"G-good a-afta'noon," Tucker managed to stutter after Benjamin led him into William's den.

William looked over at Tucker and almost laughed at the frazzled look on his face and his ridiculous attire. He had slicked his stringy hair back and was wearing an old suit that he had tried desperately to make look new again, which looked even worse now with his sweat stains soaking clear through the underside of his sleeves. "To what do I owe the *pleasure* of your visit?" William asked sarcastically, sounding very monotone.

After being so rattled by the pistol-packing patrolman, Tucker had forgotten his whole pitch and nervously bypassed any small talk that would have helped ease him into the conversation. The fact that he was slightly inebriated did not help matters much either. "Uh, umm, the whole town's abuzz 'bout y'ur, Lily," he said, trying his best not to slur his words.

Lily? William thought to himself. *What happened to calling her a monkey?*

"I-it ain't a tavern or shop I been in where I don't hear her name mentioned," Tucker continued.

William took his spectacles off and rubbed his eyes, already annoyed by the fact that he had started out the conversation with town gossip. "I can't say as though I blame them."

"Me neitha'. A lady friend 'a mine begged and begged me to go to that there dream story show a few weeks back. Said she just had to see what all the fuss was about."

"You have no friends, Tucker," William interjected, easily sensing his filthy lies. And he was right. The only thing that had convinced Tucker to go to the show was greed. He was curious to see what profitable opportunity he had mistakenly passed on. "What are you here for? I have work to do." William picked up his pen again and proceeded to start writing.

"Well, ain't no doubt about the fact that this Lily girl can play the hell out of a piano…"

"Something I remember trying to express to you months ago, but I recall being quickly dismissed by you … rather *rudely*, I might add," William pointed out, while still drafting his document.

234

"*Dismissed?* C'mon, ol' pal," Tucker replied, throwing in the endearment as if they truly went way back as old friends. "Now, I don't recall bein' dismissive at all. Matta' fact, I planned to speak to ya' the day before y'ur fundraisin' gala 'bout the opportunity for that Lily girl to play in my tavern's theata'. I-I simply needed a day 'r two to think things ova' before givin' ya' a firm answa' to y'ur request."

"Firm answer?!" William spat, suddenly glaring at Tucker. "'*I'd ratha' shoot my own eyes out 'fore I watch a Negro perform on my stage!* sounded like an awfully *firm answer* to me!" he said, mocking Tucker in his best southern accent.

"W-well, i-it was only the sorta answa' that *any* wise businessman would 'a given while contemplatin' the considerable risk he'd be takin' by entertainin' that kind 'a request."

"I've heard more subtle remarks from backwoods slave traders," William mumbled under his breath as he turned his attention back to his letter.

"Let's just be realistic, William," Tucker continued. "There's a reason why everyone you went to pleadin' for help turned ya' down. Nobody wants to disgrace the walls 'a their theata's by announcin' that a Negro is gon' be the main act. They're afraid they'd be run outta business!"

"Isn't that nice," William murmured, only half listening as he crafted his letter.

"B-but that's where things're different with me, ya' see. I-I ain't got no fear 'a such a thing," Tucker continued.

"Yes, that's exactly what I assumed after that little line about shooting your eyes out," William sarcastically reminded Tucker, while continuing to write in the midst of his nonsensical babbling.

"Well, if you'd 'a just been a little more patient we could 'a worked this whole thang out."

"Is that so?" William asked, still pretending as if he cared.

"That's right! But despite y'ur impatience, I've come here today with an offa' to help y'all out."

"*An offer*?!" William scoffed and dropped his pen in frustration. Tucker's words had finally garnered his full attention again. "Come now, spill it from your tongue then! I can go on no more listening to your insults! I have work to do!"

"W-well, I know how hard it must be for this gal to perform out there in the heat, night afta' miserable night with bugs eatin' her and everyone else alive. A girl like her needs a decent place to put on 'er show, and 'er audience deserves betta' too."

"And let me guess, you suddenly have just the place for her, right?" William hypothesized, trying his best not to laugh at Tucker's pathetic attempt at playing the role of a concerned and convincing businessman.

"Not only that, but that show 'a hers needs some work. She's in dire need of the propa' guidance. Any idiot could see all the technical problems there were."

"Proper guidance?! Technical problems?! What the hell are you talking about?!"

"Oh, come on, William, admit it! Tryna do a show like that at an outdoor facility is foolish! You need to have that show in a place where ya' have more control ova' the stage and lightin'. Hell, in a place with plenty 'a seatin', where people ain't forced to sit on the grass for Christ sake. And you can't very well make that girl continue to suffa' in the heat, lettin' mosquitoes make a meal outta her every night. In a theata' like mine, she'd be right at home! I-I can use my ideas to promote 'er show, to make it more grand and spectacula', and finally turn a true profit for ya'. You'd be rich!"

"Don't you mean *you'd* be rich?! Money doesn't motivate me, Tucker! Not the way it's motivating you right now to mock Lily's show and play like you truly care about whether or not she's suffering in the heat or being eaten by bugs!"

"Now hold on a minute! You ain't gonna question my sincerity! I'm here to offa' ya' a chance for this Negro to grow in a place where she's bein' helped by people with some integrity and…"

"Integrity?!"

"Damn right!"

"I may be old, but I'm not senile, Tucker! Everyone in this town knows that raggedy theater of yours has had more mice than people these last few years. So don't come to my home now acting like Lily's savior and pretending that integrity and making *me* rich are more important to you than your desperation to earn enough money to stop that God-awful tavern of yours from being torn down!"

"Even if there's truth in what you say, what does it matta'?! Nobody else will let that little nigga' set foot on their stage! You should feel honored to be offa'd such a gesture from me given y'ur circumstances!"

Tucker suddenly found his raggedy old suit collar in the grips of two powerful hands. "What'd you just say?!"

"N-n-nothin'," Tucker stammered, his eyes nearly bulging out of their sockets.

"I guess you didn't learn your lesson the last time you called Lily outta her name!" James growled, holding Tucker inches away from his face. "I'm only gonna say this one time, you worthless piece 'a shit, so I suggest you listen real fuckin' good," he snarled. "I'd eat a pile 'a horse shit before I let Lily walk through your theata' doors! Is that a *firm* enough answa' for you?!" he asked, shaking Tucker hard.

Oddly, James's moment of fury was yet another act that proved to William that his drive to help Lily was about far more than just trying to improve her musical ability or to help her find a way to take care of herself financially. Over the months they had lived in his home, William had picked up on James's body language and the way he lit up whenever Lily was in his presence. It was all too obvious that those were tell-tale signs that betrayed the secret of his emotions for her. But even more telling than that was the fact that this was the second time James had had an over-the-top outburst over someone disrespecting Lily. Those explosively protective moments were something William had experienced himself during his younger years after he had fallen in love with Emma. As noble as James's actions were, though, William's experience had made him wise enough to know that James could not afford to let his emotions get the better of him. So, although he was delighted by the fact that James obviously cared deeply for Lily, William prompted him to let Tucker go. "Come now James, turn him loose and let him return to preparing shows for his mice. We'll wait for the real businessmen to show up."

James continued to stare Tucker down with squinted eyes and then shoved him as hard as he could before he let go of his shirt collar. "Get the hell outta here! If you come back here again, your next stop will be to a dentist!"

"You'll be sorry you eva' put y'ur goddamn hands on me! You two nigga' lova's 'r gonna be beggin' for my help 'fore it's all ova' with! You wait and see!" Tucker exploded, attempting to walk out of the room with an ounce of his dignity.

James and William just glared at Tucker as Samuel marched in and happily escorted him off the property with his pistol pressed firmly to the back of his head.

Tucker's begging session was proof that William's plan was beginning to work. He had hoped that the shows on his land would stir up enough controversial gossip to help catapult *The Dream Symphony* to success. He wanted to garner the attention of theater owners and managers, who were willing to work out substantial financial deals to have the show presented in their venues. William

238

had no doubt that many of the same money hungry businessmen, who could not foresee Lily's worth before the success of her symphony, would be amongst the first ones to come after her like lions after a hearty meal. He knew that green would prove to be the only color that truly mattered to any smart businessman in the end. Wisely, William was now ready to use that level of greed to his advantage.

By the time the heart of winter rolled around, William wanted to have Lily in the warmth of a cozy theater, so long as it was under the right circumstances. In William's mind, the right circumstances included the assurance that the subsequent money, that would eventually roll in, would truly be equivalent to Lily's value. Just as important, he was only willing to accept offers by men who were genuinely respectful to Lily from the outset. He was not willing to beg anyone to treat her like a decent human being. He would halt the show altogether in winter before giving in to anything less. And it was apparent to William, after the way that James had so eloquently worded things to Tucker, that his feelings regarding the matter were indeed mutual. The only other thing that William felt needed to be a mutual agreement between them was the way they went about handling the sort of men who *slithered* in for their business meetings, rather than walked.

"Listen James, I understand your desire to protect Lily, but we must handle things in a certain way. We're bound to encounter tyrants and blood-sucking leaches, but despite it, our reputation must remain impeccable if this show is to continue to be a success. So, as difficult as it may be, I ask that you please find the strength to contain yourself … for Lily's sake," he added, figuring that just the mention of her name alone would be a strong motivator and would also remind him of what was truly at stake if he continued his impulsive behavior.

"Understood," James quickly replied.

* * * *

Lily was completely unaware of what had just taken place with Tucker in the other wing of the house in William's den. She was far too distracted to care about anything other than the little project she was currently working on. Despite the demand for more shows, she had gone to William in private and requested this particular Saturday off and expressed to him the reason why. He simply told her that she need not ask *him* such things for *her* show. He made it clear that she was *not* working for him, that the show was hers alone, and that *she* was the one who was to make any final decisions. As always, William's words comforted and uplifted Lily and made her decision for a day of freedom an easy one.

Lily's symphony had grown to mean so much to her, but her reason for wanting the day off held just as much meaning; it was the driving force behind the meal she was preparing. As she worked to perfect her dish, she hummed with a smile on her face, thinking about how the joy she found in sharing her music with everyone had surpassed her expectations. She was astounded to learn that something she had done as a child just to soothe herself was now giving her a feeling of purpose and a reason to breathe. When she lost James, Lily had abandoned the possibility of acceptance by anyone, except for in her fairytale fantasies. But now, with the genuine warmth she had received from William and her audience, she cautiously began to open herself again to the idea that people could see beyond her status and accept her in the way that every human should be. The positive outpouring from people, who did not know her, was overwhelming. But Lily remained humbled by it all, remembering at every moment the two people who had afforded her the luxury of escaping slavery for a while and providing her with the opportunity to bound freely within the confines of her dreams.

The consequent change that *The Dream Symphony* had caused in Lily's spirit was apparent to everyone, but especially to James, who now stood leaning against the kitchen door frame, gripping his suspenders, listening to Lily hum one of William's piano tunes, as she cleaned the last of the mess from the meal she had just made. Lily's cheerfulness was infectious and instantly melted the anger James was feeling after having dealt with Tucker. James smiled as he watched her, knowing that he now had a moment to be near Lily with the weeks of intense labor and preparation gone for a spell. With the cloud of distractions finally settled, it allowed him to see with clarity how much he missed having her undivided attention and giving her his.

"Glad to see you in such a great mood."

Lily spun around with her heart racing. "You 'bout near scared the life outta me!"

"Sorry," James laughed. "Certainly don't wanna do that."

"How long you been standin' there?"

James walked toward her sniffing the air. "Long enough for my nose to recognize that aroma."

Lily smiled at the comment. "Auntie always used to say, 'ain't a man alive who can't smell his favorite meal cookin' a mile away.'"

"That Auntie was a wise woman."

"Anna Mae and Ben was fixin' liver tonight, so I figured I'd stick with tradition."

Tradition started many years ago on the nights that James's mother insisted on Lily fixing liver for the entire family. Just for James, Lily would always secretly make a small side dish of either biscuits and gravy or his absolute favorite: spicy Jambalaya and cornbread. James always made a fuss about how much he hated liver, so Lily had taught him the trick of pretending to wipe his mouth after taking a bite of it, but then spitting it into his napkin. After dinner, James would lock the door to his bedroom and pull out the plate full of biscuits and gravy or Jambalaya that Lily always hid underneath his bed to make up for the liver that had made its way into the trash can by then. Cold or hot, for breakfast or otherwise, James would nearly swallow Lily's biscuits whole or shovel the spicy rice into his little face like it was his last meal.

The current look on James's face told Lily that his love for her spicy Jambalaya and cornbread still prevailed. He followed his nose to Lily's pot, opened the lid, and proceeded to lift the ladle to take a bite, but Lily smacked his hand down before it reached his mouth. "Now I know Auntie and yo' mama done taught you betta' manners than that!"

"*Manners?* What're those?" James laughed, scratching his head.

"Auntie would 'a whooped you good for diggin' in her food! She taught me to keep you boys on the straight and narrow. Now, get your nose outta there and let me fix you a plate," Lily said playfully.

"Yes, ma'am," James teased, enjoying the momentary return of the sassy Lily that he remembered as a boy.

By the time Lily wandered over to the table with his plate, James was ready with his napkin in his lap and his eating utensil in hand. Lily sat it down and watched him dig in as soon as the plate left her fingers. "It won't be much of a compliment to me if you choke ya'self to death on my cookin'," she laughed, sliding him a glass of freshly made lemonade.

James gulped the drink down without stopping and then took a moment to catch his breath. "I can't help it. I don't know what you put in this stuff, but once I start chewin', I can't stop."

Lily laughed as she filled his glass again, happy to see that he still enjoyed her food.

"Mighty kind of ya' to go outta your way for me like this," James managed to say in between bites.

"Well, I'd say this is really small compared to all you've done for me, don't ya' think?" Lily replied.

James stopped chewing for just a moment when he sensed the seriousness in Lily's voice, but his humbleness would not allow him to respond. He simply looked at her and shrugged his shoulders before returning to his meal.

Lily looked down at her hands as they lay resting in her lap, a place her eyes always seemed to fall whenever a wave of emotions started to overcome her. She stood up and walked over to the window that faced the lake, staring out at it a few seconds while she collected her thoughts. "I remema' the day you's in the kitchen talkin' to yo' fatha' 'bout bringin' me here," she suddenly said.

She caught James completely off guard with the topic. He stopped his spoon just as it was near his mouth and slowly put it back in the bowl, wondering where the conversation was about to go.

"When the words came outta your mouth, I remema' hopin' for…" Lily paused, feeling a sudden sense of shame for what she was about to say. "F-for God to strike me down right where I stood. Given all the circumstances ova' the years, I ain't neva' have a reason to think you wasn't tellin' the truth. Figured by now some man I ain't neva' met before would've…" She shook her head. "Well, that I'd be carryin' some man's baby by now," she said, unable to bring herself to say the dreadful things she was imagining.

However, for James it was too late. The words had triggered the thought of another man lying on top of her, which made the meal in his stomach start to churn. He pushed aside the bowl of food that he had yearned for just moments before, hoping to keep down what he had already eaten.

"All the way here, I's bracin' myself for what was about to come. I sat in the back 'a that wagon and cried and cried 'til it felt like my insides was 'bout near dried up," Lily hesitantly admitted. "I's emptyin' myself. Emptyin' my mind of all the disgustin' visions that was gnawin' away at me. Emptyin' myself of anga' and fear. Emptyin' myself 'a the ability to feel. Everythang … just empty. By the time we

243

got here, I's completely numb. Mentally, physically, emotionally, I couldn't feel no more than that oven ova' yonda',” she said, motioning her head toward it. “And 'til all this foolishness was ova' with, that's the way I wanted it … didn't wanna feel a damn thang.

“It wasn't 'til the day I walked this plantation end to end that I started to question everythang you had said to yo' fatha'. But even though I started to have my doubts 'bout why I's really here that day, I still felt numb through and through. Even afta' Anna Mae and Ben told me that incredible story 'bout what William had done for their family all them years ago, I still just wouldn't allow myself to feel anythang … I just couldn't.”

James still sat quietly staring into his half-eaten bowl of Jambalaya, silently accepting responsibility for Lily's feelings, unable to let go of the visual seeds that her words had planted in his mind: an endless stream of bodies invading hers, impregnating her with a child that was not his. His stomach and his thoughts justifiably punished him in unison.

Lily was silent for a moment before walking back over to sit down across from James. She waited for him to raise his head and look at her before she continued. “It wasn't 'til I sat outside on that porch while you's eatin' dinna' and told you all that I knew about William that I's finally able to accept the fact that you had gone and lied to yo' fatha' to get me here.” As Lily spoke, she kept her eyes trained on James. Her eyes were a spindle of rare colors that he had yet to see in any other, a hypnotizing sight he always found hard to turn away from. “The awful visions, the numbness, the coldness, the emptiness … all it took was for me to look you in the eyes that day, and I knew right then and there that I could finally set it all free and allow my body and my mind to feel all ova' again.

“The way I felt that day is a moment I'll neva' forget for the rest 'a my life.” Lily's eyes drifted down to the table, as if she could see it there replaying all over again. “It was the first day in years I felt like maybe I's worth somethin' to somebody again. And Lord knows I needed to feel that. Needed it more than anybody could eva' realize," she said, remembering how she once desired to end her own life. "Just that gesture alone meant the world to me. But now it's come to all 'a this," she said, shaking her head in disbelief with a faint smile on her face. "That stage," she said, turning for a moment to look out the window at it. "I swear I could live up there." She turned back toward James again. Without taking her eyes off him, she held his hand and ran her finger over the scar that she had stitched. "Feels like a new home you done went through hell and back to build for me with your very own hands."

James closed his eyes in the brief moment that Lily touched him, welcoming it and wanting it to continue. In an instant, he felt his stomach settle and the ugly visions fade away after her words had infused him with exuberance. After failing Lily for so long, here now, he was hearing the wonderful results of his attempt to atone for all of his mistakes. For years, he had found it nearly impossible to forgive himself, but her gentle touch and her genuine words helped to bring that possibility within reach.

"So, afta' all you've done for me, there ain't no way in the world I would eva' consida' fixin' you your favorite dish as goin' outta my way for you. Hell, cookin' is certainly the least I could eva' do for you," she laughed. "In all honesty, it don't matta' how many meals I make for you, it'll neva' be enough to repay you for all you've done to change my life to this magnitude."

"Lily, don't say…"

"No," she interrupted, "it's the truth. I owe you more than I'd eva' be able to give you in this lifetime. So, at this point, all I feel I can really do is say, thank you, James," she said, squeezing his hand with both of hers. "'Cause Lord knows I do. I thank you from the bottom 'a my heart for doin' what you had to do to get me here, and for believin' in me enough to take me on this journey with you," she smiled, fresh tears glistening in her eyes.

There was so much that James was eager to say in return, and it was all wanting to come out at once. He was taking the time to organize it all in his racing mind until the contents of his vivid night terrors rushed forward and trumped it all. He closed his eyes hard and gritted his teeth. Beads of sweat and a thumping heart followed, just as it always did whenever his recurring nightmare jarred him from his sleep. He could see the images clearly as he sat there across from Lily. The gruesome visions shut him down immediately. His desire to communicate the beautiful things that he wanted to share suddenly evaporated and left him with very little that he was willing to express to Lily from then on. "Well, I'm glad it's all helped to make a difference for you, Lily," was all he could muster the courage to say, as he slowly removed his hand from hers.

Lily was appreciative of how receptive James was, but she felt a slight emotional sting when he took his hand out of hers. The simple maneuver seemed to say a lot. Not only that, but she could feel that there was something on his mind that he refused to share with her. It bothered her that he had such a quick unexplained shift to a very cold disposition, especially since it was not the first time she had noticed such cold reactions to some of their warm interactions. Lily slowly got up from the table feeling a little embarrassed. She turned her back to James, walked over, and rested her hands on the counter, giving herself a chance to settle what she felt was an irrational need to cry about the change in James's demeanor.

When Lily walked away, James could easily sense that he had embarrassed or upset her. He blew out a breath of frustration at himself for always giving in to the powerful images that plagued him. He was beginning to realize that the images from his night terrors would take a great deal longer to overcome than he ever expected. In this instance, they had won the battle, but he was still not willing to give up on the war he was waging against them.

On behalf of this special day, though, Lily was not about to allow herself to sulk for long over James's reluctance to talk. She comforted herself by the fact that she was finally able to share with him her appreciation for his troubles, which was something she felt was long overdue. So, with that in mind, she was able to pull herself together rather quickly. For just a moment longer, she stood with her back to James, though. Before speaking again, she cleared her throat from the shakiness that would have accompanied her tears. She exhaled and finally turned back around. "Could you come with me a moment?" she asked James, completely changing the subject, wanting to lighten the mood.

James looked at her strangely at first, but then obliged and followed her into William's library. He remained puzzled by her request when the two of them arrived to a room filled with silence.

"I's hopin' I could play a song for you," Lily told him, as they stood face to face near the grand piano. "If you have the time, that is."

"If I didn't, I'd make the time ... *always*," James replied, gazing longingly at her.

After sensing that his warmth had returned, Lily found herself helplessly gazing at James as well. A pulse of heat ran through her during their silent exchange, making her even more eager to play the song she had prepared. James continued to gaze at her as she gracefully took her seat. Not long after the melody began, though, the need to close his eyes became too strong for him to withstand. He quickly found his mind drifting into another world after Lily's notes began to wrap around him.

Listening to the lightness of Lily's melody began to drum up all the repressed daydreams that James had been obsessed with in his youth. In the months since he and Lily had been reunited, all those old fantasies were slowly being unleashed. The song Lily currently played now had them quickly pelting the forefront of his mind, one after the other, beginning with the fantasy of the way in which he had once imagined proposing to Lily. His mind took him from there to the vision of the way she would have looked walking down the aisle toward him on their wedding day. He then felt his pulse quicken, thinking about what it would have been like having the honor of lying inside of his new wife in the hours after their sentimental ceremony. James continued flipping through the catalog of his old memories, next recalling the way he used to smile when thinking about the joyous tears he would have shed the day Lily gave birth to their first child. With Lily's music still tenderly whispering in his ears and those memories flooding his mind, James suddenly became overwhelmed with emotions. His stirring tears were for the fact God had yet to forge a legal pathway to make all those lifelong dreams come true, despite the countless times he had prayed for such a miracle.

James suddenly opened his eyes and stared at Lily, wondering how it could ever be punishable by law to show such a lovely woman how deeply he cared for her by giving her the sort of life she deserved. James had mentally exhausted himself over the years trying to make sense of it. Needing to get his mind off such an impossible dilemma, he let the visions fade and focused on Lily. He became fixated on the innocent look on her face as she sat playing in the perfectly sunlit library. James began examining the intricate lines of her lips, the simple style of her tight curly hair, her even features, and the beauty of her flawless honey-brown skin. Everything about her made him suddenly want nothing more than to make love to her right then and there. He was ready to happily disregard the laws, feeling as though expressing his love to Lily would be worth the punishment he would receive in a court of law.

The desire to touch Lily, to hold her, to caress and kiss her was nearly too intense for James to ignore with her sitting so close, especially with her scent pleasantly invading his nose. Suddenly, though, the room fell silent and he was jolted from his fixation.

I see us ... and the sort 'a life I wish we could have togetha', Lily thought to herself. "I see you," escaped her lips instead, as she opened her eyes and stared at the piano keys. "In my mind," she explained. "Wheneva' I play that song, I see you just as clear as you standin' in front 'a me now."

After the fantasy experience James had while listening, he was easily convinced of the truth in Lily's words. Her admission, though, suddenly made him crave to know the intimate details of her visions.

"I've played this song on this day for the last ten years." Lily finally looked up at James. "But I wanted you to hear it this time." She reached down and retrieved a box that she had placed underneath the piano earlier. "And I wanted to give you this," she said shyly. "Happy birthday to you, James."

James smiled. "Lily..."

"I-I'm sorry I wasn't able to buy you anything fancy," she explained as a disclaimer before he opened the box.

James sat his gift down, took Lily by the hand, and helped her up from the bench, so that he could look her directly in the eyes before he spoke. "Don't you eva' be sorry about that. Not eva', ya' hear? The dinna', everything you had to say to me in the kitchen a while ago, and this gift, it's all wonderful. It really means a lot to me," he reassured her. "And that song was beautiful ... *really* beautiful, Lily. It's worth far more to me than any expensive gifts, I promise ya' that. So, please don't feel embarrassed about any 'a this, okay?"

"Okay. Thank you for that." The sincerity of his words immediately melted her nervousness. She perked up and smiled. "But before you open that, I have one otha' thing for you."

"There's more?" James smiled.

"Mm-hmm," Lily smiled. "Follow me."

James happily followed behind Lily holding onto his gift. Its sentimental value immediately rose when he suddenly realized that his birthday was the reason Lily had wanted the day off. He was deeply moved by the fact that she would even consider wanting to celebrate his birthday after all the things he had put her through in the past, especially in lieu of her beloved show.

Lily guided James back into the kitchen where she then picked up a round, covered platter and carried it over to the dining room table. She lifted the lid and revealed a beautifully decorated cake. "Strawberry, right? It's still your favorite … I hope," she asked nervously.

"Yes. Yes, it still is," James answered, his mouth already watering.

"Good." Lily let out a sigh of relief. "Can't celebrate your birthday without the right cake."

"Nor without the right company," James replied. "So, can I ask one otha' thing of you this evenin', Miss Lily?"

"On your birthday, I shall humbly provide you with all that you ask, sire," she said, copying William's British accent and taking a bow. She had become fascinated by the British way of life after all the stories William had told her about his time in Great Britain as a boy.

James played along, turning himself into a British royal as well. He took Lily by the hand. "Excellent, m'lady. Then have a piece 'a cake with me, won't you?"

"Why certainly," Lily smiled, as she proceeded to sit down at the kitchen table.

"No. Not here." James stopped her, taking her gently by the arm before she could sit down. "Follow me," he instructed.

James picked up the cake and his gift and led Lily out the back door. He then guided her toward the special spot on William's land, where he always found her relaxing after grueling rehearsals. James often joined her there, wanting to spend every minute of his free time by her side. He wanted to interact with her in the same meaningful ways that they once had during the precious years when they had escaped on Sundays to their childhood paradise. However, their relationship had yet to completely return to that level of effortlessness. James could still sometimes sense Lily's reluctance to fully open up to him. But he remained determined to regain her trust and earn her forgiveness. So, he continued to be patient, feeling as though Lily was worth whatever time it took to rebuild and re-strengthen the unique bond he once had with her.

Lily followed quietly behind James, wondering why he preferred to eat outside, but when she stepped around the massive trunk of the old oak tree, the answer to that became clear. "Today is a very special day indeed," James told her, as she looked down at the array of things that were lying underneath the tree, where she loved to sit and take in the view of the lake.

When Tucker saw James in town earlier, he was shopping for this very moment. After returning to William's estate, James snuck around back to lay out the blanket, wine, and the basket of fruits he had purchased. A neatly wrapped present lay as the centerpiece to it all. The surprise was in honor of an incredibly unique occasion. After setting the cake down, James turned to Lily and held both of her hands. "Happy birthday to you too, Lily."

By sheer coincidence, James was not willing to let this unique day pass by unacknowledged either. It was a day the pair had begun celebrating together on his tenth birthday ...

After James's birthday party was over, James was out by the creek with Lily, letting her use the new fishing rod he had gotten as a gift.

She was casting the line out into the water as James stood next to her tossing grapes into the air and catching them in his mouth. "So, when's your birthday?" he had asked Lily casually in between tosses.

"Don't know," Lily replied just as casually.

The grape James was tossing hit him in the head when he quickly turned his attention to Lily. "What do ya' mean you don't know when your birthday is?!" he asked, sounding baffled by such a thing.

"Just what I said. I don't know. My mama was neva' certain of the exact date. She say I's born on the hottest day she could eva' rememba' in the summa' of 1835, just like you. But ain't nobody eva' tell 'er exactly what day it was. She say she was awful sick for days not long afta' I's born, from an infection or somethin'. So, she couldn't hardly rememba' much 'a anything from that week anyway."

"I ain't neva' heard 'a nobody without a birthday."

"Well, ya' heard 'a someone now I s'ppose," Lily said, reeling in the fishing line and handing the pole back to James.

"You mean you ain't neva' had no party, or presents, or nothin'?"

"Slaves ain't got no money to buy presents, and even if we did, it'd be kind 'a hard to celebrate when you don't even know what day to do it on."

James just sat there staring at his fishing rod, perplexed at how such an important thing could be overlooked. "Well, you would if I gave you mine."

"Gave me your what?"

"My birthday."

"You can't just *give* your birthday away, James!" Lily told him in a condescending tone.

"Can so! It's mine! I can do whateva' I please with it! And I wanna give it to ya'!"

Lily threw her hands on her thin hips and cocked her head to the side. "Well, I ain't gonna letchya'!" she fired back.

"But I want to. Just don't seem right that you ain't neva' had a birthday. I done celebrated ten 'a mine already, and I'm almost a man now," James explained, flexing his arm and squeezing his own muscle. "So, I don't need no more birthdays anyway."

"James, that's awful nice 'a you 'n all, but I can't take your birthday away from you. It's too special. 'Sides, you ain't hardly no man yet! I don't see a speck 'a hair on your face and your arms are 'bout near skinny as that fishin' rod!" Lily said, suddenly bursting out in laughter.

James sat on a log nearby and hung his head low, not finding any humor in Lily's comment at all.

Lily looked over at her friend and could tell he was genuinely hurt by the rejection of his offer, and she suddenly felt terrible about herself. She sat down next to James and put her arm around him. "I'm sorry, James. That's really kind of you."

"But you still won't take it, will ya'?" he asked, truly sounding hurt.

"No, but maybeee…"

"Maybe what?"

"Maybe we can *share?*"

"Heeey yeeeah! I like that even betta'!" James perked up and smiled.

"Me too!"

"Well then, happy birthday Lily!" James exclaimed, handing her his brand-new fishing rod.

"What're you doin'?" she asked.

"Here take it. It's your first birthday gift."

"James, I-I can't take this. Your daddy'll kill you!"

"But you gotta have a gift. I'll just tell 'em I dropped it in the deep part 'a the creek tryna reel in a big fish or somethin'. He'll get me anotha' one."

"Thank you, James!" Lily's eyes lit up looking at the brand-new pole in her lap. She leaned over and gave James a huge hug. "Thank you so much!"

"You're welcome," he coughed. "L-lily y-you're ch-chokin' me!"

"Sorry," she said, letting go of the firm bear hug she had him in.

"It's alright," he said, rubbing his neck. "C'mon! Let's do some more fishin'!"

The whole conversation seemed logical in the innocence of their youthful minds. Oddly, though, as they grew, James and Lily never challenged the validity of her adopting his birthday. Year after year, they celebrated together in their own grand way, as if their birthdays had legitimately fallen on the same date. During their celebrations, it had become tradition for James to read a story of Lily's choosing. Wilbur even joined the festivities as they ate strawberry cake on a picnic blanket underneath their favorite tree in their playground paradise. They celebrated that way up until their sixteenth birthdays. On their seventeenth, however, their tradition came to an end.

The day of their seventeenth birthdays, James sat with his head rested against his bedroom window, looking completely dejected. He had Lily's favorite book in his hand, the one he had given to her after they had spent a long summer apart. Lily loved the story so much, she had requested for James to read it during every future birthday celebration, which was something he should have been doing at that very moment. But there he sat, devoured by sadness, unable to even bring himself to leave his room. Suddenly, though, he jumped to his feet when he saw Lily sneaking from the slave quarters toward their usual birthday meeting place. James was surprised to see her headed there. A few months prior, his father had discovered his friendship with Lily. Since then, James had hardly spoken a word to her. Jesse's overbearing demands had left James feeling as though he had no choice but to begin treating Lily in the cold ways that his father expected masters to treat their slaves. So, while under the intense scrutiny of his father's watchful eyes, he was far too terrified to meet Lily at the creek. For months, James had stoically accepted his sentence of life without Lily. But now seeing that she would be at *their* special tree, celebrating *their* birthday *alone*, caused a wave of sorrowful tears to instantly spill from his eyes.

Two hours later, still immobilized by sadness, James glanced out the window again and saw Lily return from their playground paradise with her head down. Her body language confessed to her pain. He figured it was parallel to his own. "Goodbye, Lily," he whispered, as his tears pelted the leather cover of the book that he desperately wanted to share with her that day. Instead, he placed her book inside his trunk and refused to ever read it again without her.

For months, Lily had terribly missed the intimate companionship of her best friend. The night before turning seventeen, she had gotten down on her knees and begged God to bring her and James together again for just a few hours to celebrate their birthday. So, while James sat sulking by his window, Lily sat anxiously underneath their tree at the creek, hoping to hear her cherished story, being read to her by an even more cherished friend. For two hours, though, chirping birds was all she heard with Wilbur as her only company. When Lily's prayers went unanswered, she walked back to the slave quarters in tears, and finally accepted that her friendship with James was truly over.

... So, ironically, on a day that signified the official ending of their friendship, James now stood before Lily wanting to officially cement their unique bond all over again. In front of William's sparkling lake, on a tiny plot of land that he knew she cherished, James was ready to show Lily how truly sorry he was for all his mistakes. He hoped to create a new beginning for them both, one that slowly erased the pain from the past. James was ready to wipe those ugly memories away and stamp each and every day of their future together as *happy*. He felt there was no better way to begin that mission than by honoring the day that Lily came into the world with a beautiful picnic, underneath a tree where she often daydreamed of a better life for herself, the sort of life that James was giving up his own dreams to help give her.

Filled with hope, James took both of Lily's hands into his. "Lily, afta' everything we've been through ova' the last several years, maybe I don't deserve this, but please say you'll celebrate with me again, the way we used to." He squeezed her hands a little tighter. "Please?"

Lily looked down again at the spread that James had gone through the efforts of placing there for her, and she knew she could never reject such a beautiful invitation. "I'd love to," she smiled.

James smiled in return, helped her to sit down, and poured her a glass of wine. After an eight-year hiatus, they then resumed the celebration of each other's lives with a toast. James was the first to make his dedication. "To your extraordinary musical accomplishments this year and to the many more that will surely follow." They touched glasses, and each took a sip of the finely aged red wine.

"And I'd like to dedicate this next toast to my closest, most dearest friend," Lily began. "He is a friend who has always been there for me through all the ups and downs 'a my life, a friend that I once used to hold close to me, and who I have missed terribly." She raised her glass. "And so, to you, *Wilbur!* I shall collect many flies and crickets in honor of your life this evenin'!" she joked.

"*Wilbur?!*" was the only word James could get out through his laughter.

256

"Well, of course. Who else could I possibly be talkin' about?" Lily asked sarcastically.

James pointed to himself. "I have no idea," he said just as sarcastically.

"Oh yeah." Lily waved her hand dismissively at him. "And you too," she said dryly.

Lily's sarcasm set the tone for the evening. It was lighthearted and playful, the way it had been between them as teenagers. They began reminiscing with one another about the memories of their previous birthday adventures while they sipped their wine and ate the grapes and strawberries that James had packed. After sharing their thoughts for a while, Lily placed a few candles on the cake and lit them. She closed her eyes to make her silent wish, but James decided to forgo the opportunity. Instead, he chose to admire the soft features of the woman who had been the subject of *all* his past birthday wishes, one of which was coming true right there before his very eyes. After Lily made her wish and opened her eyes, they blew out their candles *together*.

Despite James's attempt to put Lily at ease about the gift she had gotten him, she still began to feel a bit uneasy when he started to unwrap it. However, she refrained from saying anything until after he had retrieved the two pair of pants that the box contained. "I-I mended 'em and cleaned 'em up good for you," she explained, feeling her nerves striking again. "I seen where you tore both of 'em up at the knees while you's workin' on the stage. Figured it'd save you from havin' to buy new ones."

James turned the pants over and scrutinized them. "I do believe you's lyin' to me, Miss Lily," he responded, a serious tone in his voice.

Lily furrowed her eyebrows and looked at him confused.

"I saw them sewin' fairies sprinklin' that mendin' dust on these just the otha' night!"

"Dang it!" Lily snapped her finger. "Ya' caught me!" she exclaimed through a sudden burst of genuine laughter.

James shook his head. "Shame on you for tryna take all the credit!" he laughed.

"I guess I sho' deserved that one, didn't I?" Lily asked, as she wiped her laughter tears away.

"Yeeeah ya' kinda did."

"Well, I'll be sure to thank the fairies the next time I see 'em," she replied, a brilliant smile on her face.

"You do that," James playfully demanded.

James continued to stare at Lily, suddenly wanting even more now to make love to her under the shade of her favorite tree, near the tranquility of the waters. Lily returned the gaze and her smile slowly faded away. The sudden sensual expression on her face instantly caused James's southern region to throb with want. Lily could easily sense his passionate desires, and she found that her desires were mutual. At that very moment, she would have welcomed him inside of her without a second of hesitation.

James swallowed hard and quietly exhaled to alleviate the mounting pressure in his pants. He then cleared his throat. "Thank you, Lily," he finally said.

"You're very welcome," Lily replied, still refusing to take her eyes off him. She rather liked the effect that she had on his body ... and that *he* was suddenly having on *hers*.

To help return his body back to normal, James forced himself to break eye contact with Lily. He turned toward her gift, grabbed it, and handed it to her. To further cool himself down, he took quiet deep breaths as he watched Lily proceed to unwrap her present like an eager child at Christmas.

After Lily tore the wrapper away, she froze, her eyes fixated on the gift in her hands. "James," she whispered, too stunned to say anything else. She immediately recognized that she was holding onto the original novel he had given to her many summers ago, one she always found herself craving to hear on every birthday since.

Lily's cherished book was the very first thing James had packed before their journey, with the specific intention of giving it back to her on this very day. He now watched her closely as she flipped through it, running her fingers down some of its pages. She was remembering the first time she had heard it and the unforgettable emotions she felt as she hung on every word. "I can't believe you still have this. I didn't think I'd eva' hear it again," she whispered.

"It's yours. I wouldn't've dreamed of gettin' rid of it."

"Thank you for this."

"You're welcome."

Eager to experience the emotional ride again, Lily handed the book to James. "Well ... aren't you gonna read it?"

"No," James quickly replied.

Lily stared at him, a puzzled look on her face.

"*You* are," he explained.

"But, James, I can't..."

"I've lost count 'a how many times I've kicked myself ova' the fact that I made a promise to you years ago ... a promise that I've yet to keep," James confessed. "But one thing I'm proud to say about myself is that I'm a man 'a my word. So, Miss Lily..." He handed the book back to her. "By our next birthday, I'm gonna see to it that you're able to read this here story from end to end, without a single word missed in between." He gently lifted Lily's face and looked into her eyes. "You have my word."

Lily wanted to keep her emotions at bay during their birthday to ensure that it was nothing but a joyous celebration, but James's gesture touched her too deeply to maintain control. Tears suddenly spilled from her eyes and christened the cover of the very first book she would ever be able to read.

James gave in to his natural need to comfort Lily. He felt no words were required this time. He simply slid over and embraced her. His embrace grew stronger the longer he held her, and so too did his desire not to let her go.

"Thank you," Lily whispered as she laid her head on his shoulder and embraced him in return.

After a few moments, James pulled back to look at her. "You don't owe me any thanks, Lily. I don't deserve it anyway. If anything, I should be thankin' *you* for your patience. I'm truly sorry this has taken so long. It's bothered me for years that you can't read this book, or any otha' book for that matta'. But I promise ya', I'm gonna do all I can to make it right."

"And for that, I'm truly grateful."

James nodded and silently accepted her kind words. "Now, c'mon ova' here," he said with a smile, patting the spot next to him.

Lily huddled close to James underneath her favorite tree on her little piece of heaven on William's land. Within an instant, her brain had shut off her tears and opened her knowledge-hungry memory vault, eager to absorb every word of her very first reading lesson. Proudly, James then proceeded to give her a gift that would literally last her a lifetime.

Chapter Fifteen

M ary Jo Parker spent a good portion of her Saturday afternoon dolling herself up for yet another business dinner meeting with her father on the Adams plantation. She rode with him in their expensive carriage with her posture perfect, her hair frozen in spiral curls, and make-up meticulously pasted on her face, waving a hand fan that matched her fancy dress. The weather had warmed considerably since the last time she had seen James in town at Albert's General Store. The swift movement of her hand fan was to ensure that not one drop of summer sweat ruined her hair or make-up before James laid eyes on her. She wanted to present herself to him looking like an irresistible prize that he would be desperate to win.

The spot Mary Jo planned to sit during dinner was just as calculated as her attire. Her chosen seat would be the one that gave James's nose the easiest access to her perfume and his eyes a constant view of her best side. She had conversation prepared in her mind as well. As she rode along, she went over the topics in her head, smiling to herself as she imagined the way in which James would be as captivated by her intellect as he was by her beauty. Her smile broadened at the thought of his eyes lighting up upon seeing her so perfectly put together. For months, Mary Jo had obsessively fantasized about James, the way she was now. Her fantasies were sometimes unbecoming of a young debutante before being honored with marriage. But Mary Jo Parker did not care. When it came to James Adams, she felt the rules of societal etiquette were worth obliterating.

Being her father's only child, Joseph Parker viewed Mary Jo as his most prized possession. He never once had the willpower to stop himself from giving his daughter *everything* she ever wanted throughout her life. Consequently, she grew up expecting everyone else to give in to her accordingly. If not, the tantrums she sometimes threw were dramatic enough to turn the head of a two-year-old in the midst of his own meltdown. She had no shame in screaming, lying, scheming, and stealing to get what she wanted. But, in the case of James Adams, Mary Jo did not just *want* him; she *needed* him, and she had no qualms about stooping to childish levels to have him. Before she resorted to such immature antics, though, Mary Jo simply tried turning herself into the most glamorous woman possible whenever she was due to be in James's presence.

In the years while James was away at school, a string of other men had attempted to court Mary Jo. She found them all boring and visually unappealing in comparison to the man she wanted. Her desires for their company usually ceased immediately after she selfishly took the lavish gifts they bestowed upon her during their quest to win her affections. She happily took their expensive trinkets and then toyed with their emotions, and sometimes even their bodies, knowing they would never be anything more than human playthings to fulfill her boredom while she waited, *impatiently,* for the one man she truly desired.

In her youth, Mary Jo always had an insatiable thirst for James. But, after seeing the sculpt-worthy man he had grown into, her simple thirst was now an insatiable hunger. With months having passed since their interaction at the store, Mary Jo was now starving to be near him. It was in that state of famine that she arrived at the Adams' plantation, hoping to finally have her voracious cravings satisfied.

Mary Jo's carriage stopped just in front of Jesse's rundown porch. Her father exited first, and then he helped his daughter down. Mary Jo emerged in her baby blue floor-length gown, holding onto her shawl, stepping down like a queen arriving at a ball in her honor. Her father then escorted her carefully up the steps toward Jesse, who waited near the front door.

It had been people like Jesse who had perpetuated Mary Jo's arrogance over the years. Jesse never failed to give her and her rich father the royal treatment during their visits to his plantation. The business relationship with Joseph Parker was essential to the lining of Jesse's pockets. Therefore, business dinner meetings with Joseph were as calculated as Mary Jo's attire. In preparation for their arrival, Jesse always demanded a few of his field slaves to scour themselves thoroughly, dress in fine attire, and work indoors to give the appearance that a crew of cooking and cleaning house slaves was the norm in his home. Even Jesse himself managed to scrub the dirt from beneath his fingernails. He got his hair cut, found his way to a bar of soap, and stuffed himself into a clean suit. All the while his temporary house slaves were setting out his deceased wife's finest china and preparing a five-course meal fit for a king and his princess at a Thanksgiving feast. Jesse rolled out the royal carpet for the Parker's to walk on, right along with his dignity.

With the utmost hospitality in mind, Jesse met the Parkers at the door with his two faux butlers standing on either side of him. The two field slaves stood tall with their hands covered in white gloves, clasped in front of them. "Evenin'," Jesse greeted, shaking Joseph's hand. "Welcome, welcome."

"Evenin', Jesse. Good to see you again, ol' friend," Joseph responded.

"Mary Jo, y'ur lookin' just as darlin' as eva'," Jesse complimented. "Hard to believe you done growed up right before my eyes. It seems like not long ago y'ur daddy was carryin' ya' up these porch steps on his hip."

Mary Jo rolled her eyes and sidestepped past Jesse faster than a pile of manure. No matter how much he scoured himself, she was disgusted by the man. She did not understand how such a repulsive human could produce one as visually stunning as James. The perplexing thought always made her question James's paternity. If it was not for the fine specimen of a man that Jesse had *allegedly* created, Mary Jo would not have even bothered to accompany her father to this meeting. It had been over five months since speaking to James in town; she was certain that he would have returned from his business travels by now. So, despite how repulsed she was by Jesse, she was not willing to pass on the opportunity to finally see James again.

Eager to lay eyes on James, Mary Jo entered the house, halted in the foyer, and casually looked around. Aside from the clinking of plates and pots in the kitchen, the house was fairly silent. She was instantly annoyed when her ears were not met with the sound of a particular voice. However, she perked up when she suddenly heard footsteps upstairs and the sound of a door closing. Deep in conversation, Joseph and Jesse breezed by her toward the dining room. Mary Jo took the moment alone to double check her appearance in the foyer mirror. She quickly smoothed out her dress and laid a few tendrils of hair neatly over her shoulders. Hoping to give James an unobstructed view of her whole body, she lingered there in the foyer, waiting on him to descend the stairs. After a few minutes there alone, though, Joseph called after her to join him in the dining room.

Mary Jo sat poised at the dinner table, trying her best not to seem too eager, but inside she was oozing with desperation. She did not care about the salad that a slave had placed in front of her or the wine that went along with it. Joseph always used such moments to groom his only child to take over the family business. Mary Jo, therefore, knew to be paying keen attention to her father's conversational business methods. But so long as James's chair went unoccupied, she lacked the ability to focus on anything her father was saying. She just sat there continuing to stare at the two other place settings across the table and the empty chairs behind them. As she grew more impatient, perspiration began to threaten her make-up. Just before the perspiration turned into beads of rolling sweat, though, Mary Jo finally heard the sound of two deep southern voices and footsteps stomping down the stairs. She instantly sat up taller, patted her hair, and a smile stretched across her face as her anticipation soared.

"Pa, this the document you's lookin' for?" J.R. asked, after he arrived in the dining room next to his younger brother, Jacob.

Jesse glanced at it. "Yup, that's it! Thank ya' boys."

"Not a problem," Jacob replied.

"Hello Mary Jo," J.R. said, a hint of lust in his tone. "Nice to see ya' again, sweetheart."

Mary Jo cringed at J.R. and his term of endearment. She quickly slid her chair a few inches away from him after he sat down beside her. Being his father's repulsive-looking twin, J.R. made her equally sick to her stomach.

"Yeah, sho' is good to see ya'," Jacob agreed, staring at her with his mouth open as he sat down across from her.

"Mr. Adams," Mary Jo said, interrupting the conversation Jesse was having with her father. "Won't James be joinin' us this evenin'?"

"Sorry to say lil' darlin' but not t'night," Jesse replied.

"Oh, I see. May I ask where he is?"

"Mary Jo!" her father snapped. "That ain't any of y'ur business."

"It's alright Joseph," Jesse interjected.

"Well, I don't mean to be nosy daddy. It's just that I had a welcome home gift I's wantin' to give James, and I can't quite seem to catch up with 'em these days."

"I see. That's mighty kind of ya'," Jesse replied. "Well, he dropped our house slave off to a breeda' a few hours north 'a here, then he went just 'cross the borda' to stay with a friend from his old university while he does some medical research with a professor there at the school. Shouldn't be long 'fore he's back, though. Lily should be good 'n swollen by now," he laughed. He then flashed his unsightly yellow smile, happy to know that Mary Jo still had an interest in James, feeling as though it was a bonus reason for Joseph to renew their contract.

"Jesse Adams allowin' a slave off his property? World must be comin' to an end," Joseph joked.

"Well, I thought it was 'bout time I started lettin' James run a few things around here. I ain't gettin' any younga'. James figured takin' Lily to a breeda' would give us a financial boost, so I went on and let 'em take 'er. He'll be takin' ova' this place soon. Won't be too long 'fore he's the one sittin' here doin' all the negotiatin'."

Mary Jo's mind faded away from the conversation after that. She did not care about where James would be sitting in future circumstances. What mattered was that he was not sitting next to her *now*, close enough to smell the new perfume she had purchased just for his nose to inhale. He was not there to see the hair and make-up that she had spent all day crafting, and the dress that she had selected, in what she *thought* was his favorite color. Suddenly not caring about her debutante poise and posture, Mary Jo slouched in her seat. She picked up the wine she had ignored earlier and quickly chugged it all, wanting to numb herself through yet another evening without the man she was craving to see.

Chapter Sixteen

A *"Quasi-free"* Slave:

A slave who is hired out by his master as free for the benefit of financial gain.

Slave Code
Article VI Section II

Every person whose grandfathers or grandmothers were Negro, although all other progenitors were white, are to be deemed as "Negro." Any person with one quarter or more Negro blood is to be deemed "Mulatto."

"What the hell is this?!" James yelled at Tucker McCormick. James had nearly knocked the hinges off the swinging doors of Buck's Tavern before walking up to Tucker and demanding answers for the article he had just read. He slammed the newspaper down on the bar, where Tucker sat flooding his stomach with whiskey. James knew he would find him there. Drowning his sorrows at Buck's Tavern had been Tucker's daily pastime since the bank had finally foreclosed on his bar a few weeks earlier.

"I don't know what the hell y'ur talkin' 'bout, schoolboy," Tucker said calmly, still sipping his whiskey. It was barely noon and Tucker had already drank enough to slow his reaction to being startled. However, the same could not be said for the few other patrons who had all suddenly ceased their conversations and turned in the direction of the ruckus. Oblivious to all the eyes on him, Tucker picked up the newspaper, held it close and then far away, trying to get his intoxicated eyes to adjust.

ATHENS DAILY JOURNAL

Sunday Edition
June 5, 1859
WARNING TO POTENTIAL INVESTORS

James Adams, a slave owner from Virginia, recently discovered that his alleged former house slave is a self-taught pianist, who possesses the ability to play musical arrangements after hearing them only once. Since then, Mr. Adams has been using his house slave's abilities to his advantage by exploiting her acts at small taverns, galas, and side shows. Mr. Adams' hope is to earn the money necessary to pay off gambling debts and bills owed to the plantation that has been in his family for four generations. Currently, Mr. Adams is in the process of propositioning owners and managers of different theaters and orchestras to hire out his alleged former house slave, in an effort to turn his usually small profits into significant gains, under the pretense that the aforementioned slave has been legally manumitted. However, sources have yet to find proof that Mr. Adams' house slave has truly been manumitted. Therefore, these sources would like to warn potential businessmen to steer clear of the Virginia slave owner and his counterpart, William Werthington. Mr. Werthington is a well-known composer, musician, and retired music teacher, who resides here in Athens. Mr. Werthington recently deceived an entire audience during a show held on his property on April sixteenth of this year, which was advertised to the public as "The Return of William Werthington." Many patrons were upset to find that Mr. Werthington had actually masked the truth about the true producer of the evening's ensemble: the alleged recently freed house slave of Mr. Adams. It is assumed that Mr. Adams and Mr. Werthington's deception was an effort to garner the attention of the public, attract potential investors, and eventually hire out the aforementioned slave. We hereby remind all citizens that the practice of hiring "Quasi-free Negroes" was outlawed in Slave Code Article XX Section

I, enacted in 1793. All potential businessmen are hereby forewarned that the penalty for breaking this law shall be carried out to the fullest extent allowed by law.

"Pppphh!" Tucker fluttered his numb lips, sending droplets of spit flying everywhere. "I ain't have nothin' to do with this shit." He tossed the newspaper aside and proceeded to try to take another sip of his whiskey.

James grabbed Tucker's hand and slammed the glass back down on the counter. "You're a goddamn liar! You make me and William out to be tyrants in this article!"

The whiskey gave Tucker the liquid courage to stumble off his barstool and stand toe-to-toe with James. "I told you, I ain't have nothin' to do with that shit!"

"Bullshit! I know you're behind this! Honestly, I don't give a damn what you or anybody else in this town thinks 'a me, but I won't let you get away with defamin' William! And you betta' hope to whateva' God you believe in that Lily neva' finds out about this slanderous garbage! For you to try to make her think any 'a this is true is low, even for a piece 'a outhouse shit like you!"

"No point in your fears then, schoolboy! Y'ur little monkey can't read anyway ... Music or otha'wise, I'm sure!"

Only the memory of William's lecture kept James from grabbing Tucker by the throat and squeezing until his lips turned blue and his beady eyes bulged from his head. James gritted his teeth and clenched his fists together, but then composed himself and headed toward the saloon exit without another word.

"That article is right, ya know!" Tucker shouted as James walked away. "You might've deceived a few people into comin' to that shit you call a show, but it won't be long before everybody gets sick 'a you and that lil' nigga'! She'll fade away like a fart in the wind!" Tucker nearly fell over laughing at himself. "Face it! She'll neva' be anythang more than the bottom-feedin' servant that she is!"

James was almost to the door before he turned back around and overturned the table that stood as the only barrier between him and Tucker. Shattered glasses and alcohol spilled on the floor.

"Oohhh, temper, temper," Tucker said, waving his finger at James. "Maybe I'm wrong. I notice you get awfully uppity ova' that lil' piano playin' bitch. Maybe you've already found out she's good for one otha' thing," he said, a smug look on his face. "Do tell, schoolboy … is brown suga's pussy any good? I've often been tempted to get a taste 'a that sweet little ass 'a hers."

James's fist caught Tucker clean across the mouth, splitting his lip wide open. Tucker saw black for a moment and then found himself on the floor lying in a pool of whiskey and broken glass. "Report that to the papers, you son of a bitch!" James said, looming over him.

Tucker licked the blood off his lip and gave an arrogant laugh as James walked away. "Her pussy's that good, huh?"

James jumped on his horse and rode away from Buck's Tavern in a full gallop, headed straight for Ohio University. Earlier in the day, another one of James's fraternity brothers had informed him that a man, fitting Tucker's description, had been roaming around the university, offering money in exchange for information about him. It was true that James had once done some gambling and borrowed money on his father's behalf, but the story published in the *Athens Daily Journal* had been embellished far beyond the truth. Now James was eager to "visit" the so-called friends whose loyalties had been purchased to bolster slanderous content.

* * * *

"Might I have a word with you, James," William called out from his den, after hearing his footsteps in the hallway.

James blew out a breath of frustration, not wanting to talk to anyone after the day he had had. He was ready to climb into his bed and sleep the rest of the evening away. Instead, he reluctantly walked into William's den with his hands gripped on his suspenders and a scowl on his face.

William sat at his desk with his hands clasped together, staring out the window. "Close the door," he instructed James.

"Listen, William, I'm a little tired, and I's hopin' to…"

"I had plans to rehearse with Lily today," William coldly interrupted. "Do you happen to know what has delayed my chance to do that?"

"No sa'."

"A knock at my front door."

"And?"

"And well, I was expecting the usual … You know, businessman, postman, old friend, things of that nature," he said, waving his hands in the air as he spoke. "But a *sheriff!* William stopped and pointed a single finger in the air. "No! Now, that I was *not* expecting. *That!* is most certainly *not* the usual, wouldn't you say?"

James dropped his head and exhaled sharply. "Yeah, about that…"

"Do you even care?"

"About what?"

"About Lily? Or about any of the things I spoke to you about not long ago?"

"What things?"

"Don't pretend to be a fool in my presence!" he said, glaring harshly at James.

"Yes, of course I do, but did you see what they wrote in…"

"I DON'T CARE!" William yelled, slamming his hands on his desk and quickly rising from his seat. "When you go into a tavern making a damn fool of yourself or go to a school tormenting your old classmates, you're giving everyone in this town more reason to believe that the garbage they wrote in that newspaper is true! We're already dealing with an extremely challenging situation for Lily, trying to navigate her through uncharted waters! And I swear, it's like you *want* to tip her boat over with your very own hands! So, tell me! What is it going to take for you to listen to me?!"

James just stared at the floor.

"Tell me?!" William insisted. "Sitting in jail, is that it?!"

Still, James did not respond.

"Or maybe, having the authorities drag Lily back to Virginia to your father while you're locked up?! Is that what you want?!" William continued. "Or worse! Giving someone reason to come here and hurt her?!"

"NO!" James spat, quickly looking up with fire in his eyes.

"Then why the hell does it seem like you don't give a damn about your actions?!" William walked from behind his desk and approached James, glaring harshly at him the whole way there. "You allowed a man as weak and stupid as Tucker McCormick to manipulate you like a puppet! He tap-danced you right into his little web! But you're too damn caught up in your emotions for Lily to see the trap he set!"

"*Emotions?!*"

"Don't insult my intelligence! Don't you dare!" William said, pointing his finger at James. "Even a blind man can see how you feel about her!"

"I don't know what you're talkin'…"

"Shut up! Just shut up! No more of your nonsense! I've had enough for today! For someone so smart, you sometimes act so bloody stupid!"

After William's tongue lashing, James felt reduced to the level of a scolded puppy. But he could not argue against the fact that he deserved it. "You're right, William, I'm sorry. I'll do all I can to fix this," he humbly replied.

William started to continue his tirade, but then caught himself and went silent. He turned and walked toward Emma's portrait. He needed the sight of her face to help soothe himself before he spoke again. "If you don't break things to begin with, James, then you won't have to crawl back, expending an extreme amount of energy trying to *fix* them," he said, calmness finally having returned to his tone. "If you truly care for Lily, the way I know you do, you'll let go of your ego and *always* do what's in her best interest from the start … *always*."

James continued to stand there silently, feeling like a soldier who was afraid to leave without being dismissed first. He simply watched as William stared at the mysterious woman in the picture. "Wh-what's her name?" James finally asked. "The woman in the portrait?"

"Emma. Her name is Emma."

"Who is she to you?"

The simple question instantly ignited William's nostalgia and gave him reason to tell a story that he felt might actually do James some good, especially considering the current circumstances. "Emma was the owner of a small country store that I frequented many moons ago. She was the type of woman who didn't know a stranger. She was hardworking, kind, patient, and always smiling. Her brilliant smile," William said while smiling himself. "It was that smile of hers that made my long trip into town to her store worth it. I often found myself there purchasing things I didn't even need, just to see that beautiful smile of hers," he admitted, chuckling at himself. "Some days, I wouldn't

273

buy anything at all. I'd just wander in and help Emma restock her shelves, just to have the pleasure of chatting with her. Our long conversations revealed that her beauty ran far deeper than my eyes could see. She was incredibly intelligent and wildly funny! With every conversation, I found myself more and more intrigued by her, and I found it harder and harder to leave. When I finally would find the willpower to go, I'd count the hours until I could see her again. It's so bizarre how the hours seemed to fly while I was with her, yet drag after I had left her for the day.

"I was helplessly drawn to Emma, but I'm embarrassed to admit that I was also intimidated by her. Oddly, I could talk to her about anything, but I could never quite get the nerve to ask her to have dinner with me ... until one December. During one of our many conversations, she happened to mention that she had nobody to spend Christmas with, and I *knew!*" William said, putting a finger in the air, "this was finally my chance! I explained to her that my family was in another country, and that I also had nobody to spend Christmas with, so I suggested that perhaps she and I should spend the holiday together. It felt like an eternity to me before she said anything. My heart was in my throat while I stood there frozen, waiting for her to answer." William smiled at the memory. "I'll never forget all the fireworks that went off inside me the moment she finally said that she'd love to join me. I swear, I felt like dancing all the way home!"

James had walked over and stared at Emma's portrait alongside William, feeling infected by his joy.

"I offered to cook for her for Christmas," William continued, "but Emma wouldn't hear of it. Instead, she came to my home and prepared the most wonderful meal for me. After we ate, we sat at the fireplace together, near the tree we had just decorated. There, I found myself telling her things about myself that I had never shared with any other. There was just something about her that comforted me enough to set aside all my fears about her ever judging me or betraying my secrets. I rambled on and on, eager to share my life with her. Oddly, though, after I told Emma a rather happy story about my mother, that smile I had come to love about her was gone. Out of the blue, she suddenly began to cry. I feared I had said something wrong."

"'Why the tears?' I remember asking her.

"'I haven't seen my mother in years,' she replied. 'I'd give anything to see her again,' she admitted, tears still cascading down her cheeks.

"It broke my heart to see Emma in that kind of pain. It instantly made me want to do whatever it would take to see her back into her mother's arms again. 'Tell me how I can fix this for you,' I asked her.

"Emma got up and walked away. She stood with her back to me near the fireplace and wouldn't look at me anymore, so I knew it was something serious.

"'Thank you, William,' she said to me, 'but there is no fixing this.'

"'Why not?' I asked. 'Has your mother passed?'

"Emma shook her head. 'My mother made me promise never to see her again,' she explained.

"'Why ever would she do such a thing?' I wanted to know. I got up and stood near the fireplace with her, and waited patiently for her to find the courage to speak again.

"'My mother ... She was a slave,' she hesitantly whispered in between her sniffling. 'I'm a Negro, William,' she boldly confessed."

James looked at Emma's portrait again and his eyes widened in disbelief. He initially saw nothing in her features that would have made him think twice about her race; her eyes were as blue as his. But after looking again, he finally noticed the fullness of her lips, the curl of her dark hair, and the slight olive tint in her skin, things he would never have picked up on before.

"Emma finally turned around and looked at me, and I will never forget the shame in her eyes," William continued. "'I'm so sorry I

275

didn't tell you sooner,' I remember her saying. I think she could feel that there was something incredible between us too, and she wanted to be honest with me before things went any further.

"After her confession, Emma began to gather her things to leave. Without hesitation, I walked over and took away everything she had in her hands. I guess she was expecting that I would be upset over her secret, but her honesty and her vulnerability only drew me closer to her. After I put her belongings down, I just held her. I didn't whisper another word. I just held her for the longest time, feeling as though my words would never have been enough for me to express that I accepted her ... *all* of her. I wanted to do whatever it took to let her know that her confession would never stop me from feeling what I felt for her ... not ever. Emma was the first and only woman I'd ever had the sort of deep connection with, and I didn't want to lose that. So, there was no way I was willing to allow her to just walk out the door and possibly out of my life. Had she done that..." William shook his head. "There's no doubt in my mind that I would've been devastated ... *absolutely* devastated.

"Fortunately, my embrace was all it took to settle her and convince her to stay. After that, she cozied herself next to me near the fireplace again and finished telling me the story of how her and her mother were both fathered by white slave owners, and that she was considered mulatto. She even said that since she was only one-quarter Negro, some people referred to her as a *quadroon,* or some strange term of that nature. Anyhow, she went on to further explain that her mother had worked hard to save money while she was carrying her so that she could buy their freedom. Her mother wanted to ensure that her child never knew one minute of what it was like to be a slave nor have the savage cycle of abuse continue with her daughter. She wanted more for Emma, so much so that she had unselfishly let her go when she was eighteen and told her never to return to the city that was her home. With Emma's fair skin, her mother knew she could easily pass as a Caucasian woman, so long as she never again claimed herself to be a part of their Negro family. Her mother wanted Emma to use the gift of her fair skin to her advantage and go on to create a better life for herself. In honor of her mother's selfless love, Emma did just that. She got a higher education, moved to a prominent town, and soon opened the little country store where she first caught my eye.

"With all that Emma had accomplished, it may have seemed like the fortune of her physical traits were a blessing. But the secret of who she really was haunted her every day. She hated denying her family and her heritage. She hated not being able to return home and see her mother and her other family members. But she knew that's what her mother wanted. Some days, though, she told me that she wanted to give her fancy lifestyle away just to have the honor of announcing proudly to everyone who her beloved mother really was.

"I was entranced by Emma's story, her courage, and her strength as she spoke to me that Christmas night. In fact, we spoke until sunrise. In that time, I learned that the woman I had gotten to know for months had actually been suffering in silence without her family. But despite it, she had never once let it stop her from always being so kind to everyone or from wearing the beautiful smile that drew me to her in the first place. I also learned that she had never once let her guard down and revealed her sorrows in front of anyone, until that night in front of the fireplace ... with *me*. It was the utmost compliment that it was *me* she chose to be vulnerable enough to share her pain and her secrets with. That meant I was special to her and that I was worth the risk. I felt so honored to have her trust in that way. It was one of the many things that made me fall more in love with her that Christmas night ... *madly* in love," William whispered, closing his eyes, forcing himself not to let his tears fall.

William pulled himself together and continued. "In the weeks that followed that Christmas evening, Emma and I were inseparable. Despite how brief our courtship was, I knew, beyond a shadow of a doubt, that this was the woman I wanted to marry. But I also knew that if people ever discovered the truth about Emma's identity, they would view my love for her as an abomination, a sin deserving of a sentence to hell, a sin that was even punishable by law. I also knew that my music career and even my life would be at risk. Taking all that into consideration, I asked myself something ... should I spend the rest of my life worrying about society's rules and take the risk, in years to come, of lying on my death bed utterly alone, regretting every moment I spent breathing? Or was I going to lie on my death bed recalling all the beautiful memories I had created with the woman I wanted to spend the rest of my life with, while she sits at my bedside comforting me as I take my last breath?" William turned to look at James. "My heart did not make it to the next beat before I knew the answer to that.

"So, the woman in this portrait," William said, pointing at her, "who was she to me, you ask?" He turned back toward Emma. "She was a woman I was too stubborn to live my life without. She was a woman I was prepared to lose my career over, a woman I would not have hesitated to lose my very life over. She was my heart, my life, my soul, my inspiration, my true love ... She was my beautiful wife and my very best friend," he said, as he touched her portrait. "She died in my arms some time ago, but not before giving me two incredible sons and forty glorious years of marriage. She was *everything* to me, James ... *absolutely* everything," he said, his voice cracking. "That's who she was to me."

William exhaled deeply before he was able to continue. "I miss her so. Every breath I take now seems like such an insurmountable task without her." He walked over to his desk to grab his pipe and to clear his throat, trying not to let the memory of his wife completely break him down in front of another man.

"Funny thing love, though, isn't it?" A much lighter tone had finally returned to William's voice. "Seems you don't have much control over who you want to bestow it upon, do you?" he asked, as he lit a match. "Can make even the sanest man do the craziest things, I tell ya!" He put his pipe in his mouth, inhaled, and let out a puff of smoke. "I spat on society's rules, and I must admit, I've never regretted it for a goddamn minute, my boy ... not a single minute!" William laughed as he pat James once on the back. William then turned his head toward the door when he suddenly heard that the faint sound of Lily's music down the hall had stopped. He took out his pocket watch and realized that he was late for a collaboration session with her. "Well now, if you'll excuse me," he said, patting James on the back again, "*Lily awaits.*" He winked and gave James a telling glance to let him know that he wanted those words to hold far deeper meaning than just their face value.

Just as William and James exited the den, Ben approached. "William, y'all have anotha' visita' at the front door," he informed them.

"Who is it?"

"Anotha' unknown. Young lookin' fella'. Don't look or sound like he from 'round here eitha'. Got a funny little accent. He sho' is mighty strange. Most folks them bandits escort to the door with them pistols look like they 'bout to mess themselves right time I open the door, but this youngun' ain't hardly broke a sweat yet."

"Interesting," William replied. Ben's description was so intriguing that he decided to greet the mysterious young man at the front door himself.

"Ahh, Mr. Werthington! Please excuse the unannounced visit," the young man said after William arrived at the front door. He extended his hand to shake. "I'm Landon." He was smiling despite Samuel's pistol near his skull.

"Pleasure to meet you," William said, looking at him strangely as he took hold of his hand. Landon's German accent was easily recognizable to him. Even his name sounded somewhat familiar, but

279

William could not quite place his face. William nodded to Samuel to let him know it was okay to remove the pistol he had pressed against Landon's skull and return to his post at the front entrance. The subtle signal wiped the giddy smile off Samuel's toothless, dirty face.

"It's an honor to see you again. I've attended quite a few of your performances as a boy," Landon explained, once his skull was free from metal.

"Is that so?" William smiled.

"Yes, I've actually…"

"What can we do for you?" James rudely interjected. He was still not in the best of moods and not at all impressed by this stranger's familiarity with William.

Landon stared at James a moment, sensing the coldness in his tone. Despite it, he pressed on with confidence. "Well, I know the two of you are probably very busy men, so I'll get on with the reason for my visit. I'm here because I was hoping to speak to the lady of the house."

"The lady of the house?" William questioned.

"Yes, the beautiful young lady from the show here on your plantation. Ms. Lily … Umm, I'm sorry, I wasn't told her last name."

"You don't need to know her last name!" James spat. "And what do you need to speak to her for?!" There was even more ice in his tone this time. William glared coldly at him, but James ignored it and continued to stare at Landon.

Yet again, though, Landon was not rattled by James's attitude. "Well, I was hoping to speak to her regarding her show."

"You can speak to *us* about that," James answered.

"Oh, I see. But it was my understanding that it is *Lily's* show, correct?"

"Yes, that is true," William replied.

"Well then, with all due respect to the both of you, I would much prefer to have a word with *her* … in private. If she doesn't mind, of course."

James was about to speak again, but William placed a hand on his shoulder to calm him. Landon's desire to speak directly to Lily had piqued William's curiosity about him even more. Normally, he would have the same skepticism and fire in his tone as James, but no other man, who had inquired about Lily, had ever bothered to consider that she was worthy of being part of the conversation. That small detail alone was enough to make William feel as though the young man deserved a chance to plead his case. Not only that, but he was also eager to figure out why his name and face seemed so familiar.

"James, go and fetch Lily, please."

"But…"

"Have her meet us in my den."

Lily was already preoccupied in the library with another guest who had arrived just minutes before Landon. Her unexpected visitor was the reason she had abruptly suspended the work she was doing on her new melody. He had walked in quietly and surprised her.

"Hello, Lily!"

"Elijah! How nice to see you again!" Lily had said after he stepped inside the library.

"Good to see you too!" he expressed, approaching her with an extremely confident stride in his step. He had been eager to see Lily again since the fundraiser, especially since Isabel went on one of her nonstop, mindless talking sessions and mentioned to him that Lily thought he was attractive.

"Oh my! What's all this for?" Lily asked, after Elijah presented her with a single rose and a box of chocolates.

"Just my way of congratulatin' you on the success of your show."

"Thank you so much! That's very kind of you!" She set her gifts aside and gave him a warm hug.

"I'm so sorry I haven't been able to attend any of your shows," Elijah said, holding Lily longer than she had anticipated.

"Oh, no need to apologize," she replied, as she freed herself from his embrace. "Your sista' told me you been busy tryna start a new business."

"That sista' of mine can't hardly hold wata'."

"Oh, sorry. Was I not s'pposed to know that?"

"No, no, it's quite alright. It's no secret. Just wish she'd leave a little left for me to talk about with folks sometimes," Elijah laughed.

"Well, I'm sure she means no harm. She's just awful proud 'a you."

"Sounds like the two 'a you talk pretty often."

"Yeah, she sort 'a feels like a sista' to me."

"Well, what otha' little secrets has she whispered to you about me?" Elijah asked, suddenly gazing at Lily in a way that hinted at what was on his mind.

Lily gazed back, knowing exactly what he wanted to hear, but she refused to betray Isabel. "Nothing. Nothing at all. We mostly talk about girly things. You know, stuff you men wouldn't have no interest in," she smiled.

"I see," Elijah replied, still gazing at her with lust in his eyes. "I must say, Lily, you have a very beautiful smile."

"Th-thank you," she stumbled, suddenly blushing. She was not yet used to being in an environment where men could so brazenly approach her. She looked down at the floor to escape Elijah's eyes when the discomfort of the moment overtook her.

"So, how have you been holdin' up amidst the show madness?" Elijah asked after she was silent for too long.

"Umm, good … really good," Lily answered, happy he was changing the subject. "Just busy most days. Me and William are constantly makin' small changes to the show. It consumes most 'a my time now. But I enjoy it."

"Glad to hear that," Elijah replied, as he walked around and fiddled with a few keys on the piano. "So, do you eva' take a little time to yourself away from this here piano? You know, to relax?"

"Every so often, but it's hard to find the time some days. I'm so absorbed in writin' music and workin' on the show. I ain't complainin', though, 'cause I love it so much."

"I'm sure you do, but it's good to step away sometimes, ya' know? Can't spend your whole life workin' hard and neva' takin' a moment to play."

"You're right. It is nice to have a break once and a while … I s'ppose," Lily nervously replied, suddenly sensing that there was an ulterior motive behind his questions.

"I've heard you put on one hell of a show. So, if anybody deserves to relax, it's *definitely* you." Elijah walked toward Lily again, staring at her in a way that intensified her nerves.

"Thank you. That's very kind of you to say," she replied with a shy smile.

"I'd like to propose a way for you to relax," Elijah said, his eyes locked on her.

"Wh-what did you have in mind?" Lily replied, her heart suddenly racing.

"You should let me cook for you sometime. A quiet dinna', a little wine, some nice conversation, no betta' way to relax than that."

"You can cook?!"

"Wow, you mean that chatty sista' of mine didn't tell you?" Elijah laughed.

"Naw, she neva' said a word about it."

"I love to cook! It's the reason I've been wantin' to open my own restaurant and bar. My motha' believed in raisin' me and Isabel to be well-rounded and independent, so she taught us both to be really great chefs."

"I'm impressed! I'd've neva' guessed that about you!"

"So, what do ya' say then? Would you like to have dinna' with me? When you have the time, of course."

"Hmm, well, I'll have to think about it."

"Okay, fair enough," Elijah nodded with a smile. "Now that I'm done travelin' for a while, I have all intention of bein' at your next show. So how about this?" He took hold of Lily's hand. "You take some time to think about my offa'. If you say yes, then maybe afta' the show I can put somethin' really nice togetha' for you. There's nothin' like a home-cooked meal afta' a hard day's work, and I'd be honored to prepare one for you, just as soon as you set foot off that stage."

"That's awful sweet 'a you, Elijah," Lily replied shyly. "I'll definitely think about it."

"Well, regardless of your answa', one thing is for sure, I can't wait to see you perform. I'll be front and centa', and I won't miss a minute. You can count on that!" He brushed Lily's cheek with the back of his hand.

"That'd be wonderful," she replied, feeling a jolt of warmth from his touch.

"Well, I gotta get goin'. Congratulations to you again, beautiful."

"Thank you!" Lily blushed.

"See you soon."

"Bye."

Elijah smiled and let his eyes linger on Lily a moment longer before leaving. He then exited the library and nearly ran into James, who had watched and listened to the tail end of their conversation from the hallway with his blood boiling. Elijah halted just before crashing into him. "So sorry, Mr. Adams. Please excuse me."

James just stared at him, refused to speak, and rudely refused to move. Elijah's attraction to Lily had solidified James's hatred for the man. Elijah could easily sense his displeasure by the sneer on his face. But he kept his wits about him, stepped around James, and proceeded out of the house.

James angrily huffed when he was finally gone. Listening to the want in Elijah's voice during his interaction with Lily was the last thing he needed to hear at the end of a brutal day. It had his irritation at peak levels by the time he stepped into the library. "Lily," he called out, sounding monotone.

"Yes." She stopped and turned around just as she was about to sit down again at the piano. As soon as she looked at James, she could tell by his face that something was bothering him.

"You have a guest here to see you."

"To see *me?*"

"That's what he said."

"Oh, okay. Where is he?"

"He's in William's den."

Lily stopped before she left the library and put her hand on James's shoulder. "You alright? I can tell somethin's botherin' you. Do you wanna talk about it?"

"Don't worry about me, I'm fine. You have a guest waitin'," he coldly replied, still aggravated by Elijah.

"You can't stop me from worryin' about you, so whoeva' he is, he can wait. We can sit and talk for a minute if you need to," Lily insisted.

"I said I'm fine!" he barked. "Go on to your meeting!"

Lily scoffed, snatched her hand off his shoulder, and looked at him like he was insane. Annoyed by his unwarranted outburst, she shook her head and hastily walked away.

James ran his hands through his hair, instantly angry at himself for taking his frustrations out on her. "Lily, I'm sorry!" he yelled to her as she stormed off, but she never turned around to acknowledge him.

Lily arrived in William's den to the sight of a tall, skinny, brown-eyed man, with sandy blonde hair, sitting in an arm chair, speaking with William as he sat at his desk. By his lavish clothing, she could tell that he was someone important. "Hello, James says you're here to see me," she said to him.

Her guest immediately stood and smiled as he made his way over to her. "Oh yes, hello. My name is Landon."

"Hello, I'm…"

"Lily," Landon finished. "Ms. Lily … Umm, I'm sorry, but I don't know your last name."

"Adams," James interjected.

Lily looked over at James, who was standing in the doorway. He answered for her to spare her the embarrassment of explaining that she had no last name, at least that was how he justified it in his mind. It was the first time Lily was hearing of any such thing. She stared at James a moment after his statement and then went along with his lie.

"Ahh, Ms. Lily Adams! It's lovely to finally meet you!" Landon said, sounding truly delighted to officially know her. He then lifted the back of her hand and kissed it gently.

"Thank you. Nice to meet you too," she replied, looking at him a bit strangely after his very formal greeting.

"It is truly an honor to be meeting with you this evening. I read the article about you in the paper this morning and…"

"Article?" Lily asked, looking over at William and James in confusion.

James instantly felt his anger flare up again. He knew he had no right to be mad at Landon for mentioning the newspaper story, so he bit his tongue and silently prayed that the day's influx of aggravations would eventually cease. He then cowardly turned his head, not wanting to divulge his knowledge of the article. Fortunately, Lily did not press further about the subject.

"Yes, I can't help but wonder if it's true?" Landon continued. "What the paper said about your ability to replay music? After hearing it only once, I mean?"

Lily looked over at James again to see if he would explain why he had not told her about the article. When he just continued to stare out the window, she turned her attention back to Landon. "Yessa', that's true."

"How do you accomplish this?"

"It's the way I first learned to play. I'd have to memorize everything I heard. Guess it's just somethin' that stuck afta' all these years."

"Simply astonishing. That's certainly a feat I'd love to see," Landon replied, looking at Lily in disbelief.

"But I much prefer to create my own music," Lily explained. "I appreciate the gift that God gave me to memorize music, but there ain't no greata' feelin' than bringin' what I hear in my head to life."

"God deprived me of any musical talent, so I'll have to take your word for it," Landon joked. "Well, anyway, William tells me that I've caught you both just before your rehearsal together, so my apologies for the interruption. But I was hoping I could speak with you about your show, if you don't mind?"

Lily curiously stared at Landon. She then turned to look at James and William, who both stood there silently, wanting her to make her own decisions. Her curiosity ultimately made the choice for her. "We can talk about whateva' you want, but only if William and James can stay," she finally answered, not wanting to be alone with a stranger.

"But of course," Landon agreed. He then took her hand and guided her to a sofa nearby, allowing her to sit first before joining her. "I guess I'll begin with just a little insight about myself, Ms. Adams, if I may."

Lily nodded her head for him to proceed.

"When I was just a small boy, back home in Germany, my father began taking me to symphonies quite regularly. I've honestly lost count of how many I've seen over my lifetime. I used to enjoy them in the beginning, but now you'd be lucky to find me awake by the third or fourth song. By then my snoring is resonating in the theater along with the orchestra," he joked.

His comment finally got Lily to smile.

"Don't get me wrong, I have an appreciation for fine music, but for decades now, it seems there has been nothing but the same old dull, redundant style of music. Many people simply try to emulate such greats as Mozart or Beethoven, and even our dear William here," Landon said, motioning his hand toward him. "During the countless symphonies I've attended, I had yet to hear anyone step outside of the molds they have created." Landon got up and walked over to the window that faced the stage. "Until I sat in the second row, just on the corner there in that amphitheater ... and heard *you*," he said, turning back to look at Lily. "What my eyes and ears were witnessing was unlike anything I've ever seen or heard before. This, I can tell you after having been to dozens of symphonies all over the world. You, your music, and the brilliance of those dancing shadows, made me feel as though I was dreaming the most unforgettable dream. As a man, I would not usually dare to admit this. But, instead of being lulled to sleep by a show ... I was moved to tears."

Landon walked back over to the sofa and sat down next to Lily again. "Ms. Adams, I have had the great fortune to see a lot in my life, and I readily admit that it has caused me to be a man who is not easily impressed by anything anymore. I now only seem to be drawn to things that absolutely command my attention and respect. And trust me, there are very few things that would motivate me to happily expend my money, and more importantly, my valuable time to attend. I have seen your show not once, but *twice*. So, I hope that serves as a clear indication about whether or not I felt it was a spectacle worthy enough to be placed at the very top of my incredibly short list of things that are worth my time and money. And if that is not a clear enough indication then let me further explain that, despite missing the comforts of my home in Europe, I have chosen to forgo my chance to depart. I have made this choice *solely* because I was so moved by what I had the opportunity to see just outside that window there. And so, instead of sitting on a cruise ship at this very moment and sailing the seas back home, you and your unforgettable symphony have motivated me to stay and sit here before you now, so that I may extend what I hope you will consider as a very valuable invitation."

"What sort of invitation?" Lily asked.

"An invitation to allow me to help you in a way that I have, selfishly, never bothered to help any other in my life."

"How so?"

"Well, my guess is that you have much more buried in that genius mind of yours. More you'd love to do with your show? Elements you'd love to add? And perhaps many other places and people you'd love to share your music with?"

"Yes, of course … so much more."

"I'm positive that I can help you then."

"Your words are so gracious; believe me they are. To know that my show could eva' touch somebody the way it's touched you, inspires me to wanna give even more of myself to my music, but..." Lily paused and looked over at William and James. "What could you possibly do for me that they haven't done already?"

Landon glanced over at both men as well and then turned his attention back to Lily. "Ms. Adams, I hope that you don't take what I'm about to say the wrong way. That amphitheater is certainly beautiful, but incredibly small in comparison to many of the grand theaters I've had the opportunity to attend, which I'm sure William can also attest to. The magnificent visual imagery that you've created should be presented on the sort of stages that will allow your ideas to flourish to their full capacity. Your show should also be able to expand inside of theaters that will be able to accommodate the massive audiences that will undoubtedly be drawn to see you. And a show as remarkable as yours deserves to reach far beyond the gates of William's estate."

"So, what're you sayin'?" Lily further questioned.

"I'm saying that I want nothing more than to take any and all limitations away from you, to tear down every obstacle in front of you, and allow you to let your dreams continue to grow in places you may have never imagined."

Lily was silent for a moment. She looked over at William and James again while she questioned Landon's sincerity. She then turned back and looked him in the eyes. "With all due respect, sa', it sounds like you're eitha' sellin' me a dream, or wantin' to sell me out to make money."

"I understand your skepticism."

"I don't need you to unda'stand it," Lily quickly replied. "I just need you to give me a good reason why I shouldn't be skeptical about you or any 'a this."

Landon paused and gazed at Lily, thoroughly enjoying the fact that she was not so easily swayed by his usual charms. A woman with confidence, boldness, intelligence, blended with unique physical features, was a combination Landon was rarely graced with in his young life. It instantly deepened his intrigue and respect for Lily. "I see that your brilliance stretches far beyond just that of music," he said, smiling devilishly. "You will most certainly go far in this business with your mindset," he said confidently. His voice then suddenly took on a more serious tone. "Ms. Adams, I will be more than happy to explain to you in detail anything that you desire, and I will most certainly do all that I can to prove myself to be loyal and worthy of your trust. But for now, in hopes of putting the fire of your skepticism out, let's just say that I am a man who has the power and the *money* to make men part the seas for you if I wanted. It's not a power that I use for anyone, unless I'm compelled, convinced, and captivated by someone ... like I am by you. It's not *money* I need, so I would *never* waste my time *selling* dreams or *selling out* someone who has warmed a heart as ice cold as mine. Anyone who possesses the sort of ability to touch me in that way is a rare and precious gift in my eyes, and certainly the last person I would ever wish to bring any harm to. In fact, it's a rare and precious treasure that I would love to help share with the world." Landon let the room fall silent in hopes that his words had a chance to resonate with everyone.

"It's my best guess that because of your life circumstances it's rare that you've been able to truly trust anyone," Landon continued after a moment. "And I understand that these two gentlemen have stood by you after proving they were worthy of your trust and that your loyalties lie with them for all they've done. But just consider this one last thing..." Landon glanced in William's direction. "William's power lies in creating, teaching, and mentoring you in music, whereas my power lies in clearing the path in whatever treacherous forest you choose to travel in." He took hold of Lily's hand. "If you let me be a part of this journey with you, I assure you that you will quickly learn how truly loyal I can be to you as well. I will make certain that it is a decision you will never regret. William and James have certainly helped you to take off, but if you give me a chance, I swear I will move heaven and hell to help you soar to unbelievable heights."

* * * *

Lily sat on the porch swing with William, resting her head on his shoulder long after their intense meeting with Landon earlier in the day. They swayed slowly with the sweet smell of William's pipe enveloping the air, sipping lemonade from time to time as they talked. The little ritual had become their nightly tradition after dinner and long rehearsals. It was in these moments that William often dove into the lighthearted and funny, nostalgic stories that Lily loved so much about his life in Great Britain. After yet another tale in the saga of his life on this evening, though, William could sense that Lily's mind had quickly strayed to other things, which was evident by her sudden question.

"William, have you eva' been afraid of anything before?"

"Well, of course. Let's see, there was the time that my brother and I were supposed to be part of a wedding when we were just five and six years old. Being the antsy little boys we were, we just had to do something to pass the time. So, we decided just before the ceremony to play hide and seek. I was always so good at that game. I'd sometimes have my brother searching for a half hour or more, sometimes until he was in tears fearing that he'd truly lost me," William laughed. "So of course, wedding ceremony or not, I had to maintain my reputation as the greatest hider in all of Great Britain. Sooo, I got the wise idea to hide … in a chimney."

"William, you didn't!"

"With a *white* suit on."

"Dear Lord!" Lily began laughing hysterically.

"Oh, it gets worse. My brother, to his credit, had learned to look for me in the oddest of places by then. He slithered his way into the chimney too, confident that he'd find me there … in *his* white suit."

Lily dropped her head in her hands as she continued laughing at William's childhood stupidity.

"Just as you are now, my brother and I were laughing, having a jolly old time ... until my mother found us just minutes before the ceremony, covered from head to toe in soot! The way she snatched us by our scrawny little necks, I was truly afraid it was going to be my last day on earth," William laughed.

"I sho' can't blame yo' mama. I'd've whooped both 'a y'all good," Lily teased.

"Oh, trust me, she did!" William laughed. "But somehow I know you're not asking me if I was ever afraid of anything because you wanted to hear another one of my foolish boyhood tales."

"Your stories aren't foolish, William. I always look forward to hearin' 'em."

"Come now, tell me what's really eating away at your mind."

Lily let out a breath, stood up, and walked over to the porch railing. "It's just that ... well, my whole life I ain't neva' had to make any real decisions 'bout my own welfare. I ain't been no different than a horse just doin' whateva' I's told. But now, here I am," she said, staring out at the amphitheater, "havin' life alterin' decisions laid at my feet. And these decisions not only affect me but nearly everybody around me. And I'd be lyin' if I said that didn't make me a lil' afraid to decide what's best."

"Lily?"

She turned to face William and saw him patting the seat next to him. She hesitantly joined him again.

"In my whole life, I've never met another as intelligent and wise as you. And please do not think that I mean only within the boundaries of your color or your gender. I genuinely mean of *anyone* I have ever met. And I have known a great many people over my lifetime. I have realized in my short time knowing you that you possess a rare and precious instinctive wisdom, musically. Effortlessly, you always seem to know just what to do. I have seen you grow more and more confident day after day in your own ability to expand on the elements of your music, the dancing, the theatrics, and the show as a whole. It is awe-inspiring to watch from my old eyes. But even more precious than that, you carry that same instinct into your everyday life." William took hold of Lily's hand. "You just don't realize it yet. You don't see it the way that I have or in the way that James clearly has. You move people in a way that you aren't even aware. You seem to know, without even trying, how to make everyone feel a sense of importance in your presence. It is that rare instinctive nature that you were born with that allows you to touch so many people in that special way.

"So, Lily, I have every bit of confidence in you that you will always know exactly what to do, be it with music, or when making decisions that could be life altering. Your ability to make the right move is there, but you've yet to grow the confidence to let it guide you without questioning it the way you have musically. Somehow, I know it speaks to you now … Listen," William paused and patted Lily's hand. "Just listen. Soon the voices of fear will begin to fade into silence. Then, and *only* then, will you hear how loudly the voices of reason are speaking."

Soothed by William's words, Lily said nothing in response. Instead, she drew her legs up into the porch swing and laid her head back down on William's shoulder. William usually would have continued to entertain her with his childhood tales, the way Lily always wanted, but on this evening he was silent. He put his pipe back in his mouth with one hand and put the other around Lily. He then pushed back on the wooden planks beneath his feet to start a gentle swaying motion in the swing and said not another word, in hopes of allowing Lily the opportunity to "just listen."

The sound of crickets and croaking frogs in the distance soon increased in volume, as the sky darkened, and the stars illuminated the crystal-clear night. After Lily and William had swayed together for a while, he turned and found her fast asleep. He brushed her hair aside, and just as he would have with his own child, he innocently kissed her forehead, silently hoping that her dreams were just as beautiful to her as she was to him.

Chapter Seventeen

Slave Code
Article X Section VII

No contract between a white person and a Negro for labor or service for a longer period than two months shall be binding on such Negro without a license obtained in writing, signed by a white person before a court justice.

"Simply brilliant!" Robert Branaugh told Landon after watching a practice run through of The Dream Symphony. After the curtains closed, Lily and the other performers retreated to the wings, leaving Robert and Landon alone in the fifth row of Branaugh Theater. Robert was the owner and manager of the small, single-story, venue in New Lexington, Ohio, two hours north of William's estate. "I must admit, every moment of the show was just as magnificent as you said it would be," Robert confessed.

Landon nodded as an arrogant smile crept onto his face. He was not surprised by Robert's reaction; he was confident that he would appreciate the artistry of the show.

"Correction, it *was* magnificent until the Negro girl showed her face at the very end," Robert suddenly added, letting the words escape as if they were not the least bit offensive.

Landon was caught off guard by his insult, but he was never one to show outwardly that anyone had an effect on his calm demeanor, no matter how tense the situation. "Pardon me?" he replied calmly in his German accent.

"She's not really going to show her face here is she?" Robert questioned. "After such a lovely and artistic performance, I don't find it the least bit necessary to ruin it all by having some Negro meandering out in front of everyone like some princess being presented at a royal ceremony."

"She's a beautiful young lady."

"Beautiful or not, she's still a *Negro!* Can't you see that? Or are you color-blind?"

"You met her already. You knew that."

"Yes, you're right, I did. But I didn't ever expect to see her face. Not here! Not on *my* stage! When you described the show to me, you never said anything about her flaunting herself in this manner. I assumed that she'd always be portrayed as a shadow behind that curtain contraption … where she belongs," he insulted again, this time with disgust in his tone.

"Well, we all know what happens when you assume," Landon snidely replied.

"Joke all you want, Mr. Von Brandt, but if you want to ensure that this little show gets to continue here, I will not, by any means, be seeing that Negro's face again on that stage! And nor will any person who pays to sit within these very seats expecting to see an elegant and respectable show."

"Then you're asking to be sued. You can't just breach our contract. You've already signed and agreed to have her show here."

"Oh, the show can go on. But certain things within that contract allow me to modify things to my discretion. And I will *not* have that girl set one foot out from behind that curtain and into that spotlight … *Ever!*"

Landon was silent for a moment. He then stood up and slowly turned around, letting his eyes absorb every aspect of the theater's exquisite interior. "Small details," he began, as he slid his hands into his pockets. "Ever since I was a child, I've always paid attention to details. No matter how small they were, they were never able to escape me. For instance, once my father took me to a symphony where the conductor wore a toupee. I could not help but notice the way it jumped slightly from his head every time he would swing his baton. Distracted me from the whole damn show. You'd think he could afford the proper glue for that dreadful old thing. Then here tonight, as I watched Lily play her last piece." He closed his eyes, envisioning it. "I watched her face and the way her eyes remained hidden behind her eyelids and the way her facial expressions gave away the secrets of what she sees behind them. Simply watching those small details of her beautiful face, I have no doubt it was the most heavenly place she had escaped to." Landon opened his eyes again. "Even now as I look at this lavish theater of yours, I can't help but notice the fine details." He turned to a particular place and motioned with his head. "The workmanship of the wainscoting." He turned his head in a different direction. "The dark and brooding eyes on all the sculptures and the design of all the light fixtures." He turned in a complete circle. "And there is, of course, all the *red* in this place. *Red* walls, *red* cloth covered seats, *red* stage curtain. Yes, it could never escape my attention how undoubtedly *in the red* this place is." He turned to look at Robert. "I'd say it matches quite perfectly with its financial state, wouldn't you?"

"What?!" Robert replied, caught off guard by his question.

"Yes!" Landon pointed a finger at Robert. "There it is again! My keen sense of small details picking up on that slight quiver in your voice."

"I don't see the point in anything you're saying, Mr. Von Brandt!"

"Details! I'm telling you, I don't miss a thing! But you don't have to have as keen an eye as I do to see that, for almost five years now, this place has run *in the red*, and not a single profit thus far this year either. There it was, plain as day, at the bottom of the financial documents I sifted through. Nothing but numbers plummeted far, far beneath zero. I believe you Americans call that being *in the red* ... isn't that right?" he asked rhetorically, while turning to look at the theater again. "Just like the dreadful color of these walls," he murmured under his breath.

"You have no access to my financial affairs, boy!"

Landon ignored Robert's comment and continued. "Honestly, I've never seen figures so low in all my life. After the first year of opening any establishment, maybe yes, that's certainly quite the norm. But here we are, nearly five years after this place has been in operation and it seems you've been robbing Peter to pay Paul. Or should I say, robbing Peter to pay..." He turned from the walls and looked down at Robert again. "*My father.*"

Robert squinted his eyes at Landon as beads of sweat began to form on his brow. "Y-your *father*?" he asked. "Christoph?"

"Christoph! Yes!"

"*Von Brandt,*" Robert murmured under his breath after realizing the connection with their last names.

"Christoph Von Brandt! That's him!" Landon replied, in an intentionally gleeful, annoying tone. "That ... is ... *thee* ... one!" he added, pointing his finger at Robert with every word. "The same Christoph that you've recently written to and asked to borrow money for ... oh, what is it this time?" He scratched his head. "A *hotel!* That's right! Yes, he's also the same Christoph that I can't wait to go home and talk to about all the fine details of this theater of yours. The lavish sculptures. The wainscoting." Landon looked up at the ceiling. "That fabulous chandelier and all of the expensive artwork." He looked down at Robert again. "I certainly can't wait to bring up the way you treat the guests in your establishment, and of course ... all of the *red* in this place. Should help you with convincing my father to fund that little hotel venture of yours, don't you think?" He paused for a moment, enjoying the sight of all the sweat suddenly accumulating on Robert's brow. "Oh well, now, I guess that all depends on which *red* I decide to detail for him, doesn't it?"

Landon's sarcasm disappeared and his face hardened. He took a step forward and loomed over Robert, piercing him with dark, unblinking eyes. "You *need* a show like this, Branaugh, and fifty more of the sort. You will *not* deny Lily from doing what she wants here! Not tonight, not tomorrow, nor during a single moment of her show when this place is packed to the ceiling … am I clear?" he asked smugly, slightly tilting his head to the side.

"You're asking me to disgrace this place! T-to defame it! To run it right into the ground!" Robert fired back.

"Seems you're doing a fine job of that already." Like an asylum patient springing back into mania, Landon's face suddenly lit up and the sarcasm returned to his voice. "Landon Von Brandt Theater!" he exclaimed, waving his hands in front of him as if he were picturing the words on a towering marquee. "Has a nice ring to it, wouldn't you say?" he asked Robert with a smile, as if there had been nothing but pleasantries exchanged between them. "Oh, the things I could do with this place! Let's see! First, I'd certainly get rid of *all* the God-awful *red* around here." His smile suddenly faded, his face hardened, and his cold eyes penetrated Robert again. "Right after I get rid of *you!*"

300

Chapter Eighteen

Slave Code
Article IIIX Section XII

Any free Negro of African race, whose ancestors were brought to this country and sold as slaves are not "citizens" within the meaning of the Constitution of the United States. Therefore, the special rights and immunities guaranteed to citizens do not apply to slaves or free Negroes. A slave or free Negro has no civil rights, and therefore is not entitled to sue in a court of the United States nor shall be allowed to serve as a witness or to testify against any white person.

Friday Night
July 1, 1859

Lily stood at the forefront of Branaugh Theater stage in front of a sold-out crowd. Moved by the artistry of The Dream Symphony, everybody in the building was on their feet, applauding for what seemed like an eternity. Much like the opening night on the outdoor amphitheater, many patrons were unaware that the entire ensemble had been composed and choreographed by a Negro, until Lily revealed herself at the very end. Once again, though, that surprise did not stop the warm reception from her appreciative audience. It was a moment that should have meant the world to Lily, a scene for her to embrace as yet another memorable highlight in her life. It should have conjured up an emotion of some sort, something … *anything*. But instead, Lily was numb. Her thoughts were elsewhere as she forced a smile to everyone who had paid to see The Dream Symphony for the very first time inside of a genuine theater.

At first, Lily stood alone at the front of the enormous stage, stiffly accepting the commendation from the crowd. But, in a spontaneous last-minute decision, the entire student orchestra trickled out from behind the curtains to stand proudly alongside her, revealing themselves to an audience for the very first time. The same body of students who once threatened to quit without the assurance of their anonymity, now all proudly stood beside her to praise her for achieving yet another milestone in her life. The warmth that the group exuded normally would have ignited Lily's tears. But, in this instance, the sadness that she was drowning in had disconnected her from her surroundings. It was that very sadness that had moved the students to join her onstage. Knowing that Lily was hurting inside, they suddenly found themselves unconcerned with hiding and secrets. Instead, they all felt the strong need to comfort a woman who had slowly become a friend and mentor to all of them. They wanted to be there for her because James Adams, the courageous man who had started this journey with her, was now nowhere to be found. He had missed every minute of a precedent-setting night that Lily undoubtedly owed to him, William, and now to one Landon Von Brandt.

Landon was the son of Christoph Von Brandt, a very rich and powerful German acquaintance of William's, whom he had not seen or spoken to in nearly two decades. During the weeks that William was searching for work for Lily, he had written a letter to Christoph. William knew that Christoph had invested in several theaters, hotels, and pubs in the United States; William wondered if he might be of assistance to Lily somehow. Landon was the first to read William's letter when it arrived. The letter was so intriguing, Landon convinced his father that it would be best to respond to William in person. Landon elected to travel to the United States on his father's behalf by playing the role of a caring son who wished to ease the burdens of his father's hectic life. In all truthfulness, Landon's desire to travel was under selfish pretenses. He wished to escape his father's command for a spell and utilize the free time to drink, attend galas, and meet an array of women.

After many weeks of sailing, traipsing from state to state, enjoying fine wines, feasts, and plenty of women, Landon had reluctantly attended Lily's symphony, only to fulfill his obligations. He had all intention of returning to his father with nothing but negative reviews. He planned to urge him not to waste his time, his good name, or his money on William's cause. Never did Landon expect to be genuinely taken aback by what he had seen the night he first saw The Dream Symphony. The show's deep impact shattered his selfishness and completely changed his future life goals to one that was far more selfless.

While attempting to accomplish his selfless endeavor, Landon could have very well divulged who his father was when he first approached William. Instead, he intentionally withheld his last name, hoping that William did not recall meeting him when he was just a small boy twenty years ago. Landon did not want Lily to feel as if he had been forced by his father to assist, as if she was some profitable pawn in his father's business deals. He chose his words carefully, hoping to ensure Lily that his genuine love for her shadow-filled symphony had been the only motive behind his desire to help her share her brilliance with the world.

Landon could hardly contain his excitement about the prospect of presenting Lily's mystical show to millions of people. He felt like a child who was eager to show off his newest gift with everyone; he wanted so badly for the masses to experience the same life-altering rush of emotions that he had while watching such spellbinding artistry. Part of Landon's excitement was knowing the opportunity that Lily would have to speak, through her music, to people who believed in a need for slavery. Landon was appalled by the institution. He was disgusted by the slave traders and slave owners who chose money over morality. He had travelled the world with his father and naturally learned that race was not the single determining factor in one's intellectual capacity, nor did he feel that one's race should ever warrant an instant sentence to lifelong captivity. Landon believed that the rampant lies that preached to the contrary were propagated by human traffickers whose businesses thrived on such ill-founded facts. His disdain for the institution of slavery further motivated his desire to move mountains on Lily's behalf; he was convinced that she could become an international sensation that exposed the propaganda of greedy elites. Landon, therefore, deemed Lily's genius, her music, and her show as an invaluable weapon in the war against flesh-peddling thugs.

After Lily welcomed Landon to join her entourage, he quickly proved himself as a force to be reckoned with. From the outset, it was clear that he was the much-needed missing piece to The Dream Symphony puzzle. He had immediately pointed out that William's first fatal mistake was telling potential venues in advance about Lily's color. While negotiating with theater owners, Landon planned only to paint the elegant mental image of the *show* and never mention who or what *Lily* is. That blatant reality was something he felt managers could witness with their own eyes when Lily showed up for stage rehearsals. By then, Landon figured the impending venue would be sold out and that it was highly unlikely that anyone would complain about Lily being brown after their pockets had already been stuffed with green.

Green was what Landon wanted for Lily as well ... piles of it. Landon's natural selfishness proved to be the greatest asset in ensuring that Lily would never receive a penny less than she was worth for presenting her one-of-a-kind musical artwork. Landon's massive ego simply would not allow him to be defeated by anyone he dealt with on Lily's behalf. While seeing her toward riches, he was willing to sting quickly with his venomous tongue, a fact that Robert Branaugh was the first to learn. After sifting through the financial files of the theaters that his father had invested in, Landon had learned of how poorly mismanaged Branaugh Theater was. He knew the struggling theater would provide the perfect place to force his way in and begin a precedent setting run for The Dream Symphony. His underhanded methods further proved how ruthless he was willing to be on Lily's behalf.

For William, having Landon eased the burdens of having to deal with things that were never his area of expertise; it freed him to focus solely on assisting a woman who had become like a daughter to him. So, while William worked tirelessly with Lily expounding on her show, Landon continued to work feverishly, manipulating, and negotiating in the shadows with prospective theater owners. Within weeks, he had already booked the symphony for three different theaters, on a mini tour of sorts, with the first leg beginning at Branaugh Theater.

All of Landon's efforts had ultimately helped lead to this very moment: Lily onstage, being figuratively embraced by the student orchestra in front of a sea of applauding onlookers, inside the beauty of her first real theater. Unfortunately, though, with the absence of James, Lily was unable to fully appreciate the joy of her grand finale. Her current state of numbness had been compounded by the fact that Landon had incessantly expressed the importance of perfection for opening night. He constantly reminded everyone that this first show would set the tone for shows to come and that the reviews would be crucial to giving strength to the legs that would carry The Dream Symphony forward. This notion weighed heavily on everyone and began to make the pressure nearly unbearable for Lily. That pressure had already been preceded by unforeseen challenges that had arisen while transporting supplies and props on their way to dress rehearsals in New Lexington. To further add to the madness of their tumultuous travels, Lily was told she would not be allowed to stay in the hotel that had been reserved for everyone. Not a single other hotel in its vicinity welcomed her either, forcing her to use the dressing room in the theater as a makeshift bedroom for the entire week. With every challenge, though, Lily did not allow herself to be broken. She pushed through her stresses with her spirits high and a positive outlook, until just hours before the opening number of the show. It was not until then that Lily allowed the dark cloud drifting over her to cast a shadow of doubt on the confidence everyone had in the fact that they would have a successful opening night.

In the hours before showtime, Lily was not enthusiastic and full of life, the way she was at all her previous shows. Normally, she was commanding professionalism from everyone, taking charge, and ensuring that every minor detail was in order ... but not on this night. With the opening number fast approaching, Lily was nowhere near her usual self. She sat alone in her dressing room, emptily staring into the mirror, her mind wracked with genuine concern over James's unknown whereabouts. The heaviness of her despair made her realize just how much strength she truly garnered from James's presence. Her despondency was so obviously crippling that the most unlikely person felt a need to speak to her before the show began.

Lily quickly perked up when she heard a light knock on her dressing room door. "Come in!" she said, whipping her head around to see if it was James. "Oh, hey, Austin," she sighed, disappointment obvious in her tone. She then turned back toward the mirror.

"Hi, Lily," Austin said, closing the door behind him. "Could I have a word with you?"

"Sure," Lily replied, more out of obligation than a desire to hear what he had to say.

Austin did not venture far from the door, feeling more at ease with talking so long as he was not facing Lily. "Look, I-I know I ain't so good with words, 'specially the nice ones ... as you've probably already noticed," he said, attempting to make a joke. He then nervously put his hands in his pockets when Lily did not laugh. "Ya' know, a few weeks ago, William gave us all the option of endin' our agreement to perform with you any longa'. He said he could try to find a professional orchestra that could take our place if none of us wanted to travel."

Again, Lily did not respond to the surprise of that news.

"A few months ago, I'll admit that hearin' that would've been music to my ears, but now…" Austin paused and took a deep breath when he felt his nerves getting the best of him. "The moment William said it, I rememba' feelin' this … this pain in my chest," he admitted. "See, it's just that my whole life I ain't eva' know what direction to go in the world. I always felt so lost until these last few months. For the first time in my entire twenty-three years, I feel like I finally have a future for myself, like I got some purpose, ya' know?"

Lily finally looked at Austin in the mirror as a way of communicating her understanding of his sentiments.

Austin held her gaze for a moment, finally feeling a sense of comfort by the sight of her innocent eyes. "So, when William told us we could escape all this, all I knew was that I didn't wanna feel lost again. And besides…" Austin paused and walked closer to Lily. She finally turned around in her chair to find him towering over her. "Playin' with you has been one 'a the greatest joys 'a my life, and I just couldn't bring myself to walk away … None of us could, Lily. We're *all* proud to play behind ya', and we're all here for *you,* no matta' what happens tonight and beyond, we'll always be here for ya'. I-I just wanted you to know that."

Lily was stunned to say the least. She would have assumed it was some sort of hoax had Austin not looked and sounded so incredibly sincere. Not only was she stunned by his words, but also by his transformation. Austin had cut his stringy, long brown hair, and shaved the shadowy whiskers off his face, unveiling his youthful skin. He was even wearing a brand-new tailored suit. Such small changes made Lily feel as though she was looking at a completely different young man. After the shock of his metamorphosis subsided, Lily gazed into Austin's eyes. It was the first time she ever noted their color. They were a deep dark brown, which gazed back at her in the most compassionate of ways. "Thank you, Austin. There ain't enough words for me to express how much that means to me," Lily replied, sounding equally as sincere as he had.

Austin nodded and walked to the door but stopped just as he put his hand on the doorknob. "I'm sorry," he said quietly, still facing the door.

"What?"

Austin exhaled, found some courage, and turned around to face Lily again. "You ain't been nothin' but kind to me afta' all the cruel things I said to ya'. I honestly ain't neva' felt more guilty for the way I treated somebody than you. And I'm awful sorry, Lily. I really am."

"It's okay, Austin, I…"

"Naw, it ain't okay," he interrupted, not wanting her to let him off the hook so easily. He walked halfway across the room again and put his hands back into the pockets of his fancy tailored pants. "Ya' know, you's the first person to hug me when you found out my mama passed away?" He suddenly tilted his head back and looked up at the ceiling, hoping to keep his tears from rolling. "Not my fatha', not my brotha's, not even my sista's … *You*," he said, lowering his head to look at Lily again. "You were the *only* person who eva' botha'd to hug me."

Lily remembered that moment very clearly but was unaware that not a single person had yet to comfort him until that day…

During rehearsals that particular evening back on William's estate, Austin was failing to keep up with the rest of the orchestra, far worse than usual. William kept stopping everyone because of how much of a disruption it was to the fluidity of the number they were learning. After the fifth scolding, Austin threw his mallets across the room and stormed out of the rehearsal session. Everyone else sat in uncomfortable silence after he slammed the library door on his way out.

"What's goin' on?" Lily leaned over and asked one of the violinists. "This ain't like him at all."

"I heard his mama just passed away," the young man whispered back. "I guess he just needs a little time."

"Take a break everyone," Lily stood and announced. She then headed out the back door to look for Austin. Ironically, she found him in *her* comfort zone near the oak tree by the lake. He was picking up rocks and hurling them into the water. Lily walked up slowly behind him, watching him angrily throw rocks, one after the other, as if he were firing his ammunition at whatever he blamed for taking his mother's life. Austin's mother was the only person who had ever shown him the slightest bit of love. Now she was gone, and he had no idea how to cope.

Lily saw Austin glance over at her as he searched for more rocks to throw, but he did not say a word or break stride in collecting his ammunition. Cautiously, Lily continued to close in on him. He had thrown a few more rocks before she reached him. By the time he went to throw the last one, though, Lily gently took hold of his wrist and slowly removed the rock from his hand. Austin could feel her empathetically gazing at the profile of his face. It took the last little bit of his bravery to slowly raise his heavy head and return her gaze. Reading the compassion in her eyes, Austin's tears were instant, but so, too, was Lily's embrace. She dropped the rock and held him tightly as he wept. Austin did not attempt to pull away. Surprisingly, he put his arms around her too. He allowed himself to be vulnerable and let go of his pain in the arms of somebody who finally dared to show that they cared about his plight. Lily felt him getting weaker as she held him, as if the strength in his body was slowly draining with his tears. In fact, he wept until his legs became too weak to hold him. It was only then that he pulled away from Lily's embrace and sat down by the tree. Lily followed suit, sitting just inches away from him.

"This my favorite spot here on William's land," Lily said, her voice adding to the calming sound of the wind rustling through the leaves above them. She was not expecting Austin to reply, but she hoped that maybe he was willing to listen for the time being while his wounded heart and mind were wide open. "I come out here almost every day to think. Sometimes about music, sometimes to daydream, or sometimes just to reflect ... especially when I'm hurtin'."

Still, Austin sat there silently absorbing Lily's words, wiping his face while he waited for his strength to return.

"I's nine-years-old the last time I saw my mama. My fatha' took me and sold me away from her," Lily explained.

It took those words to finally garner a reaction from Austin. He turned and glanced at Lily with disbelief in his swollen bloodshot eyes. His relationship with his own father was abysmal, but after hearing what Lily's father had done, he considered that maybe he did not have much to complain about.

"Far as I know my motha's still alive, but the pain 'a not bein' able to see 'er felt no different than if she'd died," Lily continued. "I used to hurt somethin' awful. Used to lie in my bed at night and cry for hours, sometimes 'til I made myself sick to my stomach. Didn't even wanna eat some days, no different than if I's truly in a state 'a mournin'.

"But then one night, afta' cryin' myself to sleep, I had a dream about my mama. Dreamt 'a this silly little song she taught me, ya' know, to one 'a those childhood hand clappin' games," Lily explained, smiling at the memory. "I woke up from that dream for the first time in weeks with a smile on my face. That dream brought back the memory of how hard me and my motha' used to laugh wheneva' we messed up the rhythm while clappin' our hands togetha' and had to start all ova' again singin' that silly little song," Lily recalled, a hint of laughter in her voice. "It was such a small thing at the time. But now, to this very day, wheneva' I'm hurtin' ova' missin' my mama, that's what I do … I *rememba' her*. I rememba' her and me togetha', laughin', and singin' and how happy we were at that moment. Or sometimes I think about this old telescope she'd somehow gotten her hands on and had hidden away in her room. It was her most prized possession. She loved that old thang! One day, when I's about five-years-old, she pulled it out and showed it to me and made me swear not to tell a soul on the plantation about it. My eyes were as wide as quarta's when I first saw it. It was the most amazin' contraption I'd eva' seen! From then on, wheneva' the sky was clear late at night, we'd sneak out into the woods, lay on our backs, and look out into the heavens togetha' and give names to the biggest and brightest stars we could find. And to this very day, I still rememba' the names of every one of 'em," Lily smiled. "Those were some 'a the fondest memories 'a me and my motha' togetha'. And now, wheneva' I reminisce about those moments, it neva' fails to numb the pain, to take all the hurt away, and put a smile on my face." Lily paused briefly and let silence take over while the memories invaded her mind. "Even been times right here unda' this very tree, I've sat here and remembered those moments," she confessed, after the vivid images faded away.

Lily turned and looked at Austin's profile as he stared out at the lake. He would not return the gaze, but she could tell he was still listening. "Close your eyes," Lily told him.

Austin did not move. He kept his eyes transfixed on the water, unwilling to do as she told him at first.

"Go on," she prompted him again. "It's alright."

Austin looked down at the ground before slowly honoring her request.

"*Rememba' her*," Lily then said softly. "Rememba' you and your mama togetha'. Rememba' somethin' that only you and her found

311

special, or somethin' that she always did to let you know how special you were to her ... somethin' that brought both of ya' the utmost joy."

At first, Austin's eyes were squinted hard while he reached deep inside of his catalog of memories to find one that meant more to him than all the others. As the minutes passed, though, Lily watched as his facial features started to relax and the twitching in his eyelids began to cease. When tears escaped from the corners of his eyes, she knew that he had finally found it. There was no smile on Austin's face, but Lily could feel the joy that he emanated. It moved her to put her arm around him while he continued to escape into his mind and *remember* a precious moment with his beloved mother.

... Austin had been profoundly touched by the whole experience with Lily that day. Now, as he stood with her in her dressing room, he wanted desperately to help her in return. After his apology, he dug deep for the right thing to say. "Lily, I know you ain't been feelin' so good about James not bein' here tonight. I'm sure there ain't a single thing that any of us could say that'll make you feel betta' about his absence. But I's thinkin' that you could, you know..." He shrugged his shoulders. "M-maybe rememba' somethin' about 'em that makes ya' happy."

"Thanks, Austin, but this is a little bit of a different situation, don't ya' think?"

"Well, yeah, I know he ain't passed away or nothin', but you said yourself that your mama might still be alive and that you always recall happy memories about 'er wheneva' you're missin' 'er. So, I just figured maybe it couldn't hurt if you did the same with James. Maybe it'll stop you from worryin' and put you in a betta' mood." Austin paused, recalling the many times he had resorted to the new ritual. "Sho' does work for me," he confessed, his voice trailing off.

Lily fought hard to think of an excuse to get out of it. She was intentionally defiant, hoping Austin would give up and let her go back to being alone before the show. "But I..."

"Go on, just give it a try, can't hurt," Austin interrupted. He refused to be deterred, fighting just as hard to help her as she had him. His persistence paid off; Lily exhaled and let her eyes drift to the floor. She was hesitant to close them at first, just like Austin had been that day by William's lake.

Austin approached her again. "Go on. Close your eyes," he said softly. Warmed by the tenderness in his tone, Lily finally relaxed and suddenly found herself engulfed in darkness. "Rememba' somethin' great about 'em," she heard Austin say just before the darkness was suddenly flooded with vivid images.

Lily could have chosen from a thousand memories from the past. But in this instance, her mind selected the most recent of her happy memories with her childhood best friend ...

As promised, James had spent every evening with Lily after rehearsals down by her favorite spot on William's lake underneath the oak tree, continuing with her reading lessons. When he learned that William planned to teach Lily to read and write music, James secretly requested for him not to teach her any more letters or words than was necessary to accomplish his goal. William happily obliged after hearing about the beautiful promise that James wanted to fulfill on Lily's birthday.

During Lily's lessons, James was as meticulous as any schoolhouse teacher. He was prepared with a small erasable writing board, pens, papers, flash cards, and instruction materials. He even gave Lily homework to help improve her writing, spelling, and punctuation, as well as a list of daily vocabulary words to look up in a dictionary. But

Lily went far beyond the short list of words and began reading multiple pages from a dictionary every night. With her insatiable appetite for learning and her potent memory, Lily was soaking up words and definitions at an astonishing rate. She absorbed all the knowledge James gave her as effortlessly as she had learned to read, write, and play music. Within just two weeks, Lily was able to slowly read every word of the book that she had treasured for years. *Remembering James* had started there. The fond memory of sitting side by side with him near the lake was fresh in Lily's mind all over again. She could see the mist of tears in James's eyes after she finally read the very last words of her beloved story to him aloud.

Remembering him continued in that dark world behind Lily's eyes as she drifted through the hours that followed the completion of her favorite book. She had sat for nearly two hours writing and rewriting a letter to James. She was determined to perfect her penmanship and the words she wanted to say to him. When Lily was finished, she then folded the letter neatly and placed it on his pillow for him to find:

Dear James,

Reading has been the most incredible escape for me, nearly as much as music. I find myself now picking through all the books on William's shelf here in my room and reading the summaries on the back of each and every one. I had hoped to find at least one book to read before I fall asleep at night, but instead of finding one, I've found twelve! I guess I better get busy! I found one called Oliver Twist by a man named Charles Dickens. It's about an orphan boy. I think I'll start with that one. They all seem like they will be so wonderful, but I'm certain there will never be one that I'll cherish more than the one you gave to me so many years ago, and that you have now so graciously taught me to read. I'm overjoyed that I can write now too, but I don't think there are enough words I can use in this letter to express how grateful I am to you for giving me the ability to abandon the tribulations of life for a while by escaping into the beautiful world of fantasy. Now that my lessons are over, I'll miss our evening reading sessions by the lake, but I'll always cherish the memories of the precious gift that you have bestowed upon me.

Thank you kindly,

Sincerely,

Lily

That very next morning Lily found a letter from James folded neatly, lying next to her when she awoke. She opened it with the excitement of a child unwrapping a Christmas gift. Lily smiled the entire time she read it, excited at how the words were no longer foreign to her, but more so at their sentiment:

Dear Lily,

No need to search your soul for any words to say thank you. Just to know that the words of the letter that I found here on my pillow were crafted by your hand means more to me than you'll ever know, and so too was hearing you speak the final words of your favorite story tonight. It honestly moved me just as much as the grand finale of your symphony. I, too, admit that I will greatly miss our lessons by the lake. So, to remedy that, how about you, me, and that Oliver Twist fella meet down at the lake tomorrow evening after rehearsals? There's nothing I'd love more than to hear you share each and every one of the stories you've chosen to escape with.

Hope to see you then,

Sincerely,

James

Those two short letters began yet another tradition to add to James and Lily's list from over the years. From that evening on, they exchanged letters with one another on a nightly basis. The anticipation of a letter underneath their doors had them both eager to get out of bed every morning. The funny messages they often shared kept the pair laughing at each other's inside jokes throughout their long daunting workdays. Their silly behavior and odd outbursts of laughter lightened the mood of everyone around them. They, too, were feeling the effects of a simple letter-writing ritual that was quickly beginning to pull the once distant pair back together.

... A slow smile crept onto Lily's face as she sat in her dressing room remembering the feeling she had when she woke up every morning to find another one of James's letters. Austin was happy to see that setting his pride and ego aside seemed to help pull Lily out of the dark place she had been drowning in before showtime. She was so lost in her joyous memories that she forgot Austin was even in the room with her. The moment was awkward when she opened her eyes to find him still standing over her. Her cheeks flushed red and she sheepishly smiled. Austin's smile illuminated as well; the Lily he knew was finally back.

After sensing a positive shift in Lily's demeanor, Austin offered a hand to help her stand. As soon as she took hold of it, there was a knock at her dressing room door that startled them both. Before Lily could respond, the knocking turned into a hard, impatient banging. "Lily Adams!" a deep voice called out from the other side, as the pounding continued.

Lily looked at Austin before walking toward the door. He shrugged his shoulders, looking just as perplexed as she did. By the elevated voices and the repeated beating on the door, they both knew that whatever lie on the other side was not something they would be happy to deal with. Lily reached for the doorknob, but Austin pulled her away and stepped in front of her, wanting to be her protective barrier before he opened it.

"Yes, can I help you?" Lily answered, peering over Austin's shoulder. Her first thoughts were of James when she finally saw the two large deputies standing there. Thinking the worst, her stomach began turning in knots. She was not remotely prepared to receive any bad news, *especially* if it had to do with James.

"We need to have a word with you," one of the deputies told her.

"Is there a problem?" Lily asked.

"What's going on here?" William asked, after suddenly showing up with Elijah by his side.

"This little show 'a hers is ova', that's what's goin' on here," the deputy explained. "We got word that this here nigga's a runaway."

"Watch your mouth!" Elijah spat, bucking up in Lily's defense.

"Who the hell you think y'ur talkin' to, boy!" the other deputy barked, taking a step toward Elijah.

Elijah lowered his eyelids and never flinched.

"The question is, who the hell's been talkin' to *you?*" Austin interjected, ending the stare down between Elijah and the deputy. "Who fed you that load 'a horse shit about Lily bein' a runaway?!"

The deputy motioned his head toward the corner. Tucker stood there chewing sunflower seeds, moving his mouth as gracefully as a cow. He was disrespectfully spitting the shells on the theater floor with a smirk on his face, his eyes coasting up and down Lily's body. "Sho' do look purty t'night, pumpkin. Gon' be the finest thang I eva' saw in handcuffs," Tucker told her, spitting out another mouthful of sunflower seeds afterwards.

"What's he talkin' about?" Lily asked. "I didn't do anything wrong."

"They say y'ur the one that created this here lil' show," one of the deputies began. "So, I assume y'ur smart enough to know that, despite this here bein' a free state, the law states that any slaves roamin' around within it will still be treated as such, and any runaways will be jailed until they're able to be returned to their owna's. You do know that, right sweetheart?" he asked in a condescending tone.

"But she's no runaway!" William interjected.

"Well, unless you can show us some papa'work as to the proof 'a that, we'll have to consida' her as such. If you ain't got no papa'work, you can forget about her settin' one foot on that stage, 'cause she'll be on 'er merry little way down to the jailhouse 'til we can straighten this whole matta' out." The sheriff took out a pair of handcuffs and began walking toward Lily.

Elijah stepped in front of the deputy. "You can't arrest her without probable cause!"

"His word *is* probable cause, boy!" the deputy replied, pointing at Tucker. "And without her carryin' documented proof, in the eyes 'a the law, I'm gonna have to consida' her a runaway! Now take y'ur ass outta my way 'fore I arrest you for obstruction!" He stepped around Elijah and proceeded toward Lily.

"You ain't arrestin' nobody!" Austin shouted, still blocking the deputy's path to Lily. "We got a show to put on!"

"I don't give an outhouse shit 'bout no goddamn show! I'm here to uphold the law!"

"No worries. Everyone calm down," Landon interrupted, walking up in his usual calm and collected manner. "Nobody's going anywhere."

"Who the hell're you?" the other deputy asked.

"I'm La-." Landon cleared his throat and suddenly replaced his German accent with a horribly replicated southern one. "Larry … Larry Adams. I'm James Adams' brotha'. He's the owna' of this beautiful young lady." He touched Lily on the shoulder, smiled, and then extended his hand to the deputy for him to shake. "Please, pardon the confusion here tonight. See, my brotha', James, is away on business, and he's left me as her ova'seer. But no worries! He's left all the appropriate documentation in my care."

"He's a goddamn liar!" Tucker shouted.

"Follow me, gentlemen," Landon instructed. "If you'll step with me out to my carriage, I'll show you both *exactly* what you need to see to clear up this misunderstandin'." He took both deputies by the shoulders and began guiding them down the hallway, completely ignoring the conniption fit that Tucker was having. Everyone else left in the hallway turned in unison to look at Tucker, who suddenly cowered in the corner.

While everyone waited for Landon, Elijah walked over to speak to Lily. Earlier in the week, he had offered to ride back to Athens to find out why James had yet to join everyone in New Lexington for stage rehearsals. He could tell that Lily was on the verge of tears when he returned with no news of James's whereabouts. Since then, he had done all he could to lift Lily's spirits and comfort her. "Are you okay?" Elijah asked her, opening his arms and inviting Lily into his embrace.

Lily hesitantly stepped forward into his arms. "As well as I can be unda' the circumstances, I s'ppose."

Elijah pulled Lily back from their embrace and touched her on the cheek. "I know this whole week has had one storm afta' anotha', but I'll do all I can to help see you through this mess, okay?"

"Thank you, Elijah. I really appreciate it."

"You! Come with us!" everyone suddenly heard one of the deputies snarl. Lily's heart began to beat wildly when she turned and saw both deputies headed toward her. To her surprise, though, they breezed right past her and grabbed Tucker by the elbow. "Get y'ur ass outta here 'fore we take ya' in for makin' false reports." The largest deputy gave Tucker a hard shove in the back and marched behind him to be sure he found his way to an exit.

"What?! Y'all got it all wrong! That man ain't his goddamn brotha'!" Tucker objected, pointing at Landon. "That nigga's a runaway! I'm tellin' ya'! They're all goddamn liars!" he continued shouting as he was marched out of the building.

"Hey, *Larry!*" Lily teased, nudging Landon on his shoulder. "How on earth did you handle that?"

"Well, let's just say, I showed those deputies the only sort of *papers* that anyone really ever cares to see." Landon had not the slightest clue what sort of paperwork the deputies needed, but figured that paper colored in green always sufficed, especially those with three-digit numbers beautifully embossed on the outer edges.

Lily laughed at Landon's devilish deceit and then turned and continued watching Tucker being hauled away, still loudly protesting every step of the way. Tucker had every reason to be upset, though. If anyone knew for a fact that James was not away on a business trip, it was definitely him ...

Just a week before, it was Tucker who once again found himself at the entrance of William's estate, stirring up a commotion with the bandits. This time around, however, he was given far less of a problem gaining access to the grounds because of the two gentlemen who accompanied him: two uniformed deputies. They were joined by Buck Harley, the owner of Buck's Tavern. The security bandits gave as much resistance to their entry as they could but were forced to step aside and let them enter after the deputies had their say.

As Tucker and the deputies trotted onto the grounds, they saw a multitude of people milling about in the yard, loading up wagons, preparing for travel. James was securing the last bit of show equipment and instruments into his wagon until his attention drifted to the sight of horses riding onto William's land. He and everyone else suddenly stopped what they were doing. By the time Tucker and his crew made it to the front of the house, almost everyone from the orchestra had gathered near the porch, staring fiercely at Tucker's entourage, like the unwanted intruders that they were.

"Can we help you?" William called out.

A rather unkempt deputy dismounted his horse. After whispering to Tucker, he turned in the direction of the man he was there to see. "You James Adams?" he asked, as he spat and wiped his mouth.

"I am," James admitted without hesitation.

The deputy held up a piece of paper. "I got a warrant here for your arrest."

In his peripheral vision, James saw William mouth a curse word and shake his head. James stepped down off the porch and snatched the paper out of the deputy's hand. He quickly read the list of allegations: simple battery, disturbing the peace, destruction of property, disorderly conduct. Each allegation stemmed from his scuffle with Tucker at Buck's Tavern after confronting him about the slanderous newspaper article. Immediately incensed over the mediocre matter, James crumpled the warrant and threw it on the ground. "I'll deal with this petty shit when I get back." He then proceeded to walk past the deputy to finish loading his wagon.

"You ain't goin' nowhere, boy!" the deputy said, grabbing hold of James's arm before he could take another step.

James looked down at the deputy's hand around his arm, then glared up at him, threatening him with his eyes. James suddenly calmed himself a bit after looking over at William, whose face spoke volumes. He then turned his attention back to the deputy and snatched his arm free. "Look, can't I just pay a few fines and be done with this bullshit? I got somewhere to be," James asked, aggravation obvious in his tone.

"That ain't up to me, boy! You'll have to talk to the judge about that." The deputy spat near James's foot and wiped his mouth. "I'm here to take ya' in," he said, slapping a pair of handcuffs on one of James's wrists before he had a chance to move.

"You're arrestin' me, now?!"

"You learn fast, boy!" The deputy wrestled James's other arm behind his back, cuffed the other wrist, and began to move him toward his wagon.

"Can you give me just a minute?!" James asked. The officer kept on walking, holding tight to his arm. "Just one goddamn minute!" he said, snatching his arm away.

"You got one minute, boy! If y'ur ass ain't in that wagon by then, I'm gonna add resistin' arrest to y'ur charges!"

James listened to his threats with his back to the deputy as he stalked off and walked up the porch steps. Lily had her arms folded and was staring out into the field, refusing to look at him. "Lily? Lily, can you look at me, please?"

She exhaled sharply before turning to face him.

"You trust William, don't ya?" James asked her.

"Of course I do," she replied, in a way that she hoped made him feel foolish for even asking.

"Good. Y'all carry on as planned. Austin, Max, and Douglas have all helped me set up equipment and lightin' before. They'll know what to do so you can get started with rehearsals." James looked over at the three boys, and they all nodded. He then turned back to Lily. "Afta' I talk to the judge and clear all this up, I'll meet y'all at the theata' and make any adjustments, if need be. This mess shouldn't take long at all. I'll be up in New Lexington lata' today or tomorrow at the latest. I promise, ya' hear?"

Lily nodded in response. It was not equipment setups she was worried about; she simply wanted the comforts of James's presence. Despite their fractured friendship, she had been comforted by having James with her while on their journey to William's home. She was terrified at the thought of being in an unfamiliar environment without him. She had long since adjusted to her new surroundings, but now the thought of venturing outside of William's estate without James instantly had her riddled with terror all over again.

"You okay?" James asked her.

"I'll be fine," Lily quickly replied, not wanting him to be privy to her reservations. As always, she believed her resilience would settle her nerves when the time called for it. She wanted James and everyone else to believe that too.

"Good," James said, suddenly looking around at all the frustrated faces staring back at him.

"We have to get going!" William announced, refusing to look in James's direction. He was eager to get out of his presence and allow his blood pressure to settle back to normal levels.

Upon William's announcement, everyone began shuffling toward the convoy of awaiting wagons and horses.

"Minute's up, boy!" the deputy called out.

Lily and James were the last two remaining on the porch. "Guess you best get goin'. Don't need no mo' trouble for ya'self," she said, her arms still folded up.

James read Lily's body language and silently cursed himself for the moment he had given in at Buck's Tavern and laid Tucker out on the floor. A moment of indiscretion had ruined his opportunity to be there for yet another important transition in Lily's life. He was already sick over the fact that he would now miss the once-in-a-lifetime chance to see her face as she walked into a real theater for the very first time. For that alone, he instantly hated himself. James loved taking care of all the details behind the scenes of The Dream Symphony. Even more, he loved being by Lily's side to see the delight in her eyes and feel the happiness she emitted as she continued to grow during her musical expedition. Watching and sharing in every aspect of her incredible journey had come to mean everything to

James. He could tell by Lily's body language that his presence meant just as much to her too, even if she was not willing to admit it.

With his hands cuffed, James could not touch Lily or hug her the way he was dying to do at that moment. He wanted so badly to help settle the disappointment he felt emanating from her. The sting of not being able to do so was made worse when Lily breezed by him and down the porch steps without another word. She did not offer a goodbye or even attempt to comfort him with a hug, despite her hands being completely free. All James could do was turn and watch her climb into the lead carriage with William and Landon and join the convoy as they trotted off and carried on to New Lexington without him. He, in turn, was carried off to his awaiting jail cell. The further Lily trailed away from James's sight, the harder the consequences of his mistakes started to hit him.

James's state of mind only became worse in the days to come when he realized that trying to clear up the issue for his *minor* misconduct was going to be a *major* problem. Every day, he begged the sheriff for his opportunity to speak to the judge, post his bail, or pay the fines necessary to be released from jail. But he was only ever fed a multitude of excuses about the delays in his case, everything from problems with processing his paperwork, to the judge just being too busy to see him. After a while, the sheriff began to ignore him altogether. James could, therefore, do nothing but wait *impatiently*, pace *incessantly*, complain *very loudly*, and try to calm himself down enough to sleep. However, his mind seemed hell-bent on denying him any serenity. Upon closing his eyes, vivid memories of Elijah enticing Lily played on an endless cycle in his head: Elijah whispering in her ear, Lily laughing in response, Elijah gifting her with candy and flowers, Lily thanking him with a warm embrace, the hunger in Elijah's eyes as he gazed at Lily's face, the curiosity in hers as she gazed at him in return, the lust in Elijah's voice as he offered to make her dinner, the smile on Lily's face as she contemplated a lovely evening with him *alone*. Again, and over again, Elijah's persistent chasing looped in James's exhausted mind, wreaking havoc on his sanity. However, his obsessive jealousy-driven thoughts and worries proved *not* to be unwarranted ...

After Lily was denied access to a hotel, William had decided to stay with her in the theater so that she would not be alone. When Elijah arrived in New Lexington, though, that arrangement abruptly changed. While James was wrapping his hands around the bars of his jail cell, Elijah decided to seize the opportunity to wrap his around Lily. With James gone, he felt it was the perfect time to prove to Lily the sort of comfort he could bring her in times of adversity, *especially* the sort of comfort that only a man could bring.

The evening of the impromptu change, William had gone across the road to retrieve dinner for himself and Lily. While waiting on her food, Lily was lying on her dressing room cot, reading one of the many books she had brought along with her. She closed her book, though, when she suddenly heard the faint sound of piano music coming from the stage. Assuming William had returned with their meals, she got up to join him but was surprised to see that it was actually Elijah playing the elegant ballad. Lily walked around to the front of the piano and Elijah smiled at her as she continued to watch him play.

"William's a wonderful teacha', isn't he?" Lily asked after he completed the simple piece.

"The best!" Elijah agreed.

"I think it's so wonderful that he taught you and Isabel to play."

"Yeah, I'm a little rusty, though. It's been a while."

"I sure couldn't tell."

"I'm certainly nowhere near your level of skill."

"Well, I enjoyed it nonetheless."

"Thank you," Elijah smiled.

The gaze that accompanied his smile sent a rush of warmth running through Lily. Needing to escape the intensity of his eyes, she turned and walked toward the edge of the stage to look out at the interior of the theater.

"Beautiful place, isn't it?" Elijah asked, walking up behind her and staring out at all the features along with her.

"Sure is."

"Amazin' what a pair 'a hands can craft."

"So true. I said that to myself when William's amphitheata' was finished. It came out to be so beautiful. But this place ... this is the grandest thing I've eva' seen in my life. Can't hardly believe I'm blessed enough to be standin' here in the middle of it, let alone the fact that I'll be playin' in this very spot in front of an audience full 'a folks."

"Is that what's troublin' you?" Elijah asked, his booming voice echoing through the empty theater.

"What makes you think I'm troubled?"

"I admire that you're tryna put on a happy face, but you seem a little tense to me," Elijah replied as he began lightly massaging Lily's shoulders. "Is it your nerves gettin' the best 'a you?"

"Naw, it's not that. I've ova'come my fear about playin' in front 'a folks. It's just..." Lily's eyes suddenly fluttered closed when the massage began to relax her.

"Just what?"

"Just that ... umm..." The soothing feeling of Elijah's caress made her lose her train of thought.

"I tell you what." Elijah turned her around to face him. "How about you tell me ova' dinna'?"

"Dinna'?"

"Yeah, I bought us some food from the restaurant across the way. I wanted to cook somethin' for you, but it's a little tough without an oven here," Elijah laughed.

"Yeah, I guess that would pose a problem," Lily nervously laughed in return.

"So, will you join me?"

"I would, but William's s'pposed to be back with some food in a little while."

"I know. I saw 'em headin' into the restaurant about to get your food. When he told me you were stuck stayin' here, I told 'em he could go on and get a room at the hotel and that I'd keep you company. A man his age don't need to be sleepin' on a cot."

"Oh, I see. I guess that's true," Lily replied, suddenly feeling a little uneasy about being there alone with him.

"Any more excuses you care to use?"

Lily smiled sheepishly and shook her head.

"C'mon," Elijah said, taking her by the hand and leading her into his dressing room. Inside, he had set up a makeshift table and laid out the dinner like they were at a fine restaurant, complete with champagne glasses, candles, and cloth napkins.

Impressed by his efforts, Lily lit up with a genuine smile. "Smells really good," she said, as Elijah pulled out her chair.

"I've heard their food is good, but I doubt it's as great as mine," he boasted.

"Well, you ain't the least bit arrogant, are you?" Lily teased.

"It's called *confidence* when it's the truth," Elijah smiled. "Go on, try a bite."

Lily cut into a small piece of the steak and let it melt in her mouth. "Mmm," she purred as she chewed.

"Mine would be far betta', but I guess this will have to suffice ... for now."

"Somehow, I just can't imagine you bein' this great at cookin'," Lily teased.

"I'm great at a lot 'a things," Elijah replied, staring at Lily with a different sort of hunger in his eyes.

"I'm quite sure you are," Lily responded, returning his gaze. His innuendo suddenly caused her mind to flood with thoughts unbecoming of a young unwed woman. The images caused her cheeks to flush red. She quickly turned her attention back to her steak to force the fantasy to fade away.

Elijah sensed Lily's sudden discomfort and steered the subject back to safer grounds as he cut into his steak. "So, I was askin' earlier, what was troublin' you? You're pretty good at hidin' your emotions most 'a the time. But I can see right through that little shield you have up."

Lily put her fork down and stopped eating when his question prompted her true worries to return.

"Did I say somethin' wrong?" Elijah asked, after feeling her emotionally drifting away.

"No, of course not."

"Well then what is it? You ain't eatin' all of a sudden. You alright?"

Lily continued staring at her plate in silence.

Elijah put his fork down as well. "Lily, you can talk to me about anything. Whateva' you say will stay between you and me."

"Thanks. I appreciate that, but I don't wanna bombard you with my troubles, especially afta' you done went through so much trouble for me tonight."

"You wouldn't be bombardin' me. Lily, I wanna help. Is somethin' goin' wrong with the show?"

"Naw, rehearsals are goin' just fine. It's just … I'm worried."

"Worried about what?"

"About…"

"Your *masta'*? William told me he's yet to make it up here."

Lily scoffed at his terminology. "He's not my *masta'*, Elijah."

"Is that what he's tellin' you these days?"

"No, it's just not that way between us. He's … He's a *friend.*"

Elijah laughed, wiped his mouth, and tossed his napkin on the table.

"What's so funny about that?" Lily asked.

"He's a *friend?*"

"Of course he is."

"A man whose fatha' paid for you at an auction is a *friend?* A man who dragged you up here without you havin' so much as a say in it, is your *friend?*" Elijah asked, sounding as if such a thing was ludicrous.

"I know what it seems like to everyone else, but James truly is my friend."

Elijah scoffed and shook his head. "Yeah, I had a *friend* once too. I knew 'em damn near my whole life. A white boy named Nicholas … Nicholas Wellington. He lived up the road from William. Me, him, and William's boys used to climb trees and fish togetha' on weekends and nearly every day in the summa's. Truth be told, we were so close for so long, Nicholas felt more like a brotha' to me than anything else.

"Nick was talented. He was good at everything. He was the only boy in town who could give me a run for my money at foot racin' and fishin'. But I couldn't hold a candle to 'em when it came to drawin' … *Nobody* could. That boy was one hell of an artist. Could draw and paint anything with the utmost precision. People, animals, landscapes, you name it. He planned to go off to school for it, so he could improve and make a livin' at it. But before he went off to college, we saved up enough money and bought ourselves some tickets to ride a steam train togetha'. We were both fascinated by trains, and we'd been dreamin' about ridin' one for years. We planned to travel from one end of the state to the otha'. It's all we eva' talked about sometimes, all the adventures we'd have while we were seein' everything Ohio had to offa'. And afta' years of savin' up, that's exactly what we did.

"So, there I was, with my best friend, our first time on a train togetha', ready to make our dream a reality. While we rode, Nicholas sat next to me starin' out the window at the landscape, capturin' everything he saw on a drawin' pad. You'd probably think that I'd've had my eyes pasted on the landscape whippin' by us too, but that's not what caught my attention at all. Instead, I couldn't take my eyes off this poor old Negro man I saw shovelin' coal into some sort 'a compartment in the engine. I realized he was shovelin' the fuel to keep the train movin'. He was hunched ova', covered from head to toe in soot and sweat. Hell, he was covered so thick, he could 'a been a white man unda' there and I'd've neva' known the difference.

"For days afta' that trip, I thought about that poor old filthy man breakin' his back. I's convinced there had to be an easier way to keep that train movin' than to force some old man to slave away and suffa' the way he was. About a week lata', I had a dream … a dream about how I could improve that train. I dreamt about a holdin' compartment for all that coal, one that could be placed high up above the engine, so that the coal could be funneled *downward* into the engine by simply pullin' on a lever. So instead 'a shovelin', all a man would eva' have to do is open that storage compartment with the lever and release as much coal as he needed before closin' it off again. No more shovelin', no more sweatin', no more soot, no more watchin' an old man damn near break his back to keep a train rollin'.

"When I woke up from that dream, I was hell-bent on makin' it a reality. I wanted to get a patent for the idea and sell it to every train

331

manufacturer in the United States. I wrote up a summary about it and tried to draw a blueprint to go along with it. The problem was, I couldn't draw no betta' than a five-year-old. But Nicholas Wellington—*my friend*—he could draw anything. So, I took my basic sketch to 'em, showed 'em the write-up on my idea, and asked if he'd do a professional blueprint for me. Nicholas was more than happy to do it. He shared in my enthusiasm because he was just as convinced as I was that this idea would be a change that no train manufacturer would eva' turn down. He had no doubt in his mind that somethin' so simple would make me rich, and my *best friend* wanted to do all he could to help. He told me to give 'em forty-eight hours, so that he could be sure the drawin' was done to scale. He said he'd have it complete by then for sure. Two days lata', I returned to retrieve it, just to find out that my very *best* friend, a friend who was like a brotha' to me, had gotten on a train and rode south with my idea tucked away in his pocket. His first stop … E.M. Baldwin Train Corporation.

"So, if you eva' have the chance to get on a steam train, just know that it'll be *my* coal funnelin' system helpin' to propel it forward. But more importantly, that my *friend,* Nicholas Wellington, will neva' have to work again a single day in his life because of it. And worse yet, there ain't a damn thing I can do about it because there ain't a court in the land that'll believe some dumb Negro actually thought of an idea like that.

"That was my ticket, Lily! My ticket to a betta' life, a life of not havin' to work like a dog to make ends meet, to supportin' a family when I have one, a ticket to givin' somethin' meaningful to my folks afta' everything they been through for me and my sista'. My so-called *friend,* he took that ticket from me, signed his name on it, and took my seat on a train with a destination to an easier life. So long as I live, I'll neva' forgive that bastard for it!

"'I'm your *friend!*'" Elijah pointed his finger down hard on the table with a scowl on his face. "White folks! That's what they'll tell ya', Lily!

They'll smile at ya'! Hug ya'! Or do whateva' they have to do to get close enough to ya', just to be sure it's easier to take what they want from ya' wheneva' it comes a time that they need it!"

Lily stared at Elijah, feeling uneasy with how upset he had become. "I-I'm sorry for what happened to you, Elijah, I really am. But how could you say that afta' everything that William's done for you?"

"William's an anomaly!"

"And how do you know that James isn't?!"

"Oh, come on, Lily! Don't be so blind! He hasn't even tried to hide it! It was all ova' the newspapa's, how he's usin' you to make money to pay his daddy's debts!"

"That ain't true!"

"If it ain't, then answa' one question for me … Of all the money you've made since performin' on William's estate and outta all the advances Robert Branaugh has given for this show, how much of it has *your masta'* laid in your hands?"

Lily leaned back in her chair and stared at her plate, embarrassed to answer truthfully.

Elijah scoffed. "A *friend*, huh?" he smiled arrogantly. "Betta' start rethinkin' your definition 'a what that really is. You should be happy *your masta's* locked up, instead 'a sittin' here sulkin' ova' him the way you are. He deserves to be sittin' in that jail cell dealin' with the consequences of his actions, not to mention for the way he's *stealin'* your money."

"Stop talkin' about him that way! You don't know James the way I do!" Lily quickly scooted her chair back, got up, and stormed out of the dressing room.

Elijah immediately jumped up and caught her in the hallway. "Lily wait! Please!" He gently turned her around to face him. "You're right. I'm sorry. I had no right. I'm really sorry. I didn't mean to get upset at you. I didn't realize how bitta' I still was about what happened to me. This whole scenario makes me so mad because I just don't want the same thing to happen to you. I know I may not have expressed myself right, but I just wanna protect you from what I went through. But, you're right … I don't know this James guy at all, so I shouldn't've said those things about 'em."

"You're damn right you shouldn't have!"

"I know, I know … but can you at least try to unda'stand where I'm comin' from?"

Lily just stared at Elijah with a scowl on her face and refused to utter another word.

"Can you give me anotha' chance? I know I was way outta line, and I probably don't deserve it, but I'm askin' for your forgiveness anyway?"

Again, Lily was cold and refused to respond.

"Please?" Elijah begged. "I know I've made a complete mess outta dinna' tonight, but to make it up to you and show you that I'm not such a bad guy, how 'bout I ride back to Athens tomorrow to see if I can find out what's goin' on with James?"

"I-I'd appreciate that."

"Then that's what I'll do."

"Thank you."

"So, now what do you say we forget about the last ten minutes and start ova'?" Elijah extended his hand for Lily to shake. "Hi, I'm Elijah … And you are?"

She finally smiled at his sarcasm. "Lily," she replied, reluctantly placing her hand in his.

"Wow! You have a smile that lights up this entire room."

"Well, thank you ... Umm, what did you say your name was again?" she responded, playing along with his game.

"Elijah," he laughed.

"Well, Elijah, that's very sweet 'a you. You have a very nice smile too."

"Well, thank you, beautiful."

Elijah took hold of Lily's hand and guided her back to his makeshift dinner table. They sat back down together and finished the meal in better spirits with plenty of wine, dessert, and lighter conversation. They later tinkered on the piano together and then sat next to one another in the theater seats, laughing at funny stories about each other's lives. They carried on with the fun of their impromptu date until Lily grew tired and departed back to her dressing room well after midnight.

From her few interactions with Elijah, Lily had learned that he was more than just a flawlessly handsome man who possessed the ability to simply look at a woman in a way that would melt her insides. He was witty, intelligent, ambitious, attentive, and had a confidence about him that was unlike any other Negro man she had ever known. She was quickly convinced that he was an anomaly amongst Negro men, the sort of rare man that women would fight over to marry and have children with. He had such an impact on Lily that she was still thinking about him well after their date. This, despite their minor argument about James. In fact, as she lay in her tiny cot, it dawned on her that she had not thought about James at all after that. Elijah's presence had temporarily freed her from her worries about James's whereabouts. Instead, she found herself wondering if she just might be the right fit for a man of Elijah's caliber. She now looked forward to spending another evening with him to see if time would tell.

... It was the mere thought of Elijah and Lily spending such precious quality time together that tortured James as he sat idly in his jail cell. Logically, James knew that he had no right to be upset at Lily for accepting Elijah's advances, if that's what she wanted. But logic was a foreign concept when it came to the matter of his feelings for her. And logic was certainly proving to have no power in stopping the graphic visions of Lily and Elijah that continued to erupt in James's jealous mind, visions far worse than any simple dinners or casual hugs. The effect of those mental images were exacerbated by the fact that James was yearning to be there for Lily behind the scenes, supporting her leading up to another monumental moment. He feared missing her first show inside a real theater and the celebratory hug that she always gave him following every grand finale. The culmination of it all had a rage building inside James that intensified the closer it grew to opening night.

Now, with only hours remaining until the opening number, the fuse of James's emotions had nearly burned through completely, leaving him on the verge of exploding. He lay in his filthy jailhouse cot with the lack of food, water, and sleep adding fuel to that burning emotional fuse. His malnourished mind continued to maliciously torture him with images of Elijah and Lily's entangled bodies. Those erotic visions finally caused his fury to explode. Angrily, he sprang from his cot, wrapped his hands around his cell bars, and began yelling at the top of his lungs. His pleading echoed down the hallways of the jailhouse and fell on the deaf unsympathetic ears of the sheriff, as usual.

After nearly going hoarse, James stood with his head resting against the bars of his cell, the vile images of Elijah and Lily continuing to add to his madness. The visions ceased, though, when he suddenly heard a familiar voice begin to berate him.

"You mean they ain't let you outta here yet, schoolboy?" Tucker teased from outside the small, barred window near the ceiling of James's basement cell.

James tore himself away from the cell bars and turned around briefly to look up at the person he was convinced had played a role in ensuring his extended jailhouse stay. After he saw Tucker's face, he turned back around and rested his head back on the bars. Despite James trying to ignore him, Tucker continued to torment him.

"Now don't you worry y'ur pretty little head if you don't get out on time, ya' hear? I'm sure somebody'll volunteer to keep y'ur honey warm t'night afta' her show. Just might be that nigga' William done raised up all them years. I saw the way he was lookin' at 'er durin' that fundraisa'. He seemed awful sweet on y'ur lil' monkey," Tucker teased. He squatted down and cocked his head to the side to be sure he had a good view of James's reaction. "Or maybe William's ol' dried up ass still got enough juice in 'em to get it up and give y'ur little honey-brown bitch a pickle tickle," he laughed. "Or hell, come to think of it … just might be *me*." He licked his dried-up lips. "I swear, I ain't been able to get 'er sweet little ass off my mind since the day you laid me out at Buck's Tavern. I been dyin' for her to give me the kind 'a lovin' that'll make me wanna knock a man smooth on his ass!" It took every bit of effort for Tucker's lungs to force his laugh through the cigar-tarred congestion in his throat. "I'm jealous of ya', schoolboy! I ain't neva' had me no ass as good as that … *yet*. I'ma fix that t'night, though," he smiled, showing his tobacco-stained teeth. "Well, I bes' get goin' if I wanna make it to the show on time. I got quite a long ride ahead 'a me. You sleep well now, ya' hear?" Tucker looked up at the sky. "You be sure 'n cova' up good, schoolboy. Gonna be awful cold layin' in that cot t'night all by y'ur lonesome," he said, letting out another phlegm-filled laugh.

James refused to give Tucker the reaction he wanted, despite his sudden desire to grab him by the neck. He wanted to squeeze until the blood drained from Tucker's face, his lips turned purple, his beady eyes bulged from his head, and his chest ceased movement. To refrain from his murderous impulse, James tightened his grip on the cell bars and waited for the annoying town outcast to leave.

After Tucker rode off, James actually felt a twinge of envy knowing that he was headed to the place that he desperately wanted to be. When he was long gone, James walked to the small window above his cell and saw nothing but the dust Tucker's horse left behind. When the dust settled, his attention drifted to two young boys playing nearby, wearing tattered clothes and no shoes.

"Heeey fellas!" James called out to them in a husky tone, trying to keep his voice from reaching the ears of the sheriff. He looked over his shoulder to see if anyone was coming before calling out to them again. On his second attempt, both boys looked around, wondering where the voice was coming from. James stuck his arm through the cell bars and waved them over. "Ova' here!"

The two boys looked at each other and shrugged their shoulders before wandering over to see what James wanted. "What is it, mista'?" the scrawniest of the two asked.

"You boys wanna make some money?" James held up two five-dollar bills that had been tucked away in his back pocket.

"Sure!" they said in unison, their eyes widening at the bills waved before them.

"Then listen, I need both 'a you to go and find a fella named Harrison Mitchell. He's a good friend 'a mine. He lives on Post Road, not far from the big fishin' creek. You know where that is?"

"Sure! We fish there all the time."

"Good, well Harrison's got the only big white house on that road, 'bout a quarta' mile from there. Tell 'em that James Adams is down at the county jail and that I need his help. Tell 'em that it's real urgent and that I need 'em to come right away, okay? Can you rememba' all that?"

"Yessa'!" both boys said in unison.

"If you get 'em down here quick then these ten dollars are all yours, okay?"

"Yessa'!" they both replied again, sounding as giddy as two boys could be over that amount of money.

"I'll give ya' five dollars now, and you can get the rest when ya' get back, ya' hear?" he promised, as he handed one of the bills over to them. "Go on, now. Go as fast as your little legs'll carry ya'."

Without another word, both boys bolted down the road, kicking up as much dust as Tucker's horse had on his way out of town. When they were out of sight, James sat on his bed and waited with his stomach in knots, hoping that giving up ten dollars would be worth it in the end.

James had been trying to summon the deputies to contact his old roommate and fraternity brother for nearly a week. Harrison had never failed to be there for James while they were in school. He had always invited him to stay with his family during school breaks, since he knew that James had no desire to return to Virginia. Despite the fact that they were close, James had never confided in Harrison about the details of the reason why he refused to go home. Harrison never pressured him about it either, sensing that it was a very sensitive subject. Instead of pushing James to get past the issues he was running away from at home, Harrison simply welcomed him to stay at his. Having been there for him faithfully in the past, James was confident that Harrison would most certainly be there for him again, so long as those two little boys were successful in finding him.

Just over an hour later, James heard footsteps outside his cell window, followed by the sound of two young voices. The two little boys had gone to the big white house near the fishing creek, but Harrison's wife informed them that he was still at the courthouse. Eager to fulfill their mission for the remainder of their money, the boys found Harrison there just as he was wrapping up a minor court case. They then quickly ushered him across the street to James's basement cell window. "He's ova' here, mista'!" one of them pointed out to Harrison.

James stood on his bed again and handed over the remainder of the money that he had promised his tiny heroes. "Thank you, boys!"

"Thanks, mista'!" they exclaimed, before running off to spend their earnings.

Harrison squatted down to see James better. "Well, well, well. What the hell kind 'a mess you done got ya'self into these days, Adams?"

James was not in the mood for sarcasm. "Listen, I don't have much time. You gotta get me the hell outta here. I've been here for almost a week ova' some bullshit charges."

"Just what kind 'a *bullshit* charges we talkin' about?"

"I got in a fight with some asshole at Buck's Tavern a few weeks back. A deputy came out to the house a couple 'a weeks lata' with a warrant for my arrest. That was a week ago, and I've been sittin' in here eva' since."

"I need to know more than that. Give me specifics. What exactly was on the warrant?"

"Simple battery, destruction 'a property ... Umm, disturbin' the peace, and disorderly conduct, I think."

"You've been stuck here a week for *that?!*"

"Yeah."

"You haven't seen a judge yet?"

"No, nothin'! I'm tellin' ya', I haven't left this goddamn cell! Somehow, I think the little shit who put me in here has everything to do with the reason I'm still sittin' here, but that's anotha' matta' for anotha' time. All I know is that you gotta get me the hell outta here!"

"What little shit're you talkin' about?"

"Guy named Tucker."

"McCormick?"

"Yeah, that's the one."

Harrison laughed. "Damn! Yeah, you certainly chose the wrong piece 'a shit to fight with. He and Sheriff Tolliva' been friends since they were boys."

"That explains a lot. Lucky me."

"Have you asked for an attorney?"

"I've lost count 'a how many times I've asked them to get a hold 'a you! I'm tellin' you, they don't give a shit! I just kept gettin' fed all these goddamn excuses, and now they're just ignorin' me!"

Harrison realized that the line of questioning was only agitating James more. "Well, unfortunately, the courts have just closed for the day, but I can draw up some papers tonight and then first thing Monday mornin'..."

"I don't fuckin' have 'til Monday! I need to get the hell outta here! *Now!*"

"Whoa man, hold your voice down," Harrison said, looking over James's shoulder to see if he had gotten the attention of any deputies.

"Don't worry, they're good at ignorin' me by now," James replied, briefly looking over his shoulder too. "Look, I'm sorry. It's just ... you gotta help me. Please," he begged. "You gotta get me outta here. I got somewhere I need to be tonight. It's important to me. *Really* important," he sighed.

Harrison let his thoughts consume him for a moment while he tried to think of a quicker solution. "Alright, I think I got somethin'. I'll be back. Just hold tight."

"What the hell else am I gonna do?" James mumbled after he walked off.

Harrison boldly walked into the front lobby of the county jail that had been James's home for the last week. "Sheriff Tolliva', how do you do?" he asked.

"Well, well, well, Harrison Mitchell," Sheriff Tolliver replied, standing and taking hold of his hand to shake. "Ned," Tolliver said, speaking to a young, goofy-looking, rookie deputy at a desk nearby. "This fella here is one 'a the finest damn attorneys I've eva' laid my eyes on." He turned to look at Harrison again. "Neva' did get to thank ya' for what you did for ma' sista'."

"No thanks necessary, Sheriff. Afta' I saw what 'er husband did to 'er face, there was no way I was gonna let that son of a bitch get away with abusin' 'er like that."

"It may seem like no big deal to you, but I can't count how many otha' jackass attorneys failed 'er. Eitha' they were too damn timid, or they were easily swayed by 'er ex-husband's money. Bunch 'a damn crooks," Tolliver snarled. "But you! You were like a goddamn rabid dog attackin' 'er ex-husband while he was up there on that stand!" He gave a hearty laugh. "In all my years, I ain't neva' seen nothin' like it!"

"Well, thank you," Harrison smiled. "I knew she needed a strong voice on 'er side, and I didn't wanna let 'er down."

"And you didn't. That's somethin' she'll neva' forget you for eitha'."

"Trust me, I'll neva' forget her eitha', nor those tears she cried durin' the verdict when it was all ova'. Tears 'a justice, that's what those were to me. I's just a rookie attorney then, and it affected me pretty deep knowin' I had the powa' to help give 'er that sort 'a justice. That's what I live for now. It's what I fight for. I crave it. I yearn for it. I dream of it. I want every one 'a my clients to know the feelin' of justice. No matta' how big or how small the offense, I wanna feel that euphoric victory vicariously through them. I ain't lost a case yet because of it, and I owe that to your sista' for given me a chance to fight on her behalf. She lit a fire unda' my ass, that's for damn sure."

"Seems you've both gained a lot from each otha' then. I tell you what, son, any man should be proud to have you as his attorney knowin' how hard y'ur willin' to fight for y'ur clients."

"You're too kind."

Sheriff Tolliver nodded and sat back down. "Well now, what can I do ya' for today?"

Harrison nonchalantly walked over and looked at a few of the sheriff's plaques hanging on the walls. "It's an election year, ain't it?"

"Sure is."

"You runnin' again?"

"Sure am."

"Must be important to ya' then ... to portray yourself to the vota's as a man who upholds and abides by every aspect of the law?"

"Of course," Tolliver responded, leaning back in his chair, starting to look at Harrison a bit oddly about his choice of conversation.

"Ya' know, I've been in that courtroom a whole hell of a lot in the last two years since helpin' ya' sista'," Harrison continued, as he strolled from plaque to plaque. "And it neva' escapes my attention how many people pack into the pews durin' those public hearin's on a daily basis. I see all kinds 'a different people driftin' in there. Everything from town gossipers who like to be nosy, to bored retired old men. Hell, some folks're just lookin' to get outta the heat or the cold. All different kind 'a people, all there for their own different reasons, but one thing 'bout all of 'em is the same ... they're *voters*. Each and every one of 'em gets to cast their ballot come election time. All those folks wanna be sure they cast their vote for the sort 'a politicians that are honest, for judges who are fair and just, and for a *sheriff...*" Harrison finally turned around to look at Sheriff Tolliver. "For a sheriff who upholds and abides strictly by the laws. The people want a sheriff that ain't swayed by money or politicians or ... oh, I don't know, old friends who ask unlawful favors. A diligent, law abidin' sheriff who believes wholeheartedly in *every* citizen's right to *swift* due process, that's what the people want! Ain't that right, Ned?" Harrison asked, while still staring at Sheriff Tolliver.

"See Ned, the people 'a this town don't wanna think that a sheriff they voted for is the kinda person who would lock a man up for minor offenses like *simple* battery, causin' *minor* property damages, or somethin' as silly as disturbin' the peace, and then neva' botha' to let 'em see a judge and post his bail, or pay his fines within a *reasonable* amount 'a time, the way the law states. The good people 'a this town would be outraged to learn that a sheriff they elected was the sort 'a man to deny a petty criminal an attorney afta' he begs for one for a whole week! Hell Ned! I've seen murderers who were granted lawya's and a chance to see a judge in less time than that! No! The good votin' people 'a this county, who pack those pews to the gills in the courthouse every day, wouldn't wanna know such a thing about their elected official, now would they, Ned?" Harrison walked over, placed both his hands on Tolliver's desk, and leaned toward him. "And I highly doubt that's the sort 'a thing that a sheriff would like to explain to a judge in front of all 'a those vote-castin' citizens loiterin' in the courtroom every day when there's a *rabid dog* questionin' 'em while he's up there on that stand!"

Tolliver jumped to his feet and fearlessly leaned across his desk toward Harrison. "You must be outta y'ur goddamn mind, boy! I don't believe you'd really be dumb enough to put y'ur career on the line for that nigga' lovin' piece 'a shit!" he growled, staring Harrison down with blood-red eyes.

"If you think that's the only thing I know about how corrupt you are, then *you're* the one who's outta his goddamn mind! I got enough dirt on you to fill the fishin' creek near my house two times ova'. I'll snuff it dry with all y'ur dirty little secrets if that's the chance you wanna take," Harrison threatened, bluffing with rumors he had heard about Sheriff Tolliver, but had no real evidence to back up.

Tolliver didn't blink, hoping to refrain from showing the slightest hint of fear. "Get the keys to the cell, Ned," he demanded, without turning his eyes away from Harrison.

"You do that, Ned. Quick, fast, and in a hurry." Harrison finally stepped back and smirked at Tolliver when he heard the cell keys rattling.

"You tell Buck Harley that my client agrees to pay for all 'a the damages done to his property within thirty days of receiving a written estimate, not a penny more or less," Harrison told the sheriff once James was out of his cell and standing beside him. Harrison was about to walk away after that but then stopped and turned back toward Tolliver. "Oh, and uh, bein' the *law abidin'* sheriff that you are, somehow I think you'll find it in y'ur heart to make all those otha' charges magically disappear."

Tolliver crumpled James's warrant and dropped it into the trash.

"Now, that's magic if I eva' seen it. You're damn sure worthy 'a my vote!" Harrison joked.

"Get y'ur asses outta my jailhouse!" Tolliver erupted.

"Good luck with that re-election." Harrison tipped his hat. "Have a fine day gentlemen."

"Don't know what kind 'a strings you just pulled in there, but I can't thank you enough" James said, squinting after the sunlight hit his eyes for the first time in days.

"Don't mention it. Neva' could stand ol' Tolliva's fat ass anyway. Felt good," Harrison replied, as they walked toward his carriage across the road. "So, I hear there's a big symphony t'night up in New Lexington. My guess is that's where you're so eaga' to go."

James didn't say a word, but the look on his face said it all.

Harrison grabbed James's shirt sleeve. "Well, I hope you're not goin' there lookin' like this." He leaned in and sniffed him. "Or smellin' like that eitha'," he laughed. He slapped James on the shoulder. "Come on, Adams, let me help my ol' fraternity brotha' out."

"Thanks. I owe you big time for this, Mitchell," James said, as he climbed into his carriage.

"No. Seems you owe it to a certain someone else to get your ass to that symphony on time," Harrison replied. He then snapped the reins to prompt his horses into a gallop toward his house, where he planned to loan James some clothes, a razor, a toothbrush, and some much-needed soap.

Just as with all James's other issues in the past, Harrison did not question him any further about why he nearly fell apart emotionally over the fact that he might miss Lily's performance. He was now fairly confident of what the answer to that would be anyway. A few weeks prior, James had invited Harrison and his wife, Lauren, to come and watch Lily perform at William's estate. While there, Harrison noticed that there was something unique about the relationship that James had with Lily. He heard the pride in James's tone when he finally introduced Lily to him at the after party. As the night carried on, Harrison continued to watch them as they interacted. He was warmed by the sight of the pair dancing, smiling, and laughing throughout the entire evening. With Lily by his side, James seemed like a dramatically different person to Harrison, one that was finally exuding genuine happiness. It only took those few hours to convince Harrison that *Lily* was the answer to *all* the questions regarding James's odd behavior in school: why he fought the desire to return home during school breaks, why he seemed to constantly drink his sorrows away, and why he used women as toys and never bothered to involve himself emotionally with any of them. Harrison did not blame James for what he felt for Lily. He, too, had been taken aback by how intelligent, funny, warm, and stunningly beautiful she was. He instantly understood how Lily could cause a man like James to feel internally torn, to the extent that he would act out his frustrations in bizarre ways. Harrison left the party that evening feeling deeply empathetic to the uniqueness of their circumstances.

With that evening in mind, Harrison was now certain that *Lily* was also the reason why James had just rushed through shaving and bathing, and why he was currently watching his longtime friend ride off his property on his strongest horse with the speed of a twister, dressed in the finest attire from his very own closet. The sight of it further proved that Harrison's assumptions about James's feelings for Lily were right. But just as with all the other intimate details of his friend's life, "your secrets are safe with me," Harrison whispered, as he watched James ride out of sight. "Ride like the wind, my friend."

* * * *

While Lily had spent two hours pushing to focus mentally and deliver another stellar performance, James had spent nearly that same amount of time pushing Harrison's horse to near death in order to be there for another once-in-a-lifetime moment in Lily's life ... but it was far too late. Lily had already taken a final bow to her grateful audience, only for her eyes to home in on the empty seat next to Landon that had been reserved for James. With all the orchestra members surrounding her, Lily finally exited the stage, feeling just as drained as the horse that James was currently dismounting. James quickly wrapped the horse's reins around a post near a trough of water and began fighting his way through a sea of people exiting Branaugh Theater. Hearing no music playing within the building, his heart sank into his stomach. He scrambled into the theater only to have his fears confirmed: the curtains had closed, and all seats were empty. He had missed every minute of the show.

"James!" Landon called out after spotting him panting in the wings, looking as lost as a puppy. "A successful night, wouldn't you say?! Did you hear that crowd?!"

With the culmination of missing Lily's show and his week-long nightmare in jail, the excitement in Landon's voice was equivalent to screeching nails on a chalkboard in James's ears. Landon's joy only managed to elevate his agitation tenfold, so too did the fact that he was not the person James wished to see at that moment.

In the midst of all the bodies backstage, Lily had yet to see that James had finally arrived. She had walked backstage toward William, Anna Mae, Ben, Isabel, and Elijah, who all welcomed her with delight on their faces. Anna Mae's eyes seeped tears of joy as she hugged Lily. "I'm so proud 'a you, baby!" she boasted.

"Thank you, Ms. Anna Mae!" Lily excitedly replied.

While Lily and her friends celebrated on one side of the stage, Landon was holding James up on the other, rambling on and on about the success of the show. Not far into the conversation, though, James became *completely* incoherent to Landon's words. He was far too busy searching for the woman he needed to settle his agitation. He kept looking over Landon's shoulder, his eyes bolting from face to face, trying to find Lily in the clutter of dancers and orchestra members. Since Landon had helped to afford Lily the opportunity to play at Branaugh Theater, James wanted to escape his meaningless chatter without being disrespectful. In an instant, though, respect became irrelevant; the woman James was desperate to see, he had finally spotted ... in the arms of another man.

After presenting Lily with a massive flower arrangement, Elijah was embracing the woman that James had been dying to hold for nearly a week. The sight of it caused him to abruptly bolt past Landon without a word, leaving him standing there alone, looking confused by the sudden change in his demeanor. The blood in James's veins had instantaneously reached explosive levels after seeing the man he loathed stealing his celebratory grand finale ritual. James's face turned a deep red and he balled his fists tight as he glared at Elijah, whose arms were wrapped as tightly around Lily's body as his were currently supposed to be. James flew in a beeline toward the embracing pair, his lips tightly pursed, his body rigid, and his ears deaf to the joyous laughter of the celebrating crew around him. All James could hear in his head was the array of compliments that Elijah had showered Lily with in the past. His eyes were fixated on the smile illuminated on Lily's face as Elijah held her. With hunger and exhaustion having completely eroded James's emotional rationale, his anger was on par with a man walking in on his moaning wife, her sacred lair happily welcoming the hardened flesh of another man.

"LILY!" James suddenly shouted.

Lily quickly turned her head toward the sound of the familiar voice. Her smile broadened and her eyes lit up, the very second they confirmed what her ears already had. "James! You're here!" she exclaimed, quickly letting go of Elijah, excited to finally hug James for the first time in days.

Lily's abrupt departure instantly enraged Elijah. His face quickly morphed into a tight-lipped grimace as he watched her damn near run toward a man that he considered as nothing more than her manipulative, money-hungry *master*.

"Get into the carriage!" James commanded Lily, as he sidestepped her offer for a hug.

"But why?" Lily asked, looking confused as James breezed by her, glaring coldly at the man who had him beyond irate.

"We're leavin'!"

"But James, I's…"

349

"I SAID WE'RE LEAVIN'!" he shrieked in an explosive belligerent tone that stopped the celebration cold, instantly silenced every mouth, and commanded the bewildered eyes of everyone surrounding them.

"James, I..."

"NOW!" he screamed, startling everyone. His jealousy and anger would not allow him to turn his eyes away from Elijah, who reciprocated with a glare that was equally as icy.

Not much had been said, but James's sudden appearance and his explosive attitude had instantaneously killed the joyous mood of the celebration. For several uncomfortably quiet seconds, the entire cast stared curiously at him, perplexed by his bizarre behavior. After such a successful night, they expected that James would be the happiest of everyone there.

The aftershock of James's nasty attitude had Lily unable to even move. She just stood there holding her bouquet, her mouth partially agape. She was wearing yet another one of Anna Mae's beautiful gowns. At that moment, though, she did not feel so beautiful in it. Embarrassment and humiliation had quickly trumped all other emotions. She was thoroughly confused as to why James was just now arriving and as to why his first order of business was to humiliate her in front of all her friends.

When James was finally able to tear his eyes away from Elijah, he looked over at Lily's face and knew immediately that his jealous tantrum had just ruined her night. Feeling the embarrassment of the moment full force, Lily shamefully lowered her head, reminding James of her reaction during the many occasions that his father was nasty to her. The sorrowful sight made him immediately regret his actions.

Already emotionally weakened from a turbulent week, it took very little to drain Lily's joy. She, therefore, conceded to James's demands without a fight. "Yessa'," she finally replied. She had quickly reverted back to her slave mentality and acknowledged him accordingly. As she walked away with her head hanging in shame, the clicking of her fancy shoes against the concrete floor sounded more like cannons going off in the midst of the awkward silence that lingered in the hallway.

James briefly watched her retreat to the carriage and then turned to glare at Elijah once more, hoping the hateful glance conveyed his anger about touching Lily. Without another word, James then began walking to catch up with Lily, leaving everyone else behind to speculate in confusion about what had just happened.

"ADAMS!"

James stopped and turned around to find Elijah walking up behind him.

"Can I have a word with you?" Elijah asked.

"What the hell do you want?!" James barked.

Elijah arrogantly smirked. "Same thing as you it seems," he replied boldly. "I see the way you look at Lily. And you're a damn fool if you think I haven't noticed the way you look at *me* wheneva' I talk to her. I've seen it from day one."

"Get to your fuckin' point! I don't have time for this shit!"

"C'mon, Adams. It's just you and me here alone now." Elijah stepped even closer, the swagger in his strides exuding extreme confidence. "I know your little conniption fit here tonight had nothin' to do with Lily, so why take it out on *her?*"

"You don't know a damn thing!"

"I *know* I was here for her tonight! I *know* I was a comfort to her while you were nowhere to be found! I *know* that she didn't deserve to be treated the way you just treated 'er! I *know* that a *real* man would've taken his anga' out on *me* ... not her!"

James took a step closer to Elijah, an evil intensity in his eyes. "I'd be careful what you ask for," he said through gritted teeth.

Elijah fearlessly took another step closer to him too. "You betta' be careful too. You don't know who you're fuckin' with eitha', greedy white boy!" he snapped. "But I can assure you that I'm a man who knows good 'n damn well that you can't possibly offa' Lily the sort 'a life that I can, and you're a goddamn lunatic if you think otha'wise." He scoffed and shook his head. "Lemme guess, you dragged Lily up here to a free state thinkin' things will be different or easy somehow, didn't ya'? Well, I can promise you that, outside 'a William's mansion, nobody will give a damn about Lily bein' free or not free anywhere else in these racist United States, trust me on that," he said, recalling his lingering bitterness over what his friend had done to him. "Outside of William's gates, without those filthy guards he hired, Lily's fair game. If anybody catches wind about the little love affair you're hopin' for, she'll have a target on 'er back the size 'a New York for hatred, ridicule ... hell, even *death!* So, I suggest you let go of any twisted fairytale fantasy ideals you have about 'er. Or betta' yet ... why don't you just let *her* go?!"

"And I suggest you stay y'ur ass the hell away from her, or the only thing left in that smart-ass mouth 'a yours will be your tongue!"

Elijah arrogantly laughed at his threat. "You're so hell-bent on tryna pretend like Lily's free, so don't you think she oughta be the one to make the decision about who she wants?" he smirked. "Go on and ask 'er, *Masa' James* ... 'cause I'm certain that afta' the week I just spent with 'er, she'll be beggin' for more of *me.*"

Despite sensing the lies in Eiljah's implications, every ounce of James wanted to swing for having the audacity to suggest such a thing. But he knew that that's what Elijah wanted: more proof that Lily need not be with a man who possessed such a volatile temper. It would have been another reason to drive her away and perhaps into Elijah's arms. James was definitely unwilling to give him that satisfaction. Instead, he stepped to within a hairsbreadth of Elijah's face. "Seems I'm not the only one with a twisted fairytale fantasy," he finally replied.

They stood there with each other eye to eye in silence afterward, both looking like two rabid animals ready to square off. After a few seconds, James finally found the strength to turn and walk away in an attempt to diffuse his fury.

"If you really gave a damn about Lily, you'd let 'er have the sort 'a life she deserves!" Elijah yelled to James down the hall.

His words rang through James's ears loud and clear, but his temper had caused him enough turmoil for the night. Remembering that fact left him content to let Elijah have the last word and gave him the strength to continue marching away from a potentially bloody battle scene.

Chapter Nineteen

Master:
A man who owns servants or slaves.
OR
A skilled practitioner of a particular art,
technique, or activity.

The carriage ride back to William's estate seemed longer than usual to both Lily and James. It was nightfall, but James did not need light to know that Lily was crying. Her body language spoke volumes, as did her silence. She sat next to the bouquet that Elijah had given her with her body turned slightly toward the window, looking out into the darkness, sniffling lightly every few minutes. James wanted to find words of comfort, but William was along for the ride as well, and he did not want to embarrass himself or Lily any further in his presence.

As soon as the carriage halted in William's yard, Lily hastily got out and trotted up to her room before James and William even reached the porch steps. When she was out of sight, William turned and scolded James with his eyes while pointing his finger toward where Lily had just gone. "That beautiful young lady up there, she was a complete and utter wreck before the show tonight, pacing and worrying herself sick, wondering what had happened to you! *Then!* After all the heartache and trouble you caused, you had the audacity to walk into that theater and treat her that way! You-you imbecile! Did you not see the instant look of relief on her face the moment she saw you?! She was herself again for the briefest of moments until you ripped it all away from her again! And to know that your little tantrum had everything to do with..." William stopped and snickered. "Yes, jealousy is undoubtedly a very natural emotion James, but only a *fool* would allow it to unravel him. And *you* ... you bloody fool!" he insulted, pointing his finger near James's face. "You are hanging by the thinnest of threads ... a very, very *frayed* thread at that!"

"I don't wanna hear any of your wisdom-filled riddles right now, William!" James replied, putting a hand up.

William shook his head. "I'm too disgusted to waste any more of my oxygen speaking to you anyway!" He then stormed up the stairs and slammed his bedroom door.

Once William was out of sight, James immediately ascended the stairs, two steps at a time, and entered Lily's room without bothering to knock. Lily still had her dress on and was standing by the fire she had just started, trying to warm herself and calm her severed nerves.

"Lily," James said, quietly closing the door behind him.

"Yessa'?" she replied with her back to him.

"You still cryin'?"

"No sa', I wasn't cryin'," she lied, trying to hide her face by continuing to gaze at the fire.

"You're not a very good liar." He approached her from behind. "Can you look at me, please?"

Lily refused to turn around, hoping to continue hiding any evidence of her lie.

James stood patiently behind her. "Please, tell me your troubles."

"I'm fine," she insisted. "Just a lil' tired is all."

James did not want to hear that. He wanted the verbal punishment that he knew he well deserved. "No need for lies. Tell me what's wrong."

"I ain't got nothin' to say ... *masta'*."

"I know you, Lily, and I ain't neva' seen you cry for nothin'."

"I'm fine," she lied again.

"I figured you'd be too angry to speak to me, and I don't blame you. But I came up here anyway because I at least wanted to tell you how sorry I am."

"For which part, huh?" Lily asked. Her arms were folded across her chest, and she still refused to turn around and look at him. "For beatin' up that moron? Landin' yo'self in jail? Missin' the show? Or for remindin' me in front 'a everybody on that stage tonight that you *own* me? Which one is it ... *masta'*?"

"Stop callin' me that!" James shouted in frustration.

"For what!?" Lily barked back, finally turning around to face James. "You *own* me, don't ya'?! You's my masta', ain't ya'?!" she berated, her tone full of venom as she began punishing him with her words the way he silently hoped she would do. "You *demand* what you want 'a me, and I'm always to oblige with a respectful answa'! Ain't that the way it is now?!"

"I don't *own* you, Lily!"

"Six in one hand, half a dozen in the otha'!"

"What in the hell's that s'pposed to mean?!"

"It's all the same! You may not have paid for me, but I still ain't nothin' but the subservient little toy yo' daddy bought for you to play with all them years ago!"

"My *subservient toy?!* You know goddamn good 'n well I ain't neva' thought 'a you like that!"

"Could've fooled me! 'Cause you always been awful good at *playin'* with me," she said smugly, throwing her hands on her hips. "Hell, sometimes I think if I wasn't able to play piano you'd've neva' botha'd to say anotha' kind word to me eva' again!"

"You don't believe that!"

"Well, what else am I s'pposed to believe, huh?! It seems awful strange that afta' all these years, you find out I can play, and suddenly you treatin' me nice and talkin' nice to me. Then tonight, afta' you and William make all that money, you go right back to snappin' at me the way you used to!"

"You think this is about usin' you to make money?!" James asked, truly in shock that she would say such a thing.

"Elijah told me 'bout that article … The one 'bout you usin' me to make money!"

That fact seared James's insides and added another layer of cement to his hatred for the man. "You can't possibly believe those ridiculous lies!"

"What I can't believe is how foolish I've been all this time! It all makes so much sense now!"

"Lily, I *asked* you if this was what *you* wanted! I neva' *forced* you to do any 'a this!"

"More than one way to get what you want!"

"None 'a this was eva' about *me* or about what *I* want!"

"Please just stop!" She threw a hand up. "I swear I don't know what to believe outta you anymore!"

"C'mon, Lily! You know me!"

"Do I?!" she fired back. "'Cause the James I thought I knew was kind and gentle! He didn't go 'round beatin' folks up! A-and tellin' lies! Or-or gettin' arrested!" she scoffed. "So, it sure as hell feels like I don't know who the hell you are anymore!" She then abruptly turned back toward the fireplace when she felt her tears stirring.

"Yes, you do!" James said, taking her by the arm and spinning her back toward him.

"No! I don't!" Lily screamed. "The James I knew was the only person who eva' made me feel like I's free wheneva' we's togetha'!" She yanked her arm from his grip. "THE JAMES I KNEW WAS MY *BEST FRIEND!*" she erupted, suddenly breaking down into heavy sobs. "H-he was my *only* fr-friend," she whispered, through a sea of now falling tears. "He w-was all I h-had … Y-you were all I had, James. But before y-you left all them y-years ago, you treated m-me like I's n-nothin'! And then y-you just … you just abandoned m-me like I ain't eva' m-mean a damn th-thing to you!" she wept, her sorrowful words broken by pain. "A-and all this w-week, I-I's afraid y-you'd abandoned m-me again."

Lily's volatile verbal attack cut James so deep that his eyes began to well with tears. He fought hard to hold them back, but her eruption of repressed pain made such a fight impossible to win. Tears were quickly greeting his eyes as he watched hers continue to pour. He wanted the verbal punishment, but he was not yet ready to hear an explosive tirade about what his past betrayal had done to her, betrayal that he was now seeing had completely devastated her. James knew that he would have to address the things about their past at some point, but he had hoped that it would be on his terms, when he had emotionally prepared himself. This was certainly not that time, and his response to her outpouring undoubtedly reflected that fact. "What was I s'pposed to do back then, huh!?" he fired back. "I had nothin'! I had no money! No job! *Nothin'!* Whateva' could I have done for you?!" He gave a sarcastic laugh, running his hands through his loose locks. "As ironic and as twisted as it may sound, my fatha' could offa' you a betta' life than I could at that time," he sarcastically laughed again at such a notion. "If anything, I left home to go and make somethin' of myself, to come back with two strong legs and two strong arms to carry you outta that *prison* my fatha' had you in! So, despite what it seems Lily, I didn't *abandon* you!"

"I ain't mean abandon in the *physical* sense," she replied in a much softer tone, as she wiped the remaining tears from her face. "*Emotionally*, though, that's sho' what it felt like to me."

"I'm sorry I made you feel that way and for the way I left everything. And Lord knows, I could neva' be more sorry for the way I treated you all those years. If I could take it all back, I swear I would. But please trust that I neva' behaved that way to hurt you. As difficult as it may be to believe, the things I did were for a good reason."

"*Good reason?!*" Lily scoffed. "Talkin' mean to me, lookin' at me like I disgusted you, makin' me feel that you hated me was for a *good reason?*" she asked, looking at him as if he had lost his mind.

"I was tryna protect you! In the best way I knew how!"

"I didn't want no damn protection! I wanted my friend!"

"Trust me! You needed it!"

"Needed it for what, huh?! 'Cause the only person I felt like I suddenly needed protectin' from at the time was *you!*"

James glossed over Lily's question, not ever willing to give her the ugly reality of that answer. But the true reasons instantly made him recall the horrific memories and graphic nightmares they had created since then. "You have no idea the things I was goin' through back then, Lily! I was young and foolish, and I admit that I didn't know how to handle it. I know I could've done things betta', but..."

"Whateva' it was, we could've figured things out *togetha'*, the way we *always* did," she interrupted, "We were a *team!* You know you could've told me what was goin' on."

"No! Not this!"

"But we used to tell each otha' *everything!*"

"You mean like the way you told me about the fact that you played piano?"

"That ain't fair!" Lily yelled, fire returning to her tone. "You can't possibly compare the two!"

"Maybe not, but the point is that I'm not the only guilty party here! We *both* had our secrets, for whateva' our own good reasons. And as for me, I can certainly say that none 'a those reasons had anything to do with me intentionally tryna abandon you emotionally, or in any otha' way for that matta'. Nor was I tryna make you feel small!"

"You really expect me to believe that afta' you's so hell-bent on remindin' everybody on that stage tonight what I am to you!"

"And just what is that?!"

"Nothin' but your damn *property!*"

"GODDAMN IT LILY, YOU'RE *EVERYTHING* TO ME!"

The ferocity in his voice immediately shot Lily's verbal assault down. She stood there frozen. The crackling of the fire was the only sound in the room for a moment.

"Absolutely *everything*," James added softly. "Can't you see that?"

Despite the conviction in his tone, Lily struggled to find the words to respond.

"Lily, I swear to you, it wasn't my intent to make you feel that way in front 'a everybody on that stage tonight. It's just that I couldn't handle it anymore!"

"Handle *what?!*" she asked, looking confused.

"ELIJAH!" James erupted again.

"*Elijah?!*" Lily repeated, once again looking thoroughly perplexed. "What in the hell does he have to do with anything?!"

"*Everything!* Seein' you in that man's arms tonight damn near drove me mad!" James fired back through gritted teeth. "Watchin' him with his arms all ova' you!" he added, a look of disgust overcoming his expressions as the images returned to his mind. "I *hated* it! Makes me sick on the inside! The way he *looks* at you! The way he *touches* you! The way he *talks* to you! The way he *smiles* at you! I don't like *any* of it!" He balled his fists up, wishing now that he had hit him when he had the opportunity. "He's been cravin' you from the very second he laid his eyes on you. And I'm tellin' you, I just couldn't handle it anymore!"

Lily put her hands on her hips again and her mouth fell open. She furrowed her eyebrows and scolded James with her eyes. She tilted her head and looked at him like he was an immature little boy who was in the midst of a tantrum. "So, all this is about you bein' *jealous?!*" she asked, disbelief in her tone.

"NO! *THIS!*" he said, pointing his finger toward the ground, "is about the fact that no matta' how fast I try to run, or how many damn excuses I make, or-or where I try to hide, and no matta' how many lies I've told myself, I can't get this-this feelin' to go away!" He pointed to his chest. "I just ... I can't make it quit," he admitted, sounding frustrated. "*This!* is about admittin' to myself that I don't want you in no otha' man's arms ... goddamn it, I want you in *mine!* 'Cause no matta' what I do, Lily, I swear to God, I can't get myself to quit lovin' you!"

The wounding words that Lily had locked and loaded suddenly faded away, along with the angry expression on her face. She took a moment to search her racing mind to express the truth about how his words initially made her feel, but her thoughts simply spiraled out of control. "Y-you don't mean that," she finally said, taking a step backward as if she wanted to get away from his words. "You don't mean it," she insisted again, truly not wanting to accept anything he had to say.

"You just don't wanna believe that I mean it. You wanna deny it. I know all too well about that. It'll get ya' nowhere ... Trust me," James said, as he began to walk toward Lily, never once taking his eyes off of her.

"NO! You're a *liar!* Th-this is just some damn illusion you tryna create to get me to keep doin' what you want!" she said, thinking of Elijah's story and the contents of the newspaper article. She continued her retreat while staring James up and down, as if he were a stranger with ill intent.

"Lily, I would neva' lie to you about somethin' like this," James calmly assured her. Like she was his prey, he continued to stalk toward her, the look in his eyes giving away the fact that there was nothing she could do or say that would stop him from approaching her. He preyed on her until he had backed her into a corner. "But go on," he said calmly, standing so close to her now that she could feel the heat of his breath. "Go on and unleash whateva' you have to. Don't shut down and shut me out anymore. Yell at me, hit me, let it out. All your anga', all your frustrations … just let it all go, right here, right now. I know I deserve it. Go on and finish openin' up all the old wounds I caused you, and then give me the chance to heal 'em right this time."

Lily refused to respond. Instead, she drew her arms up to her chest as if that would somehow stop him from attempting to remove the bricks from her imaginary protective emotional wall.

Her defensive movement did nothing to stop James, though. He took her arms and gently moved them back down to her sides. "Do what you need to, to flush it all outta your soul and make room for me to be close to you. Let me in again, Lily … *Please,*" he begged.

Lily's continued silence and her attempt at defending her barrier was futile. James pressed on with verbally tearing it down. He refused to be derailed in any way, praying silently that this time around, instead of a wall, his words would encourage her to rebuild the unique bond between them. "I know you feel like I don't deserve it anymore, but I'll do anything to be worthy of bein' called your best friend again.

'Cause, even afta' everything that's happened, I ain't neva' once stop considerin' you as mine," he confessed.

Not able to handle the intensity of his proximity or his words, Lily began to tremble. She had to look away after no longer being able to face the sea of blue that was trained on her. But yet again, despite her continued emotional retreat, James was undeterred in using his words to draw her in, feeling as though it was now his turn to release what he had held onto for years. "You're the only reason I eva' set foot back on my fatha's farm again," he confessed. "I hate that place. I hate everything it stands for. But *you* … I've *always* loved you. Loved you from the very first day I eva' met you. Since then, you've always been the center of my world, Lily. Everything I say, everything I do, my thoughts, my decisions all revolve around you. I would've died first before I let you live out the rest 'a your days in that hell there with my fatha'."

Lily still lacked the willpower to return James's gaze. Her eyes remained fixed on the floor as she blinked away the few tears that his bold confession had ignited. "I wish you would've told me these things back then," she finally said, not an ounce of fight left in her voice. "It would've left me with so much hope … instead 'a so much pain. You crushed my world, James. And I hated you for it," she admitted, as another tear trickled down the side of her face.

"I know," James replied, after the sting of her words subsided. "But I swear to you…" He gently lifted her face toward him. "There wasn't a day that went by all them years that every part 'a me didn't hurt without you too, Lily." The sudden rush of emotions caused his voice to crack. "Felt like I's dyin' on the inside without you," he admitted, slowly running the back of his fingers down the side of her face.

James had yet to shed his waiting tears, but Lily could hear weeping in the sound of his voice as he spoke. His touch and his sentimental tone triggered a flurry of butterflies in her stomach and ignited a surge of warmth all over her body.

"Tell me that you've neva' felt it…" James continued, his lips so close to Lily they grazed her skin. "How much I loved you back then…" he whispered, unable to resist the intense desire to gently kiss her forehead. "How much I *still* love you."

"Don't … please, don't," Lily replied, instinctively wanting to protect her fragile emotions. Simultaneously, though, she could not find the power to pull herself away from the intoxicating feeling of his touch.

"Tell me that you've neva' felt anything for me." James placed his hands on either side of Lily's face, forcing her to look him in the eyes. "Go on," he dared her, their eyes now locked on each other. "Lie to me." He could feel Lily trembling and hear that her breathing had deepened, but she refused to acknowledge him. "Go on," he prompted her again, running the back of his hand down the side of her face to calm her, then tracing his finger along the outer ridge of her lips. "Lie to me … tell me that you don't love me." He paused and waited, but once again Lily remained silent. "Tell me," he demanded, continuing to gently trace the outline of her lips. "Tell me right here and right now, and I'll walk away and neva' look back," he promised, caressing her face, his eyes still locked on hers as he waited patiently for her response.

"I … I-I'm scared," was all Lily could bring herself to say while she searched for comfort in the sea of blue that were gazing so lovingly at her, a gaze that exponentially drove the warmth inside her to a level she had never felt in times past.

"I know," James acknowledged, still caressing her cheek. "But I wanna take all your fears away and make you feel whole again. I wanna heal you, heal *us* … I wanna make you feel free with me again," he whispered.

Those last words instantly caused another sea of intense tears to come spilling from Lily's eyes. James was convinced that her tears were confessing that her desires were mutual. Watching her purge her true feelings drove the way in which he wanted to comfort her to another level, a level that would no longer leave the lines between them blurred. With that desire intensely burning, James descended on Lily. After years of wanting, he finally tasted the sweetness of her lips as she continued to weep. Lily did not dare to pull away. She offered no resistance whatsoever. Instead, she parted her lips to allow him further inside as a passionate sign of acceptance. James moaned after she granted him access to delve deeper. He caressed her tongue gently and slowly with his, taking his time to savor a meaningful moment that he had envisioned for over a decade.

After reveling the sweet taste of Lily's mouth, James reluctantly pulled back, feeling the need to study her facial expressions for any signs of fear, hurt, or disapproval of his actions. He wanted to be sure that the mutuality of the moment was not just his imagination running away with him. He did not want to take more from Lily than she wanted; he would take his own life before violating her in such a way. But such a thing was not necessary. Much to James's delight, he wiped away Lily's remaining tears and was happy to find that the sadness in her eyes had been replaced with want.

James had certainly read Lily well. The outpouring of his decade-old secrets, his patience, and even his jealousy, had affected her deeply. But it was ultimately the undeniable love she felt in the passion of his kiss that had her reciprocating his gaze with mutual want. Sharing his genuine emotions had finally broken through her wall and left her completely vulnerable. But the loving way he now gazed at her left her convinced that she need not fear such vulnerability.

"There you are," James smiled. He gently caressed Lily's face again after seeing that the veil of fear shrouding her had suddenly been lifted, revealing the look of innocence in her features that he adored so much. "Beautiful Lily," he whispered, still softly caressing her skin.

Lily closed her eyes and reveled in James's touch, the sound of his voice, and the sentiment of his words. It all led her desires to begin guiding her actions. She leaned toward him, seeking that connection with him again, that feeling of contentment when his lips were pressed against hers. She was like an instant addict, searching for the instantaneous high she had felt the first time he touched her in such an extraordinarily pleasurable manner.

Lily's actions were the finality that James had been patiently awaiting. The simple motion of her lips closing in on his was reassurance that they indeed possessed a mutual wanting for one another. It all allowed James to completely relax and turn his attention back to the sweetness of lips he had waited years to taste. He now felt free to proceed with expressing his feelings for Lily without the worry of potential guilt or regret.

It was Lily this time who moaned when James invaded her mouth. This time, their kiss was drawn out. It was slow and deep, filled with passion and the indisputable love that Lily had felt there the time before. After a while, James pulled back slightly to suckle on Lily's swollen lips, gently taking them one-by-one into his mouth before diving deep to dance yet again with her tongue. The long overdue passionate exchange sent every fantasy Lily ever had about James crashing to the forefront of her mind, inflaming her body with desire. The dark abyss between her thighs began pulsating with want, quickly moistening her pleasure passageway in preparation for an already much-needed eruption.

James's mind and body were unanimously in sync with Lily's. Only seconds in and the feel of her soft skin, her touch, her embrace, the way her lips moved, and the look of lust on her face left a certain part of his body aching for explosive satisfaction.

As difficult as it was for James, he stopped kissing Lily, took her by the hand, and guided her back across the room near the warmth of the fireplace. The light enhanced the flawlessness of her features, making James just want to smile at her for a moment. He then placed both hands on either side of her face and kissed her forehead again. He trailed his lips down to her ear and carried on kissing southward down the side of her neck. With every kiss, goosebumps were rising on Lily's skin from the pleasurable sensation rippling through her overstimulated body.

While James continued to delight Lily's skin, he reached behind her and began unbuttoning her dress, but felt her body tense when the buttons were all undone. He stopped altogether after sensing the change in Lily's disposition. James pulled back to look at her, wanting to be sure that he was not forcing her to go any further than she felt comfortable going. "You okay?" he asked, his eyes filled with concern.

Lily's breathing quickened. She held her loosened dress in place and looked away without a word.

"Lily?"

Still, she did not speak nor would she look at James.

He then took her face gently and turned her toward him. "What is it?"

"I-I ain't neva' did this before," she hesitantly admitted, her heart pounding from embarrassment.

James was already as hard as steel but had he not been, Lily's words would have just done the job. Hearing that no other man had ever been inside of her was like the beautiful melodies of her symphonies to his ears. He did not take her confession lightly. He felt honored to know that she would allow him to be the first and, if he had it his way, the *only* man to ever have access to her hidden treasures. Being her first, James now wanted to be sure that he treated Lily as delicately as the flower that her name represented, while simultaneously ensuring that her first time was even more unforgettable than all the other firsts they had experienced in their lives together. With that as his goal, he gently caressed her face again. "I'll be gentle … I promise," he whispered, hoping to relax her.

Lily nodded. "I-I trust you," she replied, her lips quivering from the sudden onset of nervousness.

Again, James took great honor in hearing those words. He wanted to do everything in his power to maintain the trust that Lily had just bestowed upon him. He, therefore, slowed the pace, feeling that perhaps disrobing her in front of the firelight in the middle of an open space would be too much, far too soon. Instead, he picked her up and carried her over to the bed, never once breaking eye contact with her as he gently laid her down. Seeing Lily lying there prepared to give herself to him completely, James's heart began to beat like a wild stampede, pumping more blood to his member than it could possibly handle. His nerves were misfiring, semen was dripping, sweat was pouring, and his breathing was erratic. The intense desire to be inside of Lily seemed to have broken every governor of his bodily functions.

With his knees weakening, James sat down next to Lily and ran his hand slowly down the length of her arm, examining what he felt was a beautiful contrast in their skin tones. He then intertwined his fingers with hers and raised the back of her hand to his lips to kiss it. "I'll take my time," he promised.

Lily nodded again. "I know," she replied, still feeling nervous despite the fact that she truly did trust him.

James stared at the lusciousness of Lily's full lips as her words escaped and then descended on them, needing to taste them again after already feeling the withdrawals of not having them against his. Wanting to allow her to relax again, he left her clothes alone for the time being and resumed relishing the visible areas of her body with his mouth. He returned first to her neck, softly tickling her delicate skin with his tongue. With such gentleness in the tender touch of his lips, it did not take long for James to feel the tension leaving Lily's body again. After she relaxed, he began trailing kisses down to the bare skin of her cleavage. As his lips linger there, he reached up and gingerly slid the strap of her dress down, then kissed her shoulder. While his lips were pressed to her skin, he slid the strap even further down, revealing the fullness of her breast. He then delicately slid his tongue from her shoulder all the way to her dark, hardened nipple. Repeatedly, he encircled it then gently sucked it into his mouth, immediately invoking a gasp of delight from Lily. The other strap of Lily's clothing followed suit, soon leaving both of her breasts exposed and free for the luxury of James's eyes and tongue to enjoy. He consumed each one like a much-needed appetizer before his main course. The intense pleasure sent shockwaves of heat to Lily's southern region, setting ablaze the pool of moisture between her thighs.

After savoring Lily's breasts and enjoying the sweet sound of her soft moans, James moved further on in his descent, nipping at her midsection through the silk fibers of her dress, slowly pulling it off of her as he descended. Inch by inch, he was revealing the artistic lines of her body, as if he were unveiling a priceless gem. He gently kissed every section of her skin as he unveiled it, as his way of welcoming it to the wonderment of his eyes. Once Lily's abdomen was fully exposed, James feathered light kisses across it, hoping to distract her mind with constant pleasure as he continued to uncover the hidden parts of her body. Her physical and verbal reaction to the soft touch of his lips was proof that his method was working gloriously. James carried on in that fashion and soon uncovered enough of Lily to find himself at the outline of her right hip. He could not help but tickle it with his tongue, gliding it the entire way across her curvaceous line, evoking a slight bit of sensual laughter from her, at which he smiled before christening it with a kiss. For such a lovely part of her anatomy, however, he moved in a very lax manner, wanting his lips and tongue to have the pleasure of memorizing the curvature of Lily's womanly design.

While his tongue roamed from hip to hip across Lily's tightly toned abdomen, James had worked her dress far below her waistline. He stopped, however, when his hands came in contact with the inside of her thighs. The intense heat radiating from between them caused him to ache with a burning need to bury himself deep inside of her. In an instant, he pulled the rest of her dress away and dropped it to the floor. He struggled hard at that moment to maintain his composure, fighting the urge to unleash himself and immediately slide between her folds until every bit of his hardness was immersed within her.

James's composure quickly returned, however, when he looked up from the floor where Lily's dress was lying, and his eyes fell onto the landscape of the exquisitely sculptured masterpiece in front of him. He sat on his knees between her legs, frozen in place, mesmerized, as his eyes glided over every detail of the voluptuous curves of Lily's nude body in awe. Touching her as delicately as a rare and precious treasure, James ran his hands slowly up the outside of her thighs all the way up to her hips, across her stomach, and along the side of her waist. He then traced his fingers across her breasts, leaned down and pressed his lips lightly to her abdomen. Lily closed her eyes and moaned as he then pressed them to each of her breasts. James rose up thereafter and moved his mouth to her neck. At last, he tasted her lips again before pulling back to gaze at the unique artistry of her alluring figure once more. "You. Are. *Perfection*," he whispered. The conviction of his words was evident by the way his eyes continued to glide appreciatively over the elegance of Lily's heavenly physique.

As James sat there hypnotized, continuing to imprint the images of Lily's naked body into his mind, his hands began gliding back down her sensuous frame. Eager to feel the heat on her inner thighs again, he slowly slid his hands down between them. This time, however, it was not just his hands he wished to caress them with. It was hard for James to tear his eyes away from the magnificent view of Lily's body, but he knew that his lips would soon be rewarded for the change in scenery. The heat of Lily's inner thighs singed his lips when he let a long and loving kiss linger just above the inside of her knee. Feeling Lily's legs shudder from the pleasure made the descent even more rewarding than James had anticipated.

James was still in no rush as he began trailing kisses from one of Lily's legs to the other. Slowly, he made his way north, wanting to be sure that his lips did not neglect even an inch of her delicate skin. But the closer he got to Lily's uncharted pleasure passageway those delicate kisses suddenly turned into wet, hungry suckling. He stopped just shy of tasting her dark abyss, closed his eyes, and inhaled. Her intoxicating scent turned on his salivary glands and ignited a voracious appetite. With a watering mouth, he quickly engulfed her hidden seed, ravenously suckling it from its hiding spot. Electrifying pleasure rippled through Lily's body and tore through her throat in a shocking gasp that had James drooling with delectable contentment. A long raspy purr escaped her thereafter, the erotic sound milking drops of impatiently waiting semen from James's rock-hard shaft.

Lily's fingers had been the only thing to ever penetrate her warmth, but James was eager to be the next. Hungrily, he slid his tongue inside her. He moaned at the satisfying flavor of her sweetness, his growls harmonizing with Lily's sensual purrs. She was completely ignorant to such things, but her body quickly admitted that it never again wanted to know a life without this sort of erotic stimulation. As the pleasure began to invade her nerves, she completely relaxed, and her legs fell further apart. She instinctively arched her back, thrust herself toward the *masterful* movements of James's mouth, and amassed her hands in his hair to ensure that he did not stop the wave of intense pleasure that was rolling through her body.

James was pleasing Lily in a way that he had refused to please other women in his past. He wanted her to be the *only* woman whose flavor his taste buds ever knew, for her scent to embed so deep in his mind that it turned on his erotic fantasies, and his body for that matter. As deep as his tongue was now submerged within Lily, he was certainly proving how desperately he wished to achieve those goals. Like a decadent dessert, James ravenously ate Lily, her taste equally as fulfilling to his senses as the sound of her erotic sighs. As the sound of her purrs began to rise, he suddenly withdrew his tongue and suckled hard on her sensitive protruding pearl. A ripple of pleasure escaped Lily's throat again. The glorious sound penetrated James's ears, and increased the force with which he syphoned from her. The explosive pleasure from the intense suction instantly turned on a rhythmic dance in Lily's hips, her thrusts seeming to summon James's fingers. Happily, he fulfilled the erotic demand. Delicately, he slid one finger inside her and then two, the heat setting them both ablaze. In and out, they effortlessly glided, Lily's rhythmic thrusts doing all the work, her hips now chasing the pinnacle of pleasure. Within seconds, her lips and legs began to quiver, her core began to spasm, and her back arched high off the bed. She gripped James's hair tight and cried out his name, the sensual sound erupting from her throat, much like the orgasmic nectar James had just milked from within her. James did not pull back as her nectar overflowed. He drank from her like a man in a state of dehydration, suckling every drop until her body relaxed and her moaning subsided.

Still lost in the exuberance of the explosive ending, Lily lay there with her eyes closed, stroking James's hair gently, silently thanking him for the *masterful* way he had just brought forth an unbelievably erotic eruption. James refused to release her sensitive pearl until he was certain that she was completely satisfied by the first wave of pleasure. He then raised his head and gazed at Lily. Her mouth fell open and her eyes widened at the sight of him then suckling the taste of her off his fingers, indulging like a man whose appetite had yet to be satiated. Seeing how desperate he was for more of her, her body ignited with heat again. With his body overheated as well, James finally removed his shirt. Lily's eyes widened again as she marveled at the definition in his chiseled chest and the eight hardened muscles that defined his abdomen. She reached up and guided her hands across his torso, having always wanted to know how every ripple in his body would feel, especially after seeing him working shirtless on the stage. She, too, closed her eyes, memorizing every curve, cut, and hard aspect of James's manly physique. While imprinting his rock-solid body in her mind, Lily began to moisten for James all over again.

James looked down at Lily as she stroked his skin, feeling pleased at how quickly she had relaxed. He loved that she did not seem the least bit shy about touching his body or about the fact that she was now nude. He would have been proud to learn that the sudden absence of Lily's timidness was the result of his lips gently touching every aspect of her unexplored skin. His patience, his tender gaze, his genuine words, and the explosive release his lips had just given her had completely obliterated her trepidations. The combination of it all had freed her of the self-consciousness that initially plagued her, helping her to quickly let go of the meek girl who was trembling with nervousness near the fireplace over the mere thought of removing her clothing. In a handful of significantly meaningful minutes, James simply had Lily's mind and body floating in a tranquil place, ready for yet another round of ecstasy.

Lily finally opened her eyes and let them absorb the sight of James's perfectly carved frame again. While she gazed at him, her hands wandered all the way up his chest, onto the sides of the shadowy whiskers on his face, and through his hair. She then glided her finger across his moist, reddened lips, wanting to feel the very things that had just elevated her body into the clouds. The lingering aftershocks of her eruption left her with an insatiable desire to live out years of graphic dreams that she had had about this magical man. In her dreams, she desired to make James soar. That desire now came roaring to real life, taking full control of her actions. She wrapped her arms around his neck, pulled him down to her, and entangled her tongue hungrily with his, wanting to taste herself on his lips. From there, she ran her tongue down the side of his neck, up to his ear, and began suckling on his lobe. She was eager to touch and taste more of the man who had just indulged on her in the most exotic of ways. But more than anything, she was now ready to reward him with the heat of her uncharted flesh. "I wanna feel you inside 'a me," she whispered seductively in his ear.

Lily's words induced a deep barbaric moan from James. He let out yet another carnivorous growl when she then pushed him up, glided her hands back down his abdomen, and unbuckled his belt. Her fearless craving for him had his member pulsating in desperate need of climactic deliverance. After his buckle was undone, James immediately descended again and began planting succulent kisses along Lily's inner thighs while hastily loosening his pants, feeling as though he could not free himself quick enough. He then ascended back up, continuing to kiss Lily along the way while crawling from his trousers until he was completely out of them. As his lips made their way up her body this time around, though, the knowledge of Lily's starvation for him had turned the heat up inside of James. He had morphed into a greedy madman as he navigated north around the curves of Lily's body, sucking and kissing savagely on every part of her skin. James's cannibalistic appetite and the feel of his naked hardness gliding along the inside of her thighs sent even more heated moisture rushing down to Lily's nether region, preparing her for an erection that her body was now begging to feel. Her closed eyelids and heavy panting, all spoke of how desperate she was for him to fulfill that erotic desire.

After making his way back up to Lily's face, James could easily sense that her hunger was equal to his. He sensed no objection from her whatsoever, but still, he wanted to be absolutely certain. "If you need me to stop, I will … I promise," he whispered while tenderly caressing her face.

"I won't want you to," Lily assured him, her words escaping more like the sound of her light and airy moans.

The confidence in Lily's words sent heated shockwaves through James's body, causing semen to now drip in steady spurts from his flooded, hardened flesh. His aching manhood now pulsed and waited in unforgiving agony just a hairsbreadth away from Lily's uncharted abyss. Despite the throbbing pain, James wanted to enter her for the first time with loving patience, wanting to take great care of the precious gift that the woman he loved was about to give him. Passionately, he covered Lily's mouth with another hungry kiss as he took his hand and centered himself, preparing to glide himself inside of her. Cautiously, James thrust his hips forward. The tip of his member was then set aflame with an intense, piercing pleasure as it slowly and carefully parted Lily's tight, silky virgin skin. But as the feeling consumed him, Lily broke their kiss and let out a gasp of pain, blended with the sweet sound of a pleasure-filled moan. Not yet fully inside of her, James paused and looked at Lily with great concern. "You okay?" he asked, caring more about not hurting her than with his own pleasure.

"Please, don't stop," she begged in a raspy, lust-driven tone. She was determined to push through any painful sensations, especially after James had already given her a glimpse of the exhilaration that would soon override it.

Satisfied by the conviction in Lily's tone, James continued on. He kissed her tenderly again to distract her from any more pain before gently sliding himself further inside of her. His eyes closed and his mouth parted instinctively when the tightness of Lily's insides set his body on fire, nearly shooting him straight to the pinnacle of pleasure. Finally feeling James submerged deep within the warmth of her velvety folds, a pleasurable tsunami flooded Lily's body, and she let out a deep groan of passionate contentment. "Myyy God," they both moaned in unison.

For longer than he could remember, James had fantasized about this very moment, this opportunity to satisfy Lily in every way that he knew how. Just like in those vivid daydreams, here he was, finally lying inside of the only woman he had ever loved but fearing now that he would erupt before he even had the chance to move. How James felt within Lily, just lying there between the warmth and wetness of her thighs, he could not put into words. The euphoria was unlike any other pleasure that had ever coursed through his body. The feel of her eclipsed his dreams, his fantasies, and all that he thought was possible in reality. Having been intoxicated by her scent, her warmth, the taste of her, and the sound of her breathy cries had overwhelmed his senses in a way that he was unprepared for, in a way that he had never experienced before with any others from his past. With the culmination of it all, James knew that maintaining control and preventing an instantaneous climactic explosion was going to take an act of God. And so, while stroking slowly within her, James began praying, begging God not to let his body prematurely betray him as he attempted to express his love for Lily without words.

James prayed hard, but it was simply the look on Lily's face that finally settled him. It was a look that thanked him for the hedonic tidal waves that were beginning to roll blissfully through her body. At that moment, James realized that all he ever truly needed to do was focus on Lily's lovely features while he was inside of her. It was that beautiful, intense look on her face and in her eyes that he wanted to keep there. It motivated him to keep her riding on her wave, rising, and climbing until every nerve within her was ignited in the same immense pleasure that had caused him to break down and pray, that damn near had him on the verge of tears.

James moved delicately inside of Lily, at first, covering her mouth in deep, slow, fiery kisses throughout every stroke. Lily immediately fell under the spell of his profound affections. Very quickly, any and all pain was overshadowed by the euphoria she felt while he rode passionately through the tight cavern of her body. "Jaaames," she sang in a velvety tone after his soft stroking began pushing her body faster up its blissful ascent.

The sound of his name escaping Lily's lips fueled James's desire to make this moment last for her, to ensure that she did not ever regret allowing him to be the first man inside of her. He found even more strength when he saw Lily's eyes roll back and her eyelids darken her world. He marveled at the sight of her slightly parted lips and the overall look of gratification on her face, like she had just been welcomed into a heavenly realm. James felt proud to have taken her to that world, a world in which he prayed Lily was feeling completely free in.

In response to his slow and loving patience, Lily spread her legs even wider to welcome even more of James into her. At that moment, the pair began reading and feeding off of each other, one understanding what the other needed as if they had made love in another life, merging physically just as naturally as their souls had as children. They moved in sync as their sweat-slicked bodies glided erotically across one another in perfect rhythm and harmony, all of which was illuminated beautifully by the flickering firelight nearby.

Manifested within every stroke into her body, was an emotion or feeling that James wished to silently communicate with Lily. His efforts proved not to be in vain. In every kiss, gentle touch, and soft glide between Lily's folds, she could feel the sincerity of his love radiating throughout every inch of her body. Over and over again, Lily was absorbing every anguished emotion that James had attempted to convey to her that night and throughout the years. It was because of those silent, sincere, impassioned confessions that Lily's tears began to fall, and her angelic moans began to rise. Hearing her reaction, James gently buried himself even further within her, hastening his strokes and turning Lily's breathy moans into guttural cries of elation. The heat he created within her began to rage, and she buried her nails into James's back. Her body began begging for mercy and yet more of him at the same time. Pumping her hips up toward James, meeting him thrust for thrust, Lily arched her back, her insides tightened and erupted violently, covering the length of him in her juices. She then cried out James's name again like a sultry song, as the elation of pure pleasure rippled throughout her entire body.

The look on Lily's face was a luxurious treat for James's eyes. The sound of his name erupting from her in that lascivious tone brought joy to his ears. The beautiful combination ultimately gave him the freedom to finally let go too. His body rewarded him with a long, intense, soul-piercing climax that tensed every muscle within him and reverberated into every inch of his being. He let out a guttural groan of overwhelming gratification as he ejaculated hard into Lily, pumping his seed deep within her womb before collapsing weakened and limp on top of her.

The pleasurable sensations were pleasantly drawn out for both of them, taking its sweet time to secede from the tips of their nerves. They breathed heavily in sync as they made their long descent from the heavens together, their chests rising and falling in perfect rhythm. While lying there waiting to catch his breath, James began kissing Lily's forehead lightly and caressing her face. "Are you alright?" he asked her when he was finally able.

Lily did not reply. Instead, James felt a tear trickle onto his hand.

"Are you cryin'?" he asked, suddenly fearing that he had hurt her in some way. He shifted to move his weight off of her, but she stopped him.

"Please, don't move," Lily begged, holding on to James even tighter. "Stay here inside 'a me. Just a little while longa' … Please?"

"I'm here," James assured her, continuing to caress her face. "Let me in, Lily," he whispered. "Tell me what you're feelin'?"

"Free," she said through her tears. "I feel free when you're inside 'a me."

James closed his eyes tight, trying desperately to fight back the sudden rush of emotions that threatened to surge forward through them. He kissed Lily softly in response and let his lips linger on hers for a moment while he lay there content to be inside of her for as long as she needed.

"I ain't neva' felt nothin' like this before in my life," Lily confessed after they had lain there for a while.

James kissed her again before slowly rolling off her. From behind, he pulled Lily toward him, molded his body next to hers, and wrapped his arms tightly around her. "That's what it feels like to be loved," he whispered in her ear, caressing her gently, hoping to still convey his feelings for her through his touch.

Soothed by the feel of James molded against her, Lily fell into a slumber not long after that. As she lay there, James continued his nightly tradition of watching her sleep, but this time with the honor of holding her close and kissing her soft, bare skin lightly from time to time. He then fell into a sound and peaceful sleep of his own unlike any other his body had ever allowed him in his adult life—one that was completely free from the nightmares that usually plagued him. It was a feat that only proved possible with Lily nestled lovingly in the protection of his arms: the place where James finally had the courage to admit that he had wanted Lily for years.

Chapter Twenty

THE NEW YORK TIMES
Sunday November 13, 1859

The Dream Symphony
The critically acclaimed
visual and musical showpiece
playing
one night only
at
Winter Garden Theater
Christmas, 6 pm.
Tickets now on sale!

December 1859

A stunning photo of Lily seated at a grand piano with the image of a floating, shadowed angel in the background accompanied that short *New York Times* front page listing. Within twenty-four hours of hitting newsstands, at three times the normal ticket price, The Dream Symphony had completely sold out at Winter Garden, the most prestigious theater in the United States.

In the beginning, Landon Von Brandt had helped clear the path for the journey that had led the show to this point, using his clever, relentless strategies. On this occasion, however, he did not have to use passive-aggressive verbal exchanges with the coordinators of the theater or dig up incriminating financial documents to force them to allow Lily to perform there. Instead, it was the powers that be at Winter Garden who extended an invitation to Lily after her show quickly proved itself to be the powerhouse that it was. They simply could not pass on the opportunity to welcome Lily with open arms after so many newspapers in the North began writing feverishly about her journey to success. A multitude of articles had deemed Lily as *The Prodigy Slave*: a supremely talented pianist and composer, who had earned her freedom by bringing her dreams to life as dancing shadows, infused with a style of music ahead of its time, in a mystical, ingenious, "must-see" phenomenal show.

As the demand for tickets to see The Dream Symphony continued to grow, Landon had made the tough decision, along with Lily, to let the lie about her freedom continue to further enhance the fascination about her theatrical masterpiece. Not only did the curiosity about her show continue to grow but so, too, did the respect from those who welcomed Lily and her entourage to their cities. Gone rather quickly were the days when journalists were eager to tell lies to abort Lily's musical ambitions. Gone with it was the humiliation of being rejected from hotels, sleeping in the back rooms of theaters, and of owners demanding demeaning changes to her show. With the blend of controversy and overwhelming praise from critics, Lily's color began to have little relevance. In a matter of just six short months, she was now being embraced with the dignity she well deserved, in every place her journey was taking her.

While Landon was *proudly* handling the dirty work behind the scenes on The Dream Symphony journey, William had been loyally by Lily's side, passing on his life wisdom and helping to make her transition into the world of music as seamless as possible. Through his devotion, Lily had learned to conduct herself as a true professional. Day by day, her musical expertise grew exponentially, all while her symphony traveled slowly on a tour through every major city in Ohio, Indiana, Illinois, and Pennsylvania. Lily's stint in Pennsylvania had long since ended, and she was now in the midst of yet another sold-out show at a popular venue in Jamestown, New York, playing the final show of a five-night stretch. After the completion of her show there, she would soon be pressing further east for her highly anticipated Christmas performance at Winter Garden. The state-of-the-art, well-known theater was located in Manhattan on an up and coming street that was starting to become synonymous for its artistry, eclectic entertainment, and unique performers ... a street known as *Broadway*.

To say that Lily's life had evolved tremendously while on her journey to a prestigious theater, on a famed stretch of road, would be a monumental understatement. After coming from a life where she had absolutely nothing, *everything* that Lily was experiencing during her journey managed to have a profound effect on her. But it was not the fancy hotels, the tailor-made dresses, the fine dining at fancy restaurants, performing in elaborate theaters, or the money that now poured in like a heavy summer rain that had the greatest impact on Lily. She indeed appreciated those things, but what impacted her more than anything were simply *people*. All of the perfect strangers who tearfully applauded while she bowed at the end of every performance brought Lily an immense amount of joy. The people who approached her at post-show events to confess how moved they were by the two-hour experience of her dream show had mutually moved Lily as well. Lily's massive mental collection of those accepting, appreciative Negro *and* Caucasian faces never once left her psyche. Each and every one of them had infused themselves into her soul, empowering her to write the sort of music that erupted from the warmth they bestowed upon her. Her beloved fans were always one of the many reasons why she broke down into tears as she prayed every night, thanking God for allowing her the honor of finally knowing what it was like to feel human.

But far above any other person, Lily's mother reigned supreme and remained at the root of the emotion in her music. Her mother was also the reason that Lily never forgot her tumultuous beginnings, nor took for granted the life she felt God was now granting her. Always remembering that her mother and other slaves had never been afforded such luxuries helped Lily to remain humble. She absorbed every new experience, no matter how big or small, with profound appreciation, and accepted the help she received from everyone with the sincerest gratitude, no matter how significant their contribution to her cause.

Along with her mother and her fans, there were three other people that Lily held dear to her during her time on the road. They were three brave men who had put their lives on the line and used every bit of power they had to catapult her from the filth of a cottonfield into the spotlight of a highly regarded stage on Broadway. They were three men who stood steadfast by her side throughout every step of her journey, watching in complete awe at the way she handled the transformation of her life with such grace and humility. They were three men who, while helping Lily's life change, consequently had theirs change for the better as well. *William Werthington* often thanked God for sending Lily into his life and giving him a reason to climb out of the dark hole he was living in after losing Emma. *Landon Von Brandt*, the imperial narcissist, had set his selfishness aside because of Lily and finally found a greater purpose in his life outside of himself. But none was more affected by Lily than the only man of the three who had embraced her years before he ever knew about her musical gift. Long before newspaper articles were written about her, years before there was an overwhelming demand to see her sold-out shows, and talks of performing on Broadway, Lily had changed *James Adams*. It did not take something as epic as their wondrous musical adventure to transform his life. Lily's presence, her being, simply the fact that she existed in his world, had altered James's life from the very first moment she became a part of it.

Weeks earlier, during Lily's photo session for the *New York Times*, James had stood in a corner absorbing the beautiful sight of her smiling while experiencing yet another first: a photographer creating visual proof of her existence. As he proudly watched her, James began to wonder what his life would be like without Lily, but then realized that he already knew the answer to that question. Without ever taking his eyes off of her, as she posed for the camera, he began recounting how miserable he had been during the years they had spent apart. He remembered how denying his feelings and living his life so far away from her had caused him to quickly morph into a man that he was ashamed of. He recalled how angry he then became at himself for not having the resources or the courage to stand up to his father and take Lily with him when he left home. He thought back to how he was in serious denial about the fact that mistreating Lily and leaving her behind was at the root of his rage, drinking, and promiscuity. But with the way his life had changed since he walked through the doors of his boyhood home back in January, James now knew that he could never again question that Lily was undeniably the problem *and* the remedy to all that troubled him while he was away. Simply being in her presence had instantaneously halted everything that had been ailing him through the years, no different than the day they first met. The truth in that, however, was something that James had only summoned the courage to *completely* give in to after Lily's concert at Branaugh Theater six months prior. That night, it was Lily's willingness to forgive James and express it through her words, her emotions, and the sharing of her body, that had the power to permanently seal off that chasm in his soul, the way a thousand women, gallons of whiskey, and dozens of bar fights would have failed to do. With Lily considering him once again as her confidant, best friend, and now her lover, James finally felt like the sort of man he could be proud of again, and most importantly, one that *Lily* could be proud of.

Giving in to what he felt for Lily not only healed James, but also gave him the strength and motivation to help her begin to heal too. He began sealing her wounds with the passion, patience, understanding, and love that he promised to give her. As a result, he quickly witnessed Lily's confidence explode and saw a more intimidating, courageous woman begin to emerge. James was extraordinarily proud to see how her transformation showed in the way Lily commanded the stage, in the way that she now walked with her head held high, and in the way she now looked people in the eyes whenever she spoke to them. But of course, what he enjoyed more than anything was the change in her sensual side when it finally began to flourish.

James had been slow with Lily intimately, at first, giving her the opportunity to explore and ask anything of him that she desired while she went about discovering a side of herself that was a mystery. He had catered so well to Lily emotionally and physically that being one with him and trying new things had quickly become an addiction for her, nearly as strong as her drive to create music. With her newfound obsession, all of the awkwardness that Lily once felt, when James would simply look at her with want in his eyes, had completely vanished. In place of that timid girl, a fearless lioness was born with sexual desires that proved to be unrelenting and parallel to her man's. Her desires were so strong that *Lily* soon became the aggressor on their sexual conquests, taking the lead on their spontaneous escapades, gazing at *James* in crowded rooms during large gatherings with lust-filled eyes that seductively eluded to what she wanted. And James *certainly* obliged in every way possible, never once daring to deny her.

Before her tour began, Lily had continued her ritual of leaving letters for James underneath his door, but this time containing graphic verbiage or instructions that sometimes led him out to her favorite tree on William's estate at late night hours. James would eagerly make his way there only to find Lily's clothing left behind on the shore of the lake as she swam nearby, enticing him with the knowledge of her nudity. Seeing Lily there, dying to touch her, to hold her, James would nearly tear his clothes off before diving in and chasing her down as she playfully tried to escape. All the while, both would be laughing as carefree as children at their silly antics. It was never long, though, before James caught his woman and their laughter was replaced by the sounds of soft moaning as he tasted every visible part of her skin and devoured her full lips. In those moments, the cool water did nothing to stop the heat within Lily from rising. Thoroughly aroused by James's affections, she would wrap her legs firmly around his waist, begging him to penetrate her without a single word. Responding immediately to what Lily wanted, James would quickly bury himself deep within her and passionately make love to her underneath the soft glow of the moonlight, letting the echo of their pleasure-filled sighs mix harmoniously with the sounds of the nocturnal creatures of the night. Afterward, they would sneak back into the house and lay together near the fireplace, where James would then slowly kiss and massage every inch of Lily's body with Anna Mae's specially made lotion, the way Lily had once fantasized. Once his woman was warmed and relaxed, James would pull her in close to him, arranging her in such a way that as much of her bare skin was pressed to his as humanly possible. The simple pleasure of having Lily wrapped tightly in his arms, keeping her safe and warm, continued to give James the peace of mind to sleep soundly and completely free from his nightmares.

After setting out on tour, Lily grew even bolder, initiating numerous playful trysts with James in their enclosed carriage, during their rides to hotels, or in dressing rooms after her shows. She would tease and arouse him with her lips in the most erotic of ways, tempting him in places she knew she should not, turning on his carnivorous craving to ensure that he would be ready to greet the warmth between her thighs when their hotel room door shut behind them. It was on one of those incredible nights that James realized that Lily had indeed defined for him the true meaning of passion and lovemaking, just as his dreams had predicted. The power and intensity of what they shared had further cemented their bond and added yet another layer to James's plethora of reasons to love Lily. Their newly rebuilt bond was the reason why James had stood in the corner watching the *New York Times* photographer capture images of Lily, realizing that there was no looking back, that the torture of his life without her now would easily eclipse any and all pain he had ever felt in his life.

During their past few months together, James could feel how much their newly reformed bond and their intimacy meant to Lily as well. After causing her so many years of trauma, it was gratifying for him to finally bring so much pleasure into her life. It was the reason why he reveled in the jubilance she emitted after making love to her in the late-night hours after her shows. Seeing her smile, hearing the sound of happiness in her voice, and listening to her laughter was a bright and sunny side of her that he wanted to ensure he never stripped away from her again. Knowing that Lily was happy was all James needed to feel completely settled at the end of their long days.

Lily's happiness had become so intertwined with his that James was bothered by the fact that she was so silent as they lay together following her final performance in Jamestown. Lily's hunger for him had been strong and the passion was explosive, just as he had come to love, but afterward she emitted no emotion whatsoever. James was stroking her hair and kissing the back of her neck and shoulders, waiting for her to relax, melt into his arms, and let his favorite side of her emerge as they recounted the ups and downs of the day, or laughed over silly things into the early morning as usual. But instead, he could feel the tension in Lily's body as she lay there unusually stiff, staring across the room at nothing in particular, having yet to say a word.

"*Lily?* What is it? Somethin's botherin' you."

"Nothin'," she lied, trying not to bring a dark cloud to their sunshine.

"No need for lies. Tell me what's ailin' you." James shifted his body upwards to get a better look at the profile of her face. "I can feel in your body somethin' ain't right."

Lily exhaled sharply. She was comforted yet frustrated that James read her emotions so well that she could never get away with white lies. "I just can't seem to get 'er off 'a my mind today."

"Who?"

"My motha'."

James slowly rolled Lily over to face him and was greeted by a distant look in her eyes. "What about your happy memories? Ya' know, the one of you and your motha' and that hand clappin' song? Or layin' out at night with the telescope and namin' the stars togetha'? I rememba' you told me years ago that thinkin' about those times always helped."

"I know … But not today. All day I done tried, but it ain't a thang I can do to stop myself from missin' her. Can't nothin' seem to stop the pain this time … Nothin'."

James wiped away an escaping tear from Lily's eye as he listened intently. "Maybe a new memory'll help. With all the stories you've told me about your motha', I'm sure there must be a dozen or more. Let's see, how 'bout the time when y'all were tryna take the clothes off 'a the line before it started rainin' too hard, but the both of ya' just ended up slippin' and slidin' in the mud, droppin' clothes everywhere, howlin' with laughta'. Or how 'bout that time when you both…"

"Thank you, James. But memories ain't what I need," Lily interrupted, despite being impressed by how he had remembered those stories from so long ago. "Somehow, I just know in my heart that the only thing gon' stop the pain this time is seein' my mama's face again. Until then, somehow, I feel like I deserve the pain I'm feelin'," she said, angrily rolling over.

"Why would you deserve it?"

"'Cause! All this damn money we got, and here I am layin' in this fancy hotel while she's layin' God knows where! She should be *here* …

with *me!* Not workin' in no filthy cottonfield or layin' in some damn rundown shack!"

"Lily." James rolled her back over to face him, wanting to ensure that she did not begin to shut him out again. "We can find 'er. You're right. We've got the money. I'd do whateva' I had to to bring the two of ya' back togetha' again. It should be easy. I can look through my fatha's records and find out the address of the plantation he bought you from and..."

"I'd give up every dolla' I have to see my motha' sittin' front row at my show all dressed up, lookin' just as beautiful as I rememba' her. That's what I want, James, trust me I do. But as crazy as it may sound, I'm ... I'm afraid."

"*Afraid?* Afraid 'a what?"

"Afraid 'a the truth," Lily whispered.

"I don't unda'stand."

"Last time I saw my motha', she was in the middle of a dirt field, layin' face down, *unconscious,* afta' gettin' beat like nobody's business. She was fightin'! Fightin' hard on account 'a me ... Fightin' to keep me with 'er. To this day, I don't know if she eva' woke up afta' the way my half-brotha' beat her senseless. And now, I'm afraid to know whetha' she lived or not. Right now, in my daydreams, she can be whateva' or whereva' I want 'er to be. In my mind, she's alive and well and thinkin' of me, just as much as I think about her. In my mind, she got up outta that dirt field stronga' than eva', determined not to let what happened to us tear her apart. In my mind, she's happy ... she's *alive*. And I don't think I could handle it if I eva' found out that she lost 'er life that day ... 'cause 'a *me*. I just couldn't handle it."

"Trust me, I know how the sight 'a somethin' so gruesome can scar you for life," James replied, recalling the source of his recurring nightmare. "But I'd put money on the fact that your motha's alive and well because 'a how strong you told me she was ... mentally *and* physically. Knowin' all that, I bet there's a great chance that she's somewhere thinkin' about you every day, maybe even at this very moment. So, don't you think it'd be worth it to at least *try* to find 'er?" He turned Lily's head back toward him when she looked away. "Lily, I'd be here to see you through it all, no matta' what the outcome. You wouldn't be alone in this."

"You're right, my mama was strong. Every bit 'a me wants to believe she's alive too. But as foolish as it sounds, I still can't help but be so scared of what otha' things my fatha' and half-brotha' may have done to punish her for her defiance that day. I know I'd neva' be the same again if I found out she wasn't still here on this Earth ... *especially* not if it was on account 'a me."

"Well, just know that if you say the word, I'll do everything in my powa' to find your motha' for you, okay? I swear to it." James caressed her cheek. "Wheneva' you're ready, I'll be ready."

Lily slid her hand over his and held it. "Thank you," she said, kissing him lightly on the lips. "But I s'ppose it doesn't really matta' at this point anyway, does it?" she asked, sounding slightly more relaxed after his words and his touch settled her.

"Why not?"

"This is all bound to end."

"*End?* What's bound to end?"

"All *this*." She waved her hand in the air. "This fairytale we're livin' in."

"*Fairytale?*" James sat up, now the one suddenly feeling perturbed. "Lily, this *ain't* no fairytale. It's *real*. You, me, the show ... all of it."

"I know that. I just meant that yo' daddy s'pects I'll be home soon. It's been nearly a year. Ain't no way we can carry on like this for much longa'."

The thought had crossed James's mind many times, but he was not ready to face it. "Listen to me. I don't want you worryin' about such things. You let me carry that burden. I'm gonna do and say whateva' I need to say or do to keep you away from that damn plantation!" he said with conviction, after the thought of Lily returning there began to anger him.

"Hell, you'd have to tell yo' daddy I's dead before he'd allow me to stay away from there one minute more than necessary. Even then, I think he'd drag my dead body back to his farm just to see to it that he has the honor of burnin' it."

James took Lily by the arm and helped her to sit up. "Lily, I swear on Auntie's soul, you'll neva' see that farm again." She looked down at the sheets to avoid his eyes, but he quickly slid his hand underneath her chin and forced her to look at him. "So long as I can help it, you'll neva' set one foot on that land again. I promise you that, ya' hear?"

Lily nodded. "I believe you," she said, a sparkle of joy finally returning to her eyes.

"We got a little while before I need to address anything with my fatha' anyway. 'Til then, I want you to think about nothin' but preparin' for Winta' Garden and decidin' what pretty dress you're gonna wear to that gala tomorrow night," James said, kissing Lily tenderly on the lips. "And about how much I love you." He placed both hands on the sides of her face and began kissing her again, but this time with the sort of passion that instantly brought Lily's optimism back to life and removed every bit of tension from her body.

Lily lay back down and pulled James on top of her without breaking the kiss that had just followed words that set her body ablaze. Needing nothing more of foreplay, she maneuvered her hips to align herself with what she suddenly wanted to feel inside of her. "Show me how much," she said seductively, reaching down and gliding James into her slick searing flesh. The feeling of him submerged deep inside of her reached all points of her body at once. She arched her back and let out a moan of pure bliss. James inhaled sharply when the erotic tone escaped her. Nothing fulfilled him more than the sound of her satisfaction. With long powerful strokes, he began melting away all of her anxiousness and evaporating her inhibitions. Through the sensual thrust of his hips, he was hell-bent on sending Lily soaring, once again, into the heavenly clouds of freedom, gladly showing her along the way just how much he truly did love her.

Chapter Twenty-One

Slave Code
Article VI Section XI

Any free person convicted of enticing or persuading a slave to run away shall forfeit and pay the full value of such slave to its master or owner.

Riding in the comforts of her new fancy black enclosed carriage, a team of horses pulled Lily and her entourage through the snow-lined streets of Manhattan, on the way to a fundraising gala. As Lily rode along, she gazed with pure fascination at all the towering buildings surrounding her. Manhattan was unlike any other city she had seen; she found it nearly impossible to pull her eyes away from the uniqueness of it all.

Before departing from their hotel, William had instructed the lead driver of the convoy to take a particular route on the way to their destination. When what he wanted to see came into view, William called out to the driver to stop.

"Lily come along. I'd like you to see something," William told her once the carriage halted. He stepped out of the carriage first and a cold breeze swept his scarf into the air as he helped Lily down. "Look there," he said, pointing in the air.

Lily's eyes followed his finger to the words on a towering marquee: **The Dream Symphony, Christmas night, 6 pm.**

"Winta' Garden," Lily said, a slow smile creeping onto her face.

"Winter Garden," William repeated, gazing at the prestigious building along with her. "Before we carry on to the fundraiser, I believe a brief tour is in order."

After reluctantly tearing her eyes away from the Marquee that boasted the name of her show, Lily walked into Winter Garden on James's arm. Her face lit up with a brilliant smile as she took in the sight of a theater that was three times the size of all the others she had performed in. She released James's arm and slowly turned around, looking up at the three stories of balcony seats that lined the walls. Her eyes then panned up to a ceiling that was meticulously painted like a crystal-clear, star-filled night sky. The beautiful art instantly transported Lily back to her very first performance underneath the night sky on the incredible outdoor amphitheater that James had built her, a place where her dreams had literally started to come to life and set the wheels in motion that had led her to this moment.

They had been to many theaters over their six-month travels, but William never once tired of seeing the expression on Lily's face whenever she walked through the doors of a new theater. His heart melted a little more as he watched her closely and noted her bright smile, the way her eyes widened, and the innocence she exuded. In William's estimation, it was all so pure and genuine, like the awestruck look of a child seeing the moon and the stars for the very first time. The innocence and excitement that showed on Lily's face always brought him back to the youthful part of his life. He had become desensitized to the enchantment of seeing the world since then but watching the way Lily lit up over every new thing reminded him of how grand that sort of life really was and how fortunate he had been.

William had never personally given Lily a tour at any theater before they were due to rehearse, like he was doing now. He always much preferred standing at a distance, following Lily with his eyes, allowing her to quietly absorb her surroundings as she stood on the stage or walked the aisles admiring the décor. But Winter Garden held a special meaning for William on so many levels. So, on this occasion, he felt a personal tour was warranted. After he had guided Lily and James on a tour of the view from the balcony and of the backstage amenities, the three of them stood alone in the middle of the massive stage. "Believe it or not, this theater seats 6,000 people ... 6,400 to be exact," William informed.

The number shocked Lily since it was more than double the capacity of all the previous theaters she had performed in, yet it had sold out the quickest.

After sharing that bit of information, William put his hands in his pockets, turned, and marched forward a few steps to look out into the spread of seats. "The very last time I performed here, though ... 6,397 of these seats were empty," he continued.

Lily looked at William curiously. She was in disbelief that only three people would show up to one of his concerts.

"It happened the second time I ever played here," William further explained. "I'd played here once before in my career. On that first occasion, this place was completely sold out, and the show went off without a hitch. It was flawless. Every moment of it. But what made my first time playing here so special was that my Emma was there, like she was at so many of my shows. She had seen me play at countless venues before that, and many more after that, but the night I first performed here was *unforgettable* to her." He paused a moment. "When she fell ill many years later, everything in her memory was slowly slipping away from her: details of our wedding, birthdays, the little country store she used to own ... my name." William paused to regain control of himself after that fact began to penetrate his emotions. "The names of our sons ... even her own. Such vital memories all faded away. But that night she saw me perform here at Winter Garden, on this very stage, in front of that packed audience, was the *one* performance she never ever forgot. It was as if her experience watching me play here was the *only* lingering memory that God had allowed her to keep. Even after she was suffering through the worst parts of her illness, for some reason … Winter Garden was literally *unforgettable* to her.

"'You were so brilliant last night at Winter Garden! I can't wait to see you play there again!' That's what my Emma would say to me at some point *every day* when she was ill. And I do mean *every. Single. Day.* Whenever she uttered those words, there was always a soft enthusiasm in her voice and a lovely smile on her face as she looked at me with life shining briefly in her beautiful eyes. In a matter of a heartbeat, though, her mind would quickly slip away into darkness again, taking my hope for her to get well along with it.

"'I can't wait to see you play there again,' was the very last sentence my wife ever uttered to me … and that seat over there," William said, pointing to the place he spoke of, "was the place she sat when I brought her back here for a second time to fulfill that wish. I rented this entire venue, and my sons and I traveled with her here. They sat huddled next to their mother as my old orchestra and I replayed every single song from that night she remembered from so many years ago. As sick as Emma was, as lost as she was in the depths of her mind, as disconnected from the world as she always seemed to be, I swear to you, for the ninety minutes I played here, she never once took her eyes off of me." William glanced over to where his wife had once sat. "Nor was I ever once able to take mine off of her. I just couldn't. For those ninety minutes, m-my Emma w-was back." His lip began to quiver as he spoke. "Th-that brief flash of a smile, that I looked so forward to seeing when she uttered those words to me every day, was there on her face the entire time my fingers were dancing across that piano. H-her eyes were so full of life again," he said, his voice cracking. "And mine were full of tears," he admitted, patting at the ones that now fell with a handkerchief. "To this very day, I still believe it was what she hung on so long for, to relive the one and only memory she had left … just one last time." William dried his tears and collected himself.

"Less than twenty-four hours after we brought her back home ... my Emma slipped away."

Lily struggled to control her emotions as she took hold of William's hand. Despite feeling the warmth of her soft hand around his, William still could not take his eyes off of the seat where Emma once sat. "I'm sure you already know that your Emma will be sittin' right there again in spirit watchin' you on Christmas night."

William simply nodded.

"And I promise you, I'll do my best to honor her memory," Lily sniffled. "And do my best to make you proud."

William finally turned his eyes away from Emma's old seat and let them fall on Lily. "I'm afraid it's much too late for that, my dear." He reached up and caressed her face. "You've done that many moons ago."

Lily embraced William after his kind words. The heartfelt affection finally helped to subdue their emotions. When they had calmed one another, they turned to gaze out into the empty seats of Winter Garden, both quietly staring at the area that would soon be filled by the fortunate patrons who were able to secure a ticket to watch an indentured woman emotionally free herself for two hours in the most enchanting way.

After appreciating the view for a moment, everyone returned to the carriage and carried on another fifteen minutes to their final destination. The time passed like seconds to Lily as she sat in her seat with her eyes closed, still enamored with William's story, the exquisiteness of Winter Garden, and the sentiment behind how much it was going to mean to play with William there. Before she had a chance to let it all sink in, the carriage came to a halt in front of another pristine building with tall columns leading from the top of stone steps up to the crest of the roof. The design of the elegant establishment could have easily blended in with the beauty of unique Roman architecture.

A convoy of carriages soon halted behind Lily's as well. Anna Mae, Ben, their children, and the student orchestra all began filing out, every one of them dressed in their finest. Out of the lead carriage, Landon and James assisted Lily as she exited in another one of Anna Mae's carefully crafted gowns, but it was covered in the warmth of a stylish full-length winter coat with a matching shawl and gloves. After Lily stepped down, James immediately extended his elbow for her to grasp onto to help guide her up the stone steps. The crisp, cold winter air instinctively made her huddle closer to him. Their breath was easily visible as they climbed the stone stairway together. At the top awaiting them near the massive double door entrance stood two men, both dressed as exquisitely as everyone else who had just arrived. As Lily approached and got a better look, something about their demeanor, their dark brown hair, their glasses, and their green eyes seemed familiar to her. The man to her right spoke first after she made her way to the top. "The brilliant Lily Adams, I presume," he complimented, gingerly taking her by the hand and kissing it.

Lily nodded with a smile.

"I'm Wilson," he then told her with a slight bow.

"Pleased to meet you," Lily replied.

"And I'm Emerson," the man standing next to him announced, also taking her by the hand and greeting her similarly. "By all my father has written to us about you, I'd swear you were not a stranger…"

"But rather our long-lost sister," Wilson finished, in a very proper dialect similar to Emerson's.

With their comments and the mention of their names, the familiarity of their identical faces finally made sense to Lily. "Well now, I couldn't forget those names if I tried. I've heard so much about the both of you! You must be William's twins!" she smiled. "I should've known! You both look shockingly similar," she said, looking from one to the other like her eyes were playing tricks on her. "And just like your fatha' for that matta'."

"Except we're a younger, more attractive version," Wilson replied sarcastically, pulling at the lapels on his suit.

"Less wrinkled, stronger, better hair," Emerson added, lifting his hat and a single eyebrow, with a wink that followed.

"And more of it!" Wilson laughed.

"Yeah, yeah, yeah, you buffoons! She gets it!" William interjected after finally making the long ascent up the steps. "Laugh while you can," he continued while pointing to himself. "This thinning gray hair and this face of mine are what you both have to look forward to in thirty years."

Lily laughed, already loving the playful banter between the three of them.

"How are you, father?" Wilson finally asked, stepping forward and embracing him in that special way that fathers and sons did when they truly missed each other but were too manly to verbally admit. Emerson followed suit and hugged his father as well. The twins were just as happy to see and embrace the other people they considered as family: Anna Mae, Isabel, Ben, and Elijah. They then introduced themselves to Landon and James afterward.

After the formalities, Wilson and Emerson extended their elbows toward Lily. "May we steal her from you for a while?" Emerson asked James.

He simply nodded in response.

Lily looked at the twins closely again. "I ask your forgiveness in advance if I confuse the two of you. It's gonna take an act of God for me to tell you both apart," she admitted, as she slid her arm into the crook of Emerson's elbow.

"No worries, soon your eyes will adjust, and you'll realize that I'm the slightly younger, but *much* better looking one of the two of us," Emerson joked, as he and his brother escorted Lily into the building.

Lily laughed at his remark as they entered and then immediately paused after her eyes fell on the interior of the building. She turned her head slowly from side to side to appreciate all the fine pieces of art that clung to the walls and the sculptures placed strategically about the floor.

"Beautiful place, isn't it?" Wilson asked.

"Utterly breathtakin'," Lily whispered. "I've neva' seen anything like this." The awe in her voice and the look on her face immediately made William smile.

"Well, you've yet to see the best. Come along, we'll personally give you a tour before the festivities begin in The Grand Hall," Emerson said, using words in which Lily finally heard a hint of the British accent that he had naturally adopted from his father.

"Thank you. I'd like that."

"As you can see, Lily, my boys never took after my love of music. They couldn't care less. They took after their mother with their love of art instead," William complained, after they had walked along for several minutes, and he had listened to his sons explain every intricate detail of the pieces they had shown her.

"Oh, father's always one to exaggerate," Wilson replied to Lily. "He's always felt that we loved our mother more than him and cherished *all* the things she loved more than the things he does."

"He's a delusional, nutty old man, I'm tellin' ya'," Emerson joked, pretending to whisper in her ear, but speaking loud enough for his father to hear.

Emerson and Wilson's lighthearted comedy put Lily in the most cheerful mood. She was thoroughly enjoying the way they strolled along with her on their arms, rambling on about the pieces they were passing and infusing bits and pieces of knowledge about their childhood and their parents. Their interaction indeed made Lily feel like their sister.

"So, if I remimba' correctly, William tells me both 'a you are professors, right?" Lily asked when she finally had a chance to speak.

"I see that memory of yours is just as grand as my father has eluded to. You are correct!"

"Well, maybe my memory is startin' to fail, 'cause I can't seem to rememba' which one of you teaches philosophy and which one teaches English."

"The great and wise English professor would be *me*," Emerson boasted, continuing his comical arrogant facade, making Lily smile again.

"Leaving me as the *much* greater and *much* wiser *head* of the philosophy department," Wilson said, smirking at his brother.

"But you're here to raise money for the *arts* department?" Lily asked, looking confused by that notion.

"Yes, well, you see, our mother always loved raising money to give to the charities and causes most dear to her. Our mother loved art, but she was a selfless woman and spent a good deal of her time raising money for the Ohio University music department for my father. So much time, in fact, that she rarely had the time to help the organizations that really meant so much to her. So now, in honor of her, my brother and I help to raise money every year for the arts department at our school and to help keep this place up and running," Emerson explained.

"Yes, she loved this place," Wilson added. "She'd spend hours here with my brother and me, fawning over every detail of the paintings and sculptures."

"Sounds to me like your motha's selflessness rubbed off on the two of you, right along with her love of art," Lily replied, truly empathizing with the power that a mother's love could often have on her children.

"Such a lovely compliment," Emerson replied, kissing the back of Lily's hand again.

"Yes," Wilson interrupted, stealing her hand from his brother. "From a very lovely lady," he added, determined not to be outdone by his slightly younger brother.

"Watch it you two! She's taken!" William warned playfully. "This one here is bound to turn into a rabid dog over her," he said, motioning his head toward James.

The twins and James laughed, all knowing that no harm was meant in their silly charms, but Elijah stood behind them with his blood simmering over the memory of once facing the rabid dog that had now "taken" Lily. Elijah did not appreciate William's reminder of their relationship. Over the last few months, he had already been nauseated enough by the sight of James and Lily together on a regular basis. And now, witnessing such an insignificant scene had significantly ruined Elijah's evening, yet again. Fortunately, the curator of the museum approached, finally giving cause for Elijah to stop trying to murder James with his eyes.

"William! Good to see you again old friend!" the curator said, shaking William's hand. He then turned toward Lily. "And you must be Ms. Adams." He extended his hand, gently shaking hers as well.

"I am."

"I'm Preston Mills, curator of the museum."

"Pleased to meet you," Lily replied with a smile.

"It's certainly an honor to have you here this evening. I was one of the fortunate few who was able to secure a pair of tickets for your show. My wife and I are very much looking forward to it, as is the rest of this city, it seems. Everyone is buzzing about it!"

"Thank you, Mr. Mills. You're too kind."

"Please, by all means, call me Preston."

"Well then Preston, I must say, your facility is incredibly beautiful. I can't seem to pull my eyes away from all the fine artwork. I see why William's wife used to spend hours here."

"Oh, well now, *you* are too kind."

As they spoke, another man approached. He had intentionally messy hair and was dressed in bright red flamboyant attire with white ruffles protruding from the collar and wrist areas of his outfit. Lily's eyes were instantly drawn to him.

"William, you remember Piers LeRoux, I'm sure?" Preston said, referring to the colorfully dressed man who now stood by his side.

"Of course. How could I forget?" William replied, grasping onto Piers's hand. "He's done most of the art in my home, including the magnificent portrait of my wife. He's one hell of an artist."

"Thank you, Mr. Werthington," Piers replied.

"Yes, I certainly agree," Preston said. "And fortunately for us, your sons have convinced him to display some of his most precious pieces for the auction tonight."

"Well, when your sons told me how fond your wife was of my work and of this facility, there was no way I was going to turn down an opportunity to honor her in such a way," Piers responded, in a French accent so thick that he was difficult to understand.

"You are too gracious, Piers. I can assure you that this would have meant the world to my wife," William said appreciatively.

Piers then turned and homed in on Lily. Unaware at that point that she was "taken," a devilish smile emerged on his face as his eyes glided up and down her body, absorbing what he felt were extraordinarily incredible features. One would have guessed by his flamboyant attire that he enjoyed the company of his own gender, but the way Piers looked at Lily, like she was an exotic dish that he was dying to taste, proved otherwise. "Ms. Adams," Piers announced, taking her by the hand and bowing slightly. "Pleasure to finally meet you," he said, his eyes still roaming her body.

"So wonderful to meet you too, Mr. LeRoux," Lily replied, a little surprised that he already knew who she was. "I can't wait to see your pieces this evenin'."

Piers raised an eyebrow at her. "Yes … I certainly hope to *please* you," he said, in a way that left no secret about the fact that he was alluding to much more than art.

"Well, Ms. Adams, fortunately, you won't have to wait too long then, the festivities are set to begin in The Grand Hall momentarily," Preston interrupted. "So sorry to cut your tour short."

"It's quite alright. Lead the way."

* * * *

After the bidding had gone better than expected in The Grand Hall, an orchestra began playing elegant music. Drinks and hors d'oeuvres were served, as an array of people glided around the dance floor to the classical melodies. The atmosphere was happy and light but judging by Elijah's face one would never have guessed that. He stood next to a table of drinks, holding on to a glass of liquor with a scowl on his face, guzzling it from time to time, too annoyed to pay any mind to the burn that erupted in his chest afterward. Isabel pranced over to him with a joyous grin on her face, thoroughly enjoying the festive spirit, completely oblivious to her brother's foul mood, as she typically was to all things. "Dance with me, brotha'," she smiled, taking him by the hand and trying to pull him toward the dance floor.

"Not now, Isabel!" Elijah fired back, snatching his hand away, finally making his rotten attitude blatantly obvious, even to her.

Isabel followed her brother's eyes, looked over her shoulder, and saw what had darkened his evening: Lily smiling and laughing, arm in arm with James as they waltzed happily around the dance floor.

"Sore losa'," Isabel teased, after turning back and seeing the nasty expression still plastered on her brother's face. "Everybody in they right mind knows those two belong togetha'. And I think they make a *lovely* couple."

Elijah furrowed his eyebrows and tightened his lips. "I've neva' struck a woman before." He lifted a finger from his glass and pointed it at his sister. "Anotha' word and I promise you'll be the first!"

"You wouldn't dare!" Isabel replied confidently, sticking her tongue out at Elijah like they were kids all over again. "You know I'm Daddy's favorite. He'd beat you senseless!" She threw her hands on her hips. "Hmph, I didn't really wanna dance with you anyway! I just felt sorry for you, standin' ova' here lookin' like a lonely lost puppy that nobody wants! But now I'd ratha' dance with one 'a the twins, instead of a *sore losa'*. They's always betta' dancers than you were anyway," she scoffed, sticking her tongue out at him again. "Sore losa', sore losa', sore losa'!" she chanted as she pranced off and danced her way into Emerson's arms and out onto the dance floor.

Elijah watched his sister float away and then went back to trying to kill James with his eyes while drowning his jealousy with whiskey.

"Ladies and Gentlemen, may I have your attention, please?!" Preston announced, after taking to the stage again. The music silenced, and everyone turned in his direction. "I hope you are all enjoying yourselves this evening. We will get back to the music and festivities momentarily, but if you would please find your seats once again." He waited for everyone to do so before continuing. "First and foremost, I would like to say thank you to Mr. Piers LeRoux for the lovely pieces he has provided here tonight." He motioned his arm toward Piers who stood just to the right of him with his posture perfect and his hands clasped behind his back. "His work is simply extraordinary, wouldn't you agree?" Everyone applauded in unison and Piers bowed slightly to acknowledge their warm reception. "That is why it gives me great delight to let you all know that there is one final piece that he has yet to show this evening."

Preston stepped away and let Piers have the floor. He stepped forward with his unique mannerisms and pierced the brief silence with his thick French accent. "This piece was inspired by something I saw not long ago, something that was so poetically picturesque, it awakened every one of my senses. The imagery stayed with me for so long that I dreamt of it several times afterward. Every vivid detail was engrained into my memory so vibrantly that I wanted to savor it in my mind for a lifetime. Before it had a chance to fade away from my mind, I etched it in permanence so that I may revisit the precious memory whenever I so desire. It is a memory so inspirational and precious to me that I wish to revisit it here with you all tonight." Piers then turned and dropped a black satin cover from the expansive canvas behind him to unveil his painting.

When it was revealed, Lily inhaled sharply and leaned forward in her seat. William followed suit, pushing his spectacles up higher on his nose to see with more clarity the picture that neither he nor Lily were ever made privy to.

At the very top of the portrait, the apparition of an angel with expansive wings was stretched across it. It was floating high above shadowed figures dancing in unison amidst a dragon, an oak tree, and a sword-wielding knight, all of which depicted various scenes that had been infused into the sheer tapestry during *The Dream Symphony*. In front of the shadows, an array of musicians with various instruments were scattered about the stage, all being directed by William Werthington, who stood in front of them with his baton high in the air and his signature split coattails trailing behind him. Every aspect of the portrait was in black and white except for the image in the very center. In the midst of all the orchestra bodies, sitting perched at an extravagant grand piano with her eyes closed and her fingers delicately tickling the keys, Lily Adams was painted in vivid colors, dressed in a satin gown that flowed glamorously behind her. Her illustrious spiral curled hair, her multicolor eyes, the red in her gown, her matching make-up, her piano, and even the tinted hue of her skin, were all meticulously detailed with such painstaking accuracy and colors so vivacious that every bidder in the room threw up their paddles in hopes of becoming the artwork's owner.

"I had the privilege of speaking with the creator of this unbelievable show, Ms. Lily Adams, who has joined us here tonight," Piers said, motioning his hand toward her. "And after such a lovely and revealing conversation with her, I'd now like to call this portrait *Musical Dreams* ... after learning that Ms. Adams' dreams have most certainly come true."

"Ah-ah-ah-ah," Preston said, stepping forward and waving a finger, after seeing that a slew of eager bidders still had their bidding paddles high in the air. "I hate to disappoint you all, but this portrait is not up for bids." An audible groan from all the patrons grumbled through the room as people put their paddles down. "Piers has offered this priceless piece to be added to this gallery. It will now serve as the centerpiece of our music-themed exhibit and will remain so until the day these walls come tumbling down."

Lily glanced over at the twins, who both gave her a telling smile about their knowledge of the surprise. Both were happy to see such delight on her and their father's face after hearing that the piece they were featured in would become a part of their mother's favorite museum.

"As most of you may already know, the inspiration for this work of artwork, *The Dream Symphony*, will be playing Christmas night at

Winter Garden Theater here in Manhattan," Preston continued. "However, it is my understanding that the show is already completely sold out." Another groan erupted from the audience. "But! For a lucky few of you, I have *just* the remedy for that! You see, in place of his priceless portrait, Mr. LeRoux has provided yet another way to share the experience that inspired this piece. So, although he remains adamant about not letting anyone bid on this particular piece of work, he is more than happy to let you all bid on these!" Preston raised a handful of tickets in the air. "Four center balcony seats to *The Dream Symphony* for Christmas night! Shall we start the bidding at, let's saaay … ten dollars!"

Lily heard Preston's announcement, but she simply could not pull her eyes away from what was Piers's interpretation of her show. After being entranced by it for a moment, she slowly looked around the room as the battle for tickets to her show began. She thought that perhaps it would be yet another scene where every minute detail would become embedded in her mind and added to her collection of fond memories. However, as the bidding prices rose higher, the room suddenly fell silent in Lily's world after the entire scene triggered the memory of the very first time bids were ever placed on her behalf. She was nine years old, barefoot, in a filthy dress, shivering, scared, and feeling hopelessly alone. Lily was an innocent child back then, recently stolen from her mother by her own father. Her father's callousness had left her to believe that she was nothing more than a meaningless animal to him after he so easily sold her away to serve a tyrant, a man who took pride in demolishing her spirit.

But now, after her turbulent journey, Lily had finally ended that once depressing chapter of her life where she was frozen in time as that broken young lady who once stood alone on an auction block in a tear-stained, tattered dress. She was now beginning a whole new story as a dignified grown woman, adorned in handmade silk gowns, fancy matching shoes, and fur coats. In this new chapter of her life, instead of being looked at on an auction block, Lily was being looked at on a grand stage by a variety of people with tear-filled eyes that reflected how much they appreciated her. Now, a slew of perfect strangers, both black and white, spoke to her with the sort of kindness that her father never did. They told her "thank you" after opening their arms to embrace her in a way that Jesse never had, despite all she had done for him. She was finally living the sort of life where the people that now surrounded her, while she stood on display, never once viewed her as a piece of property. In their eyes, Lily Adams was now an awe-inspiring, gifted, brilliant, and beautiful woman, who was currently sitting at an auction in the midst of a crowd full of people who were bidding not to *own* her, but instead, to *honor* her by paying to be a part of her mystical, musical dreams.

Lily sat through what she was witnessing inside of a *grand* ballroom, feeling swaddled in the *grand* warmth and love of those who surrounded her at the table—a complete contrast from the last time bidders had fought for her. That contrast suddenly struck a chord in her. Lily once believed that the dreadful day she was bid on as a child was the beginning of the destruction of her life. But now, in the midst of the current bidding mayhem and the love that she felt at her table, she realized that perhaps that day was the beginning of God's plan, that it was a means to a fifteen-year journey to free herself from oppression, but more importantly … to free her mother.

As that epiphany dawned on Lily, James took hold of her hand and kissed it, after innately sensing that she needed to feel his touch. The simple affection suddenly brought her sense of awareness back to reality. The sights and sounds of the crowd in the ballroom returned as Lily turned and stared at the strapping man who was now holding her hand. When she gazed into his eyes, she suddenly remembered one of the first things he had ever said to her when they first met by the creek as children: *I've been prayin' real hard that you'll see your motha' again.* Lily then thought of yet another of James's wonderful gestures from just the night before: *Just know that if you say the word, I'll do everything in my powa' to find your motha' for you. I swear to it. Wheneva' you're ready, I'll be ready.* As James continued to caress Lily's hand at their table, she realized that with a few simple words she would be handing him the power to answer his very own prayer, an incredibly selfless prayer that he had placed to God on her behalf nearly fifteen years ago that still resonated with her to this very day.

As the prices for *The Dream Symphony* tickets continued to rise, Lily's sudden epiphany was helping her to see God's plan with great clarity. She now felt that it could not have been a coincidence that she was sold to a home where she was able to uncover her God-given gift, to a place where the young boy who lived there, not only fell in love with her but believed in her gift enough to make such a huge sacrifice in order to nurture it. With that revelation so clear, Lily was finally able to let go of her fear of searching for her mother, especially knowing that the man who sat beside her, currently caressing her hand, would be there by her side through it all. Lily then looked one by one at all the other faces that were gathered at the table with her: Landon, the comical twins, William, Austin, Anna Mae, Benjamin, and Isabel. Lily felt that each and every one of them were her new family, and she had no doubt that they would all be there for her as well. She was positive that they would help her deal with the heartache of knowing that her mother was no longer living, or they would prepare a magnificent celebration to help welcome and embrace her mother into their family like she had always been a part of it. But with the confidence that Lily now had in what she believed was God's plan, she was thoroughly convinced that her pseudo-family would indeed be doing the latter.

As the long drawn out bidding battle finally came to an end, James placed yet another soft kiss to the back of Lily's hand. Her eyes fell on him, and she began to glow as her face lit up with a smile that brightened his evening. Lily knew at that very moment, beyond a shadow of a doubt, what the topic of their conversation would be after James made love to her and she lay melting into the loving embrace of his strong arms during the late-night hours.

After the winning bidder had retrieved his tickets, Landon walked up to the podium to make an announcement. "Good evening," he greeted. "First, I'd like to say to the gentleman who just purchased those tickets ... I can assure you that your money has been *very* well spent. By the time *The Dream Symphony* comes to a close, I swear, you will feel like you can fly."

The winner nodded with a smile as he took his seat.

"Anyhow," Landon continued, "for those of you here tonight who don't know me, my name is Landon ... Landon Von Brandt. And while you are all in your seats, I have one more thing I'd like to share this evening. At first, I thought maybe I would share this as a private matter, but while Ms. Adams is displayed so beautifully in this magnificent portrait, I suddenly feel compelled to share my news with all of you now." He paused a moment and turned to take in the sight of the artwork. "Behind the scenes of this magnificent show, I have watched the young lady in this picture work tirelessly without complaint. There is such enthusiasm and joy in her spirit as she goes about orchestrating and perfecting every minute detail of her ensemble in her attempt to bring this artistic symphony to life. To watch Ms. Adams work is truly a thing of beauty. After a short time in her presence, the happiness she exudes, and her passion for what she does, will start to infuse itself into your soul. You become drunk with it and quite frankly ... it makes you want to become a better man. At the very least, you will want to make an *attempt* to achieve greatness in the way that she strives to do. In my case ... I find that I now strive for *both*. I want to be a better man. I also want to perfect my craft the way Ms. Adams has ... Although." He thought for a moment and put a finger to his temple. "I have yet to discover a craft," he said sarcastically, infusing a bit of humor into his speech and invoking a bit of laughter from the audience. "But!" Landon put a finger in the air. "I can assure you that I'm working hard to find one." He looked at Lily. "And I undoubtedly owe that to you, Ms. Adams."

411

His words made Lily smile. James caressed her arm, gazing at her in a way that expressed how much he understood the sentiment of Landon's words.

"I presume that most of you are very familiar with William Werthington," Landon continued, motioning his hand in William's direction. The crowd applauded in affirmation of his statement. "Well, several months ago, my father received a lengthy heartfelt letter from Mr. Werthington. It is actually that letter that has afforded me the opportunity to be inspired by the young woman who is now the subject of this fine piece of artwork here." He motioned his hand toward it again. "You see, the letter Mr. Werthington wrote was regarding a certain matter with Ms. Adams. After reading such touching words, my father became extraordinarily curious and was willing to travel here himself to the United States to learn more about this fascinating young lady. But my father works very closely with the royal court in the United Kingdom. Needless to say, he is an extremely busy man under those circumstances. So, I suggested that I make the journey here for him. At first, he was not so keen on the idea because, unfortunately, he knows that I'm not easily impressed by anything, which is a fact I cannot argue. In fact, I was certain that I would return to my father after my adventure here to America and explain to him what a disappointment the journey was and to be glad that he never bothered to waste his time." Landon exhaled sharply and looked down at Lily. "Well, I cannot tell you how very wrong I was.

"I must admit, I've stolen many a heart thus far in my life," he joked, letting his narcissism shine briefly. "But after watching this beautiful young lady here, this was the first time that a woman had ever stolen mine ... But not in the *usual* manner. After seeing Ms. Adams' show, I confessed to her that what I saw captivated me like nothing else in my life. I immediately understood the passion and motivation with which Mr. Werthington had scripted his letter to my father. Because, much like Mr. LeRoux was moved to create a masterpiece after the experience of watching Ms. Adams' symphony,

I too was moved to dedicate every resource in my power to Ms. Adams' cause.

"And now the very same show that I was so hell-bent on giving my father negative reviews about, is one that I can't seem to stop myself from bragging on and on about to him. Letter after letter, it seems there is just more and more I find to tell him about this brilliant young woman and her incredible show. And now, after receiving dozens of my letters, my father has finally written back," he explained, raising an envelope in the air. "He has expressed that he has grown tired of me talking about Lily." Landon paused when everyone looked at him curiously. "My father now wants to *see* with his very own eyes, this phenomenon that has captivated his only son, a son that he knows full well is usually so cynical about *everything*. He just has to meet the woman and see the show that has transformed me: a feat that he feels he has hopelessly failed at," he joked. "He wants, at the very least, to say thank you to Ms. Adams for accomplishing what he was unable to do for the last twenty-seven years." The crowd laughed again. "But! My father hopes that he will get to meet her for far more than that." With that, Landon turned to Lily again. "Ms. Adams, would you be so kind as to join me here on stage for a moment?"

Not expecting to be in the center of attention at all for that evening, Lily looked at James curiously. He shrugged his shoulders, but then helped her to stand, escorted her up the stairs to the stage, and went back to take his seat.

"Unfortunately, with my father residing an ocean away, it would be impossible for him to journey here in enough time for your final performance at Winter Garden," Landon explained to Lily once she was standing next to him at the podium. "However, he thought that perhaps there might be a solution for that. You see, when my father wants something, he will do *everything* in his power to acquire it. That, coupled with the fact that he knows I am rarely excited about anything, makes my father trust that you are more than worthy of this," he said, handing Lily the envelope he was holding.

Lily looked down at the folded letter that Landon had placed in her hand, which had an official red wax seal with the emblem of a winged horse holding its folds together. She then glanced back up at Landon with a perplexed look on her face.

"Go ahead, open it up and read it," Landon insisted.

Lily loosened the seal, unfolded it, and took a moment to read it silently. She looked back up at Landon again when she was finished. "Is this real?" she asked, tears starting to well in her eyes.

"Every word of it," he assured her.

Lily then turned to look out into the crowd. "William?" she questioned, seeking reassurance from him as well while staring at him with hope glistening in her eyes.

The artwork was a secret that William's sons had kept quiet from him. He was genuinely unaware of that surprise. For two days, however, he had remained tight-lipped about the contents of the letter that Lily now held as she questioned him with her innocent doe-like eyes. In response, William simply nodded, afraid to utter a word for fear that he might let loose the waterfall of emotions that had quickly built in his chest after sensing how emotional Lily had suddenly become.

"Well, don't leave everyone in suspense," Landon chimed in, breaking Lily's fixation on William. "Tell everyone what it says."

Lily cleared her throat, but was still unable to keep her emotions from saturating nearly every word as she began to read:

Ms. Lily Adams,

It is our pleasure to extend an invitation for you to present The Dream Symphony in the United Kingdom, here at Buckingham Palace. Upon affirmation of this invitation, you will be furnished with any and all necessary equipment and items required to complete your show. All measures will also be immediately put into place for you and your entire cast to journey here. Further details of this arrangement can be discussed in future correspondence after receipt of your response, which we very much look forward to, with the hope that The Dream Symphony will soon be here to witness.

Sincerely,

Queen Victoria

Lily's eyes met William's again. "The very same Buckingham Palace you've told me stories about playing in?" she asked him, her voice still wracked with emotion.

"Thee *one* and *only*," William replied.

"I've been dreamin' about playin' there eva' since you told me about your experience there."

"Now here the chance lies before you," William replied, still fighting hard to swallow the swell of emotions in his chest. "Took me half a lifetime to get an invitation there, but *you* … only half a year!" he smiled. "What's your secret?" he asked, infusing humor into the atmosphere to settle the rising dam threatening the overflow through his eyes. It worked momentarily, bringing lighthearted laughter to everyone in the room. But for Lily, it was no laughing matter.

"Havin' one hell of a mentor to help guide me there," she replied, with extreme sincerity in her tone.

With those words, the dam that held William's tidal wave of emotions back finally crumbled, allowing tears to gush from his innocent green eyes. He removed his spectacles and lowered his head, attempting to hide the moisture accumulating on his face as both of his sons placed a hand on his back. It was the second time Lily had seen William cry that night. His passionate response, the sight of his sons comforting him, and suddenly imagining that Emma was there with them, added to the sentimental river flowing down Lily's own cheeks.

Landon walked over and handed Lily a handkerchief. "Well, one word from you, Ms. Adams, and I have no doubt that you are capable of infusing your Buckingham Palace dreams into one of the scenes in your extraordinary symphony," Landon said to her. "*One word*, and I'll prepare a letter to my father *and* the Queen this very eve, giving them the much-anticipated news that you have graciously accepted their request ... just *one* simple word."

The room was silent for a moment while Lily pondered something she thought would be so easy for her. She looked down at the invitation written by the Queen herself and then looked over at William, who finally held his head up and put his spectacles back on. She then glanced to William's left and met the eyes of the man who had initiated this journey with her in a beat-up wooden wagon as she sat in the back, barefoot, in a dress nearly as old as she was. James had sat at those reins driving his horses forward with nothing but hope and a deep belief that Lily's talent would lead her to a better life. His faith in her was evident when he began the journey, even without a single guarantee of the outcome. And it was certainly evident on this evening in his body language and in the way his eyes lingered on Lily with pride and admiration dancing in them. With their eyes locked on one another, James nodded to let her know that he was behind her, no matter what.

"Say yes!" Lily suddenly heard Austin shout, breaking the eye contact she had with James.

An array of scattered "say yeeess's" then began to erupt from various members of the orchestra until it began to build into a slow chant with rhythmic applause to support it. "SAY YES! SAY YES! SAY YES! SAY YES!" they all continued to chant, the sound crescendoing like music toward an intense climax.

Lily scanned the room of happy faces, all chanting in support of her. A brilliant smile then illuminated on her face as she finally nodded her head.

"Yes?" Landon asked her, after seeing the slight movement that he was certain nobody had noticed.

"Yes," Lily replied, barely audible over the sound of the crowd.

"You're certain?" Landon asked.

Lily looked back down at her letter written by the Queen. "YEEESSS!" she suddenly erupted, no longer able to contain her enthusiasm after seeing the words *Buckingham Palace* there in front of her again. "YEEESSS!" she shouted again, holding her letter in the air this time, bringing the entire student orchestra to their feet. They all suddenly disregarded the formal nature of the ceremony by applauding loudly, whistling, dancing, and hugging one another in a youthful energetic fashion. They could not help but to share in the excitement of Lily's good fortune and to celebrate the fact that they would soon be performing for a queen and an entire royal court, in a place they thought they would only ever visit in their dreams.

Even the older crowd, who were only there to bid on art, could not help but be entranced by the celebratory spirit enveloping the room. They all stood as well and applauded Lily's decision. "Bravo!" echoed throughout the room, blending in with the sound of the giddy students.

Landon took his assistant by the shoulder and leaned in toward him so that he could better hear amongst the noise. "Prepare a letter to my father immediately." He then turned to look at Lily. "Send him word that *The Dream Symphony* will soon be on the steps of *Buckingham Palace*."

"As you wish," his assistant replied, before trotting off to do as Landon had requested. The assistant breezed right by James, who had finally made his way over to Lily and lifted her from her feet in a warm, long, and loving embrace.

* * * *

After thanking Piers LeRoux, William stood on the stage alone, unable to turn away from the portrait that eternally depicted him and Lily. He was wishing that he could see his wife's reaction to hearing that a piece of art he was featured in would soon be hanging in a gallery she cherished. He closed his eyes attempting to visualize the joy on her face, but he knew that his imagination could never do Emma's true emotions justice. "I wish you were here, Em," William whispered after opening his eyes, needing to stop the visions of her before he cried for a third time that evening. He collected himself and turned when he heard footsteps approaching.

"Mr. LeRoux certainly outdid himself," James said, standing off to the right of William, staring in awe at Piers's creation. "Feels like I'm sittin' front row at the show."

"It's incredible. No doubt about it," William replied. Both men then stared in appreciation for a moment before William completely changed the subject. "I've been hard on you, James." William turned toward him. "When it comes to Lily's welfare, I know."

James nodded and slid his hands into his pockets. "Ain't nothin' been said that I didn't need to hear. I deserved every tongue lashin' you've given me thus far."

"And I don't apologize for any of it. However, it seems that I always forget about how extraordinarily unique the circumstances really are for you and Lily. I now admit that it was a mistake on my behalf not to take your frustrations about that into consideration."

"Jesus! That's somethin' I sure wish everybody else in this world would forget about as easily as you do!"

"Trust me, I know. Even though it was much easier for Emma and me to hide our secret, I still very much empathize with how much you wish the differences in you and Lily didn't matter so much to everyone. With your differences being so obvious, I know it must be far more taxing on the both of you than it ever was for me and my wife."

"I'd be lyin' if I said it was easy."

"I know. And that's why I must say, it's truly commendable the way you've come to handle it all. Despite the weight of the situation, though, I still couldn't help but be hard on you before. But I want you to know that that's only because I truly love Lily. I love her as if she were my own child, and I truly want nothing but the best for her." William put a hand on James's shoulder. "And as of late, that's all you've given her, James … nothing but the best of you. I see now how much you truly love that young woman. I see that you're now being the sort of man that she needs by her side. I think I was always so angry at you before because I was convinced that that was the sort of man you could be for Lily from the very beginning, and I wanted so badly for you to just let him emerge."

"I think it just took a while before I could convince myself that that's who I could be for Lily too. Just had some growin' up to do, I guess. Needed to learn my lessons the hard way."

"Ha! Don't we all?! We're all just a bunch of stupid men after all!" William waved his hand dismissively. "We're all guilty of losing our wits over a woman from time to time," he laughed. "I guess I was just trying to do what I could to keep you from making the mistakes that us men all fall victim to at one time or another. But hell, maybe it's best just to let every man fall flat on his face and pick himself back up. After all the scars and broken bones, he'll be a stronger, wiser man."

"I couldn't agree with you more."

"Well, anyhow, I'm just glad that you've come around, and I just wanted you to know that I'm proud to see that you make Lily so happy, because that's all I ever truly wanted for her."

"You and me both, William ... You and me both."

"What are my two favorite men in the world ova' here plottin' and plannin'?" Lily asked, approaching the two of them with a smile.

"I," James began, greeting her with a smile and a kiss on the cheek, "was just plottin' and plannin' to go and take advantage of some more free alcohol," he joked.

"Can't blame you for that!" Lily teased.

James kissed her again before heading to the bar and leaving her alone with William.

Lily then walked over to the portrait that she was featured in and gently touched it while absorbing all of its fine details. "Emma would be so proud," she said, as she admired the painting along with William.

"Just as I am of you." He turned to Lily. "Have I ever told you that?"

The sound of those words brought instant warmth to Lily again. "Trust me, I don't think I'll eva' forget that moment tonight when you did," she admitted, recalling exactly where they stood at Winter Garden when he said it.

"Please, forgive my repetitiveness, but I am, Lily ... So very proud of you," William confessed again.

"No need to ask forgiveness. I don't think I could eva' tire of hearin' that."

"If not for that then, perhaps I'll require your forgiveness for keeping the secret about Buckingham Palace. I'm so sorry I had to withhold it from you. I wanted so badly to be the one to tell you, but Landon swore me to secrecy. He was insistent that he be the one to deliver the news."

"I could neva' be upset with you for that eitha'."

"Happy to know that," William nodded. "But, more than anything, I'm happy to know that you'll soon be able to make yet another of your dreams come true ... an incredible dream that I absolutely believe you deserve to live out."

"Thank you, William," Lily said, touching him gently on the arm. "I can't even tell you how thrilled I am to be travelin' there! But what makes me happier than anything, is knowin' that you'll be there to experience it all with me."

"Trust me ... Nothing would give me greater joy," William replied, thinking about how much he loved to live vicariously through her. "It will certainly be unforgettable. Most often people say that the anticipation of an event always far outweighs the reality of it. But in this instance, I can assure you that the reality of performing in Buckingham Palace will far supersede the way you have dreamed it up in your mind. *That!* I can truly promise!"

"Oh, I believe you!" Lily smiled. "And I can hardly wait! I'm ready to get on that ship tonight!"

William laughed at the effervescent child in her emerging once again. "If you left tonight, there would be 6,400 people sitting at Winter Garden who will be awfully disappointed come Christmas night!"

"Lord, I'm so excited, I 'bout near forgot!"

They both gave a light laugh and turned to continue appreciating the portrait together in silence for a brief moment.

"Ya' know, William, I guess I should take this opportunity to apologize to you too."

"Why is that?"

"This gon' sound horrible, but I have to confess that I hated you before I eva' even met you."

"Oh!" he replied, shocked by her candidness. "Is that so?"

"Unfortunately, yes, that's the truth," Lily said sheepishly. "But let me explain ... Ya' see, James neva' told me the truth about why he was takin' me to meet you. In fact, he neva' directly said anything to me at all about where we were goin'. I just so happened to ova'hear him tellin' his fatha' that he was takin' me to a slave breeda'."

"To a what?!"

"Yeah! That's exactly what I said in my mind ... along with a few otha' *choice* words," Lily laughed.

"Well, James admitted to me that he was going to get you away from his father by any means necessary ... I guess he certainly wasn't lying. But after using such extreme measures, I certainly can't blame you for the way you felt about me. My God! Under those circumstances, I would've hated me too. No wonder you seemed scared to death the first day I met you."

"Oh, I's terrified! No! *Petrified,* more like it. Actually, I don't think there's really a word to describe how I truly felt when James first rolled me through your gates."

"I'm so sorry he tortured you in that way."

"It's alright. I think we both know by now that James isn't perfect."

"*Really?* I never noticed," William joked.

Lily laughed. "As always, he was just doin' what he thought was best ... in his own *odd* little way. Now, in hindsight, though, I can say that I appreciate what he did. It shows me just how desperate he was to get me here. But I admit, it sho' would've been nice if he'd've explained everything before I had the chance to meet you. Hell, I don't think he said more than five words to me the whole two-day trip to your estate!"

"With the way you two carry on now, that's certainly hard to believe," William laughed.

Lily smiled. "Yeah, things have certainly changed since then. But at that time, that's the way it was between James and me, and he just wasn't willin' to say a thing to me about who you really were. He let me walk through your mansion doors believin' that you was nothin' more than a slave breedin' monsta'."

"The thought of such a vile, so-called *profession* makes me sick to my stomach. Makes me even sicker to know that you had to suffer, even for a second, believing that I was about to destroy your life in such a cold and heartless manner."

Lily turned to William. "That's exactly why I feel the need to apologize to you. Because believin' that awful lie left me hatin' you before I eva' laid eyes on you. Even afta' we met, I had horrible nightmares about you, because James had still yet to say a word to me about who you were. For days, I didn't want no parts 'a bein' near you, talkin' to you, or even lookin' at you. Didn't wanna eat your food or sleep in the bed you's kind enough to let me use. I didn't want a single thing you's offerin' me ... not even your incredible piano. Because, despite how nice you's bein, deep down I figured you's nothin' but a monsta' in sheep's clothin' tryna lure me in." Lily turned to admire the huge canvas in front of her again. "And now I look at this portrait and think about all the things you've done for me since we've met, and I can't believe I eva' thought anything of the sort about you. All the beautiful things I see here on this paintin'...." She turned back to look at William. "There's no way in the world I could've accomplished any of it without you. You've been so much more than a mentor to me, William," she said, taking hold of his hand. "You've felt more like a fatha' to me ... a fatha' who's used all his heart and his valuable time to help build my confidence and my courage. Then you protected me enough to let the real woman that's been hidin' inside 'a me step outta the darkness and into the sunlight. And I can't even begin to tell you how good it feels to finally stand in its warmth with you.

"It's for all those reasons that I stand before you now confessin' the sin of my evil thoughts about you. I wanna let you know that I regret every single nasty thought that's eva' crossed my mind. Because with everything that's transpired in this last year, I've grown to learn that you're the kindest, most generous, and gentle soul I've eva' met in my life … and I wanna thank you from the bottom 'a my heart for all you've eva' done for me."

"Lily…" William whispered, his kind eyes welling with tears again.

"If only your heart beat in the chest of every man alive, this world would be like heaven on earth," Lily added.

"Your words touch me very deeply. But in my estimation, it is *you* who has given so much to *me* for all these months. It is *I* who has not the words to express how much working with you has been one of the greatest joys of my life."

"Mine too," Lily smiled, touching his arm again. She then looked over at the twins after she heard them laughing together while talking to two ladies. "I hope your sons know how lucky they are to have a fatha' like you," she commented, after watching them for a moment and realizing that they always seemed to be so happy. "William, I know you've done so much for me already, but…"

"But what m'lady?"

"W-will you dance with me?" Lily asked shyly. "The way a fatha' would with his daughta'? I-I've just always wanted to know what it would feel like."

"Lily." William took both of her hands into his. "You have no idea how truly honored I'd be," he replied, his voice cracking with emotion again.

James was still near the bar drinking a glass of whiskey when he turned and saw William and Lily step out onto the dance floor together. On his way to get a drink, James had walked by Elijah, whose evil expression was powerless to take away the joy he was feeling that evening, especially as he watched Lily being waltzed around the dance floor by William with a smile on her face. James did not know what Lily and William had talked about after he left them alone, but he could tell by the way they danced that there was something special about the moment, something that made him even more impenetrable to Elijah's nasty attitude.

"She is your lady, no?" Piers suddenly asked James, motioning his head toward Lily. Seeming to have appeared out of nowhere, he stepped up alongside James and watched Lily drift across the dance floor as well. Piers had finally come to realize that James and Lily were probably a couple after watching the pair closely during the night's festivities. But despite it, he still boldly questioned James, with a sliver of optimism that maybe Lily was still fair game.

James looked over at Piers. "She is my *lady,* my *queen,* my *best friend.* She's..." He turned for a moment to watch Lily smiling as she danced with William. "My *everything.* I'd give up my own life for her."

Piers stared at James's profile as he watched Lily. By the expression on his face when he looked at his woman, Piers was left with no doubt that James meant every word that he had just uttered. "A beautiful answer such as that makes you even more worthy of this." Piers handed James a drawing that he had crafted on a piece of paper earlier in the evening. It was a picture of James and Lily dancing closely together. Lily's head rested on James's chest and James rested his head on top of Lily's. Both of them had their eyes closed, completely lost in the essence of one another. Piers had captured with perfection a moment that screamed *love,* and he did it with splendid accuracy. "A man with a woman, who has been blessed with such lovely features, should have her beauty to admire whenever he so desires ... Cherish it."

"Trust me, I will," James replied, truly appreciating how accurately he had captured Lily's beauty. "Thank you for this Mr. LeRoux."

"You are quite welcome. It was most certainly my pleasure," Piers said, with thoughts of Lily's illustrious body dancing close to his instead.

James had become aroused by simply looking at the image of himself so close to Lily. At that moment, ironically, he glanced up from the picture to find Lily staring at him with a hunger in her eyes that he was pleasantly familiar with. It was a hunger that James was always willing and able to satisfy at a moment's notice, whenever, wherever, and however Lily wanted. And with the way he was feeling after staring at her picture, James knew he would certainly have no problem fulfilling whatever erotic desires were invading her mind. His eyes spoke back to Lily, letting her know that his body was ready to meet her demands. Lily read his mutual longing and bit her bottom lip in anticipation of yet another fantasy that was on the verge of coming to fruition. James then quickly tucked the drawing away neatly into his inner jacket pocket. "Will you excuse me a moment?" he asked Piers.

"But of course," Piers replied, a devilish grin on his face. After watching the enticing exchange between them, Piers understood full well the nature of the sudden urgency. He actually felt a twinge of irrational jealousy as he watched James and Lily disappear down a dark corridor.

Piers was not the only jealous person who had witnessed the lust-filled exchange between the couple. All evening, Elijah had rarely taken his eyes off Lily. He, therefore, saw the look in her eyes when she gazed at James and the sensual desire on her face as she bit her bottom lip.

Elijah simply could not purge himself of *everything* about Lily Adams. The time he spent alone with her at Branaugh Theater had cemented his feelings. For every day that James had sat in jail, Elijah had sat enjoying evening dinner dates with Lily. Laughter and long intimate conversations carried on between the pair while sitting next to one another in the middle of all the empty theater seats, or sometimes while sitting on the stage with their feet lazily dangling off the edge. Elijah was happy for the time he had alone to connect and learn more about the incredible woman that Lily was. It deepened his attraction for her far past her physical beauty and talent. Lily's humor, intelligence, charisma, strength, and her willingness to openly share her life story had completely enchanted Elijah. Even five months later, he was still utterly obsessed with her. After their short but intense time together, Elijah genuinely thought there was a spark that ignited the beginning of something special between him and Lily. He was convinced that the deep feelings that had roared to life were mutual. It, therefore, angered him how quickly all of that had evaporated when James returned, as if their cherished week in close quarters meant nothing to Lily.

Since then, Elijah had graciously offered to step in and take the place of a percussionist in the show, who was suddenly unable to travel. As a new member of the cast, Elijah tried to take advantage of the fact that he was now around Lily every day. He was constantly asking her to lunch, offering his help with changes to the show, or doing anything else he could that would allow him a little more intimate time alone with her. But he could feel the emotional distance that she had placed between them. Suddenly, the ease with which they once spoke to one another was gone. Elijah even noticed that she rarely laughed or smiled anymore when she was alone with him. In fact, all of the things that had drawn him toward Lily were completely absent in his presence, and it infuriated Elijah to know that James was the root cause of her sudden coldness.

James understood the necessity of Elijah's new role with the cast, but he still hated him being a daily part of Lily's life. However, James trusted that Lily would always do right by him and never once felt it was necessary to voice his opinion on the matter. Unbeknownst to James, though, it had become a challenge for Elijah to take Lily away from him. But, time and time again, Lily proved how worthy she was of James's trust by always politely declining Elijah's constant onslaught of advances. Lily kept quiet about his disrespectful behaviors, feeling the need to keep the peace for the sake of the show. Most importantly, she wanted to prevent James from the sort of explosive rage that would likely have landed Elijah in the hospital and him back in jail.

With no knowledge of Elijah's disrespectful behaviors, James had quietly breezed right by him at the bar, like he did not even exist. In his haste to satisfy his woman, James had not even noticed the look of pure hatred on Elijah's face as he glared at him. Elijah's look of disdain was the result of the mere prospect of what James was on his way to do with a woman that he had developed serious feelings for, a woman that he *still* felt had no earthly business submitting herself to a man who technically owned her. The notion of it all disgusted him on an immeasurable level. In this ironic mirrored twist of fate, Elijah was now the one feeling jealous and sick to his stomach after digesting the sight of James and Lily enjoying themselves together, in the same way that James felt watching Lily with him. And, yet again, much like James, the alcohol in Elijah's veins made it far easier for his vile thoughts to seep through his rational filter. It left him with no inhibitions about putting a quick end to any impure acts the pair had planned at that moment. Hazily turning and stumbling in his inebriated state, Elijah began to quietly pursue James, who was eagerly pursuing Lily. Elijah was hell-bent on doing *anything* he had to do to shake Lily from her foolish fairytale. He wanted to force her to realize the massive mistake she was making by submitting herself to a slave-owning white man, rather than opening her eyes to the potential they had together.

Unaware that she was being pursued by both men, Lily was walking briskly, well ahead of James, down a dimly lit hallway. She was sashaying with an intentional provocative sway in her hips, initiating a chase of sorts, which James was more than happy to partake in. James, however, got halfway down the corridor and lost sight of her in the darkness. He paused and no longer heard the sound of her shoes clicking against the stone floor. A few minutes passed, and Lily did not hear a thing either. She peered from behind the stone column she had playfully hidden behind to find the hallway empty. She began to walk back, wondering what had happened to James, when a hand reached from an empty office room, pulled her inside, slammed the door shut, and locked it. Her lips were instantly devoured as strong hands held her pinned against the wall of the moonlit room.

Just as Elijah had watched Lily, Piers had watched Elijah curiously from time to time throughout the evening as well. He was uncomfortable with how rude Elijah seemed to be toward everyone. Piers noticed that he was the only one not joining happily in the festivities and that he showed no excitement whatsoever after Lily's epic news. Elijah's disturbing behavior led Piers to keep watch over him, especially after noticing the way his eyes obsessively followed James and Lily throughout the night with an evil intensity in his glare. Piers could easily sense Elijah's displeasure for the couple. Ironically, they were a couple that Piers was obsessed with as well; so much so that he was motivated to etch them together in a loving embrace. And so, as Piers had enviously watched James and Lily escape on a passionate rendezvous, Elijah quickly caught his attention again. Piers saw him creep curiously down the hallway behind James. Something in the pit of Piers's stomach told him that there would undoubtedly be trouble erupting from the darkness of that corridor without a quick intervention.

"Another drink, my friend?" Piers asked, holding tight to Elijah's arm. Piers had slipped with cat-like precision through the dancing crowd to catch Elijah midway down the corridor.

"What the hell! Get your fuckin' hands off 'a me!" Elijah protested, his drunken state causing his words to slur. He tried to escape Piers's grip, but the alcohol had made him too weak to snatch his arm away.

"Perhaps you've had a little too much to drink this evening. Come. Sit with me," Piers insisted calmly, pulling Elijah along. "A cup of coffee might suit you better." Within seconds, Piers had put a quick end to Elijah's pursuit. He wanted to ensure that the beautiful young lady, whose show had invaded his dreams, would have her fantasies thoroughly fulfilled by her lover—a man he truly envied—without any interruption from the likes of a drunken imbecile. Piers turned back momentarily to look down the hallway with an envious curiosity sweeping through him. He then devilishly smiled at the visions of his fantasies as he hauled Elijah away.

Piers's brazen interception left Lily happily in the arms of the man who had playfully abducted her. "Makin' me chase what I want, huh?" James asked, barely able to find the willpower to pull his mouth away from Lily's for the two seconds it took to ask her that question. "You want me here?" he asked, his tone heavy with lust. He then covered Lily's mouth again with his.

"I don't *want* you…" Lily replied, suddenly tearing herself away from James and walking in a tantalizing stroll to the other side of the room. With the full moonlight casting through a nearby window, James had no problem seeing the sensual look on Lily's face when she turned around. She began slowly unlacing the strings of her dress. She then let it slide down her body afterward, revealing her silky form-fitting lingerie and the length of her long, toned legs. "I *need* you," she corrected, calling him with her eyes to come to her.

Watching the aggressor emerge in Lily made the bulge in James's crotch threaten to tear a hole in his trousers. He began licking the taste of her off his lips as he made his way over to her, never once removing his eyes from hers. In record speed, he threw his suit jacket aside. He had broken into an immediate sweat from the swell of heat coursing through his veins, ignited from Lily's seductive show and her impassioned verbal confession. As much as James loved the look of the sheer two-piece ensemble hugging the curves of his woman's body, he was beyond ready to tear it off of her by the time she was within his reach. He was dying to have access to what was hidden underneath, wanting nothing more than to satisfy her appetite. With the way James ached to plunge deep inside of Lily, it took every bit of his willpower to leave her lingerie in one piece. Instead, he turned her around and impatiently slid her top up and off of her body and dropped it to the floor. With his hands now free, he traced the curves of Lily's thighs, back up her hips, around her waist, and up to her supple breasts, all the while suctioning soft wet kisses along the nape of her neck, drawing soothing purrs from her with every touch of his lips. Lily gasped at the tingling sensations of his fingers tickling and tugging gently at her nipples, then tilted her head back, and caught his mouth in another fiery kiss. As their tongues still danced together, Lily guided James's hand down her stomach into her panties, through her light thread of hair, then forced his fingers into the moisture of her searing insides. James growled at the feeling of her heat igniting his fingers. Lily's body relaxed and pleasure forced a moan through her vocal cords as he began repeatedly dipping his fingers into her wetness.

Lily wrapped her hands around James's neck, and her mouth parted as the blissful sensations began rolling through her. "Taste me," she suddenly moaned.

Upon her demands, James withdrew his fingers. Lily then turned to watch him carefully. The heated liquid between her thighs began to pool again after her arousal was heightened by the sight of James relishing the taste of her. The enjoyment of her flavor showed in the look on James's face as he indulged, slowly sucking the moisture of Lily's creamy insides from each of his fingers. Suddenly, though, Lily grabbed his wrist and guided his fingers from his mouth into hers while looking seductively into his eyes. Her erotic delicacy triggered a guttural groan that roared through James's vocal cords like the sounds of a primordial savage. The sight and feel of her tongue sent a rush of blood to his groin that had his member mercilessly throbbing.

Hungry to taste more of her, James ushered Lily over to a sofa in the corner, laid her back, tore her panties off, spread her legs wide, and immediately began suckling on the sensitive skin of her inner thighs, heading quickly northward to get to the prize he was yearning for. Like a starving beast, he greedily wrapped his mouth around Lily's pleasure pearl, causing her to sing out his name in a breathy tone. Forcefully, James then began suckling her, wanting desperately to taste the sweet flavor of her nectar. The power of his lips instantly caused Lily's legs to quiver and her cries of elation to soar. She nearly tore James's hair out as a euphoric rush triggered intense spasms that flooded James's mouth with the nectar that he was so eager to taste. His name, once again, sensually escaped Lily's lips, causing his hardened shaft to pulsate and drip with envy.

Lily had been spoiled by James enough to know that this first wave of pleasure was only her appetizer. She knew that he would soon serve her body the main course, something that she was desperately craving as she breathlessly unbuttoned his shirt, pushed him down onto the couch, and descended on his reddened lips. Her forceful ways evoked another growl from James. Submissively, he laid still and let her have her way with him. His heartrate increased and his breathing quickened as he watched her hastily unbuttoning his pants like a madwoman trying feverishly to unleash what she needed to finish satisfying her ravenous cravings. Lily's unabashed savage hunger for James, stroked his ego in a way that her words never could. Her actions left him already on the verge of climax as she mounted him and slid him deep inside of her in one smooth motion. "Yeeesss," she cried out, as his hardness electrified every nerve in her body.

The moment they were one, James and Lily were immediately oblivious to everything, despite an entire room full of people a short distance away. Much like drifting in their tiny fishing boat as children, they were now in a world where only the two of them existed, in a world where they were hugged by happiness, love, and the pleasures of their bodies. It was a phenomenon that never failed to occur whenever they were joined in this way. While they were suspended in their desolate fantasy world together, James pulled Lily in, held her close, and ran his hands up her back and down her waist, loving the look and feel of her soft honey-brown skin contrasting against his. As he caressed her, his eyes coasted over the landscape of her curves. He paused and marveled at the sight of himself buried deep inside the thickness of Lily's folds. Simply the essence of her had pleasantly overloaded every single one of James's senses, leaving him on the cusp of bursting inside of her with one more thrust of her hips.

Lily pushed James's hands down onto her buttocks, forcing him to grab her cheeks tight. Her domineering actions made James's need to erupt even more intense. To release the building pressure, he exhaled sharply, fighting hard with his body to settle down. Such a thing was impossible, though, as he watched Lily place one hand behind his neck and the other on his thigh to settle in for a pleasureful ride. Once steadied, she began maneuvering her hips, rocking back and forth in a slow motion, at first. Seconds later, she began picking up the pace, riding him swiftly, bucking up and down, mimicking a rider at full gallop on her horse. The intensity of the pleasure left neither of them able to hold back the erotic sighs that accompanied the blissful sensations that Lily's alluring ride had cascading through their bodies.

Sensing James was near, Lily began to ride him harder, coming down with forceful strokes, choking his hardened rod in a death grip, building the volcanic pressures within him quickly. Usually, it was Lily's release that ignited James's eruption, but the immense pleasure of her body became far too much for him to take. In an instant, he unleashed with cataclysmic force inside of her, belting out virile groans of gratification in deep tones that penetrated Lily's ears with ferocity, pushing her over the edge, bringing her to yet another explosive ending along with him.

They lay limp afterward, still connected in a mound on the couch, tired after another unforgettable climb together. Both were breathing like two horses that had just run in a derby, their chests heaving in unison as they silently allowed the high to linger for a while longer.

"That ... was ... heavenly," Lily breathlessly purred.

"You ain't lyin'," James replied, sounding just as out of breath. "I swear I just saw the stars up-close."

Lily giggled at his comment. "Sorry I couldn't wait 'til we got back to the hotel. I couldn't help myself."

"Trust me, I am *not* complainin'!"

Lily laughed again.

James smiled at her reaction. Quietly, he then gazed at her while gently running the back of his hand down the side of her face, taking a moment to absorb the exquisiteness of her features. His sudden need to gaze at her was owed to gratitude. After everything they had been through, he was grateful that his best friend—a beautiful, strong, intelligent woman—was truly *his,* in every way imaginable. He drew Lily in and kissed her tenderly as his way of silently thanking her for that fact.

James pulled back from their kiss and gazed at his woman again as he thought quietly to himself for a moment. "We don't eva' have to come back here, ya' know?" he suddenly said, while slowly caressing Lily's arms.

"Why wouldn't I want to? It's a beautiful museum, and I haven't had the chance to see the rest of it yet."

"No, I'm not just talkin' about this museum. I mean *all* 'a this ... These *entire* United States. We could leave and neva' come back to this place."

Lily looked at James with questioning eyes, wondering if he was being serious.

"I mean it," he replied after reading her mind. "This has become a country that I don't want no parts of anymore, and I certainly don't want you bein' a part of all the ugliness here." He sat up taller. "Lily, I really think this is our chance. We're goin' to the United Kingdom soon, and who says we eva' have to come back here?"

"James, what are you sayin'?"

"I'm sayin' we can start a new life ova' in Europe, in the Old World as they call it. We can escape this place. As soon as you read that letta' from the Queen, I knew this was the answa' I've been prayin' for. This is our chance to start ova' in a place where you'd be a world away from my fatha's reach. And, most importantly … in a place where slavery doesn't exist anymore. I'm certain William and Landon would be more than willin' to help us settle in and make a life there," James explained, still caressing Lily's arms, waiting for a smile or some sort of excitement about the prospect of his idea. But instead, she was expressionless and silent while the possibility of it rolled through her head. Without a word, she then suddenly got up to retrieve her dress.

"Lily, are you alright?" James questioned, confused by her odd reaction. He expected a joyous response, especially after knowing how obsessed she had become with British culture.

"But what about your family, James?" she finally asked while trying to get her dress into place. "You'd just leave 'em all behind?"

James stood, buckled his pants, and then went over to help Lily with her dress. "*Family?*" he scoffed. "My fatha' gave me life, yes. But outside 'a the blood we share, I feel not one ounce of a connection to that man. My motha's dead and my brotha's have hated me since the day I's born … and trust me, the feelin's mutual." He turned Lily around to face him. "They ain't no family to me, Lily." He placed his hands gently on her face. "*You are* … you and the beautiful children I pray you'll give me someday. You'll all be my family."

"B-but your home is here," Lily replied, sounding as if she had not heard a word he said.

"*Home* is whereva' you and our children are, no matta' where we are in this world."

435

"James that's a serious move. Don't you think you might regret makin' such a drastic change in your life just for *me?*" she asked, her puzzled eyes staring straight into his.

"Maybe you haven't been listenin' to me these past few months when I tell you every day how much I love you. Or maybe you just don't believe me. I know afta' everything I've put you through in the past, maybe I don't deserve to be fully trusted by you yet, but Lily..." James made her look at him after her eyes drifted to the ground. "You are my world. I'd *do* anything for you, and I'd most certainly *go* anywhere for you. If I haven't proven that to you already, then I don't know what else I could possibly do to make you believe me." He threw his hands up. "Hell, except for lettin' you watch me get on that ship and sail away from here without hesitation or one single solitary reservation about it. And so, for *us* ... would I have any regrets about makin' such a drastic change in my life? Hell no! I'd leave this place with you in a heartbeat and neva' give it a second thought!"

"I believe you," Lily replied, but there was still no excitement in her eyes or in her tone.

James could sense her reluctance, but he did not understand why. "Lily, what is it?"

She removed his hands from her face and turned away from him.

"Lily, tell me that you want this too, so we can sail away from this place and neva' look back. Tell me that you wanna start ova' a world away from here and take nothin' but all 'a the wonderful memories you and I have created. When we get there, we can create a lifetime full 'a new unforgettable memories ... and a beautiful family of our own."

Lily was still silent. Her mind already seemed to have drifted a world away.

"Lily?" James persisted. "You'd want that too, wouldn't you?"

"You really are serious about all this, aren't you?" she asked, still staring across the room at nothing.

James walked around to the front of her and turned her face toward him. "I've neva' been more serious about anything in my whole life. I want you an ocean away from my fatha' and my brotha's ... in a world where I can finally feel secure that he has no way of gettin' access to you. Where I know you and our children will be safe."

"I can't do it, James," Lily finally replied.

"*What?* Lily, w-why not?" he stammered.

"Not without my motha'," she answered, instantly bringing clarity to her reservations. "I don't wanna go ... not unless I can take her with me. I can't leave her here."

"If that's what you want, then I'll find 'er. I swore that to you, and I will. As soon as we're settled in Europe, and I know you're outta harm's way, I'll come back and find 'er for you. But..."

"But what? You made a promise to me," Lily reminded him, a serious look in her eyes.

"I know, and I swear I'll stand by that. It's just that I know your fears about wantin' to find 'er, and I don't want you to feel rushed into this because 'a what I'm askin' here. So, I'll do it, but *only* ... only if you're *truly* ready for me to do it."

Lily stepped past him and walked over to glance out of the moon-filled window at the troubled world that her mother was still trapped in. It was a troubled world that Lily had the power to help free her mother from with just two simple words. Ready to exercise that power, Lily closed her eyes and let out a cleansing breath. "I'm ready," she announced.

Feeling great relief after hearing the sincerity in Lily's tone, James walked up behind her and slid his arms around her waist, and they gazed out the window together.

"I know I can do this, so long as you're with me to give me the strength to get through it," Lily added.

"So long as I'm alive, I'll *always* be here for you ... through *everything.*"

"Then I'm *truly* ready…" Lily finally relaxed in the arms of the man who continued to prove that he genuinely loved her. "Ready to start our new life … *togetha'*."

"*Togetha',*" James repeated, letting a soft kiss linger on the side of Lily's face. "In the Old World," he continued, swaying gently with her in his embrace.

"The Old World will be our *new* world," she whispered.

Chapter Twenty-two

What Lily was currently feeling was a familiar anxiousness that began to manifest the very first time she ever saw James roll out of sight in a wagon to stay with his aunt and uncle for a few weeks during the summer. That anxious sick feeling in her stomach grew worse every time she watched him leave every summer thereafter. That anxious pain in her stomach led her to regurgitate the day she watched James pack up his wagon for college and ride out of her life for six long years without so much as a goodbye. That same unsettling feeling in her stomach struck again when Sheriff Tolliver had come to haul James off to jail. James's unknown whereabouts in the days that followed had her stomach teetering on erupting again when he failed to show before her performance. Now here Lily was, sitting snuggled next to James in her carriage, headed to the train station with that all too familiar sickness brewing in the pit of her stomach again.

In the few days before the Manhattan art museum fundraiser, Anna Mae had struggled to rid herself of a cough that rattled her whole body, brought pain to her chest, and hoarseness to her voice. She had fought it for as long as she could, but it had gotten progressively worse. Amidst the art museum festivities, the invading bug caused her to collapse. James had returned to The Grand Ballroom after his intimate rendezvous with Lily to find guests circled around Anna Mae as she lay on the floor. He immediately put his medical training to good use. He found that Anna Mae's symptoms pointed to dehydration, brought on by her inability to hold much of anything down. James had forced her to drink as much as she could on their way back to their hotel. By the time they arrived, she was feeling slightly better. William insisted on finding a doctor in town who had the sort of equipment and medication that James lacked, but Anna Mae refused. She accepted whatever help James could offer, but she was fearful of what some other white doctor may do to a helpless Negro woman. Instead, she insisted on being treated by the doctor she had trusted for years back in Ohio. Her family tried to convince her that traveling while ill would not be wise, but she remained stubborn. After months on the road anyway, she was longing for trusted medical care in the comforts of her own bed.

Since James was best suited to handle medical emergencies, he decided to escort Anna Mae and Ben back home. In between a fit of painful coughs, Anna Mae thanked James for his willingness to help. He told her it was the least that he could do in light of everything she had done for Lily.

Before departing the hotel, Anna Mae's children and everyone else said their goodbyes to her and Ben. And now, Lily took a moment to bid them farewell while they sat on the train, waiting for it to depart. She held Anna Mae tight and kissed her on the cheek. "I feel guilty, like I'm the one that done worked you clear to the bone tryna keep up with all the madness for the show. Don't seem like you eva' get a minute 'a rest."

"Don't you feel a lick 'a guilt, baby," Anna Mae replied, coughing into a handkerchief. "I'm the one been foolish enough to push myself too hard. I neva' trusted that absentminded daughta' of mine to make the costumes and yo' dresses by herself." She tried to laugh but began coughing again. "Guess I ain't got no choice now," she wheezed.

"I've seen Isabel's work. It's just as beautiful as yours. You taught 'er well. You should be proud."

"I am proud … proud 'a both of ya'."

"Thank you, Ms. Anna Mae," Lily said, taking her by the hand. "I'm gonna miss you. I don't know how to adequately thank you for all you've done for me."

"Seein' the joy on your face every time you put on one 'a my dresses has been all the thanks I eva' needed, baby," she replied, breaking into another coughing fit.

"No mo' talkin'. You go on and rest now," Lily said, patting her free hand. She then turned toward Anna Mae's husband. "Ben, I know you'll take good care 'a her."

"Always have, always will," he replied, as he covered his wife with a blanket. "Don't you worry about her. All I want you to do is go put on a show that queen ain't neva' gonna forget, ya' hear?"

"Yessa', I promise I will." Lily embraced him. "For all the hard work you put into the stage, I wanna thank you too."

"It was my pleasure, sweetheart. I finally got to put these old muscles to work for a change. Had all them young'uns lookin' like a bunch 'a sluggish snails," he joked.

"I sure am gonna miss you ... and that sense 'a humor of yours," Lily laughed.

"I'll miss you too. Take care, sweetheart."

After Ben kissed her on the cheek, Lily exited the train and walked up to Griff, the leader of the misfit security bandits. There were already two bandits back on William's estate guarding the grounds, but William still felt it was best to send Griff back with Anna Mae and Ben for added protection, since death threats still trickled in from time to time. Griff was the closest to Lily of all the bandits, and she suddenly found it hard to say goodbye to him as she approached him. As always, Griff had his thick, dark mustache perfectly twisted and turned down at the sides. He was wearing his typical all black clothes and boots, his black Stetson hat, and had his two pistols hanging crooked in his holster from his hips. Lily had never once seen him without "the punishers" dangling from his waist, as Griff jokingly called them. She swore he probably slept with them. By all accounts, Griff looked mean and hard as nails. But all he ever did was talk to Lily about the fondest memories of raising his three grown daughters. The tenderness he exuded as he gushed about them left her convinced that they had melted his ice-cold heart.

Lily found Griff's combination of soft and tough endearing. Griff never said it, but she could tell that he never stopped missing his girls since they married and moved away. So anytime they were back at William's estate, she would walk out to Griff at the front gates in the morning and serve him fresh brewed coffee, strong and black the way he liked it, along with a towering stack of her homemade pancakes. The pancake on the very top was always made in the shape of a heart, the way Griff said his daughters used to do for him when they were younger. It was not only Lily's way of thanking him for risking his life to protect hers, but of trying to make Griff feel like his girls were there with him again, at least for a little while.

"I sho' am gon' miss them famous flapjacks 'a y'urs," Griff confessed to Lily when she stopped in front of him at the train station. "But *you* more than anything, Little Flowa'," he said, referring to her by the nickname that he had given her.

Strangely, his term of endearment would always remind Lily of something that once happened to her while she was standing near an apple tree on her father's plantation when she was only three. Hearing Griff call her that now triggered the memory again. She began to wonder if the event she was recalling was real or perhaps just a dream. Once her mother joined her in the Old World, it was one of the many things she wished to ask her about.

"I'm gonna miss you too, Griff," Lily admitted. She then threw her arms around him. Griff wanted to keep up his hard demeanor, but with his "Little Flower" hugging him, he easily lost his willpower and gently returned her embrace.

When Lily let him go, Griff returned to his usual intimidating self. He then walked over to one of the other loyal bandits and slapped him on the shoulder. "Take good care 'a my Little Flowa', Samuel ... Or I'll blow y'ur goddamn head off y'ur shoulda's and mount it on my wall," he threatened.

Samuel swallowed hard, flashed a nervous smile, and touched his forehead after imagining the wound. Griff then strolled by him to get on the train in his usual calm strut.

After her goodbyes to everyone, Lily had to turn and face the inevitable: a goodbye that had already begun to sicken her. Knowing that James was leaving for a noble cause, she felt foolish for her anxiousness this time around. Meekly, she approached him. Her hanging head spoke volumes to James. He took her by the hand and ushered her to a dark corner of the station. Samuel stood guard nearby as an added layer of protection from prying eyes.

"You okay?" James asked, once they had some privacy.

"I wish you didn't have to leave tonight," Lily admitted.

"Me neitha', but I wanna be sure Anna Mae's well taken care of on the way back. Besides, once I can get 'er to her doctor, it'll give me time to tie up some loose ends, take the money outta our account, and gatha' up all our things to take to the Old World, just like we talked about on the way here. The soona' we can leave this place afta' you perform, the betta'."

Lily nodded. "I know."

"Speakin' of your performance ... I just looked at that train schedule, and it looks like I'll be runnin' a little behind gettin' back here in time for the start 'a the show Christmas night," James said, the cold air making clouds out of his breath. As with all things regarding Lily, he noticed the quick change in her disposition after he mentioned when he would be returning. "Lily, it's alright. I'll be back for the show. I may be a little late, but I'll be there."

"I know. It's just that…"

"Just what?"

"Nothin'," she said, determined to ignore the sick feeling in her stomach. "But will you do me a favor?"

"Of course. Anything."

"All of our letters … I keep 'em in the chest at the end 'a my bed. Would you gatha' 'em up and bring 'em too?" she asked, thinking of everything she could to keep from having to say goodbye until she absolutely had to.

"I'd be happy to."

"I know it might seem like such a petty thing, but those letta's mean so much to me."

"It's not petty at all. They mean a lot to me too. Anything else you can think of?"

"My book … *Our* book. I'd be sick if I left it behind."

"I already had it on my mental checklist," he said, pointing to his temple with a smile. "Anything else, m'lady?" he asked, playfully mimicking a British accent, attempting to cheer Lily up.

Lily wanted to laugh, but she felt a lump starting to form in her throat. "*You*." She closed his large overcoat and pulled his scarf a little tighter, trying to distract herself from the tears she felt brewing. "And don't you dare be gone away from me long this time."

James brushed back a lock of her hair after the wind swept it into her face. "I won't be gone from you a minute longa' than I need to be, Miss Lily."

"Not *one* minute, ya' hear?" she warned.

"Not one," James promised, not wanting to hurt her the way he had during his last absence. "Not one damn minute," he whispered, caressing her face.

"AAALL ABOOOARD!"

James looked back at the conductor and watched the last few people funneling toward the train entrance.

"Well, you best get goin'," Lily said, dropping her head, still refusing to say goodbye first.

"I'll see you real soon, beautiful," James said, raising her head and kissing her quickly on the lips before turning to walk away.

"You were right all those months ago, ya' know," Lily called out to James before he had gotten too far.

He stopped just feet away from her and turned around.

"I've always felt it," she continued.

James looked at her a bit confused. "Felt what?"

Lily approached him and ran her hand down the front of his overcoat. "How much you've always loved me," she answered. "And I hope you've always felt it too." Her eyes were suddenly fixated on his. "How much I've always loved you."

James froze for a moment and let his eyes drift across the softness in Lily's face after she had spoken the words. "*Always*," he assured her, in a faint whisper.

"Good. 'Cause I do," she admitted, blinking away the tears she could no longer hold back. "I really do love you, James Adams. Through *everything* all these years ... I *always* have."

James's eyes suddenly closed as an uncontrollable swell of tears surged forward and threatened to fall from the warmth and sincerity of her confession. In the six months since he had confessed his love to her, Lily had been willing to share her worries, her joy, her concerns, her happiness, her fears, her laughter, and even her body with him. But never had she shared those words ... until this very moment. After his egregious errors of the past, James knew that such words did not come lightly and without great meaning. He viewed those invaluable words as

445

a symbol of her willingness to completely trust him. It meant that the healing was complete, that all had truly been forgiven, and that he was finally worthy of having *all* of her. Lily was now willing to be totally and completely vulnerable with him, without so much as a grain of the wall she had once erected around herself standing in between them.

As the train whistled in the background, with tears welling in his eyes, James descended on Lily's lips. He kissed her with the sensitivity and finesse that he hoped would convey how much he understood the magnitude of her admission. Lily's confession and the caress of her soft lips suddenly made James feel impervious to the freezing temperatures, and to everything else for that matter. He closed his eyes again while he kissed her and let the sentiment of Lily's declaration seep into his heart, his soul, and his spirit as he mentally recorded the time, the place, the look on Lily's face, the tears in her eyes, the tears in his own, the sound of the train engine, the direction her hair was blowing, and the slight break in her voice as Lily professed her love to him for the very first time. He *needed* to be sure that *everything* about that moment implanted itself deep in the recesses of his memory for the rest of his natural life.

As the conductor called out for the last time, with great reluctance, James pulled himself away and let Lily go. Lily stood on the platform huddled next to Samuel and watched him board and take his seat near Anna Mae, Ben, and Griff. As the train began to roll, James looked out the window and kept his eyes firmly planted on the woman who loved him, until she was no longer in his sight.

* * * *

Lily was taken back to the hotel in her carriage with Samuel at the reins, and with James's passionate kiss having freed her from that sick feeling in her stomach for the first time ever after one of his departures. She quickly realized that it was all she had ever needed from James to feel settled whenever he left. Lily would have much preferred to be wrapped in his strong arms on such a cold night, but she was comforted by the warmth that his lips had left her with, and by knowing that they would soon have the rest of their lives to spend curled up together across the sea.

"Good night, Samuel," Lily told her security bandit before walking into her hotel room.

"Night, Ms. Lily," Samuel responded as he closed her door and took his post right outside of it.

Lily wearily entered her room after a long day, removing her shoes as she walked in the dark toward her oil lamp. "Do you love him?" she suddenly heard a deep voice asking her from the corner of the room. She nearly jumped out of her skin after turning and vaguely making out a dark figure sitting in a chair near the window.

"How the hell'd you get in here?!" she shouted.

Samuel quickly opened the door. "Ms. Lily!"

"It's alright Samuel … It's only Elijah," she said after her eyes adjusted in the darkness.

Samuel grimaced at him. Despite knowing Elijah, he felt uneasy about him breaking into her room, like a night crawling criminal. Samuel looked at Lily once again to be certain she was okay being alone with him.

"It's alright, I'll let ya' know if I need ya'," Lily responded to the questioning look on Samuel's face.

Samuel furrowed his eyebrows at Elijah and then hesitantly closed the door.

As soon as the door latched, Elijah immediately continued with his line of questioning. "Do you?"

Lily finally lit her oil lamp and turned to get a good look at how unkempt and pathetic Elijah looked, hunched over in the chair with his elbows on his knees and his suit jacket and shirt loose. "Do I *what*, Elijah?" Lily asked, sounding annoyed.

"Love yo' *masta'?*"

"His name is *James*, and I don't see how that's any of your concern."

Elijah suddenly pounced to his feet, startling Lily again. "It *is* my concern because I don't wanna see you hurt! And that's exactly what'll happen if you keep bein' foolish enough to let yourself believe there can eva' be anything honest and pure between you and *your masta'*," he emphasized again.

"He's *not* my masta'!" Lily yelled, aggravated with his blatant disrespect. "And I don't know if you've noticed, but I'm a pretty big girl, and I don't need *you* or anybody else to tell me how to conduct my affairs!"

"*Affairs!* You couldn't've used a more fitting word!"

"And just what the hell's that s'pposed to mean?!" she asked, throwing her hands on her hips.

"It means, that's all you'll eva' end up bein' to *yo' masta'* in the long run! An *affair!* Open your eyes Lily! He can't legally marry you! And even if he could, I'm sure he'd neva' *want* to! Afta' he marries a woman he'd actually wanna be seen with in public, you'll end up bein' nothin' but his secret little *affair* in backrooms and alleys unda' the pitch black night sky, where he can hide his shameful activities from pryin' eyes!"

"James shows me love and affection openly all the time!"

"Yes! And have you noticed it's *only* in front 'a all of us! Around people who care about you, where he knows he won't be puttin' himself in harm's way, or *embarrassin'* himself, or shamin' his family by bein' seen with a *Negro!* But in the real world there's no way in hell he'd display you proudly on his arm!"

Lily thought briefly about how James had ushered her to a dark area of the train station to say his goodbyes, but then quickly shook it from her head, not wanting to fall victim to Elijah's mind games. "He'd be tryin' to keep *me* outta harm's way!"

"Is that the lie he's been tellin' you?! Or worse yet, is that the lie you're tellin' *yourself* now?!" Elijah approached Lily and touched her shoulder, but she shrugged him off and stepped away. "Lily, you're brilliant ... a damn prodigal genius! That's why it anga's me to see you bein' so stupid and naïve about this. I just wish you'd stop bein' blinded by what you *think* is love."

"It's not just what I *think!* It's what I *see!* It's what I *sense!* It's what I *feel* runnin' through me like wildfire!"

Elijah backed up and looked her up and down with scathing eyes. "So, you *do* love him?"

"You're damn right I do!"

"Then why'd you lead me to believe there was somethin' between us?"

"What?!" Lily erupted. Her face twisted in anger. "Are you still drunk?!" She put her finger in his face. "How dare you have the audacity to accuse me of such a thing! I neva' *led* you to believe *anything!*"

"You'd be lyin' if you stood here and said there wasn't somethin' between us back at Branaugh! In all these months we've worked togetha', you know good 'n damn well you *still* feel somethin' between us! You can't tell me my mind is just playin' tricks on me!"

"Yes! I *can!*" Lily erupted again, after having had enough of Elijah's intrusion, not only into her room but into her personal life. "You dismiss my feelin's for James like I'm some kind 'a imbecile who needs your permission to know how I should feel! Then you have the nerve to disrespect me, him, *and* our relationship wheneva' he turns his back, by pawin' all ova' me and smotherin' me 'til I feel like I can't breathe ... and I'm sick of it! So right here and right now, I'm *demandin'* for you to tell me just how many times I have to turn you down for you to accept that there ain't a *damn thing* between us?!" She continued to glare at Elijah, her chest heaving after her verbal blows, waiting to see if he would actually answer her insulting question. When he cowered like a puppy and remained silent, she continued her tirade with just as much ferocity in her tone. "Tell me, dammit, so I'll be sure to meet my quota!" When Elijah refused to respond again, Lily finally took a bit of the steam out of her voice. "There has *neva'* been anything between us, Elijah … and there *neva'* will be. All along, this ain't been nothin' but your damn imagination, and your undyin' hope that your twisted fantasies will come to life! Now it's time for you to get ova' it!"

Without warning, Elijah covered Lily's mouth with his while holding tight to her face. The taste of whiskey instantly seared her lips as she pushed hard on his chest to get away from his unwanted invasion. He held her so tight, she was forced to pry his mouth off her with her fingertips. After disconnecting him from her face, she gave him a hard shove and slapped him with as much power as she could muster.

"Don't tell me that meant nothin'!" Elijah had the audacity to demand afterward.

"GET OUT!" Lily screamed, wiping hard at the residue he left lingering on her lips.

"YOU CAN'T TELL ME THAT MEANT NOTHIN'!" he still insisted.

"GET YOUR DRUNK ASS OUTTA HERE!"

"I'M IN LOVE WITH YOU!"

"I SAID GET OUT!"

"LILY, I'M SORRY!"

"GEEET! OOOUT!"

Lily's door flew open, and Samuel grabbed Elijah by the throat. "I done heard enough from you t'night," Samuel said, wrestling Elijah into submission. "Get y'ur goddamn sorry ass outta here!" Knowing that Elijah was part of the family and that he was inebriated, Samuel spared him the feel of cold steel against his temple. After a brief tussle, he simply dragged him out of Lily's room. Elijah conceded quickly after the contents in his stomach began to churn. He stumbled down the hallway, out of the hotel, and wandered off into the cold night air to clear his head, along with the alcohol that finally erupted violently from his stomach.

"You alright, Ms. Lily," Samuel came in and asked her after he was certain Elijah was no longer a threat.

"I'm fine," she replied, sitting on the bed in disbelief while wiping her mouth with a wet cloth, trying to get the repulsive taste of whiskey and Elijah off of her lips. While she sat there, Samuel walked around the room and checked the windows, the closet, and even under her bed, just to be sure all was clear before bidding Lily goodnight and walking out to stand guard outside of her door again.

Once alone, Lily undressed and laid down, feeling beyond angry that she had been violated in such a disgusting way. After giving it much thought, though, she decided, once again, that it was best *not* to tell James about what Elijah had done. She feared the heinous offense would literally land James on trial for murder. After crossing the line, the way Elijah had, Lily wanted him immediately tossed from the show. But she also decided to let his participation at Winter Garden stand so that nobody would question her reason for firing him so close to the Christmas performance. After tolerating him through the end of the show, though, she looked forward to telling Elijah that he would *not* be setting one foot on the ship bound for Buckingham Palace, a place that she suddenly began to sail to in her subconscious to help escape the memory of Elijah's liquor-covered lips violating hers. With thoughts of that distant land finally overtaking her mind, Lily's horrid encounter with Elijah faded away altogether. Instead, her mind began to replay the vivid visions of her erotic encounter at the museum with a man she currently wished was making love to her again. After making the euphoric climb together, she wanted so badly for James to swaddle her nude body against his while caressing her softly and lulling her to sleep by his gentle touch, as she fantasized about what the future held for the both of them in the Old World.

Chapter Twenty-Three

LOVE:

A profound, tender, passionate affection, or feeling of warm personal attachment, deep passion, or sexual desire for another person.

Christmas Night 1859
Winter Garden Theater
On Broadway

Now Playing:
THE DREAM SYMPHONY

OVE: With a sea of shadowed hearts drifting around it, that was the one word written into the sheer tapestry halfway through *The Dream Symphony*, Christmas night at Winter Garden. In front of a packed house, two grand pianos sat facing each other in the middle of the massive stage with William Werthington seated at one and Lily Adams seated at the other. It was just the two of them, no strings, no percussion, no horns to add to the mix. There was just the sound of two masterfully played pianos, mixing harmoniously together, projecting a simple yet elegant ballad that Lily had written just a few days prior for this special night: a ballad inspired by the power of ... **LOVE.**

In quiet moments, be it near her favorite tree, in her hotel room, or riding in her carriage, James sometimes peered at Lily in admiration as she scribbled music notes onto sheets of blank paper. She would write feverishly, whenever, and wherever her creative juices began to flow while swaying softly from side to side, closing her eyes from time to time, and dancing to the symphonic sounds in her head. James noted how Lily seemed not to be in the same world as he was when she wrote. He could see in her face and body language that she had tuned out everything around her and was completely lost in the musical wonderland of her mind, the place where her memories and experiences were giving birth to all the wonderful elements that made her shadowed show so extraordinary. From James's perspective, Lily seemed so lost in that glorious world that he often wondered if she ever noticed him stealing glances at her. He gazed at her in utter fascination, pondering to himself where it all came from, why, and how music erupted so easily from within her. Although those answers eluded him, one thing was accurate: music came with ease for Lily. The melodies and harmonies flowed effortlessly, so fast that her hand sometimes could not keep up with the speed with which they exploded from her creative factory. The array of musical sounds in her head would fill dozens of blank papers in a matter of an hour or less. And for as many times as James had witnessed the phenomenon, it never ceased to amaze him.

While watching Lily script lines and dots that he could barely comprehend, James was unaware that he had actually watched Lily transcribe a song that his love had inspired. Lily wanted to perform it for him for the very first time during this one-night-only Christmas event. But after being deeply affected by the story of Emma reliving her cherished memory at Winter Garden, Lily decided to blend her new love ballad with a song that William had written for Emma years ago.

And so now, the beautiful duet that Lily sat playing across from her beloved mentor, was one that she hoped would honor the undying love that he had for his wife. Simultaneously, Lily hoped that the remastered melody would adequately thank William for summoning the courage and the strength not only to return to Winter Garden, but to return to the piano at all after the pain of losing the love of his life. The new duet was the least she felt she could do to express her appreciation for the emotional sacrifice that William was willing to make *solely* for the sake of helping her pursue her musical dreams.

The sentimental ballad surprise brought tears to William's eyes when Lily presented it to him on the piano and he heard Emma's song infused within it. After hearing the blend of melodic perfection, William insisted that the song did not require the company of an elaborate show of shadow dancers, only two grand pianos and two people playing them for the people they loved. He felt that the passion with which they played would be more than enough to ignite vibrant memories of every personal love story embedded in the minds of all who listened.

Hoping to convey those emotions to the crowd on this cold Christmas night, William certainly played with an immense amount of passion. He was fighting to hold back tears after looking out into the audience and seeing his beloved sons in the front row, sitting on either side of a seat that housed not a person but, rather, an extravagant bouquet of white lilies: Emma's favorite flower. The elegant arrangement sat on display in the very same seat that their mother was seated in the day her loving husband had brought her back to Winter Garden to let her relive the very last remaining memory she had left in the fading last hours of her life.

Much like everyone in the crowd while the ballad was played, William's mind drifted to the memories of his love. Those flowers in her old seat faded away and he imagined Emma was there nestled between their boys again. He closed his eyes and the memories of when he first met Emma came crashing back to him: the way he walked into the little country store she owned and stumbled when he first caught sight of her, the way she wore her hair that day, the way he felt warmth flow through his body when she turned and smiled at him, how he struggled to pull his eyes away from the beauty of hers, and how he suddenly forgot how to speak when she said hello. He even still remembered her sweet scent as she approached him, and how he could not figure out how to move after she briefly touched him on the shoulder while asking if he needed help. As William played the blended ballad Lily had written, he recounted every minute detail of the moment he had gladly made a complete fool of himself in front of a woman he had instantly fallen in love with.

The passion with which Lily played was obvious to the audience as well. Samuel had gone to retrieve James from the train station just before the opening of her show. She had yet to see him, but she felt James's presence there while she played across from her mentor. As she played for the man she loved, Lily was suddenly happy that there were no dancers present to tell the secrets of her mind when that melody was born. She realized that the only person who needed to see the story had already lived it along with her. He had shared the laughter, the heartache, the birthday celebrations, great sorrow, the pain of separation, the books, the tears, the losses, and the lovemaking. Through every peak and valley, James was there. And as she sat at the grand piano expressing her love for him through her music, in Lily's mind, she was there with him all over again.

Just like William, Lily sat playing with her eyes closed, lost in the memories of her love story, the emotion of it all showing on her face and in the way she moved her body. It showed in the way she swayed gently while remembering the wind whipping by her as she jumped down from an old oak tree, and raced with James along a creek, seeking out the turtle they had named together. It showed in her smile while remembering how a jumping fish once had James jumping overboard from their fishing boat. It showed in the anguish on her face, thinking of the years they had spent apart. And it showed, yet again, in the delight on her face when she thought about the moment he had returned. The passion Lily felt even displayed itself in all the tiny goose bumps that covered her body as she remembered the very first time James pressed his lips against hers. Passion then reached its peak and overflowed from her eyes as she recalled the first time he ever made love to her. Every sentimental memory sent warmth rushing through her with each musical bar she played that represented the times over the last fifteen years that she felt showered in the love of James Adams.

There were so many of those glorious moments to recount that Lily could have done an entire two-hour show with that song alone. But with the ending of the five-minute melody, William stood and walked to the front of the stage, waiting for Lily to join him and take a bow, just as they had rehearsed. To William's surprise, however, his sons emerged from the wings on either side of him and began walking toward him, holding onto the bouquet that had sat in their mother's seat. Overwhelmed by the surprise that his twins and Lily had planned, William's emotions began to swell in his chest, and so, too, did the lump in his throat when Lily began to play the original melody that he had written for Emma. On cue, Lily crescendoed into the piece at the exact moment the twins reached William and handed him their mother's flowers. Emerson and Wilson then put their arms around their father and turned him to face the sheer tapestry, where William found it already brilliantly illuminated with the figure of a shadowed angel. The angel's wings were spread far and wide, floating above the image of three shadowed men, two of whom had synchronized and mimicked the movements of Emerson and Wilson as they entered the stage and stood next to their father. While Lily continued to play Emma's song, the shadows that represented William and his sons stood together holding the beautiful flower arrangement, still mimicking the stance of William and the twins as they watched the silhouette story play out in front of them. The tears that William had fought so gallantly to hold back suddenly began cascading in streams down his face the very moment the shadowed figure of his angelic wife slowly floated down and took hold of her flowers. She then wrapped her wings around the shadowed version of her family in a loving embrace, in perfect timing with the last few notes Lily played, just as the light slowly faded away.

Once the audience's long-standing ovation and tears ceased, the dancing shadows returned again for the rest of the show. Their elegant movements in front of elaborate lighting gracefully glided across the sheer tapestry, telling stories through dance, driven by the rhythm of Lily's brilliantly written classical pieces. For two nonstop hours, every stagehand, every dancer, every student orchestra member, William Werthington, and Lily had come together to complete another spellbinding show that riveted a sea of people, finally ending Lily's musical journey in the United States. After delivering the gift of her music on Christmas night, well over six-thousand pairs of hands continuously applauded for a genius woman. The delighted audience was on their feet, cheering on and on for a prodigal woman, who, by law, was only considered three-fifths of a human being, who had no right to vote, no right to own land, no rights to education, no right to learn to read or write, nor any of the other basic freedoms they all had when they walked beyond the doors of the theater they were in. In the eyes of the law, the creator of *The Dream Symphony* was a woman who was *still* figuratively bound by chains, *but*, despite those ugly truths, as she took her final bow at Winter Garden, Lily Adams felt as free as a bird in a summer sky.

After absorbing the unbelievable ovation of the crowd, the curtain finally closed, truly symbolizing the end of Lily's unbelievable journey to Winter Garden. But, ironically, instead of it feeling like the end, it felt more like a new beginning to her, something she was eager to celebrate with a particular man that she had not seen in days. Lily turned with a smile and watched the stagehands lowering the sheer tapestry behind her while all of her close friends mingled around it in different modes of celebration. While she searched for who she really wanted to see, Lily was greeted with huge bear hugs and innocent kisses on the cheek from many of the orchestra members as she made her way through the chaotic scene. Her happiness and enthusiasm were fueled after listening to the sounds of everyone's cheers and champagne bottles popping around her as they celebrated not only another flawless night, but their excitement over soon drifting off to the Old World.

After being hugged and congratulated by nearly everyone in the crew, Lily had yet to spot James. While she had the chance, she retreated to her dressing room to retrieve a Christmas gift that she had wrapped for him. Before she could grab it, though, Landon caught her there. "Lily, do you have a moment?" he asked, peeking his head inside of her door after knocking.

"Sure."

"I have a few people here who have requested to meet you, if you don't mind."

Always having a true appreciation for those who attended her shows, Lily never once turned down an opportunity to meet anyone who wished to speak to her afterward. "Absolutely! They're more than welcome!" she exclaimed.

After giving her permission, Landon brought in a tall slinky man with a rugged beard and a top hat that made him seem even taller than he already was. Tagging along with him was a much shorter woman with a round plump face, dark hair, and two young boys that held tight to her hands.

"This is Abraham Lincoln, his wife Mary, and their two sons. Mr. Lincoln was once a member of the House of Representatives in Illinois, and he happened to see your show in Chicago. He's currently campaigning for the presidency here in New York and has brought his family along to experience the show with him this time," Landon explained.

Hearing that Abraham was such an important person suddenly made Lily a little nervous, but, as always, she quickly pulled herself together.

"Ms. Adams," Abraham began, extending his large hand toward her. "Mr. Von Brandt is correct. I had the pleasure of seeing you perform in Chicago not long ago. I told my wife and children about it, and they've been eager to see your show ever since. I thought it would make a wonderful Christmas present for all of them."

"Thank you. That's very kind of you to say," Lily replied, gently shaking his hand.

"And I must say, seein' your show truly has been, far and away, the best gift he's eva' given me," his wife smiled, walking up and giving Lily's hand a dainty shake as well.

"Best gift I've eva' gotten too!" their oldest son concurred.

"How do you make all those shadows dance?!" their youngest son asked, speaking with a severe speech impediment that Lily was somehow able to decipher.

The curious little boy looked to be no more than five-years-old, so Lily knelt down to his level before answering. "It's magic!" she said, waving her hand in front of him. "You believe in magic, don't you?"

He nodded, gazing at her in wide-eyed fascination.

"What's your name?" Lily asked with a warm smile on her face.

"Thomas ... but everyone calls me Tad," he explained through his impediment.

"Well Tad, magic starts right up here." She pointed to his tiny head. "Whateva' you dream, if you put all of your heart and your soul into it, and you work real hard, you can bring it all to life."

Tad nodded again, still staring at Lily like he was mesmerized. He even had a huge smile on his face, which was something his parents rarely saw him do, since his older brother always poked fun at the deformity of his teeth: a side effect of his cleft pallet.

"Always rememba' that, okay Tad?" Lily continued.

"I will," he replied, suddenly wrapping his little arms around her neck.

Lily brushed her finger against his nose before standing up and being greeted with the warm, appreciative smiles of his parents.

"I read that you were once a slave, but that you've since earned your freedom by playin' the piano," Mary said to Lily. "Afta' seein' you play, I unda'stand now why your owna' felt you deserved to be freed. Somebody with your level of skill should neva' be forced into slavery," she smiled, attempting to compliment her.

"Well, in my mind, yes, I feel free. But on paper, I ain't no more free than any slave workin' in a cottonfield at this very moment. Truth be told, whetha' any of us can play piano or not, I think we *all* deserve to be freed."

"I'm so sorry, I didn't mean to offend," Mary replied, feeling a bit embarrassed after realizing her mistake.

"Quite alright, ma'am. None taken. Forgive me, I was just expressin' my opinion."

"Papa, how come only brown people are slaves?" Tad suddenly wanted to know after paying close attention to the conversation. He gazed up at his father with curious, big brown eyes, waiting for a reply.

Abraham nervously looked down at him then up at Lily. They held each other's gaze as the wheels turned in his head. He did not want to answer the question in front of Lily. However, he quickly realized that even if she were not in his presence, he still would not have had a logical explanation to give to his inquisitive son.

Lily scrambled to ease the tension of the situation when she saw the look of extreme embarrassment on Abraham's face. "Do you boys like chocolate?" she finally thought to ask.

"Yeah!" they both announced in unison.

"Mrs. Lincoln, would you mind if they had a piece?"

"No, of course not. Only *one* piece, though, okay boys?"

461

"Yes, Ma'am," they promised as Lily handed them a bowl of candy to sift through.

Once the boys were occupied, Abraham turned his attention back to Lily. After learning that the newspapers had embellished the truth about her freedom, he was suddenly curious to hear the truth about her life. He wanted to hear in her own words how she had come to play piano in such an elaborate show. In response to that initial question and many more that followed, Lily began to satisfy Abraham's curiosity with the details of her long, turbulent life journey to Winter Garden. She was very open about the fact that her father had sold her, her unique friendship with James, and how she had secretly taught herself to play piano. She went on to explain how James believed in her talent so much that he had taken her to meet William and that he had even built her an amphitheater. She talked about Landon paving the way for her tour, the ups and downs of her journey along the way, the ridicule and rejection in the beginning, and finally being embraced and accepted in the end. Lily was not shy at all about sharing the vivid details of the events that eventually led to the rise of her musical success, as well as emphasizing the fact that she was *still* nothing more than a slave.

Abraham had hung on Lily's every word as she spoke. He was absolutely intrigued by the entire phenomenon, as was his wife. However, Mary had become fixated on a particular part of Lily's story. Being a woman, she could easily sense Lily's emotions and hear the sentiment in her voice when she spoke of James, and she suddenly could not help but want to know more about him. "The piano piece that you played ... the one about love. Is James the one you played it for?" she asked.

There was a gentleness in Mary's voice that made Lily feel as though she could trust her with the answer. Whether she could or not, though, Lily suddenly did not care if the Lincolns, or any other person, was appalled by the fact that she loved a white man. She was not ashamed of her relationship with James and wanted to feel free in expressing how she felt about him. She knew they would be sailing away to Europe soon and felt confident that no harm would come to her between now and then anyway. Lily stared at Mary for a moment before answering. She felt a mutual understanding being exchanged between them in their eyes, expressing that her words would remain between the three of them. "Yes ma'am, he is," Lily finally answered.

A smile illuminated on Mary's face, and she encircled her arm around her husband's and snuggled closer to him. "That song was beautiful," she replied. "Simply beautiful."

"Thank you, ma'am."

"I'd sure love to meet this James you speak of ... and Mr. Werthington too. I've been to several of his symphonies when I was just a girl."

"Well, come right this way!" Lily gestured with her hand toward the door. "I can certainly arrange that," she smiled. She was beyond eager to see James too anyway.

"Come on, boys," Abraham beckoned to his sons, who had both disobeyed their mother and were indulging on their fifth piece of chocolate.

"Yes, sir!" they said, their voices muffled by the chocolate that they had quickly shoved into their mouths.

Before exiting, Lily picked up the Christmas gift she had meticulously wrapped for James, wanting to share it with him there at Winter Garden while everyone still celebrated in the back halls. She wanted to give him more than that, though; her deprived body was begging to erotically prove to him how badly she had missed him. The thought of it brought a mischievous smile to her face as she escorted her guests out into the hallway.

Lily walked down the hallway with the Lincolns, answering their questions about the production of the show while she went in search of William. The conversation, however, came to an abrupt halt when Lily stepped around the corner and gazed down the corridor. She immediately froze where she stood. There, straight in front of her, stood the man whose gift she held, a man she had just admitted to loving just a few days before, a man who had gone above and beyond the clouds to prove that he loved her, and was responsible for helping her to seize this rare moment at Winter Garden. Lily's eyes immediately widened, and she became weak all over. But her reaction had nothing to do with James. She owed her moment of shock to the person standing beside him, a person whose presence immediately brought profound memories of her childhood flashing back to her, a person Lily thought she would never again see in her lifetime. She stared in silence and utter disbelief as tears began to well in her eyes.

"Why the long face, girl?! You mean you ain't happy to see me?" Jesse snarled, glaring at her while standing wedged in between two deputies.

The hatred Lily had harbored for Jesse instantly ignited every nerve in her body, rendering her incapable of even replying. Paralyzed, she simply stood there and stared at the man she believed was the devil himself.

After Lily failed to reply, Jesse stepped toward her with his face twisted in anger. "I'd've snatched y'ur ass clean off 'a that stage had I not stopped and realized I's finally gettin' a return on my investment," he told her, standing a hairsbreadth away from her face, while holding up a briefcase full of her hard-earned money. "'Cause Lord knows y'ur cookin' and cleanin' ain't been worth a goddamn penny all these years!" he growled.

The blood in Lily's veins began to go cold as Jesse loomed over her, letting the anger in his eyes and body language continue to speak on his behalf. His proximity, the growling sound of his voice, his vulgar stench, and the sudden flashbacks of the countless times his open hand had made its way across her face as a child, all held enough

464

weight to crush her in a matter of seconds. The woman that Lily had blossomed into over the last few months, with confidence, strength, and courage, instantly shriveled and died. She quickly reverted back to the submissive shell of a woman that Jesse had violently molded her to be. She immediately dropped her head after not being able to withstand the menacing look on his face that she had seen in times past, a look that was often followed by grave pain. As Lily looked down, her eyes drifted to the briefcase filled with thousands of her hard-earned dollars, money that Jesse now declared as his own. She then glanced over to the papers in his other hand, documents that legally declared him as her rightful owner. At that very moment, Lily conceded to the fact that it was all truly over.

Landon, Wilson, Emerson, and William all suddenly approached and stood in a circle around Jesse, Lily, James, and the deputies, as if in a standoff. Their eyes were all darting from one to the other, each waiting for someone to speak. Easily sensing that something was horribly wrong, Austin, the other students, Elijah, Isabel, and the Lincolns, all slowly gathered on the outskirts and watched on, wondering who this strange man was berating Lily with his words and his devilish presence. They watched and waited, somehow knowing by the look on everyone's faces that a war was likely to erupt if someone did not intervene, but fearful to do so because of the presence of the deputies.

After staring at the ownership papers in Jesse's hands, Lily finally looked up at James through a haze of tears that had yet to fall. He just stared back at her with no expression on his face whatsoever. He had yet to move, or say a word in her defense, or attempt to stop his father from making any claims over her. While Lily was holding James's gaze, Jesse suddenly snatched her by the arm, twisting her skin tight. She inhaled sharply, cried out in pain, and dropped James's Christmas gift to the floor, shattering the contents inside. "Come on here!" Jesse snarled as he grabbed her, his fire-red eyes piercing through her.

Without another word, he yanked Lily along and began to walk with her down the corridor, still holding her arm in a death grip.

"Sir, please, I beg you to let her go!" William interjected, his heart racing after watching Jesse handle Lily like a meaningless object. The realization of what was happening was setting in hard for William as Jesse dragged Lily further away. He immediately began to fight to regain control over the situation since it seemed that nobody else cared to bother, not Elijah, not Austin, not either one of the Lincolns, who stood horrified by what they were witnessing … not even James. William was the only one who proved that he was not deterred by the deputies nor by the evilness that Jesse exuded.

"Who the hell're you?!" Jesse demanded to know after stopping for a moment to look at William.

"Please, sir, I just beg you to turn her loose!" William pleaded again, his hands visibly shaking.

Jesse responded by tightening his grip on Lily and yanking her toward him. Again, she cried out in pain.

"Please! You're hurting her!" William erupted.

"Shut the hell up!" Jesse shouted at Lily, his face turning a darker shade of red. He began to stomp away again when William refused to answer his question.

The thought of Jesse taking Lily away sent William's mind racing to find a solution. "Sir! It's my understanding that you've appointed your son to take care of matters involving your slaves, correct?!"

Jesse stopped. "I'm gonna ask you one more time, Brit! Who the hell are you?!"

"Just someone who wishes to help resolve this matter…"

"I got my resolution," Jesse replied, holding up the briefcase full of money and shaking Lily hard with the other. He then proceeded down the hallway.

466

Yet again, William jumped in front of him and blocked his path. "There must be a better way than this!" William continued to plead, his tone oozing desperation. "Can you please speak with your son?! Please?!" he begged, pointing to James, who had still done nothing but stand there silently staring at Lily as she begged for his help with her eyes. "Please allow James to work things out with you! I beg you not to do this!"

"My son," Jesse replied, turning around to look at James. "*My son?*" he repeated slowly, saying it in a way that sounded as if he questioned whether or not he truly was his own flesh and blood. Jesse suddenly walked toward him. James had already divulged to his father how and why Lily had ended up at Winter Garden. But Jesse suddenly felt the need to know where his youngest boy's loyalties truly lie. Jesse wanted to test his son in front of all the people surrounding them. "Maybe this ol' fucker is right. I gave you control ova' Lily," Jesse said, approaching James with his face still crippled by a menacing expression. "So, tell me, *son* ... what do you think is best, huh?" He stood face to face with James. "You decide." He dropped the briefcase full of cash in between them. "Do we take *my* property home where she belongs?" He shoved Lily toward William. "Or do we hand 'er ova' to this ol' fucker, huh? If you wanna hand 'er ova'...." He held up Lily's ownership document. "I'll sign 'er papers right now and set 'er free right where she stands. The choice is y'urs ... *son.*"

James read the look in his father's eyes as they stared each other down in cold silence while everyone else watched on in suspense. It had never been a secret to anyone in the show how James felt about Lily, so many of them suspected that his choice would be an easy one. Feeling the heat of their glares, James turned to face Lily's entourage and saw hope radiating from every set of eyes that stared back at him as they eagerly waited for him to speak. He then peered over at Lily and caught sight of a pair of innocent multicolored eyes that sparkled with unshed tears, gazing back at him. James knew that the waiting tears in her eyes had nothing to do with the pain in her arm after being manhandled; he was certain her tears had everything to do with the thought of being taken away from a man who treated her like his beloved daughter and being returned to a man who treated her like an animal. As James continued to stare at Lily, he realized that his words had the power to decide the definition of her waiting tears. The answer that he uttered would be the difference between tears of great sorrow and misery *or* tears of great relief and joy. Even through her brimming tears, James could see the hope in Lily's eyes as to what his answer would be. He could see the trust that she had bestowed upon him and the confidence that she had in him to prevent her from being cast back into a torturous life. Even through the swell of tears in Lily's anguished eyes, James could see that she still even managed to look at him with an infinite amount of love. The way she looked at him was so intense that it caused him to quickly snatch his gaze away without a word, leaving the definition of Lily's tears to await his decision for a moment longer.

"Speak, goddamn it!" Jesse barked at him with great impatience.

After quickly pulling his eyes away from Lily's, James finally turned his attention back to his father. "Well, it's like I already told you earlier, Pa. I played the role ... with *everyone* here," he emphasized, turning to look back at Lily again. "I said what I had to say, did what I had to do to orchestrate all 'a this. We needed to earn money for the farm, didn't we?" He bent over and picked up the briefcase full of money. "I'd say this little scheme was far more profitable than any baby breedin'," he said, pulling out a stack of one hundred-dollar bills and flashing it. "Wouldn't you agree?" He then thrust the briefcase back toward his father with a sinister smirk on his face.

Jesse snatched the briefcase filled with every dollar that Lily had earned. "*My son*," he said proudly. He then turned to glare at William. "I do believe *this* belongs to me," he told him, snatching Lily away from his embrace.

As Jesse grabbed hold of Lily's arm again, she stared briefly into James's eyes and saw that ice had returned to them. Then, suddenly, the silence in the hallway was pierced by her heart-stopping shrill. It was an agonizing, stomach-wrenching shrill of a woman who had, *yet again*, been emotionally shattered and betrayed in the most evil of ways by a man that she thought loved her. James had finally defined Lily's waiting tears, and he was now forced to watch as sorrowful tears of misery began to rain down like a sudden flash flood from her eyes. The way Lily cried was unlike anything anyone there had ever heard or seen. Her body convulsed as the sobs of pain continued to erupt. Her chest heaved, to the point that she nearly hyperventilated. It was like watching a woman cry who was dying an incredibly slow and excruciating death.

Realizing her fate, Lily's fears caused her to reflexively snatch her arm away from Jesse's grip. When she momentarily escaped, Jesse backhanded her brutally across the face. The move was swift and powerful, and the result of the force he exerted was instantaneous. Lily found herself on the ground after a moment of seeing black, her eye pulsating and swelling fast. The heads of all her friends turned away quickly when the heartbreaking brutal scene was too much for them to handle.

"Dear God!" William cried, rushing immediately to be by Lily's side, crouching near her and helping her to sit up. "Have you no soul?!" he screamed, looking up at Jesse, who hovered over the both of them.

Elijah looked down at Lily lying on the floor, and his actions were quick and unexpected. He lunged at Jesse. Before he could grab him, though, one of the deputies caught him with a fist to the jaw.

"Know y'ur goddamn place, you uppity nigga'!" Jesse spat, after turning around and realizing who had just tried to attack him.

Elijah held his jaw after being briefly shaken. He quickly composed himself, looked down at Lily, and met her eyes as she lay there. Even through the swelling and blurred vision, Lily could easily read the expression on Elijah's face. It caused her mind to instantly replay the heated warnings that he had given her in the past regarding James. Elijah then turned and looked at James in the most menacing of ways before storming out of the building.

Abraham and his wife had retreated just before Elijah. Appalled by the horrific scene they were witnessing, they had covered their sons' eyes and ushered them out in the opposite direction. Everyone else who remained did not dare to intervene, fearing that they would be met with the same force as Elijah.

Once all was settled, Jesse pried William off of Lily, who was still trying to comfort her. Jesse then picked Lily up off the ground in one quick motion.

"Please let her go!" William continued to beg, rushing to jump in front of Jesse as he began escorting Lily out.

"Move aside, damn it!" Jesse demanded.

"Please! I'll purchase her from you!" William begged, walking briskly to keep up with them.

"She ain't for sale!"

"Name your price!"

Jesse stopped and turned toward William. "I *said* ... She! Ain't! For! Sale!" He had leaned in so close that his tobacco-coated spit particles were pelting William in the face as he spoke.

Still undeterred, though, William suddenly reached deep into his pocket and pulled out a wad full of folded one hundred-dollar bills. "How much do you want for her?!" William suddenly threw a bill at Jesse. "A hundred dollars!" he shouted, then threw several more. "Five hundred?!" He then took every bill in his hand and tossed them into the air. "TEN THOUSAND?! YOU SICK SON OF A BITCH!" he erupted, as a rain shower of money floated to the ground. "Tell me how much money it will take to make you realize that Lily is *not* an animal?! SHE'S A HUMAN BEING!" William shouted, his hands shaking with rage. "And by far one of the finest I know," he said, with softness in his voice as he referred to her. But the fire in his voice immediately returned upon addressing Jesse. "And *you!* Are by far the most *despicable!*" William snarled, his face etched in the most hateful expression his sons had ever seen.

"Get outta my goddamn way, you old fucker, before I snap you in half!" Jesse growled, grabbing William by the neck and shoving him back hard.

"At least give me a moment to say goodbye to her!" William managed to choke out while holding onto his throat. "Please!" he begged. He reached his hand toward Lily, but Jesse snatched her away from his reach and quickly fled from the building with her. William fell to his knees and began sobbing uncontrollably into his hands, crying like a man who had just witnessed the abduction of his own child.

As his father marched off with Lily in tow, James looked around at the swarm of people left standing in the hallway. Every last one of them had grown to care very deeply for Lily, and he could feel the heat of their angry eyes burning holes into his flesh. He gave a quick, sweeping glare to everyone before he boldly walked off to catch up with his father, without so much as an attempt to explain the irreparable damage he had just caused not only to Lily, but to William as well. On his way out, he glanced down at the heap that William had been reduced to and did not even bother to assist him in getting to his feet. He just kept on walking callously through the minefield of money on the ground, kicking some of it up in the air in the light trail of wind he left behind from his swift departure.

Hundreds of miles away from Winter Garden, by sheer coincidence, the very moment that William's knees had hit the floor, a bullet had ripped through the shoulder of Griff Buchanon: Lily's favorite security bandit. While sitting in the very place that he always sat enjoying Lily's homemade heart-shaped pancakes, Griff was now bleeding profusely.

After seeing smoke billowing in the air from the fireplace, a group of men riding on horseback, with torches blazing, all assumed that William was home, along with all the Negroes that he housed there. It was the signal they had eagerly waited for in the hours before flooding onto Werthington Estate and instantly turning the cherished land into a battlefield. Adorned with ghostly white robes and sheathed faces, a crew of over twenty deep ambushed the property, waging a virtual war against William and every Negro who lived there. They intentionally attacked on Christmas night, feeling as if they were delivering the gift of justice to a white man who they felt lived with corrupt morals, and who openly defied the unwritten rules that white society had set forth. In the minds of the ghostly-looking riders, housing a family full of Negroes was one thing, but helping with the uprising of one of them was another matter altogether. Knowing that William was assisting the sort of woman who had the power to use her success as a platform to speak on giving Negroes rights—rights that they never wanted to see come to fruition—was a major infraction that the night-riding terrorists planned to deal with in the most permanent of ways after they galloped with ferocity onto William Werthington's land.

Back at Winter Garden, where William was still crouched on the floor in tears, another gunshot rang out outside of the theater. It crackled through the air just minutes after James had walked out of the building. The sound penetrated the ears of everyone left in the back hallway, instantaneously commanding their attention. Wilson, Emerson, William, and the entire cast immediately turned in unison toward the piercing sound that lingered in the air like the rumblings of a distant thunder. Soon, they would all learn that the thunderous blast ultimately proved fatal for the victim, whose skull contents were slowly seeping into the dirt below it. Screams from the crowd outside, the whinnying of reacting horses, and carriage wheels being swiftly dragged away were the only sounds everyone heard next. Still, everyone in the hallway stood there frozen, shocked into silence, fearfully speculating about what scene their eyes had to prepare for on the anterior walls of Winter Garden, in the aftermath of the storm-like force of Jesse Adams' wrath ... a devastating storm that had just completely ripped everyone's world apart.

Slave Code
Article I Section I

Be it enacted that if any slave resists his or her master while being corrected, or for refusing to surrender him or herself contrary to law, and shall happen to be slain in such correction, the master shall be indemnified from any prosecution for such incident, <u>as if such killing never happened.</u>

TO BE CONTINUED IN:
The Prodigy Slave
Book Two

About the Author

Londyn Skye is a comical 43-year-old mother of two, ex-all-American collegiate athlete, million-mile lady trucker phenom, and romance novel junkie! When she was a child, Londyn began creating stories in the fantasy world of her mind as a way to escape life's troubles. As an adult, she decided to challenge herself to turn her comforting fantasies into a novel. That challenge led her to write *The Prodigy Slave* Trilogy. Wanting the utmost quality for her readers, she has diligently worked to balance the saga with humor, drama, romance, unpredictable plots, and devious, neurotic characters that are equally as captivating as the erotic love scenes between the fascinating heroes and heroines. She has painstakingly painted her fantasies with words that she hopes will help readers see the images just as beautifully as her unique mind does.

Most importantly, she hopes that everyone will feel just as emotionally moved and inspired by the heroes and heroines in her love story.

Connect with Londyn at
www.facebook.com/AuthorLondynSkye

Made in the USA
Columbia, SC
05 February 2021